Bloom books

Dear readers,

Are you jumping up and down!? Because I am jumping up and down! I'm so happy we get to go on this journey together. It feels like only yesterday you were screaming my name in vain at the top of your lungs with the plot twist in book one. Every part of this book is for you, my amazing readers. With each of these stories, a little part of my love for Caly and Mendax goes out into the world like a glowing firefly. As the crispy pages of your book open, my firefly emerges from the pages to stay with you. Thank you for reading my stories and keeping my fireflies. Without you, I would never have been able to fully embrace my love of fungi and not wearing pants during the day. For that I am eternally grateful!

With love and gratitude,

ALSO BY JENEANE O'RILEY

The Infatuated Fae
How Does It Feel?
What Did You Do?

WHAT DID YOU DO?

JENEANE O'RILEY

Bloom *books*

Copyright © 2024 by Jeneane O'Riley
Cover and internal design © 2024 by Sourcebooks
Cover design by Cat at TRC Designs
Cover images © Gerard/Adobe Stock, maykal/Adobe Stock, dule964/Adobe Stock, tomert/Depositphotos, alexlabb/Depositphotos, Oliver Klimek/Adobe Stock, Anja Kaiser/Adobe Stock

The characters and events portrayed in this book are fictitious or are used fictitiously. Any similarity to real persons, living or dead, is purely coincidental and not intended by the author.

All brand names and product names used in this book are trademarks, registered trademarks, or trade names of their respective holders. Sourcebooks is not associated with any product or vendor in this book.

Published by Bloom Books, an imprint of Sourcebooks
P.O. Box 4410, Naperville, Illinois 60567–4410
(630) 961-3900
sourcebooks.com

Cataloging-in-Publication data is on file with the Library of Congress.

Printed and bound in the United States of America.
KP 10 9 8 7 6 5 4 3 2 1

To you.
The pleasure of a chapter is surpassed only
by the torment of a story.

AUTHOR'S NOTE

Dear reader,

Hi. You look great.

Listen—this book is dark. If you are sensitive or easily triggered by horrible, nasty, disgusting, vile things, then congratulations, you are quite normal (though is anyone actually normal?), and you still have time to close this book. I will close my eyes and turn the invisible key in my mouth and never speak of it again...unless we run into each other at the grocery store in one of those awkward *your eyes hit mine at the same time we were both trying to hide, and now it's too late* moments. Because then I'll obviously need something to say.

In all seriousness, your mental health isn't a joke. I do my best to list all the triggers I can think of, but that doesn't mean one might have slipped past, so please do not chance it if you are in doubt at all. The last thing I would ever want is to cause you pain or discomfort in any way.

This book contains BUT IS NOT LIMITED TO: **mature sexual content, abuse** (verbal, physical, emotional, mental), **breaking bones, kidnapping, decapitation, blood, gore, excessive amounts of growling men, death, loss of parents, sexual assault, mental health**

issues, rough consensual sex, murder, cheating, unreliable narrators, voyeurism, plot twists, animal death (I SWEAR the bad guys get what's coming to them though), **stalking, belt play, knife play, car crash, amputation, child murder** (...I said dark. It's kid on kid, he's a bully, and it's about three sentences from the past), **poisoning, somnophilia, alcohol, consensual non-con** (I only add this because someone thinks they dreamt something, but it really happened and they were into it, but still thought it was a dream?), **and physics**—yeah, I said it.

Okay now, one or two good things that happen.

You are transported to another realm with Caly and Mendax. You learn that labels and looks mean nothing, and that you are capable of greatness, no matter how unlikely. There are several cute animals, smart women, and handsome fae.

Now another warning.

I know, a bit of a reverse shit sandwich there, huh? Bad—good—bad.

This is the second book of a four-book series. There is more backstory in this one than will be in any of the others. Along this journey, you are going to hate and love each character several different times. You are going to get very confused about who's really the hero and who's really the villain of the story, and that's what I want. To show you that no matter what we look like, act like, have, accomplish, where we live, where we come from, etc., it's up to *us* to decide who we want to be, not what the world thinks we should be.

XOXO,
Jeneane

PLAYLIST

"Castle"—Halsey
"How Villains Are Made"—Madalen Duke
"Inferia"—Eternal Eclipse featuring Merethe Soltvedt
"Soul Without a Home"—Glasslands
"Mirage"—Eternal Eclipse
"Come Hell or High Water"—Imminence
"Darkness Inside"—Astyria
"noose"—Nessa Barrett
"keep me afraid"—Nessa Barrett
"Sand"—Dove Cameron
"Not Strong Enough"—Apocalyptica
"Change (In the House of Flies)"—Deftones
"Be a Hero"—Euphoria featuring Bolshiee
"No Time to Die"—Billie Eilish

CHAPTER 19:

"Suicide Note"—Jurrivh

ALL SPICY SCENES:

"Karma"—Amanati
"Invicta"—Amanati
"9/8"—Amanati

CHAPTER 1
THE SEELIE QUEEN SARACEN

B LACK ROSE PETALS DROPPED TO THE FLOOR OF THE CASTLE'S
foyer as I plucked them one by one from the vase.

"There you are." Relief weighed down my sequin-covered
shoulders as tiny gold reflections danced off the dark walls in
response. "Your commander took the subjects through the back
entrance. You will be very pleased with this batch. A few of
them are what the humans call 'serial killers.' I took the transport
carrier down on its way to one of their high-security prisons,"
I stated, struggling to steady my voice when he came nearer.

He was terrifying. His presence alone made everyone else
shrink into themselves out of fear he would focus on them
and then they would become his prey.

The king didn't say a word while he continued to walk
toward me, backing me up against the wall next to the console
table.

My stomach tightened and flipped in anticipation, as if
the butterflies that followed me were dancing on my insides,
rather than fluttering around the Unseelie castle.

Thanes pushed me against the wall and began to ravage
my neck with hungry kisses.

I swelled with pride.

I had pleased him.

"How is the testing?" I inquired through heavy breaths. His large, domineering body pressed against mine like a vise.

"Few have lived," he grunted while unbuckling his pants with one hand as the other caged me in against the wall. "I need them more powerful if this is to work."

His hands hoisted up my gown, rough and demanding. The gold sequins grated over my thighs like tiny nails.

Suns, he was incredible.

A pulse of heat flared in my stomach at his words.

This had to work. It had to.

It was the *only* way.

"Well, my love," I purred. "Something more powerful wouldn't be a human, and you can't get inside of their minds if they aren't human," I reminded him.

His strong hands grew rougher as they pulled and squeezed at my ready body.

A putrid green moth landed on his shoulder for a moment before leaving to join one of my monarchs on the wall.

"The blood witch from the north believes she can take some of the Smoke Slayer powers." He slid himself inside of me with a deep thrust and low groan. "Add a bit of Smoke Slayer to a few of them. She is to test it on my son first and take from him."

His eyes closed, and I had to stifle my own moan just from knowing I caused it.

"He got my ability to impel, as well as Tenebris's power as a Smoke Slayer. Mendax will be far stronger than all of us one day. It will work. If it doesn't, then it will be all the better that I be rid of him. With so much power, he's bound to get out of control."

I tightened my legs around him.

My teeth pinched at my bottom lip as I focused on the feel of him. I loved when he used me like this.

The small buttons on the sides of my shoes dug into my

ankle as I pulled him closer. Deeper. My eyes rolled back in my head, reveling in the tight, slick feel of him being pushed harder inside of me with every thrust. Felix was always too gentle with me, too respectful.

It was always dirty and gritty with Thanes. Exactly as I wanted.

An alarmed cry fell from my lips when Thanes bit into the skin of my neck like a feral animal, breaking the sensitive flesh. Sometimes I worried that one day he *might* actually break me. I reveled in it.

It made me stronger—for him. His wife would never take his aggression like I would.

"Get rid of her," I moaned. Tilting my hips, I pushed against him until it burned. "Get rid of them both, or I'm done," I said, tightening myself like a sheath around his length.

"The fuck do you think we are building these creatures for?" he growled before he pulled himself out of me and dropped my legs.

I had pushed him too far.

He was dangerous like this: full of lust and rage.

I couldn't help myself. "You are an *Impeller*. You don't need her to rule," I volleyed.

I may not match the Unseelie King Thanes's magnitude in abilities or powers, but I did in title.

Making certain that my armor—the Seelie crown—was still upright on top of my head, I shoved my golden dress down, wiping away the wet wrinkles where our juices had stained my hoop skirt.

"Of course I don't *need* her, but the Smoke Slayers are revered. I'm already hated by the Unseelie fae for getting banned from the human realm. Killing their last two heroes would only bring about more enemies."

His semi-hardened length, still free from his pants, glistened under the warm glow of the wall sconces.

"I am taking care of that, darling, I've told you. Every human I bring you is physically strong, mentally weak, and has the *perfect* mind for being melted and molded into evil little cretins. The plan is finally coming together, my love," I whispered as I took his half-hard length into my hand. "Get rid of Tenebris and Mendax," I purred, pulling on his once-again-hardening cock. "I want it to be only you and I. Think of what we could do together when we rule Seelie, Unseelie, *and* the human realm." I swiped my thumb over the rock-hard tip in my palm.

I did that to him.

Thanes let out a low moan before his hand shot out and gripped my throat.

"What is *she* doing here?" A voice bounced off the expansive walls, shrill and irritating, like nails being dragged over slate.

Startled, my eyes flashed over Thanes's shoulder just before my lips curled into a cunning smile aimed directly at his wife.

Thanes didn't flinch as he continued to roughly grind himself into my hand.

"Hello, Tenebris. I'm afraid he's busy," I purred, the smile still on my lips.

This was too perfect.

"Husband, I thought I asked that you fuck the whores *outside* of the castle. Do make sure you pay this one. She appears to be in desperate need of the assistance," Tenebris sang sardonically.

The Unseelie queen crossed her arms and watched us. She squinted her eyes in irritation, but unfortunately for her, it didn't hide the glint of pain I saw in her icy-blue eyes.

And everyone thought it was so hard to wound a Smoke Slayer.

"Leave now," Thanes barked at his wife.

My smile widened beyond anything I thought capable. He was already choosing me over Tenebris, and our army hadn't even been completed.

How sad and pathetic she must feel to watch this incredible man pick me over her…in her own home.

Me, a near-powerless Seelie, rattling her. I was giddy at the thought.

I barely had enough powers to have warranted my being groomed as an option for the Seelie kings. *Everyone* knew my husband had only chosen me for the irony of my small gift. Felix loved the symbolism.

The bright orange-and-black wings flared slightly at my back. They never caused me to feel more powerful. Instead, they only amplified how weak I really was as I stood alongside the king and queen of the Unseelie realm.

Tenebris snorted. She easily beat me when it came to powers, and she knew it.

"I should kill you both right now. No one would miss you. The courts wouldn't even falter with the two of you gone," she snapped with a smile.

Inky blackness began to crawl up her fingers, climbing up her wrists like a creature.

I was getting under her skin.

Thanes pulled away from me abruptly and turned to her, leaving me feeling empty and slighted.

"Go ahead." He stalked toward her. The arrogance in his easy stride made me shiver. "Tell your son that *you* killed me, his best friend. His idol. His *fucking father.*" Thanes's laugh thundered through the castle as he moved in close to Tenebris's porcelain face.

The woman who always appeared so frightening and powerful to me suddenly looked weak and timid. I nearly felt sorry for her the way Thanes's presence caused her to shrink in on herself.

To everyone else, she was unstoppable, an unyielding force of power, but with her husband, she submitted like a dog.

Love made you stupid. No one would ever understand that more than me.

"He'll get over it," she growled back at him.

Smoke from the queen's feet formed a protective barrier between them.

"Mendax idolizes me, Tenebris. You kill me, and the first thing that boy will do is end you," he said with a cocky smile. "It doesn't matter though." He grabbed her blackened hand. "You wouldn't hurt me. You *love* me. The fae believe you Smoke Slayers to be so tough, but I know the truth."

He bent down and kissed her tenderly. Despite her eyes falling shut, she remained stiff as a board.

My fists curled until my long, peach-colored nails threatened to pierce the skin on my palms.

"I know that once you are in love"—he kissed her again softly—"and once you have bonded to another"—another kiss to her forehead—"you Slayers are *incapable* of stopping it or hurting the one you've chosen. It doesn't matter how it destroys you." He brushed a piece of straight, black hair from her face as I watched with horror. "It seems that it's you, my love, who fucked up when you chose me."

Jealousy flared inside me like the fiery sun. If I'd have been granted the SunTamer's abilities, I would have burned them both with the heat of a thousand suns.

I knew he was manipulating her and that he didn't really love her.

He loved me.

But as I stood in the cold, dimly lit castle, something blossomed inside of me. Something dark and jagged with thorns and teeth flourished.

I would make her regret ever challenging me—regret *ever* making me feel less than worthy because I couldn't match her powers or beauty.

I was no Smoke Slayer, but I wouldn't let that stop me from ruining her whole life and everything she ever cared about. I would make certain of it.

This wasn't just about Thanes anymore.

Her realm was mine.

I was the better woman, and I would watch as he killed both his wife and son for me.

I could be powerful too.

CHAPTER 2

MENDAX

W ARM BLOOD TRICKLED DOWN TO THE DRIED LEAVES THAT blanketed the ground, making a soft noise that would have gone unnoticed by most. But not by me.

My ears always searched for that sound, perking forward with the hopes of being blessed with its sultry notes. It was the orchestra that fueled and ignited me, the essence of my soul that demanded I hear the song of blood being shed—that I be the maestro.

I stole the deepest breath my aching chest was capable of and let the humid forest air push into my immortal lungs. Even the earthy forest scent made me think of her.

Everything made me think of her.

Not yet, I sang over and over in my head as I let out my breath and willed some of my impatience to exit with it.

I was faltering already. I could feel it. The impatient rage had already commenced its siege on my body and mind. Faster it came, every day since she had left. Simply beating this man's face in wasn't enough.

"Do. Not. Hide her from me," I warned the man.

Not yet! I pleaded with myself while feebly attempting

to loosen my grip around his throat. The pads of my fingers rebelled, pressing tighter into the coarse stubble on his neck.

"I-I told you, I kn-know nothing. I would *never* keep her from you, My Lord," the wiry man stammered.

"Dirac! Take him now!" I shouted as I lost all composure. I threw the trembling man to the only other fae in the dim and smoggy forest.

My friend, if that's what he was, gathered the weathered TreeTamer and slammed him against the tree directly behind us.

I was losing it, and I couldn't afford to lose it—not now. Not when he might have answers. Different answers. Answers that I *needed* to hear.

Dirac spared me a concerned look before turning back on the man with a smirk.

"You feel it, don't you, mate?" the large fae whispered. Dirac grinned wide at the bleeding man and pushed the smooth, gray blade harder against the weathered skin of his throat. "You thought him unhinged before, eh? Look at our prince now." He nodded in my direction with a smirk. "We have word you were seeing to the whispering oaks a few miles from the Elf and Hanabi portals the same day the human assassin left."

Of their own accord, my feet began to pace in an all-too-familiar rhythm. The skin covering my knuckles tightened until I was certain I would crush my own bones.

She belonged to me.

I wanted to kill him for putting the goddess—*my* goddess—in the man's mind.

She was *fucking mine.*

She didn't belong in anyone else's head but mine. Stars knew she had taken up every empty space of it in her absence. She was all I could think about.

I snarled in frustration while my fists started to pull tufts of wild, black hair from my head. The scar on my back where she had stabbed me stretched with tight, new flesh, further reminding me of how much I ached to get ahold of her.

Both men shifted uncomfortably. My wings of smoke pulsed, but like usual these days, they remained pinned to my back. Black smog billowed around me, inching its way closer to where Dirac held the villager.

"I swear!" The man grew frantic at the sight of my smoke.

A Smoke Slayer was only as dangerous as his smoke, and I was practically fuming wisps of acid.

His heart beat like drums in my ears—drums that pounded out a symphonic crescendo, begging me to include his cries of pain.

"I swear, I saw no one! There was no one in the woods that entire day. You—you know who was behind this. *We all know it!* Just like all the other traitorous humans! Everyone knows she's with the Seelie prince—"

His head snapped in my hands with a resounding crack the instant I grabbed him. It sent enough relief down my spine, I may as well have cracked my own neck.

My eyes burned a hole in him as I dropped him to the ground and coiled my smoke around each of his arms and legs while replaying his final sentence in my mind over and over.

I watched the man's limbs pull free from his body with a soothing sound. He had been dead since I snapped his neck, but I *desperately* needed to release some of my fury.

If I couldn't get a handle on myself, all of Unseelie would soon be dead, and I would have a throne but no one to rule.

Even that—a thought that would have normally shaken my soul—didn't matter anymore. If she and I were the only two left in all the realms, I wouldn't care.

I would rule her.

I would worship her.

I would punish her.

My chest vibrated with a growl, thinking of that worm calling Callie—or whatever my pet's real name was—a traitor.

I pulled his lower jaw off with an easy tug and threw it into the misty forest. A bit of tension ebbed as the sharp tang of black blood teased my nose.

"You know he's right," Dirac said.

Nearly tripping, I spun to throttle him. Friend or not, he wouldn't speak about her.

The dark forest where he had stood was now empty. He was smart and fast, I would give him that.

"He was *not* right," I barked into the empty forest air, my desperate voice echoing off the old trees.

I couldn't take it if he was right.

If he was right, it meant that I may never get her back— not really.

"Who else in all the realms would send a *human* to do their killing, Mendax? You *know* she is with the Seelie. You've heard the rumors." His disembodied voice echoed behind me now.

I spun to shout at him. "She is not with the Seelie. Those rumors are nothing more than peasant gossip," I bellowed, feeling my body shake from the scream.

Distant cicada chirps blended with my heavy breath and the scratch of bare branches in the cool night breeze.

The space in front of me blurred slightly before the seven-foot-tall tank of a fae reappeared in front of me with palms held high in surrender. His sharp eyes pierced mine with concern and gentleness that made me want to stab him.

"If you had a brain, I would impel you," I grumbled as my shoulders sagged.

"You mean like everyone else you've tried to interrogate?" He grinned, showcasing his missing incisors.

I had been unable to harness myself since the day she left. I had no control without her. The last four people who I had tried to interrogate died significantly harsher deaths than this TreeTamer.

Once inside their minds, I hadn't been able to stop myself. I hadn't wanted to.

I *needed* them to snap and break so I didn't have to.

I missed the way she made me feel, and if the only thing I could feel was their pain, then so be it.

This was on her hands.

She had forced me to feel something powerful and deep, and then just took it all away, along with her soft skin and fiery eyes. Their deaths were her fault.

Needless to say, we hadn't gotten the most promising answers out of anyone before I melted their minds into unhelpful puddles that sloshed about inside their thick skulls.

"You know where she resides, mate. I came back to help you—or should I say help all of fuckin' Unseelie with the way you've been rampaging. Stop dickin' around killin' everything with a pulse, and make a plan," Dirac said firmly as he slapped my arm. "I'll hold things down while you're gone. Go get her, Mendax. Teach her a lesson for leavin' ya. Don't worry about nothin' here. I heard your mum likes the company of Hanabi commanders," he said with a wink before vanishing from sight.

Deep in the back of my mind, I knew who had sent my pet—I had known all along. She had said as much, but still, I refused to believe she had joined the Seelie. Not after everything they had done to the humans already. If it was the Seelie that she worked for, then she was in a lot more trouble than she realized.

Which meant so was I.

CHAPTER 3

CALYPSO

B REATH WHEEZED OUT FROM MY CHEST AS I LOWERED another cardboard box to the floor of my closet. My trembling hands ripped off the clear packing tape to dig through as fast as they were capable. My bloodshot eyes found the small crack of the closet doorway and landed on the tall fae admiring one of the paintings of various wings on my bedroom wall. My eyes hesitated only a moment before returning to the disheveled closet floor. I quickly added a few more things to the leather duffel bag that waited at my feet. My heart—the half I still had anyway—beat like an overused drum. I needed to hurry. It was getting late, and Eli had promised we could go today.

I heard once that if you are angry about something, it was really because you were sad about it. Maybe it was true, maybe it wasn't. All I knew was that I was always angry, but if I let myself think about the reason why, I would cry until my tears drowned every bird in the sky.

What would it feel like to not have anything but a hollow cavern inside?

I should have been happy. I'd slayed the dragon. I'd

checked the last box. Now I would finally get to go to my family.

My family.

"You know you can't take all of this, right?" The deep voice skittered over me, startling me from my thoughts.

My eyes closed for a second, then I opened them once again to refocus on the man looming over me, smiling with the most contagious, charismatic smile that was ever created.

Eli is here.

I'm the only one who gets to call the large fae by this name. Prince Aurelius of the Seelie kingdom—or something similarly pompous sounding—is what everyone else has to call him. But I'm his best friend, so I could (and frequently did) call him all sorts of things and get away with it. I claimed the right when we first met, ages ago, as kids. I could never say his long name correctly, and after many laughing attacks of shouting *Or-ell-ee-usssss* later, we both agreed *Eli* was better.

It was also special. Something we had had just between the two of us that no one could take away.

The closet light reflected off his dark-honey eyes, almost making them glow.

"Cal? You okay?"

Eli's tan skin and blond hair stuck out against the white walls of my cabin. He looked so out of place here.

"I'm nervous. I know how much the fae still hate humans, and it feels weird to finally be going. I can't wait to see where you went every time you two…left me." I shook my head and choked down the words, not wanting my thoughts to go there right now.

I was barely keeping it together as it was. I was so close now. Soon everything would be made right.

My eyes absently took in the room past Eli's large frame. I had enjoyed this house the most out of all of them. My entire adult life was nothing but relocating town to town in search of the luna moths.

The luna moths were attracted to the fae portals, especially

13

the Unseelie portals. It made a lot of sense, as I later found out from the...from *him*. The luna moths were the chosen symbol of Unseelie—their mark, if you will.

The rare moths were meant to guide me toward a portal so I could complete my final test of loyalty. The last big task that needed done before I was able to go to Seelie and be with my family again. Everything had depended on it.

I had done it all for her.

Looking back, I occasionally wondered if Saracen wasn't testing me more on how long I'd continue to persevere, despite my wasted efforts, before I gave up. Perhaps that was the true test of loyalty after all. The moths were the crumbs to follow until I found my next—my last—mark. The last ordered kill I would ever make. The fee I was required to pay to become an official Seelie and be rejoined with my family.

My temples pounded painfully—too many internal wars.

The memories from just a few short weeks ago flooded me, impatient from being constantly pushed to the side.

The cold dungeon. Brown rat... Walter helping me escape.

A genuine smile touched my lips at the thought of the shifter. I was so lucky to have met him, but my smile was short-lived remembering him being pushed to his death from the castle's rooftop.

The gravelly voice of the Unseelie prince calling me his pet. His mother bonding us against my will, in preparation for a marriage ceremony, one that *thankfully* never happened.

The velvety feel of his tongue between my legs.

The way he saw through what I was the entire time and still wanted me. He saw so deep into my soul, it shouldn't have been possible. A connection we should never have had but couldn't stop.

Among the flood of memories was the drowning stare of his eyes widening when I stabbed the dagger into his back and killed him.

The box of seed envelopes in my hand fell to the floor with

a rustling slap as my body fought against my brain, wanting to collapse onto the floor along with the seeds. None of this was as easy as I'd thought it would be. The effort of breathing felt too hard...too painful.

You don't love someone full of hate and depravity.

But most of all, you don't kill someone you love.

Even monsters didn't do that.

I bent down and collected the envelopes from the floor, biting the inside of my lip to stop the tears from coming, the spot in my mouth raw and tender from the familiar action. Copper-tasting saliva coated my tongue, and the tears remained in their bastille.

Bleeding for me already?

The box dropped to the floor again as I spun around so fast, I fell back into the wall of the closet.

That was *his* voice.

Just like when...

Eli was in front of me before I could blink.

"What's wrong? What is it, Caly?" Eli scanned the small room, his amber eyes flashing with the quickness and ferocity of the fox he was capable of shifting into.

"I-I... You didn't hear anything?" I asked, shaking myself free from whatever delusional fog had just tricked my mind into hearing voices.

Malum Mendax couldn't talk to me through our bond. It was impossible...because I had killed him.

And killing him was the *only* reason I was granted passage into Seelie tonight.

"No, nothing."

"I'm so fucking nervous, I'm hearing things," I grumbled.

"Well, it's been a chaotic few weeks since you've been back from that forsaken land. Suns knows you haven't had a decent night's sleep since your return. Every night I wake up on the couch hearing you pacing about your room, mumbling. It sounds like a ghost is in the house." He chuckled softly.

Every hair on my body rose.

15

I had slept like a rock since my return, always waking up in the exact spot I fell asleep in. It wasn't me he heard.

The dreams were the only thing that soothed me anymore.

My fae best friend moved in for a hug, and my whole body tensed.

Our eyes locked as he stepped back quickly, noting the small display of black smoke that rose from my exposed forearms.

It had been happening since I awoke in the hospital.

Every time Eli got close enough to touch, the onyx smoke seemed to whisper a dark warning. We had decided it must have something to do with my being bonded to Mendax and him dying, but neither one of us could fully explain away the oddity. Every time it happened, I didn't miss the millisecond of sadness that filled Eli's eyes, as if he knew something I didn't.

"Once I'm in Seelie and Saracen mends together the other half of my heart, all of this darkness will be over. All of the thoughts of *him* will end, and I will finally, *finally* feel at peace again. I will finally get to be with them," I whispered, needing to believe it. Whether he deserved to die or not didn't matter to me. I wished I hadn't had to kill him, but if it got me to Seelie, I'd do it all over again. I'd do anything to get to Seelie.

Mendax was nothing more than the dragon who needed slain to get to my treasure. He didn't love me; he didn't even know me...and I didn't love him.

I don't.

People like us couldn't love—or not in that way. It wasn't love.

It just wasn't. Lust, most likely.

Maybe if he'd have let me orgasm instead of edging me to the point of death, I wouldn't be thinking about him so much.

Whatever it was, it wasn't love.

This had been my mantra since leaving the hospital. I had

berated and chastised myself a thousand times already, but none of it mattered.

I still missed him. Painfully so.

No one had ever seen the real me—all of me—and it was a horrible irony that when I did actually, willingly allow him to see the real me...I was pressing a dagger into his back and killing him.

What had that made me?

What kind of a monster had I become?

My jaw felt stiff and tight.

Sometimes you become the monster for the ones you love.

"You're thinking about him," Eli remarked.

I flinched, immediately wishing I hadn't said anything out loud.

I shook my head, unsure of what to do other than continue hoping that the memory of Mendax would stop haunting me for five fucking minutes. I ought to be thinking about how I was *finally* going to be with my family. It had been years since I had actually seen Eli; I should have been enjoying this.

I smiled, pushing aside everything else and suddenly feeling a swell of elation in my chest. I had gotten good at that. Ignoring things I shouldn't.

"We should head out tomorrow morning, as soon as the sun is out," Aurelius said.

I nodded. I was anxious to get to Seelie and feeling a little awkward with Eli in my space. There were still parts of my personality I hid from him, and he wasn't the same teenage boy I used to play in the stream with. His charming, handsome, comfortable presence was definitely not helping to sort out my whirlwind of emotions.

"I can't wait to see Saracen," I said, a little giddy at the thought of seeing the small blonde woman. "I'm going to hug her so tight when I get there. Will I be empowered as an official Seelie tomorrow?"

He moved to lean against the wall, crossing his large

arms in front of him. He was muscular and trim, but nothing like Mendax. Malum Mendax's body had been built for war, muscles coiled and waiting for an attack, wanting it. Eli reminded me of an athlete, still large and muscular, even powerful…but missing something.

"Cal…"

My eyes snapped up. "Aurelius," I said as I waited for whatever was coming. We hadn't spent much time together as adults, but I recognized the tone immediately. His face had somehow roughened over the last three seconds. A muscle jumped in his sharp jaw, and he suddenly looked unrecognizable to me. The normal golden-retriever best friend was replaced by a fierce defender I had never met as he stared out my bedroom window, completely frozen.

I rubbed my arm in an effort to soothe the hairs standing on end while I stepped out of the closet to see what it was that had caused the change in him.

A single pale-green luna moth fluttered calmly on the screen of my bedroom's open window.

For half a second, blinding hope swallowed me whole, before it disintegrated into the dust-speckled air.

"It has to be the bond," Eli said, still staring out the window. "The smoke, the moths…they must still be following his magic, not realizing he's dead. They will stop soon."

Our eyes locked together.

"What if…what if…" I began, feeling my pulse pick up.

"It's not him, Caly. You're safe. And it's not another Unseelie. They were forbidden access to the human realm after King Thanes—" He paused, shaking his head, suddenly looking a little angry. "The Unseelie were allowed access long, long ago and still find it occasionally, I suppose. Those powerful enough to get through the veil sometimes find a way, but it's rare. The Smoke Slayers have broken through before, but because of you, there is only one remaining who won't risk leaving the throne."

My stomach tightened.

"King Thanes?" I asked cautiously.

Getting information out of Eli and Saracen had always been a bit tricky. As much as they trusted me, they were still hesitant to tell my kind anything. There was only so much they would ever share until I was in Seelie, as one of their own.

Eli's eyes flickered at the mention of the old Unseelie king, Mendax's father. We both stared, waiting to see what the other would say. The air felt suddenly heavy.

"No, King Thanes wasn't a Smoke Slayer. He was an Impeller, and they would *never* let him cross. He's the reason they are banned from entry," he said with a familiar look. A look I had seen frequently as the queen's personal assassin—one that I only got when they were trying to hide something.

I looked at the red nail polish peeking up through my white socks. I couldn't look him in the eye.

Mendax had been a Smoke Slayer, like his mother. Only unlike the Smoke Slayers, he had also been blessed with the ability to impel your mind, like his father. It never quite occurred to me how dangerous that combination really was until this moment.

Eli was still talking, so I shook away the ever-present thoughts of Mendax.

"I still don't understand why I couldn't just sneak into Seelie. You could have told me where it was. I'm the fae killer of the human realm. Did I really need an escort?" I grumbled.

"You wouldn't have gotten past the sentries, even if you had managed to find the Seelie portal on your own. They would have killed you on entry. The royal guards are nothing to mess with."

He was right. This was not the time for me to be angry about being kept from Seelie—foggy smoke rose around me, confirming that thought. These powers were weird. I was suddenly grateful for my own abilities.

"What are you going to do with all of this stuff?" he said, waving to the plethora of things I was unable to take with me.

My fingers reached out to touch a framed luna moth painting. Eli watched as I lifted it off the wall and smashed it to the ground with a crackling shatter. My hands grabbed for more.

"What are you doing?" Eli shouted.

"What does it matter? None of this is *really* me, is it?"

My hands landed on my prized microscope. The most expensive thing I had ever owned. The one possession that had felt like a piece of hope. Something that had let me escape myself and all my obligations for a little while.

But it wasn't ever me, was it? What good would human science be in the fae realm? Science had been the only escape my mind had, but I needed to adapt. There were new things in Seelie I needed to learn. More important things. Science was a tool I had used.

A warm tear ran down my cheek as I opened the case. The snap popped with a solemn sound. Nineteen years. Nineteen fucking years, this had been the plan.

The darkness that fought to consume me was getting harder to tame. Weighty, lurking thoughts that would only settle for one thing.

It was a part of me that Eli *could not see.*

Something touched the top of my bare foot and caused me to jump back with a kick, sending whatever it was at least a foot away.

"What the—" I said, grabbing Eli's arm.

As tiny as a daisy, the little field mouse looked up at me with glistening black eyes.

"Oh my gosh!" I cried out, hurrying to the ground to scoop the little mouse up.

I may hate most people, but I had a soft spot for animals. They always reminded me of my little sister, Adrianna. I could never hurt an animal because of her.

Just people.

Without hesitation, the tiny mouse nuzzled against my hand, rubbing its white belly to my skin as she pressed a large, rounded ear to my palm.

Instantly I felt better. The anger ebbed from me, replaced with comfort. It made me feel close to my family.

"She's so sweet. It's like she knew I was upset," I mumbled as I continued petting her.

Silence caused me to glance up and catch Eli watching me, an odd expression cloaking his features.

Agh. Could he know?

My sandwich from lunch turned in my stomach. Well, this was all going to happen eventually. This was the plan.

He snapped out of it and smiled. "How do you know it's a she?" he said.

"I don't know," I said with a laugh.

I gently rubbed the tiny mouse against my cheek as all my worries seemed to get further and further away. Just for a moment.

"I just feel like I can tell. I guess that's weird, but..." Once again, I trailed off, noting the way he was watching me. I refocused on the sweet animal in my hand as I moved to open the front door.

"Caly, where are you—"

The warm, humid air hit my face. I inhaled, closing my eyes. The night air smelled like summer—fresh-cut grass and nearby bonfires.

I moved to the side of my house, where I kept the buckets of bird feed. The mouse began to skitter about nervously on my hand.

"Ssshhh, it's okay," I whispered softly.

The smell of smoke was stronger on this side of the house. Woody and smooth like burning cedar or juniper.

She must not like the campfires. I scanned my mind, trying to think of who could be burning so close. There was a campground a ways off. I opened the metal trash can a small crack and set the creature on top of the bird seed that filled the inside.

"Thank you. Stay under the lid until morning and eat as much as you would like," I said, giving her one last pet.

I turned around and slammed into Eli's chest.

21

How had he gotten behind me so quietly?

"Fuck!" I shouted. "I didn't even hear you."

"Sly as a fox," he said with a grin.

I snorted and moved to his side, where he tucked me against him and returned to the open front door.

Three luna moths were on the screen door.

"They must be attracted to you," Eli said as he shooed me inside and closed the door behind us.

After Saracen and I had made our deal, I knew I had to go to Unseelie and kill whoever the son of the queen was, but I had known nothing other than they had been hated by my family. And I didn't care about anything other than finishing the job. I hadn't even been certain how to get there. Saracen would only tell me to follow the luna moths and that she would send word when it was time.

I took the old leather book from my desk and threw it in the fireplace to burn with the next stack of wood.

"You're throwing out the opus?" Eli asked.

"I don't need it any longer. You and Saracen won't have to send me letters through a magical book. I'll be right down the hallway," I said with a smile.

"I'll kind of miss writing you letters," he replied with a frown. "What else am I to do in the evenings now? How am I ever going to gossip with you about Chef Samuel's crush on the new stable master? Or the horrid perfume Tarani insists on wearing? Honestly, you think I'm kidding, but it smells like seahorses."

I turned from the fireplace, wishing more than anything I could laugh about perfume and gossip.

"She sent me to die in Unseelie, Eli," I said as I walked back into the bedroom.

"You're her assassin. Isn't that what you signed up for, technically? She knew you could handle it," he replied as he took a stance at the window.

"Assassin or not, she knows I'm human," I said as I watched him like a hawk.

"You know how she is. This was the only way. Believe me—I tried to think of any other possible way. But Seelie rules are different, and you don't understand them. She loves you, whether you believe it or not. Mother knew you were the only one out of all of us who could outsmart those particular monsters. She knows how strong and clever you are. Tartarus, why do you think she trained you the way she did? You were being trained to kill him since the beginning."

Interesting.

As far as she was concerned, I was a weapon indebted to her, and she used me to extinguish her enemies while they were in the human realm. Only the most powerful fae could even get in here. She couldn't kill them in Seelie without breaking rules and appearing just as dark and evil as her enemy, the Unseelie queen. I didn't know much about the fae realms, but I did know the Seelie were supposed to be good and wholesome.

And I also knew that wasn't true.

They were the "good side" so to speak. But that didn't mean Saracen didn't have enemies, or that people weren't after her crown. And if they were sent to the human realm and a human took them out, the queen's hands were free of blood.

They all hated humans, so it was easy to blame us.

I rubbed my temples, trying to stop the headache that had taken residence. God, this hurt. All of this was taking a toll on my body that I hadn't suspected.

I had known our deal. I had suggested it. I owed Saracen a lot for taking me in when my mom and sister died, and as soon as I got to Seelie, I would repay her.

I was a part of the Seelie royal family now.

I turned and walked back to the main room of the house, taking one last heavy breath before picking up my most prized possession. The thing that embodied me. The prize of all my hard studies as a scientist searching for those sherbet-green moths.

23

I hurled the microscope against the tile floor. My eyes couldn't stop the tight squeeze shut when I heard the delicate pieces shatter.

How often had I driven to my biology courses, crying because I missed Eli?

I turned around and scanned the mess I had created. Strong arms pulled me in against a hard chest that smelled like mandarin oranges and sunshine.

"She loves you so much—we all do. We are your family, Cal. I don't pretend to understand half of what or why she does what she does, but I promise you, we want you to be with us as much or more than you can imagine. You are my best friend, and I can't wait for you to come to Seelie. I'm sorry I haven't been a part of your life these last several years. I hate it, but it's over now. We will go first thing tomorrow morning, and Mother will explain everything."

He squeezed tightly, and though something in my gut sent up warning flares, I relaxed into the hug. He felt so warm—almost too warm.

"Is there anything else you need to grab?" he asked.

Eli released me from the hug. The glittering gold feathers caught the light as he unfurled his right wing and began sweeping the shards of broken glass toward himself and away from me.

"I need to grab my sister."

CHAPTER 4

MENDAX

R OUGH, TEXTURED BARK PRESSED INTO MY BACK WHILE I stood against the old tree, my body too large to be completely shadowed by the night, but it didn't matter. I was the night. I was the darkest thing this human land would ever see.

A piece of hair fell into my eyes, darkening my view further. I didn't raise my hand and brush it away though; I didn't move. I couldn't move. Instead, I watched her.

She moved quickly, placing items in a traveling satchel. I could feel her heart from where I stood, watching her through the windows of her human shack. The black hair that had fallen in my eye shifted to the side with a breeze filled with the earthy smell of a forest at night.

My eyes tracked every move she made, every wrinkle in her shirt, every nervous tap of her fingers. I would never miss another move Callie—or whatever her name was—made again.

A noise sounded behind me. I wanted to turn and look, but I couldn't pry my eyes away from her. It didn't matter anyway. I watched my only threat in this world.

A pop sounded from my jaw, and I felt the deep, grinding pressure of my teeth clenching when the golden fae entered the same room as her.

Turning my head to the side and closing my eyes for a beat, I pressed my ear to my shoulder and cracked my neck with a loud snap.

My body thrummed with the need to kill the Seelie for being in the same room. He had no idea how fortunate it was he was a SunTamer and I couldn't impel his mind, because if I could, I would have decimated him.

The old gods thought they were being fair when they made the stronger powers infallible to each other.

A shiver of excitement ran over my skin as I imagined everything I would make him do had I been able to crawl inside his mind.

I listened as they talked.

He spoke differently to her. Gently, softly.

He called her Calypso, and I nearly laughed into the night at her brilliance. Giving me a misspelled nickname was smart. It wasn't tied to her strongly enough for us to use, but it was close enough that when spoken, no one would have doubted her reaction to it. Calypso did not seem like a normal human name though—perhaps she'd lied to him as well.

I knew she was human. I had felt her broken heart in my hand.

I didn't give a shit what her name was.

Mine was the only name she deserved.

She was clever, so she would realize she was only mine quickly.

Her eyes scanned the poorly lit room they stood in before gazing out the window I watched from.

For a moment our eyes locked.

She saw only darkness, but holding her gaze for a moment caused my breath to halt in my chest.

She was a goddess.

Anger boiled under my skin as I watched her return to

26

her tasks. It wasn't anger that she had betrayed and lied to me the entire time I had kept her. No—I had known the moment I saw her that she was different, that she attempted to blanket a fire inside of her. I just hadn't realized I would be drawn to it like a fucking moth to a flame. I wasn't even angry that she had stabbed and tried to kill me…that she *believed* she *could* kill me. If anything, that made me want her more, made me want to set her darkness free and see what it could really do once its shackles had broken.

I gripped the tree so hard, flaky, pale wood crumpled, creating a divot where my hand had been.

The old tree creaked in protest.

Aurelius moved closer to her while they continued to talk.

My face hardened, now with pure fury.

She had left me.

She had left me when she hadn't really wanted to. That meant someone *else* was pulling her puppet strings, and that wasn't going to work for me. It wasn't going to work out very well for them either. I knew who it was. I just needed to see if there was anyone else to add to the list.

The Seelie and the Unseelie queens had always been on the verge of a war, and I was afraid this human had probably doomed us all—unknowingly. I *knew* she wasn't aware of all there was to the Seelie queen, or she wouldn't have been packing a bag as a human to join her right now.

The only thing that might have saved her and gotten her away from them safely was our bond. Funny how much she fought against it, when it was probably the only thing that would keep her alive in Seelie. If she thought being a human was unsafe in my realm, she was in for a shock.

She definitely received some of my powers when we bonded, though how much or why was unclear. My mother and I had never heard of such a thing happening. Typically the bonded receives some of the Smoke Slayer's powers once the marriage ceremony is completed, but I've watched the smoke cascade from her soft skin enough times to know that wasn't the case with her. Through the bond, I can feel her emotions. They are watered down and faint, but they are there. She feels mine, too, when I'm not keeping them in check, even though she thinks they are her own.

This will be fun.

A tight grin lifted one side of my mouth.

The golden shit tried to hug her. She recoiled, likely repulsed by his sunshine glow, then they watched as the charcoal smoke caressed her skin.

I shuddered, feeling my smoke dance across her skin. She liked the feel of it. It reminded her of me.

"Fucking stars," I growled.

Aurelius finally left the room to collect something from her kitchen. She shuffled frantically through another box, stuffing odds and ends into her bag in his absence, checking every so often if he had returned before hurriedly placing more odd-shaped items in the bag.

For the first time since she left me, I smiled so wide I could feel something crack open in my chest.

I couldn't wait to play with my little hellhound. I couldn't *wait* to see the look on her face when she realized I wasn't dead, and I *especially* couldn't wait until I punished her for leaving me.

I told her she would never, ever be free from me, and I fucking meant it. Whether she had killed me or not, I would have returned to haunt her—and that's exactly what I planned to do.

CHAPTER 5

CALY

THE MOMENT WE CAME THROUGH ON THE OTHER SIDE OF THE portal to Seelie, we were greeted by a beautiful woman with warm brown skin and an orange-tipped sword that matched the color of her shoulder-length curls.

Stepping out from the ring of mushrooms, I nearly hurled all over the vibrant green grass, still unused to the dizzying sensation of passing through portals.

"You okay—"

Eli's words were cut off when the guard pressed the large sword flush against his neck.

My pulse picked up seeing a blade at my best friend's throat.

"Who are you?" she demanded.

I took a step toward them, ready to remove the blade from Eli's throat and turn it on her.

Eli rolled his eyes and held up his palm to wave me off.

"Mia, you know who I am. I helped train you," Eli grumbled.

The woman smiled. "Proof. Hurry up, my shift is almost over," she barked at him as if he weren't the Seelie prince.

She had sharp hazel eyes that held a threat every time they landed on me.

He let out a sigh and held the pinky finger from his right hand out to her.

As she pierced the pad of his finger with the tip of her sword, I rushed her.

"Caly, it's—"

The breath knocked out of my lungs and I realized I was lying on the grass.

The guard had one knee smashed against my throat while she held a small ball of light in the air.

"Mia, let her up. She is with me and is only granted access to the portal if I am with her, all right?"

I glared at the nodding guard while he helped me to my feet.

"It's for your protection, trust me," he said.

He smiled when my glare turned on him.

"She had to check my blood. Seelie fae bleed gold, but Seelie royal blood is iridescent. It is two different shades of gold when held against the light."

As we continued our journey up a neat and tidy dirt path, Eli informed me that Mia was a Lumins guard for the Seelie portal. Apparently they had recently needed to ramp up protection, placing guards at every portal into the realm.

Appreciation rose within me that they had women guards.

"Wait, how will I travel once I become a Seelie royal? Will magic make my blood change or something?" I asked with a laugh.

Eli's stare kept to the ground. "I suppose that's a question for my mother."

My hand absently covered the cylindrical pendant hanging from my neck, rubbing the intricate design, the white-gold vines encasing the small capsule that held my sister's ashes.

A neighbor behind our field happened to be one of the paramedics that tried to save them…or what was left of them.

She had brought some of my sister's ashes to me, and I've never been more grateful for anything in my life.

The sturdy necklace was only removed from its place around my neck when I had an order from the queen. Then it was removed and kept in a tiny red velvet bag until my return.

Adrianna didn't need to see the monster I'd become.

I tucked the pendant back against my skin and adjusted my butter-yellow sundress.

I despised dresses.

After my last trip to a fae realm involved being trapped in a dungeon, wearing the same blood-caked dress for ages, I'd vowed I would never wear a dress again.

But here I was, as usual, the need to please this particular fae family outweighing all of my own feelings. I knew Queen Saracen expected me to look the part when I arrived, and I would deliver.

She preferred me in girly dresses and had made no qualms about letting me know.

I wanted to please her—kill an evil prince, wear a yellow sundress... Whatever it took, I desperately needed her to accept me.

"I hope lunch is ready when we get there; I'm starved. Human food is horrible compared to our food," Eli groaned as we continued walking.

"You didn't seem to think half of my refrigerator was horrible last night," I quipped.

"I was doing you a favor and cleaning out your disgusting fridge," he replied while pretending to be offended.

I rolled my eyes and laughed so hard, the unfamiliar sound startled me. I never got to feel like this.

My eyes caught on the white dress shirt pulling across Eli's chest. His pecs tightened the fabric as his arms moved at his side. When had he gotten so...manly?

"I bet Mother had Chef make pistachio ice cream for you," Eli chirped.

I quickly steeled myself and smiled as we continued up the dirt path.

When I was seven, shortly before my eighth birthday, I had watched an ice cream commercial where a *very* happy family dug into bowls of pistachio ice cream. They smiled and laughed, each full of the deepest love I had ever seen. The father laughed and teased the kids.

I knew immediately that I was no longer a vanilla girl.

No, pistachio was my new flavor.

It didn't matter that I'd never so much as *tasted* a pistachio. I wanted what they had, that love and closeness. I craved everything they had in that commercial—even the ice cream.

That week was the same week that held the day, the hour, the *minute* that would be forever etched into the darkening recesses of my mind.

That was the week my mom and sister had been killed in the car accident.

The same week Saracen stayed with me and brought Miss Claire to watch over me.

I remember quite distinctly how numb I had been.

A lot of things changed for me that week.

I didn't want Saracen and Miss Claire near me.

I wanted Mom and Adrianna back. I should have been in that car accident too. It felt like my punishment was that I hadn't been allowed to go with them.

It *was* a punishment—and a terribly painful one.

To this day, I've never wished for anything more than that I'd died in that car with my family.

But no. So it was up to me to make the best use of my time here.

After I had stumbled upon the Seelie queen in her tiny form and protected her from the blackbird, a few things had happened. I'd learned that fae in the human realm who spent too much of their magic would shrink until they could return to their realm. I had learned that the blackbird was actually the Unseelie Queen Tenebris in a different form. And I'd seen the golden queen often, as she'd visited and left her son frequently while she tended to business, leaving me to play with him.

Queen Saracen had been the one to relay the news of their death.

I remembered the way she struggled to get the words out of her pink lips when she showed up at my door.

She and Eli had stayed with me for weeks to make certain that I was safe and wouldn't be shipped away to some foster family I didn't know.

Mom didn't have any friends that I knew of, and there was no family left besides me. My grandparents had long since passed, and my father wasn't a part of our lives. I had no one. Mom was always a little anxious and paranoid about the people in our lives.

A short time later, Eli had gifted me the tiny, vined pendant to keep her ashes in. He had snuck it in from Seelie and had even had it engraved. Amongst the delicate white-gold vines that held the ashes, a tiny oval citrine sparkled on a small hinge, and when you unlocked the hinge, it revealed an inscription that had been etched unto the vial:

FEUHN—KAI—GREEYTH

Eli told me it was an old fae language and that it meant "eternal love and friendship." It's something we said to each other all the time now. It must be a really old language because even other fae like Miss Claire had no idea what it meant. That made me like it even more—something else special just between us.

Saracen tried to be kind and tender. But she was the queen of a fae realm that humans were forbidden from entering. Eventually she and Eli had to return to rule their kingdom. (Well not Eli, he was close to my age, an infant by fae standards, though the aging of fae was unbelievably incomprehensible for me.) In her place, she had left a nurse-maid, Miss Claire, to take on my care between her very scattered visits to the human realm.

That week, the modestly sized freezer of my small house had been packed with tubs of every flavor of ice cream imaginable, the tiny freezer threatening not to close if even one more pint were to be added. Apparently word had gotten around our small town about the accident, and everyone assumed ice cream would be exactly what a newly orphaned child needed.

I didn't want to drown in ice cream, I just wanted to drown someone.

I had a really hard time controlling my anger back then.

One day, on a particularly hard afternoon, I opened the freezer and found pistachio was among the many pints. At that point, I was willing to try anything that could help me grip hold of even a tendril of comfort.

Flashes of the commercial played in my head, and I knew it would give me that same, sought-after experience.

That was the first day I realized how hard everything would be.

I remember one day, not long after that, when Saracen's gorgeous monarch butterfly wings had appeared at her back in the garden behind my house. Eli had been red as a beet while she yelled at him for skipping his courtly duties. Instead, he had snuck in to visit me and run through the fields of poppies, where we used to race the falcons across the big meadow.

It was Eli's favorite thing to do.

I only knew a few things about faeries at that time: fae who have wings are usually of a royal bloodline of some sort, and they generally only release them when they feel something so strongly that it takes over their system. It is completely out of their control, and it's usually a sure sign something bad and dangerous is about to happen.

At least in my experience.

Queen Saracen had been so mad at me for distracting Eli, she had threatened to put a magical block on the portals, barring Eli from reentering the human realm to see me. She didn't, of course.

Not then anyway.

He returned a few weeks later, but that afternoon, she had left with Eli in such a rush, I had been upset for days. Was she going to hurt him? Would they come back? Would she be so mad she would take away Miss Claire? I would be left completely alone.

As far as the system and anyone else was concerned, I didn't exist. It had been the only way to keep the state and everybody else from questioning who was actually caring for me. Queen Saracen had erased any evidence that I had ever existed.

It worked well—so well that no one ever came and tried to take me away or see me.

I had been beside myself when they left that day, wishing more than anything that I could go to the golden castle and tell her it had been my fault and not Eli's.

But I couldn't.

No matter how badly I wanted to be with them, I just couldn't.

Humans were forbidden from entering the fae realms— they had been having problems with humans trying to assassinate royalty. So instead of being able to go to the Seelie realm, I drowned my worries in pistachio ice cream, needing it to give me everything the people in the commercial had felt.

I loathed it.

The second the sharp, faulty sweetness touched my taste buds, I *despised* it. It was a terrible, false flavor masquerading as something wonderful. Pistachio was disgusting, but still I forced myself to eat the entire tub of disappointment. Every single bite reminded me of something I couldn't have, couldn't feel. It reminded me of how strong my commitment to the plan needed to be. How important it was that I didn't falter.

From then on, pistachio was the only ice cream I ate, remembering each and every time the foul taste touched my tongue that I needed to be strong so I could finally be with my family. Only then would I experience the loving feeling of those in the commercial.

That was kind of how I felt now as I stared at the golden castle—the castle that I had spent my entire life trying to get to.

I stood on the brick path of the field and stared at the obnoxious golden monument. The sun pelted off the shimmering gold turrets and shot straight in my eyes, blinding me.

I couldn't help the nagging feeling of disappointment that had settled in my belly.

I could do this. I had to—for them.

But it was too large, too bright.

Too…happy.

I had thought a feeling of happiness would flood me or that I would immediately get a feeling of accomplishment.

In the short walk from the portal in the royal forest to the front entrance of the Seelie castle, it seemed as though the sun had focused on burning my skin, giving it an unpleasant pink hue I'd only seen on baby hippos. It was obvious that this was not the same sun I was accustomed to in the human realm.

"Once we get inside, I'll ask the monarch witch to spell your skin with some protection from the sun," Eli said sympathetically as he made a face at my neon-pink forearms.

I nodded in response, unsure of what else to say.

Having spent a significant stretch in the Unseelie realm, predominantly in the dungeon and inside the Unseelie castle, my eyes and skin had grown even more accustomed to darkness.

Much like my taste in men apparently.

"You okay?" Eli asked, grabbing my hand as we both stared at the giant castle's entrance.

My stomach churned from nerves—it was showtime.

My eyes stung as I squeezed Eli's warm hand. Light wisps of smoke lifted from mine, and this time, we both looked away in an attempt to ignore it.

"Yeah," I said, shaking myself out of my wallowing. "Just nervous, I guess, and tired."

Tired wasn't the half of it. I had gone from tirelessly fighting to get close to Mendax, the Unseelie prince, to fighting to keep myself away from him.

He had been nothing like they had told me.

I sighed, feeling it down to my ankles. I had fought for my life in the trials Mendax and his bitch of a mother had forced me to partake in. I trembled, still able to feel the weight of the blade in my hand.

Ouch!

I gasped, dropping Aurielis's hand to clutch at my chest.

It hurt—emotionally *and* physically.

It hurt in a way I'd never be able to forget.

My time was running out.

"It'll be okay. Mother is going to be so happy to see you," Eli said.

I noted the uneasy cracks in his typically smooth voice. Warm droplets of sweat dripped down what felt like every inch of my body. I squeezed my eyelids shut tightly and held still for a moment before forcing them to reopen. I refocused on the giant, shimmering castle once again.

The tall wildflowers rustled in a soft breeze, tickling my leg. I grabbed a handful of the stems and tore the clump out, throwing them to the ground.

"Maybe you should rest before we see the queen," Eli said gently as he stared at the crumpled pile of flowers at my feet.

"No," I stated firmly. "I want the pain to stop—I want my heart whole again as soon as possible."

Maybe if my heart was whole again, it would fill this horrible ache that filled it.

"Caly?" Eli questioned, resting his hand on my lower back.

"What, Aurelius?" I snapped, instantly regretting the use of his full name as soon as he shrunk backward.

Relief washed over me though when our eyes locked. I knew he understood.

I had noticed the way his touches seemed to linger now. How his eyes darkened sometimes when he watched me.

That couldn't happen.

It had nothing to do with Mendax.

Aside from seeing Eli briefly at the trial with Mendax, it had been years since I had seen him in person. And now, the comforting best-friend touches held something deeper, something that felt more breakable.

In my eyes, Aurelius was always the golden boy who somehow, no matter how tough, always seemed to do and say the perfect things, always put a Band-Aid on me when my broken bits felt too rough. He was my hero.

So why couldn't I stop thinking about the villain?

If Mendax had been the villain though, then what did that make me, the person who stabbed *him* in the back? In some stories, the person who slayed the villain instantly became the hero.

I knew I wasn't the hero. Which was just one more reason Eli needed to stay away from me. He'd hate me soon enough.

I had sacrificed every facet of my life to stand in the exact place I was standing now.

So why was I dreading it?

It was beautiful. A hint of briny sea was on the breeze. Perhaps the water was nearby? Hundreds of vibrant monarch butterflies fluttered around. Several had been with us since the human realm and were now dancing atop the swaying flowers. Birds chirped happily, swooping merrily across the bright-blue sky. A fluffy bluebird with a teal crest fluttered in front of my face before landing on a nearby oak branch to watch us with a joyous expression, and I swear to god, I think a squirrel smiled at me.

My wide eyes turned to look at Eli.

"What?" he said with a shrug. "You're in Seelie now."

I turned back to the flowers in a riot of colors assaulting my eyes. Don't get me wrong. It was beautiful—it just felt like someone else's beautiful.

I shook my head, not sure of what to say that wouldn't hurt his feelings, unsure of why it rubbed me the wrong way.

What, it's too happy? Everybody wants to be happy.

This was what *I* wanted. I was being too harsh, too jaded.

The hair on the back of my neck tingled like I was being watched, and the training that had been drilled into me took over, and my palms began to sweat. Eli seemed oblivious as I whipped around and peered back into the far-off edge of forest. Had the guard followed us?

There was nothing.

But I could feel it—that sense of panic animals got when the predator marks them.

As if sensing my thoughts, Eli broke the silence, letting out a soft chuckle. "This isn't like the dark and monster-ridden Unseelie realm," he said with a smile. The sunny prince waved me onward, to the last stretch of narrow path between us and the castle's main entrance. "This is the good side, Caly." He tucked a daisy behind my ear.

And just like that, I was reminded of which parts of me to hide.

CHAPTER 6

MENDAX

C ALY HAD TOLD ME I WAS A VILLAIN.
     She must have learned what bad guys are from someone meaning her harm because she has no fucking idea what a villain really is.

She thought I was awful when I hated her. She's about to learn just how horrible I am when I'm in love with her.

My skin itches in anticipation.

I lower my chin and reach for my powers. Like a crack of lightning, the ghost of smoke appears over my skin, eagerly whispering sweet, masochistic nothings to my black soul as I shadow through the portal.

Unsurprisingly, there's a guard at the entrance. With everything taking place with the Fallen fae, of course they would have guards at the royal portals. The Fallen were the same ones who had been attempting to take over my castle.

The guard couldn't see me—not that a small Seelie guard would stop me anyway. The Fates themselves couldn't stop me from getting to that woman, and anyone that got in my way would sorely regret doing so.

I reach for her tooth dangling on a cord around my neck

and rub the smooth, white edge methodically against my bottom lip, mindlessly aching to feel her closer and remembering the fire in her eyes when she spat the molar at me in the Unseelie dungeon.

Would she fight me when I got to her? Probably. It didn't matter. She was as deeply in love as I was. She just might not know it yet.

I would make sure she knew.

I walked past the guard unseen, his beady Seelie eyes flickering in my direction. He could sense something awful was near him, the feeling when your primal body recognizes that you are in danger. That's all he would notice though.

I meant to let him live. I had intended to slide by unseen before making my way to the Seelie castle and retrieving my things—but I couldn't.

My black blood prickled under my flesh, overcome with the need to rattle his Seelie bones.

I squinted, standing in front of the guard. It was bright as could be in this star-forsaken land. In my shadow form, I was completely invisible to the naked eye. I preferred blending into the darkness and night, but I could conceal myself enough in broad daylight for short periods. It was one of the reasons Smoke Slayers were considered some of the most powerful fae.

It was incredibly easy to kill when others couldn't see you.

I didn't want to just kill this guard though.

I wanted to make a scene.

I had barely killed anything since I watched that golden bastard put his hands on my pet in the human realm. I knew in that instant, he would experience a death unlike any other. That would be the price he paid for tangling himself with my love. Aurelius certainly knew better than to fuck with me, but I would be pleased to remind him.

That was the difference between a so-called villain and hero. It wasn't about who had the greater powers or tricks. It was about who felt the strongest and to what capacity. Even some of the best thieves and murderers have a surprisingly strong moral compass. The gauge that tells them it's okay to steal bread or rob someone in the village for their starving family but not to hurt innocent people.

I didn't care who I hurt. I've never needed something in return for hurting anyone, and I didn't need motivation to inflict pain. I was built full of rage.

I used my strengths to get what and where I wanted. No matter what accomplishments, praise, accolades, titles, or companions I ever had, I had never felt the way I've seen others feel. I had had friends, family, lovers—if you wanted to call them that—but I had never *felt* anything from it. Not the way I felt when I unleashed myself and killed. Sure, I had people who I would have helped: Alistair, Walter— before I dropped him off the roof and into the Seelie portal anyway.

The thought of what would have happened to my love if she had managed to get through the portal with Walter and land in Seelie without being bonded to me made a guttural growl rip out of my throat.

The guard in front of me froze, stopping his pacing to look straight through me. Tiny goose bumps rose on his sweaty flesh. What horrible armor they had.

I was within arm's reach of him. His golden-tan cheeks sagged just slightly. There was the barest tremble to them as his eyes darted around in an attempt to find the cause of his terror. His heart rate doubled, nearly deafening to me.

Walter would be easy to find. I would start with him so he could help me with Caly. The portal I had dropped him into went straight to the golden seas that butted up against the small village beyond the Seelie castle. If he was smart, he would have shifted into a rat in the confines of the village, but knowing how much we both hated the Seelie, I was betting he had already exposed himself with a fight and landed in a dungeon somewhere.

"Aye, who goes there?" shouted the Seelie guard in front of me.

My smoky wings unfurled with a soft thrum, enthusiastic to kill. Smoke tendrils crawled up his body leisurely but gained speed with every inch they touched. The smoke wasn't as easy to hide, its darkness too great to be covered completely in this light. His nostrils widened, taking note of the woody, amber scent of my smoke just as his eyes found mine.

It didn't matter. All of the Seelie realm was about to know I had arrived.

CHAPTER 7

CALY

Y OU'RE HERE!" THE WOMAN SHOVED ME ASIDE TO LAUNCH AT Eli with enough force to send us all onto the perfectly manicured lawn.

Thankfully Eli had anticipated his sister's move and steadied me as he greeted Princess Tarani.

The fae squeezed her arms around Eli so tightly, I listened for the soft cracking of a rib up until the moment she released him. Her golden-blond hair, draped across her shoulders like a cape, caught the sparkling sun. I couldn't remember how old she was, not that it mattered. Fae didn't age in the same way humans did, and it had never made any sense to me anyway. Once they hit around twenty, their looks remained the same for decades.

She looked young, like a fresh-faced and sheltered eighteen-year-old human. Like all fae, she was unbelievably beautiful. Her large amber eyes were the focal point of her slightly rounded face. What her sweet eyes didn't take up, her contagious smile did. She had the same bright smile as Saracen and Eli—the kind that, even if you didn't want to, you couldn't help but smile when you saw it.

"I'm so glad you're back! I've been bored stiff since you left." She smiled. Her twinkling eyes landed on me as though she'd just noticed someone else was with them. "You are the human I hear so much about," she said, losing the smile. Her face hardened, and I was completely caught off guard by the venom that dripped from her words.

"Uh—I—" I stuttered.

"Suns, Tarani, let us in the door first before you start. Cal, as I'm sure you've guessed, this is my younger sister, Tarani," Eli said with a large grin. He reached out to tousle his sister's hair.

They fondly looked at each other, and I couldn't help but feel a pinch in my chest.

They smiled and teased each other, and it dawned on me that I'd probably never been as happy as the two of them appeared to be in all my life. While these two had been pampered and waited on, surrounded by a family that loved them, I had been stuck in my own realm, without a family, tracking insects and killing fae that rubbed their mother the wrong way.

The smiles fell from the sunlit pair as they noticed the few tears falling down my cheeks, breaking through the dam I'd built.

"What's wrong, Calypso? Tarani didn't mean anything, she's just protective," Eli said, stepping closer to comfort me.

I wiped the tears away with the back of my hand and silently threatened the other tears before they thought about falling as well. "I just can't believe I'm finally here," I lied, emphasizing it with a smile and a limp wave of my hand.

Eli's eyes held mine for a beat before he ushered us inside. The guards all moved around us, one of them grabbing for my bag.

"I'll carry my bag, please," I said, turning my attention to the sentry and attempting to take the leather duffel from the gold-armored guard.

"It's part of his job, Caly. Let him. You'll need to adjust to

45

people helping you now that you will be living in the castle. The bag will be taken to your room for you. Let's go inside; I know Mother is dying to see you," the princess said, sounding more than a little annoyed. She laced her arm in Eli's, who linked his in mine, and guided us forward—away from my things.

I smiled wide, making certain it reached my eyes. I gave Eli's arm a light squeeze before deftly unlinking it as they continued. "Just give me one second," I mumbled in their direction.

With the smile still plastered on my face, I walked back to the guard who held my bag and scanned his gold armor. They were either really powerful and didn't need very good armor, or they were foolish and it was for decoration. Either way, it was ineffective. I noticed several arteries fully exposed. Even their helmets left their faces open for an attack. I didn't deal with magic very frequently with the fae I killed in the human realm though, so I had to assume that they were far more dangerous than they appeared. It didn't help that every one of the guards also had a small, creepy grin on their face. I would need to adjust to that.

The guard with my bag paused for a second, likely trying to figure out why I was approaching him.

Smile still plastered to my face, I leaned in and whispered into his slightly pointed ear where small tufts of hair white hair peeked out, "You are going to hand me my bag." I leaned back to look in his face, gave him a bright smile, and let out a giggle. His smile faltered but returned once I giggled again. "You are going to give me my bag right now, or I am going to take it from you, and trust me, you don't want that." I laughed, reaching out to touch his shoulder.

Like a good guard, he glanced to Eli, who rolled his eyes and nodded, no doubt having heard every word I'd whispered with his foxlike hearing. My hand tingled slightly on the guard's shoulder, and I pulled it away to take the bag from him just as he and everyone else noticed the wisps of smoke trailing into the sky from my hand.

What the fuck was going on with this? I needed to run some tests and figure out exactly what caused it to react. It hadn't gone off when the portal guard had touched me and had even stayed dormant a few times when Eli had. It didn't make any sense.

I shifted my bag's strap over my shoulder and rejoined the group, smile still in place. I wanted to make a mental checklist of things to test for, but I wouldn't even know where to begin with this kind of thing. As soon as I got settled, I would ask Eli about a library.

My arm once again looped through Eli's, I began to walk before he caught my gaze, tilting his head a fraction. The customary best-friend check to make sure I really was okay. Barely hidden concern leached out of his pretty honey eyes. I nodded back with a real smile this time, and we continued up the mammoth-sized stone steps into the Seelie castle.

If I had thought for a single moment that the outside of the Seelie castle had been obnoxious, the inside was like a punch to the face.

Mendax and Queen Tenebris's castle had been opulent, but the Seelie castle made theirs look like a small manor in comparison. It was deceptively large, even considering the outside made it look like an absolute monstrosity. The inside felt repulsively grand—and gold.

Bright, shiny gold—not the deep, dark gold of human jewelry, but a neon, sparkling, gleaming gold that bathed every inch of the interior, making my eyes tremble and squint. The unbelievably tall ceilings, marble floors, intricate molding, and carved doors that seemed to go on endlessly down a hallway were all gold.

Holy shit.

What was I doing here? I didn't belong here.

"I'm going to go find Mother. She is going to be so excited to see you," Tarani said with a sly quirk to her smile as she left Eli and I in the entryway.

I craned my neck and saw the ceiling wasn't simply gold,

47

but bright rays of sunshine also beat down harshly on every crack and crevice.

I already missed the gentle comforts of the darkness. This hurt my eyes and made me feel...exposed. Did everyone feel this way under the scorching ceiling? Perhaps they had done this intentionally.

"Just the hallways are spelled to have the sunshine on them," Eli added as he watched me try and relax my face. "The Seelie royals are the house of the sun, and we are light wielders. The queen, Princess Tarani, and I are the only SunTamers left," he said proudly, tracking my reaction.

"Was Langmure a SunTamer?" I asked, regretting my words the moment I said them.

"Yes. My brother was a SunTamer before Mendax killed him," he snarled and looked at his shoes.

"I'm sorry, Eli. I–I didn't mean to bring it up," I apologized.

What the fuck? This was the worst possible entrance to the Seelie castle I could have made.

"Cal, you have nothing to apologize to me about. You killed my brother's murderer. I should be thanking you."

The burning in my lungs threatened to knock me down.

When would I feel good about what I had done for my family? Would it ever feel right?

I had killed many times before. As an assassin, I had killed *a lot*. It was all I knew.

In all the times I had taken someone's life, not once had I felt as broken and hollow as I had after Mendax.

What a fool I was.

There was no hiding that I had started to fall in love with Mendax. I deserved every hollow moment that I got for being such a fool. Once I got the other half of my heart back, I would feel differently. I had to. I would stop thinking about him. Stop missing him. It would all be a part of the past.

If I could go back, I would kill Mendax all over again just for making me feel so miserable without him.

"Are you certain you do not wish to get settled and

cleaned up before you see Mother? It's been a long time since you have seen her." Eli spoke to me with the same gentle undertone he would a child.

"Please, Eli." I fought it, but another tear freed itself. "I just need to feel whole again," I mumbled, looking into his amber eyes. Being with my best friend again was so nice. Just the thought of being separated from him again was painful.

He nodded solemnly, and we continued through the castle. A few incredulous looks came our way from the servants. I wasn't certain if it was due to my now-rumpled sundress (even these servants wore fancy clothing that was much more garish than what the servants in the Unseelie castle wore) or if it was due in part to me being so clearly a human with my non-pointed ears and boring, ungoddesslike features.

"Stop this very instant, Prince Aurelius." A stern, clipped voice came from behind us.

Eli stopped moving instantly, grabbing my arm just as I had begun to reach into my bag for a weapon. I scowled at my friend before I shook my arm free.

"What on sun's soil is the meaning of this? You cannot be bringing a human into this castle. Do you want the Ancients to kill you?"

"It's all right, Samuel," Eli said gently, putting his hands up in surrender.

I barely hid my disapproval as I turned to observe the man responsible for such sharp words.

My eyes found a stiff, angular man no taller than myself, with lowered, fluffy brown eyebrows that sat above his slightly asymmetrical green eyes. He looked a human sixty, so there was no telling how old he truly was. He could have been hundreds of years old with the way the fae aged. I expected to see the gleaming armor of a guard or the white ceremonial garb I had seen Eli wear at the trial in the Unseelie realm, but to my surprise the assertive man wore something that bore such a striking resemblance to a human chef's jacket that my mouth dropped open in surprise.

"Don't you dare *it's all right, Samuel* me, Aurelius!" the man shouted, taking an erratic step toward me.

Eli quickly stepped in to block me, though I did notice he seemed to be protecting the old man more than me. "It's *her*, Samuel—it's Calypso." Eli grabbed the curmudgeon's shoulders.

I stepped back a little, my brown ballet flats sliding a bit on the polished floor. Something about the way Eli had responded seemed odd, like he was speaking to a close family member, not a cook.

The man stilled instantly, and they continued to look at one another for a moment.

"I'll be," the man muttered.

They stood grinning at one another so long, I lost interest and took the opportunity to try and map out exactly where I was with regards to the castle's layout.

Out of nowhere, a warm force pressed into my chest and gripped tightly to my shoulder blades. My nerves got the better of me, causing my somatic reflex to snap. Just as your hand flees from a hot stove, I moved quickly—so quick I surprised myself.

Within a second I had dropped the force—now noticing it was the old chef—and stood over him with my shoe pressed firmly into his trachea.

"Oh my suns! Calypso!" Eli hollered, quickly moving to push me off of Samuel's neck.

"Calypso! Get off him! Is this what you do to someone who tries to hug you?" His voice held alarm, but his eyes danced with a hint of amusement. "Samuel is my dear friend—he's like a father to me, Cal. Let him up. He knows *all* about you," he exclaimed with a wide, boyish grin.

Crimson crept into my cheeks. "Never sneak up on an assassin," I nervously sang.

Eli shot me a harsh look.

"I-I am so sorry, Samuel," I stuttered as I helped the man up. "I guess I'm a little more on edge than I thought. Please forgive me. Eli has told me so much about you."

I weakly hugged the chef.

I needed to get it together before I ruined everything. I cleared my throat, readying a more convincing apology and chastising myself for further embarrassing humans in the fae world, when a beautiful voice poured in from the hallway in front of us.

"And you thought I acted harshly about my overcooked oats this morning."

As though the voice held the strings to my expression, my mouth pulled up in a wide smile.

She was a vision of grace and beauty standing in the bright hallway, watching me, her smooth, tanned face overflowing with laughter and joy.

I swear, even more rays of the sun appeared inside of the bright castle to backlight the queen. Her dazzling flaxen gown shimmered, the train of it in a small pool behind her. A deep breath let loose from my tight chest as I felt for the V-shaped scar on my hand.

"Queen," I said. Talking was hard right now. I didn't want to say anything I shouldn't.

I couldn't believe I was here. Finally.

Chef Samuel had taken my distraction as an opportunity to roll away from me, but he never stood. Instead, he kneeled, bowing.

A noise kind of like a forced cough came out of his throat, and I immediately felt a little bad for hurting Eli's friend.

It was almost over. I was here. I looked to Eli, who was also making the same weird noise as his friend and was also in a deep bow.

Samuel's side-eye caught my gaze as he nodded his head in short flicks, signaling for me to bow.

Realizing I was the only one not bowing, I immediately stumbled over myself and into a clumsy curtsey like I'd seen in the movies. I felt so stupid.

In the human world, I had never been told to bow to Queen Saracen. Nor had Aurelius bowed to his mother. I noticed several servants and guards had moved out into the hallway from the dozens of rooms all around to get a look at the queen. A quick glance up showed a few leaning over the intricate gold railing that seemed to climb never-ending heights.

"Calypso. My Unseelie destroyer, my favorite child!" She winked at Eli. "Come, Aurelius, bring Caly into the drawing room. There is much I wish to speak with you about. I have hardly slept a moment since sending you that last letter. Tell Tarani to join us for some tea."

I breathed out, preparing to see the princess again. It was touching how much Eli doted on her.

It was a shame I had to kill her.

CHAPTER 8
QUEEN SARACEN

T HEY WERE SO HAPPY.
Tarani and Aurelius gracefully chased after the small cluster of butterflies. Langmure sat by the fountain, reading whatever human tale his nurse had gifted him this week. From the library's tall window above, I watched them dance and laugh in the sunlit garden.

They were too young to know it was actually the butterflies that chased them and their pureblood Seelie bodies. Thanks to the marriage arrangements, these children had been bred to be the purest of Seelie.

A heaviness in my body grew, knowing what was about to happen. Aurelius began picking poppies like he didn't have a care in the world—the perfect example of a happy, light-hearted Seelie faerie.

He would never work. He was never going to be the leader necessary for the world Thanes and I were creating. I suppose very few true Seelie would.

Langmure might have worked, but he wouldn't be here long. The child had been cursed by Kaohs in a deal gone bad and was owed to the pits of Tartarus as soon as the king of the Nether decided to take him. He didn't even know it.

I noted the position of the sun.

Any minute now.

I grabbed the leather-bound tome close to me and took one last glance at the lighthearted children playing below. Tonight, I would take Aurelius and Tarani to the human realm, where they would remain.

I would leave them.

It was weak, but I couldn't bring myself to kill them. I really did love them—they just weren't useful to me anymore. Thanes could never know I let them live. The Unseelie king would be killing off Mendax and Tenebris at this very moment.

Earlier today, he had told me several of his "Fallen fae" were immeasurably stronger than anything we could have hoped for and that he was going to test their powers by using them to kill the Smoke Slayers.

My eyes, heavy and tired, dropped closed while I took in a deep breath of leather-scented air. I could almost *feel* the world lightening with Tenebris and Mendax finally dead. If Thanes had been able to rearrange and infuse the human minds to be that powerful—powerful enough to kill two Smoke Slayers—then maybe we were aiming too small just working on the humans. As I began to turn away from the window, I stilled at the last moment, the unusually dark look on Tarani's face while she glared at her brother catching my full attention.

Aurelius had begun to scream at her, his voice raw and shrill. He was close to a meltdown, throwing himself on the ground at her feet.

My lips started to curve into a smile as I watched.

Tarani larked about, grabbing ahold of the butterflies that fluttered near her. She giggled as her tiny fingers masterfully pulled their wings off before dropping them to the ground and grabbing another as her older brother wailed at her feet.

Pride swelled in my chest. She was different—I could see it now.

She would stay.

Thanes and I could see to it that when the time came, she had felt enough pain to rule with a strong and steady hand. She was far too beautiful to be allowed in the castle with us though, where she would definitely catch Thanes's attention, but I would make certain her darkness was properly fed.

On second thought, maybe catching Thanes's eye would be good for her. He would toughen her up.

It was settled. Aurelius would go to the human realm alone.

A soft tap sounded at the door. It was time.

"Your Highness?"

My fingers clenched around the book I held. This had to happen. I needed to prove I wasn't just some frolicking, simple-minded Seelie. Just because I couldn't shift into a fox didn't make me less than them. I would show them all *exactly* what I was capable of.

"You asked me to fetch you when King Felix was ready for his night's tea," the maid murmured softly, averting her eyes.

"Yes, thank you, Evelyn. His Majesty requested that I prepare it tonight." I picked up the leather pouch from the small desk as I moved toward the young maid who held the door open.

My knees threatened to drop me as they trembled with each step.

I could do this. It would all be for the better in the end.

I paused briefly before stepping out the door to lean toward the girl, speaking as if in confidence. "How have you been liking your new position, my dear?" I asked kindly. She'd only been hired a fortnight prior.

"Oh, her ladyship is too kind. You could not have bestowed the employment on a more grateful family, ma'am," she replied softly as a blush crept up her neck.

"That does please me. Tell me, what did your family think of your bonus wages? You did receive them, did you not? For starting on such short notice?"

She stared at me, bewildered, unable to speak.

"I thought as much. Here," I said, thrusting the leather pouch into her hands. "A token of our gratitude, from King Felix's personal collection. I've added a few tokens from the royal treasury as well."

"Oh! Ma'am!" she cried, her face filled with joy.

"You deserve it." I leaned in and lowered my voice. "I shouldn't tell you this, but if you go to the servants' quarters and make a big stink about it, they will trade you anything you could possibly desire to be in your favor. Mary makes the most gorgeous day bonnets. You would look absolutely divine in one!" I squeezed her palm lightly.

"You think? Would they not be upset with me?" she asked.

"Oh, good heavens no! They were not lucky enough to receive such a gift. They will be thrilled to share in the excitement." I smiled, making certain that it reached my eyes.

"Oh, thank you! Thank you so much! I will go now! Are you certain her ladyship doesn't need my help to prepare King Felix's tea?"

I leaned in even farther now. "Strictly between us, my husband has recently brought up concerns that his tea has been tampered with the last few weeks. Apparently, every time he drinks it, he becomes violently ill," I whispered just loud enough that the two butlers who had just appeared down the hallway could also hear.

"But, ma'am—"

"Oh, I'm sure it's nothing. Though I did hear he looked rather pale while I was in Duneberry last week. Once the healer returns from his trip, please send him up immediately. I don't know what I would do if something were to happen to my Felix."

She curtseyed deeply and nodded before running off to the servants' quarters as I continued to my parlor.

Unfortunately, the healer would not respond to their summons when the time came, as he was floating in the Golden Sea, dead as of two days ago.

I turned the corner into my parlor and pulled the poison sachet free from the hollowed-out book. Next, my trembling fingers collected the small green tin of loose tea that sat next to the small memoillusion cube of Felix and I on the desk.

I stared at the little glass box and watched as our tiny figures of light danced together in a perfect waltz. The gold glow of our opaque bodies moving with grace.

We looked so happy. It was the first time we ever met, at our wedding ceremony.

I had been brought up knowing that I would wed the crown prince of Seelie. He only had a few brides to choose from, and my wings almost guaranteed me the position. I had no other powers, which was unheard of for a pureblood. It would have damned me had I not been blessed with monarch wings. They all believed it was destiny, but I knew I was just a mascot.

Royalty weren't allowed to choose their partner, not really. It was a matchup of pure, royal-blooded families. The men were the ones that chose. It was based purely off of dancing with the eligible women in a ballroom and then marrying them hours after. I held the memoillusion cube, feeling its solid weight settle in my hands. Felix's handsome face stared back, his deep amber eyes stabbing into my soul from behind the glass.

I had loved him from the moment he swore he wouldn't treat me the way the other queens were treated. That he wanted me to be an equal and rule beside him. That was unheard of for a king.

Felix worshiped me. Anything that made me happy, he made flourish as only a king could do. When I asked for a novel, he built me a library. When I showed interest in war strategy, he allowed me to sit in during briefings on the procession of the Unseelie War. He always treated me as an equal, showing me anything and everything I could ever want to know.

But then that was the problem.

He had shown me how much I didn't wish to be his equal. I wanted his power.

Putting the memoillusion cube down, I grabbed the poison, poured the dried herbs into the tea sachet, and tightened the small, cream-colored strings, setting it in the teacup and hurrying out of my parlor before I could lose my courage.

"There you are, my flower."

I bumped into Felix's chest, causing me to nearly drop the fragile cup. "Felix."

His familiar hands wrapped around my waist. "Agh, the woman with the tea. Chef Samuel mentioned that you wished to deliver my tea tonight. I *desperately* hate to be a pest, but after the day I've had, I'm afraid I need *quite* a strong brew," he said squeezing my middle.

Oh, I'd give him a strong brew.

I'd have doubled the dose had I thought I'd have to sit and listen to him talk about his boring day. He had no idea what a tough day was. He and everyone else in Seelie were oblivious to the horrors outside of Seelie's veil.

"I was just bringing it up, my dear. Will you be taking it in your study?" I asked, taking note of the faded scroll he carried under his arm.

"Yes, I need to place a few things in the burnaway." He removed his arm from my waist to rub at his forehead.

We continued up the stairs and into his study without words. I made my way to the warm wrought-iron kettle in the corner of the well-lit study. I poured a bit of the hot water, filling the teacup I held. The black kettle refilled itself with hot water before I had a chance to set it back on the table. The tea sachet leached a small swirl of purple into the clear water as it steeped.

I couldn't do this. This was foolish and wrong. Felix was a good man, a good king. He had been so kind to me.

What was I doing? I was Seelie. I didn't do things like this.

"You and I will be unmatched in power. You will show all the realms what you are truly made of. No one can stop us with an army so powerful."

Thanes's dominating promises echoed in my head, the words he said to me every time I delivered another group of humans for him to break, each more sinister than the last. Though I was having a harder and harder time impressing him with my finds. We needed someone more powerful than a regular human, but the trouble was, anyone more powerful easily blocked him from entering their mind.

My eyes clenched shut.

This was the only way to get power over the other realms.

I needed to claim the throne for myself and become the most powerful queen in existence. It wouldn't matter that I couldn't shift into a fox or that I was just a chosen bride. For once, it would be me with all of the power.

I opened my eyes and moved the teabag around. The water deepened in color.

Felix had gone to the fireplace, waving his hand in front with an easy flick that caused a bright glow of sunlight to cast upon the sooty-black inside and burst into flames.

"Here is your tea, darling. It must have been an eventful day if you have scrolls for the burnaway," I said, sending up a silent prayer that he didn't feel the need to tell me about it.

Felix began to set the scroll in the fireplace, then paused. The fire of the burnaway would seal it from all eyes but his until he requested to see it again. It was where he put all of his most important documents.

Taking the ivory teacup from me, he sat with a great huff in the dark-green love seat facing the fire.

"It's been a day straight from the seven levels of Tartarus. I was in the confidence of Zef this afternoon." He paused to take a sip of his tea.

My breath stilled. Would he taste it? Would he know that I betrayed him?

He let out a relaxed sigh.

I gripped the gold-and-white dress hanging heavily over my legs and sat in the love seat across from him, my back to the fire.

I'd rather watch the hedges grow than listen to him talk about Zef. The Ancient had been close with Felix prior to his Ascension, and he had always hated me.

I couldn't have cared less. Zef was Artemi, and as such, could ascend to Moirai and preside over the veil with the other grandchildren of the gods. He thought he was better than *everyone*. It was no wonder the Artemi had gotten themselves wiped clean off the realms.

I hated Zef.

As he was the god that created all shifters, I couldn't help but wonder if he had something to do with my not being able to shift.

"How is your tea, dear?" I asked with a little more bite than I meant to.

"It's lovely. Bring Eli up here, would you? He would *love* to taste the berries in it," the king mumbled.

"Oh, I'm afraid he's resting. I'm taking him on his first trip to the human realm tonight." I smiled as I watched him take another large gulp of the tea.

"The human realm? Oh my. Do be careful. I know Unseelie can no longer cross, but I've heard the Smoke Slayers can. From what Zef tells me, all hell broke loose at the Unseelie palace today. Such an unpleasant lot they are, murdering their own family, such vile nonsense." He shook his head, causing the purple tea in his cup to tremble.

He had done it. Thanes had killed Queen Tenebris and that little nitwit of a son.

Pure euphoria coated my insides. I could have sung. In one swift motion, I moved to the seat next to my husband and tipped the cup more deeply as he drank, emptying it in his mouth as I leaned an elbow on the back of the seat.

"Oh my, good heavens," he chuckled as he pulled the empty cup away and set it on the small table next to the sofa.

Already his normally tan skin had taken on a pale, waxy sheen. The heavy wrinkles under his amber eyes were moist with sweat. Tiny beads of sweat lined his reddish-blond hairline.

"Is it warm in here?" he asked. "I suppose it will be safe enough in the human realm, if it's safe enough for Zef..." He trailed off. His bloodshot eyes snapped to the scroll still hovering in the fireplace before catching mine. "Oh no..."

He clumsily moved toward the blaze, realizing he hadn't sent the scroll away with the fire yet. Just as he reached for the scroll, he fell to the ground with a heavy thud.

King Felix struggled a moment to sit up, looking to me in alarm. "You...you must send the scroll away. Zef entrusted me... I-I have to watch over them," he said as the poison did its job and he struggled to breathe.

He had a sickening gray pallor now as he leaned back against the sofa, clutching at his chest.

Wait, what did he just say?

"What do you mean, Zef entrusted you with watching over them? Watching over who?" I asked.

"I've... Get the healer. I've been poisoned." His head lolled to one side as he began to cough. "Burn the scroll, Saracen. It's a matter of life and death. There are more Artemi. Zef has them hidden... Wait...my—my tea," he whispered as his fading mind struggled to put the pieces together.

My handsome fae husband looked up at me with so much hurt in his eyes, I nearly felt bad.

I grabbed the scroll from the fireplace and sat down next to him. "It will be better this way, Felix, I promise you," I whispered into his ear as his breathing slowed. "You wouldn't want to see what's about to happen to this realm. I've joined forces with the Unseelie King Thanes. We've created an unstoppable army. We will rule the Seelie, the Unseelie, and the human realm before we take the Elven and Hanabi realms. Soon all the realms will bow to me."

"How could... The kids...swear to me that the kids... will be safe, Saracen...swear to me!" He struggled to keep his eyes open.

"I can't do that," I whispered with a frown.

I'm not sure why I had thought it would be hard to watch him die. It wasn't.

It was invigorating.

His last breath sputtered from his chest with a low, rattling sound. I unraveled the thick, tan scroll, letting out a lungful of air myself.

Unit 1 No. 11 Upper Morn St.
Donegal Town, Pennsylvania
Human realm
Calypso, Jennifer, and Adrianna

Interesting.

I leaned across the couch and grabbed the old iron scissors from the small wooden table behind the sofa, lost in thought.

"Don't worry, darling. I have no doubt a good soul like yours will visit Aether in the Elysian Fields." I pressed my lips against his damp, slightly warm forehead. "I have a feeling I won't be meeting you there in the afterlife either, after what I'm about to do."

With a firm grip and the most force my arms could muster, I grabbed the hair on top of his head with one hand and forced the iron scissors into his skull with the other, hitting the exact place I had planted my kiss.

I had to push and fight a bit to get the scissors all the way through, the odd squishes and pops catching my attention as the scissors tunneled farther in.

The more pure-blooded the fae, the harder they were to kill. Most pureblood immortals were immune to illness and recovered from poisons and superficial wounds easily. Shifters of pure blood, like Felix, required a severe and thorough head injury.

Steadying myself, I tugged until the scissors exited the dripping hole in his forehead. I was nearly mesmerized by the slow drips of metallic blood that dripped off the point, shining against the warm sunset rays that came in through the large windows of the office.

Calmly walking toward the door, I patted the pleats of my gown until I found the hidden pocket and placed the textured scroll inside, trading it for the few tolkiens and gems from within its hidden depths.

Soft thunks sounded as I opened my hand and the blood-ied scissors and tolkiens crawled across the intricate carpet by the door.

A sharp twinge of regret suddenly rippled through me at the realization that Felix was truly gone from my life forever. I didn't look back. I didn't dare. This was what had to happen.

I reprimanded myself for being so weak. This had to be done. For Thanes and me.

I stepped out of the room and into the hallway before clearing my throat and letting out a blood-curdling scream.

By now the new maid would have already shown the entire castle staff her "bonus": the prized pouch of Felix's most sought-after and collected treasures.

The ones the entire staff knew he would never part with.

There were no bonuses for the staff.

The elder staff had likely restrained her already.

CHAPTER 9

CALY

T HEY'RE SCISSORS."
"Yes, Eli, I know they are scissors," I said with an eye roll. "Why are you holding them to me like that? Where did those even come from?" I asked with a nervous laugh. He looked as if he were scheming.

He stood in front of me with the bright light of the unfamiliar castle glinting off of the office supply in his hand. The sharp tips pointed at me as my focus shifted slightly over his shoulder to see Queen Saracen smiling from the hallway.

Eli's face suddenly looked pained as he reached out to me. His warm fingers gently skated across the back of my neck. Tachycardia overtook me, propelling my broken heart at least 120 beats per minute. I shifted nervously, my eyes volleying between the scissors and his handsome face.

"What are you doing?" I asked.

Time froze. I flinched a little when he dominantly stepped into me, holding the back of my neck firm. A creak of scissors opening. What was he doing? What was happening?

"You have a tag still on your dress," he whispered. His searching eyes slowly ran over my face. "Hold still, it just looks like we're talking," he whispered with a wink, slowly moving his hand down the back of my neck until his fingertips caressed the T1 nerve of my thoracic vertebrae, causing a shiver to vibrate across my skin. "There, you're good. I don't think anyone saw it," he said with a sneaky grin as he handed me the stiff, barcoded price tag from my new dress.

Eli winked, and his eyes roamed my face slowly before he stepped away and returned the scissors to a filigreed cup on a stand by a giant vase of fresh flowers.

"Chef, return to the kitchen. Bring Caly that special tea in the cabinet please," she snapped in Samuel's direction before spinning to walk off.

Eli and Samuel immediately caught each other's gazes. Nothing was spoken, but I couldn't help feeling a lot was being said by the odd look they shared. Samuel nodded once to Eli.

"Yes, immediately, Your Highness," the old man said softly with a look in my direction.

"You can't drink the tea," Eli whispered softly.

"Why not?" I whispered back.

"Because I don't want you to. You won't be able to handle it," he said sternly.

Immediately, stubborn fire poured through my veins. I knew faerie food acted differently on humans, but I was strong. I could take it. "And just how would you know what I can and cannot handle? Because I'm human? It's tea." I scowled back at him.

"No, Cal, it's—"

"Make yourselves useful and bring us tea and cold cuts. You may gawk at the poor human whilst you serve her," Saracen snapped in the direction of a group of servants that had huddled nearby.

I may as well have been an animal at the zoo by the way they all clamored to get a better look at me as I passed by. Eli let out a loud, dramatic breath as he touched my elbow to gently guide me through the castle.

The queen had just made her way into a sitting room, leaving them free to whisper and stare at me as they liked. For the first time in a really long time, I felt weak and self-conscious.

"Leave now," Eli commanded in a tone I had never heard him use.

A little startled at his tone, my head whipped around to look at him.

The crowd scattered in a frenzy. Eli looked down to give me a wink and smile, instantly transforming back into the charming, fun boy I used to play in the fields with. He paused at the doorframe a moment to let me enter the room before him.

His mother sat on a small, Victorian-style sofa in the center of the grand room. Intricate molding and chandeliers seemed to be in every spot my eyes landed. A tingle in my nose made me sniff abruptly. It smelled sharp and clean—the kind of clean that stings your nose.

Thump, thump, thump.

My heart pounded unusually hard. Was that because it was near its other half?

"Caly, my dear, please sit. Chef will be here momentarily with your tea. You *must* drink it quickly before it gets cold, that is one thing I specifically remember the apothecary saying. Sit, sit," the queen playfully scolded as she waved a hand, indicating the spot next to her on the clean, delicate-looking sofa.

I should have changed my clothes.

I felt disgusting in my dirt-speckled sundress sitting next to her. Why could I not seem to keep my clothes clean? Ever? Even fresh, new ones? Somehow I had managed to ruin my pretty dress on the way here.

Not a pale-blond hair was out of place on Saracen's beautiful head, and a small, modest crown of citrines caught the chandelier light, sparkling atop it. I glanced at my feet the second her eyes caught me staring.

I needed to get it together.

"I just collected Caly, Mother. She has been traveling all day and has hardly had a moment of relaxation since she was in Unseelie—" Eli began, but was quickly cut off by Saracen.

"Is he truly dead, Calypso? Is that vile blotch of a disease finally dead?" she asked, leaning her angelic face closer to mine.

Her warm, polychromatic eyes danced, alive and excited. The reflection of the fire in front of us reflected eerily as it filled her irises, adding a strangely sinister edge to her question.

The words lodged in my throat, cold and hard, but I reluctantly forced them out. "Mendax, prince of the Unseelie realm, is—is dead," I said as confidently as was possible with a lump clogging my throat.

As soon as I spoke, a shiver trickled down my spine like phantom fingers raking over my skin.

"I had heard as much, but I wished to hear it from your lips, Calypso. It's quite the accomplishment, even for a skilled woman such as yourself." Saracen squeezed my forearm kindly. "You know what it would mean to the Seelie court, to me, if you had not been capable of killing him...and you were bonded to him." She clenched her jaw, and a cold look hardened her typically warm features.

"She fought against the bonding, Mother. It was against her will. I was there." Eli rose from his chair to defend me.

"Yes, of course. I would *never* betray you, Saracen...or Seelie," I stated, quite surprised. It felt foreign and sour for her to doubt me. She had never even questioned me after other hits, other than to ask if it was completed. "I-I have done everything you have asked of me," I said, beginning to feel defensive. "Every mark you have given me in the human realm, I have killed without so much as a question. Mendax was no different," I replied. "I have ached for this day for as far back as I can remember. The day I could be here—that we could all be together. *You* are my family. I would do—I have done—anything for you!"

Careful, I warned myself.

I glanced at Eli as he hovered by the door, letting Chef carry in a small tray with a single teacup. "Though I am anxious to have my heart restored, I would have given all of it as proof of my undying allegiance, had it been so requested, Saracen."

"*Queen* Saracen," Samuel interjected harshly.

My eyes snapped to him. The older man was setting the tray on the table near my side of the sofa. He gave me a tight-lipped smile and left, pausing only to take the tray from the servants who had just arrived with a separate tea for Eli and Saracen.

One more remark like that from him and there would be a kitchen fire soon.

"Drink your tea, dear. Tell me about your time in the Unseelie palace. What is that gloomy old bat Tenebris up to now? What a horrid time I imagine her to be having with her only heir dead. Right under her rigid nose too." A glassy, pleased look tightened the corners of her eyes and pulled at the corners of her lips.

Whoa. I knew they hated each other, but this felt like something deeper than what little information I had. The Unseelie must have hurt Saracen horribly.

The hairs on my forearms rose, and there was a rush of adrenaline in my system.

Nerves. It's just nerves.

Thump, thump. My heart pounded like a timpani. Why did I suddenly feel so sick? I grabbed my teacup and took a drink, hoping to calm myself.

"The tea is wonderful. Thank you," I murmured, locking eyes with Eli.

Cinnamon, but what else was in it? I knew it but couldn't put my finger on it. Strong but surprisingly calming.

Within seconds though, every part of my body was humming. My foot began tapping on the floor, attempting to release the sudden fuzziness.

Fuck. Was this because it was faerie tea and I was a

human? Why couldn't I remember what Eli had told me it did to humans? Saracen no doubt hadn't thought I would have a reaction.

All of my senses felt tense and overwhelmed. The obnoxiously bright gold-and-white room, the pungent scent of floor polish, even the closeness to Saracen and Eli were suddenly too much.

"Yes, dear, drink up. Aurelius, for sun's sake, open the flue. Smoke is pouring in. Incompetent staff, honestly! We can't even have a proper fire."

"Yes, Mother," muttered Eli as he dutifully moved to the large marble fireplace.

"After tea we will sort out all of that heart business, Caly. Aurelius tells me that the Unseelie prince was intensely fond of you. Obviously so, if you got him to bond with you. I can't help but find it quite odd though. It is absolutely unheard of for that psychotic fae." She tilted her head to the side slightly. "Such a shame that their bonded do not receive the Smoke Slayers powers until after the wedding ceremony. You truly could have had it all," she laughed. "You would have been quite the force, my dear. Could you imagine? Had I even thought you could affect him that strongly, I—for the love of sun! Aurelius, what is the matter with the fire?" the queen shouted as she waved her dainty hand in front of her face, pushing a haze of smoke away.

My teacup's smooth edge grazed the bottom of my lip as I prepared to take a drink when the cause of the scentless smoke dawned on me, and I froze.

The queen's mouth dropped open, her wide eyes locked on my forearms. Petrified, I watched as Saracen's teacup fell to the floor, accompanied by the sharp sound of porcelain shattering into a million pieces. The queen stood, covering her mouth with trembling hands and hurriedly stepping away from me to move her frightened eyes over my still figure.

"Mother, the fire is absolutely fi—" Eli turned and froze. "Oh, suns."

"What is it?" I scanned the empty space behind me,

praying a threat loomed behind me—a threat I knew wouldn't be there.

The light trails of smoke filtering through my clothes and across my bare arms grew thicker. I hadn't even felt it this time. Was I already so comfortable keeping part of his powers?

My body was producing enough smoke now that a small black cloud hovered where I had sat only a moment prior. I took in a deep breath, searching for the familiar smoky, masculine scent of pine and cardamom to comfort me, but this time I smelled nothing. Not even a hint of charcoal burning, like I'd smelled so many times at the picnic areas at the state park, and it most certainly was not the incredibly seductive, smoky fragrance I'd smelled before.

How incredibly odd.

"It can't be! How can this be?" Saracen cried as she clutched at her son.

My heart thundered so fast, it felt painful as it flooded my ears. How could this happen now? I had just gotten to where my family was. I wasn't even a Seelie royal yet! I'd thought I'd be able to spend a little more time with Eli, but if Saracen tried to kick me out for having her enemy's powers in my veins—or worse—then I would have to make my moves sooner. I needed to stay. I couldn't let everything come undone now.

Thump, thump, thump.

"Please, Saracen," I said, hurling myself to the hard marble floor at her feet. *"Please!* It's just residual from the bond. It will leave as soon as my heart is put together again. *Please, please*, I'm begging you. We agreed you'd make me a royal!" I cried as I clutched her skirts.

"Some of his powers have fastened to you…even with the lack of a wedding ceremony and his death." She looked at Eli, seemingly dumbfounded. Her wide eyes just stared for a moment before she collected herself and hauled me up to stand barely an inch from her face, startling me with her closeness.

Lines of smoke traced the outline of her body. Every part of me trembled, waiting to hear her tell me to leave.

"How is it possible that his powers still *live* while he is *dead*? Unless you have absorbed some of his powers through your own."

Her sunset eyes narrowed, searching mine for the tiniest flicker of falsity. I fought desperately to will the tendrils that still flowed to cease. I didn't like her this close.

The ball of my foot dragged over the floor as I attempted to take a step back and give myself some space. This was all too much. The weight of her gaze felt like it would crush me. Every second, it was harder and harder to not run into Eli's arms and cry.

"It's unusual. Something about her must have caused the powers to hold." Eli's jaw flexed.

He and his mother locked eyes in a silent conversation.

"I'm certain it's because of the magic that you used to keep me alive with half of a heart, or maybe a reaction to the Seelie gift of animal companionship you blessed me with," I broke in, beads of sweat gliding down my forehead, glancing nervously at Eli.

"He already knows. Tarani does as well," Saracen stated.

"You told them?" I said, my anger rising.

"Only the basics. They can fill you in later." Her eyes held mine a moment too long.

I needed to know how much they knew.

"Calypso's powers may have neutralized a bit of his," she said to Aurelius.

I glared at her. She was going to wreck everything for me.

"Oh, the cat's out of the bag now that you're back from Unseelie," she chuckled. "No one would have believed you were human and returned alive as it was."

Tell her I just needed to be inside of you in one way or another, pet.

A scream ripped free from my throat as I fell over the small love seat, tipping it and myself to the ground.

No.

No!

What the fuck?

What. The. Fuck?

The voice in my mind was the same gravelly voice I had heard during the trials when Mendax had spoken to me through the bond.

My entire body trembled, making it impossible to get up.

No.

He couldn't talk through the bond anymore.

He was dead.

It was my subconscious talking. *I* had thought that.

Flashes of Mendax's face appeared in my mind—the look of shock and appreciation that creased the corners of his cold blue eyes when I had stabbed him.

I swear I could feel him laughing at me from his grave now.

God, I'm exhausted.

"Cal! What is it?" Eli helped me up, alarm and worry filling his voice.

Thump. Thump. Thump.

"I-I—" My head was shaking. Trembling. I gawked at him, unable to find the right words. "I thought I—I thought I heard something, and it scared me. I-I'm just tired," I said, reaching out to squeeze the tanned arm of the kind fae.

"Mother, she needs to go to bed. Look at her—"

"Nonsense. There're things we need to decide now that everything is out in the open. Tarani, I know you are listening outside. Stop being so troublesome and take Calypso on a tour. Eli and I will join the two of you shortly. We have something of importance to discuss."

❧

I had finally calmed myself—at least enough to appear unaffected—as Eli's sister reluctantly showed me a few rooms, side-eyeing me the entire time. Her glare felt like knife points piercing the back of my head when I walked in front of her.

I had never met the princess before today. Queen Saracen and Eli were the only two who had ever visited me. But I didn't need to know her to realize she was upset with me being here.

The moment we were out of earshot of the others, she confirmed as much. "You don't deserve him," she bit out coldly.

She was right. I didn't.

We both continued to stare straight ahead. Her outburst hadn't surprised me. She was used to getting everything she wanted, including all of her brother's attention. I would bet what little money I had that she had never been told no. She was as spoiled and pampered as they came. They both were.

I bit down on my lip hard, nearly running into a door in shock as the sensation forced my eyes shut and sent tingles of pleasure deep down into my belly.

Mhhmmm....

Was that me?

My chest filled with three deep, belly-expanding breaths before I dared continue.

Okay then...

Anyway, Eli had been Tarani's best friend, and she'd had him entirely to herself forever. I didn't blame her one bit for hating me. In fact, I respected it.

"I know I don't," I returned.

She glanced at me, hate filling her yellow irises, and for the first time since I was in the Unseelie realm, I was genuinely uneasy.

Maybe she hated me because I was a fae killer. I couldn't help but wonder if she knew the work I had done for her mother in the human realm as well. Did they tell her I lured fae in with smiles and charm, and then killed them simply because her mother had told me to? Did she know that most of the time I didn't even know what crimes they had committed to deserve death? That I didn't care? I was given an order and I carried it out. Every time. And I enjoyed it.

It was all so I could get here and finally be with my family again.

Anyone who ever tells you they wouldn't kill for that is a liar.

The princess barked at me to follow her, guiding me to yet another large, opulent room. Her flowing, white dress trailed behind her, reminding me of sheets on a clothesline, flapping in the wind. She was so young and vibrant. Not tarnished and broken like me.

I choked the memories down as I continued to follow her. Things were going to be amazing from now on.

This room was different. I could feel the shift in the air immediately when we stepped inside. It felt...permanent. Powerful. The ceilings seemed to grow before my eyes with painted Rubenesque figures. They looked to be in a battle of sorts, but it was unclear who sided with whom. When my eyes touched them, the characters snapped their heads to watch me with hauntingly intense and empty, black eyes. Some wore all gold, holding what looked like handfuls of light, while others were cloaked in dark grays and browns. I took note of several slightly pointed ears in the battle scene... but then, I also noticed some with rounded, human-looking ears.

They looked horrifying.

A poor attempt at humans from a fae painter, I supposed. Their faces were empty and gaunt, soulless but for the eyes that seemed to stare straight through me. They reminded me more of zombies than humans. Especially in contrast to the godlike figures in gold. They seemed to be on the same side of the battle as the fae in gold, several even kneeling at their feet.

Tarani pushed me, and my perusal of the mural ended. I could still see them look at me in my peripheral vision, creepy grins on their faces and all.

I really had a lot of adjusting to do in the fae realm. Human science didn't apply here.

In the back of the room, two large thrones loomed on a short platform. One seemed slightly more feminine than the other, encrusted with citrine set deep into the glistening gold. The other bore no gems or glittery accoutrements; instead, it was adorned with a regal fox head carved intricately on both of its tall back posts. The room was almost entirely bare, with the large, white-cushioned thrones the obvious focal point. It felt wrong and oddly dangerous to be standing in this room. The heavy, suffocating air even advised me to leave.

"This is obviously the royal throne room," Tarani said, gazing at the throne to the left with a hard-set jaw. Did the queen and princess get along? They were close from the small amount Eli had said.

"It's beautiful," I mumbled, uncertain of what else to say. She seemed a little more excited in this room, but I still couldn't shake the feeling we shouldn't be here. Maybe she was hoping to get me into trouble. It seemed like something she would do.

"The fox heads are very impressive." I smiled, nodding at the second throne. I'd never met King Felix, but from the small amount Eli had told me, he had been a truly kind and loving father.

"Yes." Tarani's face dropped.

"I'm sorry," I said, trying to backtrack.

"No, you're right. It is a beautiful throne. The fox heads were designed to look like my father in his shifted form." She stepped closer to the throne, transfixed by the wooden heads. "I wish he were here. He could have fixed this," she said with a wave.

Tarani turned back to face me, tears brimming her eyes. She reminded me of a fisher cat—small and innocent looking but ready to rip the flesh off my bones.

"How long has he—"

Tarani cut me off. "Since that horrible woman murdered him."

I looked at her, shocked, but remained silent.

She looked up to the ceiling, a tear overflowing and swimming down the side of her tanned nose.

I craned my neck to focus on where her angry eyes had landed. More of the classically painted mural encompassed the ceiling. I could see the figures swathed in dark much clearer on the ceiling. Among the darkened areas were large, shadowy-looking figures. Maybe five or so of these ominous shadow monsters fought against the figures in gold. A few wore the familiar billowing, white robes with gold vines artistically draped across their bodies—the Seelie.

My eyes were still captivated by the hazy shadows.

They were terrifying.

The soft *tap-click-tap* of footsteps preceded Eli and the queen as they entered the echoing room, still speaking heatedly to one another.

"Queen Tenebris is the only known Smoke Slayer alive... for now," the queen stated icily. "It's quite likely she has something to do with this. I'm unsure as to why, but it doesn't matter now. What's done is done. We must act accordingly."

The murmurs of Eli's deep voice grew closer. "Mother, that is not how she wants to become a Seelie royal. You know I will never allow you to hurt her, and I refuse to let you banish her from me again." Eli's pinned wings twitched ever so slightly, either from fear or anger.

"Banish her?" Saracen shouted in a shrill tone. "Banish her? Darling, how can you not see what a gift we have been blessed with? With Langmure dead, you are the heir to the throne. I can hardly imagine a more powerful duo than a SunTamer and an Artemi. Our dear Calypso, so suddenly left with such overwhelming powers—no matter how little of his powers she now possesses, retaining even a tenth of that fae's power is more than most of the elevated fae put together. Once her heart is returned, her Artemi powers should be fully restored. Do you know what that would do for Seelie? The depths which we could reach with that type of power?"

Eli shifted uneasily, glancing nervously at me as they came to a halt in front of us. "You want me to marry Cal…because she has some of *his* powers?" His lip curled, and he let out a small animalistic sound, instantly moving closer to me.

It was so foreign to see anyone move to defend me. My chest squeezed at Eli's movements. I knew it wasn't practical and I knew it wasn't intelligent, but I leaned into the comfort of being the helpless one for one singular second.

I had been strong for so long.

"She will have her own powers as well. Powers greater than you children have ever witnessed. The Artemi went extinct long before you were alive to witness them. You think Chef Samuel is the only one who knows how long you've been in love with the girl?" the queen chided Eli playfully, casting a wink in my direction.

A blush burned my face. "When will you empower me as an official Seelie?" I cut in.

"Calypso is one of our own. She is family, and we don't just leave our family in danger, unprotected." The queen's voice softened as her eyes danced between Eli and Tarani.

I focused on my breathing.

Her satiny voice grew louder. "It is no secret that the Smoke Slayers are among the most dangerous, albeit sublimely powerful, creatures the Fates ever created. Besides the Artemi and the old gods, there has never been such power. Imagine a realm, no, *a family*, that possessed the Smoke Slayer, Artemi, *and* SunTamer abilities?" She paused, her warm eyes beginning to widen dreamily. "Imagine the bloodline they could create. They would have rights to both the Seelie and Unseelie crown, and quite frankly, anything else they wanted. There could hardly be a more advantageous marriage, and it's no surprise you two are in love. I knew the moment Aurelius laid eyes on you that the two of you would one day be together." Her smile was so wide, it nearly closed her eyes.

Princess Tarani shrieked. "You cannot be serious, Mother! She can't take the crown. Eli doesn't need her to rule! No one"—she snapped her head to me—"and I do mean *no one* cares about him more than myself. She will hurt him! How can you even trust her? She's a liar and a fae killer by profession!" The small princess snarled at her mother. "Imagine what she'll do once she has her full powers!"

She wasn't wrong.

A haze of black smoke once again danced down my arms and rolled onto the marble floor.

"She's a liar and a very skilled fae killer because I trained her to be. Well, technically Commander Von trained her, but that's semantics. She has gifted us with half an organ in a show of loyalty, Tarani. What have you given us?" Saracen retorted. "And, darling, it might behoove you to remember just how proficient she is at her particular set of skills."

Tarani glared at me.

"I don't want to marry Eli," I said, looking between all of their faces. What was happening? How was my plan turning to shit every five minutes when I'd had it since I was eight?

Eli scoffed at his mother. "Calypso is my best friend. She doesn't want to marry me, and Tarani is right, I don't need Caly to rule. You're talking nonsense. And furthermore, if I'm not enough for the throne alone, then maybe Tarani should take the crown. She is more capable than me anyway."

The queen gave a short laugh as she stared at Tarani. "Your sister couldn't lead a blazing lindwurm into a fire filled with offerings," she chuckled.

Tarani gasped. "No one could! Blazing lindwurms are obstinate and uncontrollable!"

What in the fae world was a blazing lindwurm? I shook away my thoughts. "I-I was painfully unaware a marriage was an assumed part of our deal," I said.

"Okay, fine, then. I suppose a marriage isn't necessary for you to be impregnated," the queen suggested.

"What? Oh, god no! I thought you'd be upset at what's

inside of me now," I said, grabbing my pounding head. "Instead, you want Aurelius and I to—to make a baby?" Was there a possibility I was still in the hospital with brain damage?

I would *never* marry Eli for a position as a Seelie royal. Of all the people in the world, he was the only one I cared about not hurting.

Eli's sharp eyes snapped to mine, his light-brown eyebrows so high they nearly blended into his hairline.

"It's as if the old gods have rewarded us for the horrors we Seelie have endured," Saracen said, tilting her chin up slightly.

She moved with a smile as she grabbed both mine and Eli's shoulders like a football coach about to share a play, lightly pushing Tarani out of the way in the process. Her touch sent a truly odd sensation of excitement down my arms and up my neck.

"Aurelius, you will marry Calypso, solidifying her as a Seelie royal. We will then claim the Unseelie throne, as Calypso still carries rank as partial Smoke Slayer. Aurelius will likewise take the Seelie throne as king, thus combining the realms under our control."

Fuck!

Eli and I both recoiled slightly as we looked at each other with wide eyes. Rage bubbled in the back of my mind, but it felt different, out of place even, next to the fear I was really feeling.

"No. I will be empowered as a Seelie royal once my heart is restored. That was the agreement," I snapped angrily.

Everyone's eyes snapped to me, taken aback by my angry tone.

Fuck. I was ruining this.

Eli jumped in. "Hello, Calypso! So lovely to have you in Seelie with us. Would you like a tour? Perhaps some weird tea? Oh, gee, look at that, you have the devil's powers! Let me force you into an arranged marriage with my son!" Eli said sarcastically. "She is a person, Mother. She is special without this horrible smoke and not a tool to level you up. I haven't even seen her in some ten years! Nothing more than letters since she was eighteen and you barred my entry."

In the few minutes since Eli had arrived, my last bit of smoke had settled, aside from a few small, translucent tendrils from my fingertips.

"You and I both know, as a SunTamer, you were always going to have an arranged marriage. Would this not suit you more? I could think of worse pairings than your best friend, Aurelius. Especially when she looks as yours does." The queen winked at me with a laugh.

"I'm sorry and I mean no offense, Saracen. You have done so much for me, but I will not be marrying anyone. I am not a prized heifer at the auction house. Eli should take the throne and find another bride of *his* choosing." Why did the thought of him marrying someone suddenly sting? "The Smoke Slayer effects—I would hardly call them powers, as fogging up a room seems the most I am capable of—will all go away once I collect the remaining half of my heart. I'm certain of it. Which—that will be soon, right?" I held the queen's gaze and my own breath.

I was so close. So close to being whole again.

Saracen matched my stare for a beat before answering with a smile that didn't meet her eyes. "Yes, of course. We will host a ceremony, allowing me to return your heart properly and for all of Seelie to recognize your allegiance and witness your title change." Her soft voice dropped. "Once your heart is fully restored and whole, we will provoke you."

"*Provoke* me?"

That could be a big problem. Thoughts of how Saracen would provoke me until I used my powers caused a worried shiver to slither down my spine.

"If you show any sign of the Smoke Slayer powers after the return of your heart, then you will be married to Aurelius in front of everyone." Saracen's eyes sparkled. "Unfortunately, the Seelie realm has no place for such a powerful Artemi as a wielder of dark magic, unless you are to become a part of the monarchy. The Artemi are far too dangerous to be independent from a royal court. Their ability to absorb another's powers and leave them a powerless mortal is unforgivable in the eyes of all fae, and that is only one of your gifts." She paused, as if challenging us to interrupt, but no one dared, not even Tarani. "If, as you so confidently claim, the Smoke Slayer powers are nonexistent after rejoining your heart, then you will continue to live under our roof as an associate of the royal family with our full protection. I hope you understand I'm doing you a grand favor with this deal." She removed her grip on our shoulders with a beautiful smile.

"But…that wasn't the deal! I need to be a Seelie royal, not an associate!" I yelled.

Everyone looked at me, but no one spoke.

Eli's eyes were like a closed book—filled with untold stories. My eyes snagged on his soft-looking lip. I wanted to bite it—badly.

The fuck was happening today?!

A very low growling sound reverberated from somewhere.

I rubbed my arms, shaking away the goose bumps that had suddenly covered my body.

"Aurelius, darling, take the poor girl's bag and show her to her room in the east wing. She must be exhausted, and I'm sure you two have a lot of…catching up to do."

Saracen smiled coyly, looping her arm around Tarani's shoulders before the princess pulled away and stomped toward the door ahead of her mother. The queen paused for a moment to glance back to where Eli and I remained, staring at each other as if we were strangers.

"Actually, I've changed my mind, Aurelius. Take her things to the north wing. You two will have the entire section to yourselves. Calypso, I'd like to meet with you in the gardens tomorrow evening to discuss a few things," she sang, slyly smiling at us before following Tarani out the doors.

Eli and I remained. The large throne room was so quiet now, I could have heard a pin drop. Why was my heart racing? Had I moved closer to him, or did he just move closer to me?

"Cal, are you all right? I'm so sorry. I had no idea she would be like this. I would have hidden you until we could get your smoke stuff under control had I known."

"You're a pushover," I snorted, suddenly feeling loose-lipped. My emotions were like a roller coaster.

His eyes creased with laughter. "I'm a pushover?"

"Yes, and I think maybe a little weak also," I said quite seriously. I felt like I had so much to tell him.

He chuckled, surprising me, not at all offended that I'd just called him a weak pushover. "And what have I done to deserve the prestigious title of an unappealing pushover?" He smiled, leaning in a little closer.

Why couldn't I stop looking at his mouth? There was serious shit happening right now. "You're enticing," I whispered. *What?*

"What?" His own volume lowered.

"*Unappealing* wasn't in the title I gave you. *Weak* was." I bit my lip hard to stop from biting his. Fuzzy, mind-numbing tingles rippled down between my legs.

He filled his hard chest with air, lifting my hands. When had I touched him? What was I doing?

"You should know better than anyone, looks usually only tell what you want them to." His breath skated across my closed eyelids.

I needed to be touched. Now. I knew it wasn't normal, but I didn't care. I couldn't think straight. Couldn't even remember why I was standing in this room with the moving mural.

Eli cleared his throat roughly. "Tea, one; Calypso, zero. You need rest. Come on. You'll remember everything tomorrow, so don't be weird. Also, don't worry about Mother."

I followed Eli out and down another long corridor. I needed to map the castle, but my mind was spinning, and something in my stomach didn't feel right.

My body had begun humming when Saracen had touched my shoulder. Even then, I had been forced to bite my tongue in an effort not to say the most random, malicious things to her.

His voice faltered a second before he spoke again. "Is it *that* repulsive to think about marrying me?" Eli laughed.

The truth was, there was a time I would have killed to marry him. I think at one point, I basically thought I was.

It seemed like a good idea to tell him that now, so I opened my mouth to speak just as he reached over and squeezed my hand. Immediately all words left my brain, stopped by the way his large hand felt on my vibrating skin.

I wanted to clench my thighs together at the thought of those hands other places, but we continued to walk. The room felt fuzzy, and tracers had started up in my vision if I moved my head too fast. I couldn't seem to think about anything other than how much I needed to be touched.

"Have you ever thought about what you'd feel like inside of me?" I blurted.

Eli coughed and choked next to me.

"It's just that—" But Eli had stopped helping me stand, and I stumbled onto the ground, hitting my shoulder with a thud.

"What in the suns?" Eli mumbled, trying to help me up.

"Do you know I can kill you, even from down here?" I laughed.

"Well, isn't that an alarming thing to giggle about," he said, fighting a smile.

I couldn't seem to get my bearings with the heat of his body so close to mine. Instead, I ended up pulling his shirt loose from where it tucked into his pants and running my palms up his warm skin. I raked my fingernails down over the ridges of his stomach.

"Ouch!" he said, giving me a shocked look.

"I've always wondered what your abs would feel like. They are so hard. Where else are you hard?" I rasped, running my palm over his crotch.

Fuuuuuck.

I gasped in surprise. "Has bestie always had this package?" I smiled, reaching for more, but his hands grabbed my wrists and pulled them away.

I moaned at his hold on my wrists.

"Oh my Fates! She gave you faerie mead!" Eli said with a cackle. "To bed with you immediately, you lush."

I lost the fight to stand up again, and Eli didn't hesitate to scoop me into his arms. My head spun under the bright lights of the sun that shone in the halls and the rocking of my tired body as Eli carried me, batting my hands away every time they wandered away from his chest.

I wanted to turn my body over and grind on him. In fact, I was feeling aggressive about it.

What was that smell? Oh god, I loved that smell. Cedar? Ambrosia? Why did I always smell that? Whatever it was, I wanted to roll it up into a good-smelling, sexy ball and then climax on top of that ball.

I couldn't discern my thoughts. All that was left were feelings and urges—pent-up, angry, rough, supposed-to-be-kept-quiet urges.

It wasn't until I felt myself drop slightly that I realized Eli was setting me on a bed.

Yesssss.

The room was darker, and I struggled to take note of my surroundings.

Was that still Eli?

"You're all right. I'm just setting you on the bed and then I'm going to get the maid to start a cold shower and get the witch to make an elixir for you," Eli whispered. "I'm afraid Mother gave you faerie mead, knowing how it affects non-fae."

"I don't want a cold shower. Faerie mead?" I grabbed ahold of him, locking his arms in place.

"The cold shower is for me, I'm afraid," he chuckled, trying to shake my hold.

I squeezed harder, easily gaining more leverage.

He wouldn't leave me. He couldn't leave. I didn't want him to leave me ever again—if only that was how it could be.

"Faerie mead usually causes those who aren't fae to get… umm…quite frisky. Artemi are not technically faeries, so I suppose that's why it's hit you so hard. It causes a loss of all inhibitions, sort of like human's alcohol, only about a million times more potent and aimed specifically at making you horny and honest. It's as good as a truth serum with non-fae. They typically hide a lot, and it seems to…ugh…come out with the mead," he chuckled.

He surprised me with his own skills as he gently disengaged my hold on him.

"Don't leave me, please?" I begged, my voice husky and full of pleading.

He paused, still holding me and touching my skin. His godlike face froze above mine with a dreamy expression. A hint of reddish orange I'd never noticed before brightened his honey-colored irises. Was that his heart racing? How could I hear that?

Maybe we could get married, and I could take him with me.

No. I frowned. I wouldn't make him go where I was going.

"I need to go," he stated. "You don't want this. Not really."

"Maybe I do. Maybe I've wanted this for a long time," I whispered, feeling slightly dejected, still holding tight to his shoulders.

"Not like this," he whispered back.

"Because you don't want to ruin our friendship?" I asked, rolling my eyes. My hands tightened around his hard biceps when he attempted to move away from me. "No! I won't let you push me away and leave me so you can forget about me again. You'll have plenty of time to hate me later, and eons of immortality to forget me."

"That's not true, and you know it."

"Then why, Prince Aurelius? Why won't you be with me tonight?" I snapped.

He stilled, and sorrow crossed his features for a moment before it was replaced with something I didn't recognize on his face. Anger?

"Because I know you like no one else in this world will ever know you. Because I know you grieve him. As much as you will deny it, I saw you two together. You were falling in love with him and had to take his life."

I pulled away. "I didn't love him. He tried to kill me. He is awful—"

"You needn't convince me of anything, Calypso," Eli said softly.

"I didn't love him...but I could have. I was starting to before I...before I..." I could feel each stone from the wall I'd so carefully built beginning to tumble down. "Before I murdered him."

Thunk. The last brick of my fortress fell with the assistance of mead. I was a horny, crying, angry, drunk assassin—a terrible combination.

"It's okay, Cal. It's just me here. You don't need to be ashamed of anything. I can't imagine how hard this has all been on you. We haven't even talked about you being Artemi. I didn't know you knew." He moved to the other side of the bed like he was going to hug me.

A torrent of salty tears poured from my eyes. "You can't imagine. Do you know the most fucked-up part, Eli? Do you? After all these years, the only reason I'll fail is because of you," I yelled, picking up a crystal bottle from the nightstand and hurling it at the wall and then continuing with whatever was in reach.

"Because of me?" Eli repeated calmly, not flinching as I threw every breakable object I could get my hands on.

"Yes! I need to destroy the castle and everyone in it." Out of objects to smash, I moved for one of the large windows.

Eli intercepted me, grabbing both my wrists and holding them tightly.

Shit. Not the wrist holding again.

"Destroy everyone in it?" He held me firm as I growled and tried to free myself.

"All except you! And that's why I'll fail. You've made me weak," I screamed, my voice bouncing off the walls of the semidark room.

He blocked my kick to his groin with surprisingly fast reflexes.

I doubt he could even understand my words the way they ripped out of my throat in great heaves and bellows. "I need to go to Moirai." I froze. Even in the state of mind I was in from the mead, I knew I had never wanted to say that out loud.

"Moirai? Okay, remind me never to get an assassin drunk." Eli's grip softened. "You are talking nonsense. You need to go to bed."

I tried to head-butt him, but he avoided it like it was nothing.

"Mendax was so different from what you both described," I blubbered on. "He was kind and mysterious! It was just so... He saw through me! He saw every little dark shadow inside of me. And even seeing all of me, knowing I was there to kill him, he still couldn't stop himself from *wanting me.* He—he was unhinged for me! The evil fuck loved me just as I was. Every dark nook that I was embarrassed of and hid from you guys, he ached for! How could I not have felt something for him?" I stopped my physical assault and sunk even deeper into my words, letting myself believe Eli held my hands out of comfort instead of restraint. "When I pressed the blade into him and I had finally completed my last order, I thought the evil and hate in me would leave, Eli—that everything I had done would somehow change me, make me finally feel normal, like you guys. But the dark corners only grew. They took root and then added smoke. I hate that I had to kill him!" I wailed as I lost myself in a rare burst of hysterics.

"Shhhh, it's okay," Eli whispered. His breath tickled the wisps of hair around my forehead, reminding me who it was who was hearing my broken rant.

At some point, Eli had pulled my angry, upset body into his and folded his arms and wings around me in a tight, solid hug-cocoon. He hadn't gotten upset at my confession, it seemed. His sole focus seemed to be comforting me as he continued to hold me and whisper soft, undecipherable words that cascaded over my forehead.

"I'm just...so confused," I mumbled softly as I deflated into the damp, tearstained fabric on his warm chest.

"It's okay, Cal. Anyone would be confused with all of that. Maybe you did love him, and that's okay." His hand gently held my head to his chest, stopping the loud protest I was about to make. "But even if you didn't see it then, he was a truly horrible man, you understand me?" He tilted my chin up and looked deep into my tear-filled eyes. "He would have killed you eventually, Calypso. But of course he loved you. He would have been a fool not to, and Mendax was many awful, terrible things, but a fool was not one of them."

He put my head back against his concrete-hard chest. I could feel the strong, steady thump of his heart against my cheek, the heat of his body causing even more confusion inside of me.

"It kills me to think that you are struggling with all of this alone, Cal. You don't ever need to hide anything from me. And just so you are aware, I could be unhinged for you too."

"You don't know what I've done for her, Eli." I shuddered.

He looked hard at me for a moment, searching my eyes for something. "And you don't know what *I've* done for her," he whispered as his arms tightened around me.

❧❧

When I had first started taking orders from Saracen, as a teenage girl, I learned very quickly—and unpleasantly—how strong and awful the fae could be if they got to you first. I stopped letting that happen. I found it much easier—and I suppose a bit more rewarding—to take my marks out in a different way, when they least suspected it. I learned to be whatever that individual least suspected to be dangerous. It became a game and a way to release some of my pain and anger.

Queen Saracen and I agreed that the explanation for my power would be that she had blessed me with a bit of Seelie magic for saving her life. This strange and amazing gift caused animals to be drawn to me. That's what we would say until it was time to tell everyone I was Artemi. We had to hide it from everyone somehow, and Saracen was happy to take the credit. She had even convinced them it was a Seelie royal gift of hers that had skipped them, just as shifting into a fox skipped her.

The truth was, my magic always made me feel bad for the animals. If they understood what a horrible person I was, I knew they wouldn't be drawn to me anymore. It was only the Artemi powers that attracted them.

I groggily lifted my head, and a shock of cold air hit my warm, damp cheek. My eyes began to adjust. Where was I?

Gold renaissance-style swirls covered the expansive, white walls. I wiped the sleep from my eyes and methodically marked everything's location on a map in my mind: a great white fireplace in the corner. One large four-poster bed. A wardrobe against the wall near a few other small tables. Broken porcelain and glass everywhere. Two large, arched windows with cream-colored satin curtains. Two doors, one an exit, one a bathroom. The nearest one about twenty paces to my left.

Deep reddish-orange sun poured through the windows, causing odd shadows to hang in the corners of the room. The small crackling fire caused the shadows to move in deceptive shapes. Eli must have lit the fire last night.

The mattress below me rumbled, and I nearly hit the ceiling.

Oh. My. God.

Eli was the rumbling mattress. Eli was under me in the bed! Had we...?

No, I knew I would remember that.

In shock, I backed away toward the foot of the mattress, not realizing until it was too late that I had moved my chest down between Eli's widespread legs. I let out a silent scream. I was still too tired for this.

Urging my hands to stop shaking, I pushed them onto his thighs to slowly lift myself up.

Eli snapped awake, sitting up and grabbing my arms before I had a chance to even blink. His pupils widened, darkening slightly as he took in the situation. Eli's golden wings snapped out, knocking something over on the nightstand.

Oh no.

Eli masked it well, but I had seen his desire. His manners thankfully took precedence, and he stood immediately and helped me sit on the edge of the bed. Alone. The sun-hazed room blurred slightly with my movements, the soft notes of smoke and spice dragging against my senses.

"I-I'm so sorry, Calypso. I tried to leave last night, but you put me in choke hold and told me you'd replace me with a new best friend." Eli smiled. "Nothing happened. Though I will say the smoke chains were a bit excessive," he snorted.

"I didn't... Oh, Eli, I'm so sorry." I covered my face with my palms. "Wait...smoke chains?" I remembered the choke hold, but...I couldn't make chains of smoke...

"You did. Oh, don't be embarrassed. To be honest, the chains were wildly impressive. Here I thought you were asleep, and suddenly my legs were bolted to the bed, my arms and hands tied to my sides. Even my throat was chained to the headboard," he chuckled. "Don't show Mother what you can do with that smoke, or she'll drug us both."

I'd only ever seen one chain of smoke before, and it had been around my throat.

That was impossible though. Mendax was dead.

"Oh my god."

"I'm sorry, bad joke. Caly, please don't feel bad. I hope you trust me enough to know I would never touch you without your consent. Tartarus, even when you said you wanted it last night, I wouldn't touch you." He was almost wheezing, he laughed so hard now. "I will say though, whatever makes you feel safe, I support you fully, but next time, could you lighten up on the throat chains? I think you may have drawn blood. You should have heard the crazy things you said."

I stood up in alarm to look at his neck. Sure enough, link-shaped indentations and bruises encircled his neck, his gold Seelie blood drying in spots.

"Eli...I didn't..." I trailed off. I hadn't done this. I couldn't have if I'd wanted to. I had no control over my smoke. But if I didn't do it...

"Suns, Caly, all the blood has drained from your face. I will get the healer for your hangover, even though I know that you will heal quickly. I wouldn't worry, just the afteref fects of the mead," he said, patting my arm.

I sat on the bed, trying to reason out the situation.

He was right though—ever since my time in Unseelie, I had healed oddly fast, even before bonding with Mendax. I didn't think my powers could do that...

"I am glad you are here, Cal."

"I want the stream back," I rasped as tears began to threaten. The scent of the cozy fire was the only thing grounding me.

"The stream?" he asked and moved to sit on the edge of the bed next to me.

"I want to go back to when everything was right. When I was whole and a good, normal person. When I still had Mom and Adrianna. I want to go back to when I thought I would grow up to be an astronaut. To when you and I would spend all day in the stream, playing pirates. I want the stream back, where we were just best friends, Eli." I choked on the words.

The prince looked hurt, recoiling slightly. "We are and will *always* be friends, Calypso." He stood from the bed and straightened his shirt as he walked toward one of the large, arched windows. "I would give anything I have to bring your mom and sister back, truly I would," he said, turning to face me, his shadow darkening as he stood next to the barely illuminated window. "I don't know the details of what you had to do for my mother, and I know it's not something you ever want to talk about." He sped on to cover my protests. "But I also know the basics of what you had to do, and you are still *very much* whole and good." He brushed a hand over his golden hair and handsome face. "I had hoped my mother wouldn't discuss us marrying. At least not on the day of your arrival. She is being unreasonable, but I will not lie to you and say I haven't thought about it a thousand times on my own."

My stomach flipped nervously. "You can't be serious," I bit out gruffly, startling him. "It's been years since I've even seen you. Hell, we are only even best friends in absentia at this point!"

He was suddenly in my face with fire in his amber eyes. "Yes, and why was that, Caly? Why was that?" He gripped my shoulders, and though his touch was gentle, his expression was anything but.

I'd never seen him like this. I was too stunned to say anything back. After a pause, Eli continued.

"Because my mother banished me from the human realm! Do you have any idea what happens when you disobey a faerie queen, Caly? Death! Do you think she'd show mercy just because I am her son?" He was gripping my shoulders tighter now, and I fought the girlish urge to slap him or, worse, the assassin's urge to suffocate him with the fluffy pillow that brushed against my thigh.

"Queen Saracen would never kill you, Aurelius. Especially just for going to see me," I replied with a wavering voice.

His expression suddenly softened. His hands slid down my arms, and he clenched his jaw with a pained expression. "No. She would have forced you to kill me," he whispered.

"The simple fact that you don't even realize that means you don't know her as well as you think you do."

"You have no idea what I know about her," I snapped back, fighting the urge to grab the pillow.

Smoke had begun to fill the space between us, and for once I was thankful for the charcoal smog. I wanted to hide beneath its dark mask. I didn't want to cry in front of him anymore than I already had. Maybe I was delusional, but the smoke from the fire now had the most calming scent I'd ever inhaled. I wanted to bury myself in it and hide. It was a shame my own smoke couldn't smell like this. It never smelled like anything.

"Fuck. This is not how I wanted your first days in Seelie to be." He rubbed his hands down his face in frustration, absently swatting at the thick smoke between us. "This was too much, I'm sorry. The healer will be in shortly to check on you. I think I'd better go so you can rest. This entire wing is yours. Get some rest, and feel free to roam it whenever you like."

CHAPTER 10

CALY

M Y NERVES DANCED A THOUSAND TINY PIROUETTES. TINGLES
erupted across my skin. The eerie sensation of invisible fingertips ghosted over the sensitive skin on the backs of
my thighs and knees. I groggily turned my head to the side,
shoving the pillow off my face where it nearly blocked my air.
Was that the sheets making that sound?

I groaned, adjusting the pillow over my head once again
to dull the bloodred glow that poured from the windows.
The light abruptly shifted, and a large black shadow dropped
over the bed. Flinging the pillow off my head with a gasp, my
eyes darted to the window directly in front of the bed.

My breathing stopped.

Pressed against the window was the silhouette of a man.
A very large, broad-shouldered man.

I bolted up from the bed, reaching for my glasses with
the blades hidden in the temples on the nightstand, only to
realize all of my weapons were still in my bag in the bathroom.
Feeling the familiar hum of exhilaration, I moved for the
nearest weapon.

Of course I had nothing nearby in this luxurious,

pampered space but a small bottle of linen spray that had somehow escaped my earlier destruction. At best, my attacker would end up smelling like freshly tumbled sheets.

Fuck!

I grabbed it; maybe the ethyl or isopropyl alcohol would at least cause bleeding in the stomach and intestines. I needed to be better prepared than this.

As soon as I turned back to the window, the large silhouette was gone and back was the eerie red glow of the sun.

What the fuck? Was I seeing things?

I was seven stories up in a heavily protected, royal castle. Nothing should be hovering outside of this window.

I shook myself, remembering I was no longer in the human realm. Something winged could be hovering outside of my window; in fact, it could have been a royal guard for that matter.

I raced to the opposite window, scented weapon in hand, and checked.

They would have expected me to go to the other window to look for them, so I at least had a better chance of seeing someone hiding from this side.

Nothing but the warm red sun blanketing the flower-speckled fields and turning what looked to be a sea off in the distance a bloody-gold color. A few dark birds, maybe crows, took off from one of the turrets overhead.

I tried to convince myself that was all it had been—a bird.

After thoroughly checking the room, I grabbed the squishy comforter off the bed and hung it over the window by carefully wedging a few corners. I would work on getting better curtains made, but this would have to work until then. I could barely sleep with a crack of light under the door at home, let alone the creepy, red sun pouring in. Granted it was closer to a murky glow than a full sunset, but I needed it as dark as my tainted soul when I slept.

I let out a sigh so deep, it seemed to rise from my toes as I crawled back onto the bed and under the cool, white sheets. I shivered with the lack of a blanket, but the newfound darkness quickly lulled me to sleep—a sleep so deep I dreamt the wildest things imaginable. Like so many times in the last few weeks, I let myself fall deeper and deeper into the paradisiac dreams of *him*.

In this unconscious state, no one could reprimand me, no one could make me do a thing I didn't want to. I didn't have to be the betrayer. I wasn't forced to be a different person.

I was just me, and he was just Malum.

Deep in my wondrous dream, a powerful hand flattened on my hip. A warm, sharp jaw pushed into the crook of my neck as I inhaled the clean, masculine scent of him so close. My mind burrowed into the dream, savoring every sensation.

I moved to roll over, but the strong hand gripped my hip tightly, keeping control and keeping me on my stomach. Did it tremble slightly?

The fingers splayed, gliding over the side of my rear and onto my thigh. Less controlled this time, they indented my flesh with an unchecked need that coursed through my own body.

His barely audible whisper rolled over my ear and neck. "I cannot watch you for another minute without touching you. It *will* kill me," Mendax growled into my neck.

I arched, moving my back into his hard chest and exposing my neck for him. My butt followed, nestling into his crotch. Even in my dreamy state, the bare skin of my legs burned with excitement. His pants and body felt so hard and solid behind me. I lifted my ankle and rubbed it against his outer leg, wanting to feel the texture of his clothing and body.

He groaned softly into the back of my neck. The sound vibrated in my head and chest and ran all the way to the soles of my feet. My lower stomach hummed, his small noise making my thighs quiver.

I lifted my arm to wrap around his and head, needing desperately to pull him to my lips. I needed more than anything to feel that connection with him one last time, dream or not.

Normally my dreams were just of his mostly shaded silhouette watching me. Occasionally they'd be of him saying the most heinous, absurd things to me. He'd usually just be standing by my bed or in a doorway, watching me broodily. This was by far the most exciting.

"Are you ready to play, pet?" he whispered as he hovered his full lips just out of reach.

"Play what?" I drunkenly asked, continuing my attempt to crane my neck so I could push my lips into his. But all it did was push my body against the length of his arousal, stoking a frustrated fire between my legs.

"A game." I could hear the cocky smile in his rumbly voice.

I pressed back harder, arching against his hardness and letting out a groan.

"You should really stop that, Calypso. I've had a lot of time on my hands to miss this body of yours," he stated in something of a command and a whisper.

My whole body tensed—the sound of my real name flowing from his mouth did something to me. It sparked a sensual danger that both frightened and ignited me.

I wished I could have actually heard him say it like that... before he died.

"You don't really want me to stop, do you?" I purred. "I can feel how hard you are, and you've barely even touched me," I whispered triumphantly, grinding my ass into his hardness.

"Never in my immortal life have I ever wanted anything more than I want to feel you under me right now, pet, but I am not a gentle, benevolent man. I have hurt others I barely desired and killed others because of my lack of control; others, I haven't wanted a modicum as much as I crave you," his voice whispered across my neck. "I won't allow myself inside of you in that way until I can control myself enough to know you will still remain with me forever. Unharmed."

His hand trailed down my cheek and grazed across my

breast before rubbing my nipple between two fingers for a moment and then pinching it roughly.

I inhaled a sharp breath.

It hurt, but only enough to cause a torrent of arousal to heat between my legs. I was sure there were oceans that weren't as wet as I was.

Yes, I know, him saying he literally killed someone as they fucked shouldn't turn me on, but something about how rough he was sent an absolute fire through me, like a challenge.

"You wouldn't hurt me. I know it," I practically moaned, slipping my palm between our bodies to feel his cock.

My hand found my reward immediately, and I salivated like a monster. He was as hard as a fucking brick.

"As frequently as I have been getting off to the mere thought of you, love, I would fuck you into the dirt under this castle," he groaned into my neck before grabbing my wrist roughly and stopping my massaging hand. "And you're very, very wrong. I *do* want to hurt you. I plan on it. Why do you think I'm here?"

I recoiled slightly at his words and his harsh grip on my wrist. Even my dream senses heightened, readying me to fight or run.

Mendax was an unpredictable, menacing fae predator. Even in my dreams, he radiated danger and raw power.

The bed shifted, and cold air hit my back.

Immediately my happiness ebbed at the absence. Mendax left the mattress and stood at the foot of the bed. His large silhouette was outlined eerily with the deep red of the scarlet sun behind him.

I rolled on my back to protest, prepared to sell my soul to whatever fae devil existed for a few more moments of him in this dream. I wouldn't even try to unpack how fucked up that was until morning...or maybe never.

"Please come back, Mendax," I whined.

He took a step forward, leaning over and grabbing my

knees, pushing them wide apart. The bed lowered when he kneeled in the space between my legs. My heart kicked into overdrive while my body thrummed with excitement.

Finally.

The Unseelie prince braced his body over mine, grabbing my face roughly in one hand, my lips puckering out above my teeth.

This close, I could practically see the collagen fibers in his iris, causing the ice-blue streaks of color as they looked straight through me. Like the rope of a noose pulling tight and strong, our connection was unwavering. Even if it was unwanted, we were coal to the other's flame.

"For *forever* you are mine. I alone own you. Do you understand that yet?" he asked, dropping his hand from my face to graze across my chest and stomach before settling it between my legs, cupping me firmly.

I heard the breath catch in his throat before his grip grew firmer, more intense. The sultry rhythm of his breathless chant made my head spin with need.

I pressed myself harder into his palm, causing my eyes to flicker closed as I opened my insolent mouth to tell him exactly what he owned.

I wasn't generally a passive sort of woman, as he had figured out by now. No man or fae would *ever* own me.

But it was a dream, and an unbelievably good one at that, so I wasn't going to ruin it.

"A good pet should always listen to their owner's commands, don't you think?" he questioned softly as he hooked his thumbs into the sides of my sleep shorts and underwear and slid them slowly down and off my legs.

My knees pulled up and now rested on either side of his body as he knelt between them.

I was fully exposed and vulnerable to him.

"You are immaculate," he murmured after a moment of stillness.

Mendax leaned his muscular frame forward, hovering

over me and grabbing my hand and tucking in all but my pointer and middle fingers.

Hot, wet need pulsed violently between my legs as he pushed my fingers inside his mouth, his eyes angrily glowing at mine. He ran his hot tongue over my fingertips, closing his mouth around them before pulling them from his mouth, then pressing them on my exposed sex roughly, all in one motion, still warm and wet from his mouth.

I let out a small whimper, shocked by how much I liked his angry touches and the unbelievable realness of the dream. Is this how we would have been if he were still alive?

The prince removed his hand with a groan to stand at the foot of the bed again, towering over me with his large arms crossed.

"Wait—"

"You will touch yourself gently because I cannot. Do not move your hand from that spot until I command you to, my queen." His gravelly voice held so much roughness, I swore I felt it.

I was so shocked and so turned on, I didn't even realize I'd started moving my fingers over myself. The heat from our angry stares, though shadowed with darkness, had jumped from being coal to chlorine trifluoride. I was on fire.

"I want you to touch me, please, Mendax," I begged.

Unable to bear another moment of his lustful stare, I slid my fingers lower to feel my pulsing clit—I wouldn't be taking orders well.

Without warning, my throat choked, something tightening around it with heavy pressure. I gasped for air while I tried to sit up, but I couldn't rise.

"Did I tell you to move yet, love?" Mendax said nonchalantly from where he stood.

I clawed and ripped at the force strangling me until I saw the smoke coiled around my throat like a fucking python trailing back to Mendax's large hand.

The grip lightened slightly as I stilled and heaved large

gulps of air into my straining lungs. The mixed sensations of arousal, fear, and aggression swirled into a confusing puddle of desire between my legs. I glared harder at the towering fae. Since when was I into rough sex?

"Be a good girl and listen to your owner, pet, or I won't let go next time. I do owe you for stabbing me, after all."

My hand had already moved to rub me.

I wanted him wild and violent with need. I wasn't afraid of him. I wanted him so badly, I could feel the desperation in every cell of my body. My thalamus was going to explode trying to regulate my arousal.

"Touch yourself while I watch you. Back and forth," he commanded in a deep, sultry tone. "Good, now slower."

My toes curled as I listened for more requests.

"Fuck, Caly. I would die for you all over again if it meant I got to watch you in this moment," he groaned breathily as his hand moved to his hardness.

A moan escaped my mouth as I watched his eyes drag over me—harsh eyes filled with such intense affection and desire.

I began to move my hips to the rhythm of my fingers.

"I want you to press your two fingers as deep inside of that needy, little pussy as they will go. I wonder how hard you'll come for me knowing you lay beneath me, a smoke curl away from death. Rub yourself in a circle with your thumb," he stated, a deep, raspy breath escaping his cocky grin.

I didn't need another nudge. I pushed into myself, letting out a silent cry as I thrust my hips up, wishing it were him. He was so close to touching me.

Like a viper, a coil of smoke snapped out and tightened around my throat, causing me to falter and gasp, tightening my stomach.

"*Do not* come until I tell you to," he whispered before loosening the smoke from around my throat but not letting it off completely.

The blood and panic seemed to rush from my neck

straight down to my clit. I had barely touched myself, but I was already on the edge of an orgasm from the intense sensations.

"Oh fuck, Mendax," I moaned, feeling all the tension coil in my lower stomach while I resumed fucking myself in front of his hungry, unsated eyes.

"Fucking hell," Mendax cursed as he peeled off his shirt, revealing the body of a god.

Another breathy moan slipped out of me watching the shadows dance across his broad shoulders and muscled stomach. I was so fucking close. Any second now, I would slip past the edge and my orgasm would be unstoppable.

The smoke around my neck tightened the tiniest amount, reminding me of his orders to wait for his word. With the hand not controlling the smoke, Mendax undid his belt buckle with a small jingle and pulled out his rigid cock, fisting it roughly.

"How badly do you need me to move between your legs and slide my cock inside of you, love? A little?" he rasped as he stroked his cock up and down, staring at me like a hungry lion.

Oh. My. Suns.

"A lot. Fuck, please, Mendax," I panted, biting my lip hard in order to move myself away from the orgasm that was so close, a draft in the castle might send me over the edge.

He gripped himself so tightly, it looked painful as he slid his fist up and down wildly.

"You shouldn't have left me then, Calypso. Maybe then I could be a bit more gentle. I wouldn't have spent so many hours thinking about all the things I would do to you once I found you. How much I'd make you hurt. How hard I would fuck you."

"I'm going to come if you don't shut up and get over here," I moaned, knowing I was about to fall into the abyss.

The Unseelie prince was at the side of the bed near my head in an instant. He grabbed my throat with his right hand, continuing to fist his cock with the other right next to my shoulder.

"Men—"

"You want to come? Then admit it: say it out loud, and I'll let you come, my pretty little hellhound. Admit you are in love with me," he whispered slowly, emotion turning his voice gritty.

"I love you," I said without hesitation. It was a dream, and no one could hurt me for admitting it. No one could weaponize it or tear me apart for owning such an absurd declaration.

"Then come for me now, my love," he whispered with a smile, straightening to his full height to watch me. He fisted himself faster now, his hand still tight around my throat. "Now," he said squeezing my throat firmly.

I lost it. The tingles and tension built and built and built until there was nothing left for it to do but explode from within my body. I shuddered as my body clenched, no longer in my control.

Mendax tightened his hand around my throat. I couldn't breathe at all. It was terrifying, but I continued to move my fingers in circles on my sensitive clit, knowing he would let go.

He didn't.

My wild eyes shot to him in blind panic. My mind became fuzzy, and my vision had started to speckle. Instinctively, I lifted my arm up to turn and slam my elbow down on his arm, but my orgasm burst forth like a gift from the heavens, and I came again.

I came harder than I'd ever come in my whole goddamned life.

Just as it ebbed out and I was positive I was going to black out or evaporate, Mendax released my throat, letting out a low groan at the same time.

He was coming too. Warm ribbons of cum shot onto my chest as he slowed his fisting, now leaning on one shaking arm next to my head. He removed his hand from his cock and leaned over my face. "You look like a goddess veiled in my cum," he whispered, leaning in and kissing me so tenderly, I couldn't imagine never feeling it again.

He pulled away to bite his lower lip while he moved his thumb through the trails of his cum that marked my chest.

Mendax dragged the same covered thumb slowly over my bottom lip before pushing it inside my mouth. Saltiness and a shockingly smoky flavor swirled on my tongue with the taste of him. It tasted just a hint like how a roaring campfire smelled.

He removed his thumb and then gently trailed his hand down the side of my face, leaning down to kiss my shoulder.

"I'll see you soon, my pet. I hope you're as ready as I am for the second part of our game." He smiled a crooked smile that forced one of his dimples to show while he pulled his black shirt over his head and fastened his pants.

What was he talking about? I pinched my eyes shut tightly, willing myself to wake up.

Something wasn't right.

"Game?" I fumbled over the simple words.

Clothed now, he stepped back into the shadows of the room until the only thing I could make out was the black outline of his profile.

"The part of the game where I slaughter every member of the Seelie family that took you away from me, starting with the prince."

CHAPTER 11

QUEEN SARACEN

I SCRUTINIZED THE SCROLL, DOUBLE–CHECKING THE ADDRESS that had been neatly written on the mottled papyrus paper. Squeals of high-pitched laughter came from the back of the small, run-down cottage I stood before.

They were young. One looked roughly the same age as Aurelius, the other younger.

So this was what the almighty Zef had hidden.

It was brilliant. I wouldn't have been surprised if he had hidden in the human realm with his offspring until he was called to ascend. No one would ever bother to look for them here. Most of his enemies weren't even permitted across the veil.

Zef must've trusted Felix to check in on them when his full Ascension to Moirai took place, his best friend making sure they were taken care of.

They would definitely be taken care of.

A smile crept onto my lips. Artemi usually didn't come into their full abilities until their twentieth red chariot made it past Tartarus and through the Elysian Fields. I've heard of some getting them early if they were really powerful.

Which made them perfect for our army.

I could hardly believe the goldmine of luck that today had revealed. Felix's lifeless body would be found while I was leaving Aurelius and bringing Thanes back the Artemi he deserved.

Leaning against the corner of the cottage, I settled back to watch my trophies play.

A rickety screen door slammed at the back of the house and a plain, weary-looking human woman with dirty-blond hair appeared. She looked tired and nervous at the same time, not even bothering to tidy herself, letting the hideous skeleton tattoo emblazoned on her chest hang out of her filthy blouse.

"Calypso! Adrianna! Girls, please don't go any farther toward the field!" the woman shouted, looking stressed and rumpled but at least adjusting her shirt to hide the odd tattoo—a skeleton holding a ring of skeleton keys. Where had I seen that before?

"Yes, Mother," the girls singsonged in unison.

The woman adjusted her shirt again, and I was able to get a closer look at her weathered face. Aside from the clothing and hair, her features were surprisingly striking. So much so, that had it not been for her energy being completely and utterly mortal, I would have assumed she was fae.

I could hardly believe it.

Zef had defiled himself with a human! My mouth hung open as I continued to watch the mortal wipe her eyes on the sleeve of her shirt as she closed the door behind her and returned inside.

I could hardly believe it. Zef, the last of the extinct Artemi, had hidden a partially human family in the smallest nook of the smallest human town.

This changed everything. It was highly unlikely that he would have two full-blooded Artemi after procreating with a human. Most fae could impregnate humans, but Artemi's powers were so strong-willed, they refused to be shared or diluted by blood. The powers grew in strength with every generation, and being so strong, it was the parent with the most concentrated Artemi powers who chose which of their children would be most well suited to receive the immense gift of powers themselves, which child would have the strength and kind heart to take on such obligations of holding the feared powers of the Artemi.

It would be almost impossible to tell which one had it until their powers came.

The horrible stench of misplaced smoke caught my senses.

"You almost did it."

I whipped around to see the Unseelie Queen Tenebris standing mere feet behind me. Her hands were coated in black all the way up to her elbows, while the rest of her porcelain skin was covered in veins of black. Her dark, butterfly-shaped wings of smoke pulsed. Though normally pristine, she was disheveled, black streaks of blood staining her lips and eyes.

"You're alive," I whispered.

How could she be here? Thanes was to have killed them. News of the violent bloodshed that filled the Unseelie castle had been running rampant all evening.

Her pale eyes took in the oblivious, laughing children around the corner of the house.

"Children, Saracen?" She wrinkled her pointy nose at me with a look of disgust.

How dare the empress of darkness and evil pass judgment on me?

"Yes, Tenebris." I smiled. "Apparently your husband and I need something significantly more powerful to kill you, as it seems our creations were unsuccessful," I bit out.

"Unfortunately, you and Thanes are quite finished running experiments on humans. You really haven't the need for any more monsters. Even with no powers, you could pass as one," she said with a smile that left her eyes hollow.

I held firm, but truthfully, doing so provoked every sense

in my body to scream at me to flee. With no real powers, I stood next to her feeling weak at best.

"Seems as though they did quite a number on that bony face of yours. I can hardly see your sallow skin, covered in all of that blood. Thanes will never be happy with you. Never. He loves me," I snarled, taking a step closer.

"Such an adorable noise. Tell me, how did you learn it, being unable to shift like the rest of the royals?" Tenebris looked at her torn black dress and arms covered in blood. "But yes, it's true. The creatures Thanes made were quite... equipped, but you are mistaken in assuming that this is my blood."

"Wha—"

"Mendax has killed Thanes, and I am here to finally kill you, Saracen. Something I've been wanting to do since you involved yourself with my king and husband."

"No..."

Tenebris stepped into me.

My vision began to blur, and my stomach tightened into a thousand knots as her words started to sink in. "No! No! You wench. You lie, you didn't kill him! You didn't!" I screamed at her.

The sun filled my entire body with shimmering gold beams of light. This was about the extent of my powers— shimmering. Thankfully I had pocketed some of Aurelius's light before I left him in the forest.

The smoke in her palms shifted into long, tentacle-like talons.

"You're right. I didn't. My son, Mendax, killed him," she said with a pained look.

She was lying. There was no way Mendax would kill his father. "You lie. That child adored Thanes. He would *never* kill him!" I shouted.

"You are correct," she said with a pained crease of her brows. "Mendax did adore him. But he also loves me, and between Thanes and your...whatever you call them, Fallen fae creatures, I would have been dead had it not been for my son." Her eyes glimmered.

"No! Noooo!" I bellowed, feeling my protest rise from the soles of my feet as I hurled one of Aurelius's orbs of fiery light at her.

This couldn't be happening. She had ruined everything. I had just killed my sweet, kind Felix. I had left my own son in a human forest.

"I have lost *everything* because of you!" I screamed. "You and your son will pay for this if it's the very last thing I ever do!"

She dodged the orb easily, pushing out a gust of smoke to repel it.

I sent every morsel of power I had collected at her, one giant ray of fiery SunTamer power after the other, but somehow, everything I sent to her was either pushed away or absorbed with her smoke.

She effortlessly held the upper hand.

I had depleted myself of both Aurelius's stored power and the insignificant power I had. Being so far away from the Seelie sun like this was foolish, and I began to lose my size as well as my dignity, shrinking into the small, helpless fairies the humans were so used to finding and writing stories about.

It was already too dangerous for me here now—I needed to return to Seelie as soon as possible.

I took off toward the girls. They were of no use to me with Thanes dead. Let them at least serve by being shields.

I had already shrunk to the size of a toad. Any longer in this horrible realm, and my wings wouldn't bet able to get me back to the portal.

I made it to a mushroom, just in front of the older girl. Quickly, I looked back toward the front of the house. If the human or Tenebris caught me now, I was as good as dead.

A crow cawed above the mushroom I hid under.
Fuck!

Tenebris's shadows replicated a crow, concealing her now-tiny body from the humans.

She hadn't needed to shrink; she had done so in order to kill me with a clear conscience.

Queen Tenebris unleashed her full powers on me. The black smoke penetrated my skin painfully, crawling down my throat when I began to scream.

This was it. I would die with nothing. No power, no love, nothing.

Suddenly the older girl, the one with the big eyes, flung her bouquet of meadow flowers and mushrooms to the ground to hurl herself over me, taking the wrath of Tenebris.

I was stunned. The girl's chest heaved even after a few minutes.

She had taken the dark queen's full onslaught and remained alive. This was unheard of, even for an Artemi—especially a supposedly powerless Artemi child.

A few moments later, the girl dropped to the ground, passing out while still covering me. Her sister had brought out the mother and what looked like half the neighbors, who were suddenly running in our direction.

A sharp flicker of pain shot through my wings.

Tenebris took off as the humans were approaching, flapping away just as a crow formed of smoke would. She had lost a lot of power, but nothing that should have...

It was her—this one was the Artemi child, I could feel it.

My suns, her powers had to be strong. She had begun to draw the Smoke Slayer's powers. I could feel her strength trying to take hold of every part of my body. If she was this strong and didn't even have her full powers yet...

I smiled, and my tearstained cheeks lifted with a wild tremor.

I doubted the Unseelie queen had even realized the child wasn't human. Artemi were forgotten, extinct—aside from the ascended Ancients—as far as anyone else knew.

This was fate.

I would take my revenge on Mendax and Tenebris for everything they had ruined, and this Artemi child was going to help me.

CHAPTER 12

CALY

M Y EYES REFUSED TO COOPERATE, REMAINING TIGHTLY closed behind the layer of fluffy, lemon-scented pillows I had pressed against my face. Between the excitement of finally being here and the anxiety I felt when Queen Saracen demanded I marry into the family, it was no wonder I just had the most vivid dream of my life.

The warm and toasty smell of wood burning mixed with something delicious and spicy caught my attention, and I smiled. The smell seemed to be everywhere I was—the comforting scent that reminded me so much of Mendax. I had even gotten myself to believe it belonged to Mendax last night in my dream.

A great honk of a snort left my nose with a short laugh that was thankfully muffled by the pillow that remained on my face.

They used wood-burning fires to cook. That's why I smelled it last night at dinner and again now for breakfast.

I couldn't help but wonder why they didn't use magic to cook. It seemed like it would be so much easier. I made a mental note to find out everything I could about their magic and idiosyncrasies. Perhaps I could take it easy the next few days and read up on Seelie fae. I was sure I could find my way to a library in town if they didn't have one in the castle.

My body sank deeper into the large, comfortable bed as I really let myself relax unguarded for the first time since... well, since I could remember. This was dangerous. I could have stayed inside of this dreamlike serenity for days.

I stuck my leg out to test the temperature of the room and immediately pulled it back into my homey pocket of warmth. The air outside of the bedding was crisp and cold, while the heat I had cultivated under my sheet was surprisingly warm and cozy. I was in blanket prison.

It would be best to stay here until someone came for me. I just knew the marble floor would be like ice on my bare feet. The unrelenting scent made my muscles relax and settle even further. I had made it here. I could finally relax.

Today would be a great day. I felt happy and rested—not something I was able to declare very often—but if I didn't get up now, blanket prison would keep me trapped and lazy all day.

At last, I shoved the mound of white pillows away and rose from the bed. Stepping out of the tangled white sheet and bracing for the touch of cold marble, my foot landed on something soft instead.

My plaid night shorts.

I suddenly realized I was completely naked from the waist down.

Heat rushed into my face as I remembered the details of my dream. I must have taken my shorts off and touched myself while I was dreaming.

The dream.

Oh my god, what the hell—or Tartarus now—was wrong with me?

I nearly fell to the ground pulling my shorts back on. I couldn't even think about that right now.

What an absolute mess of a person I am. Dreaming about the enemy, the one who viciously terrorized my family, watching me finger bang myself?

I scanned the room, taking note of the now yellow sun blazing across the empty fireplace. The smoky scent was so potent now, I expected to see the fire going.

Could he have...?

There was no way. No. See? This is what happens when you never relax. The first time you get to, you forgo calm and immediately turn paranoid and lonely.

I had no idea what time it was here. One of the few things I did know was that time worked differently in each of the realms. The difference in proximity to the moon and the sun made things faster or slower. I couldn't help but feel a little disheartened realizing that science, my one real comfort, was basically nonexistent here. Those laws didn't apply in these realms. Magic didn't care about molecular structure or quantum particles.

Still, it would be a new area of study for me. Excitement gently stirred in me. I loved learning and was excited to understand more about Seelie and its inhabitants. I climbed back onto the fluffy bed, my legs dangling over the edge. Would I marry Aurelius if that was the only way to become a Seelie royal? Saracen still retained half of my heart. What more did she require?

I pulled in a deeper breath, my nose searching for the comforting scent only to be disappointed when I couldn't grasp hold of the spicy, warm fragrance. My mind scanned its cabinet of memories for an impression of comfort in its absence.

My mother sat on a tattered picnic bench in our old backyard—at least I thought it was my mother. Most of my early memories had blurred a bit as soon as the more... unsavory memories were created. I didn't really mind. They didn't belong in the same space.

Adrianna, my younger sister, cuddled on her lap while I sat atop the gray-brown table, painting my mother's face with one of her metallic-blue eyeshadow palettes. Acorn, a friendly squirrel we had made friends with, sat on my lap nibbling one of my shirt buttons.

Tears filled my eyes at the memory. I had been only a child then, almost eight years old and my sister a few years younger. That was right before they were taken away from me, before they left me all alone. That was the last time I had felt whole. Now it only ever felt like my soul was shredded and furious.

My mind threatened to cave, as it so frequently did whenever I thought about Mom and Adrianna. The sheets dragged against the back of my thighs as I slid to the hard floor, my eyes filled with tears.

A loud knock sounded at the door, startling me.

"Calypso, get up. Eli sent me to wake you while he gets ready. Apparently I'm no more than a lady's maid now." Tarani's voice was muffled from the other side of the door.

Quickly wiping my eyes and smoothing my hair, I leaped up and flung the door open to a very disgruntled princess.

Twirling blond hair around her fingers, Tarani looked up at me coldly from under her sparkly gold eyelids. She waltzed into the room, making no secret of inspecting it as if making certain I hadn't ruined anything.

"Is that what your kind sleep in?" she asked, looking me up and down with a flat expression.

Princess Tarani was once again in a beautiful white dress that trailed just slightly behind her. It had to be absolutely horrible to wear these dresses every day. Didn't she ever get to wear pants? I looked to my barely there yet obnoxiously comfortable sleeping shorts and then back to the princess, who was so sweetly scowling in disgust. I wouldn't hold it against her—she had obviously never worn flannel pants covered in kittens and didn't know what she was missing.

"Yeah, this is pretty much what humans sleep in. Feel how soft though!" I said, grabbing a wad of the buttery-soft fabric and pushing my hip out.

"But what about *your* kind?" she asked with a small smirk and a mischievous twinkle in her eyes.

I took a few steps back from her. Ah. She came to rub it in my face that she knew I was Artemi with no real powers.

"You probably don't even know what shorts are, do you? Do you always wear such fancy dresses?" I questioned, watching the blonde woman continue to wander aimlessly around the room with her hands clasped behind her back. I stole a glance at the hallway, hoping Eli would save me from this awkwardness, but it was empty.

"Not always. Unlike you, I'm able to wear the fur of a fox on occasion," she sang matter-of-factly.

She poked her fingers in one of the corners next to the window, where I had hung the bedspread, slightly scratching the molding in the process. She had found the one goddamn blemish in the room in less than thirty seconds. She was smart and perceptive. I had a feeling she was underestimated quite a bit.

It was clear she was still angry about my arrival and was trying to show how different I was, to make certain I knew I didn't belong here.

But I would try to play nice. It might be important that she like me if I was going to become a Seelie royal. I didn't know how much sway she had with her mother.

"Your brother was beautiful in his fox form. From what I can remember though, a much thicker, shinier coat than yours," I muttered as I leaned on the wall near the window she was still inspecting.

I said I'd try.

Tarani's smug expression fell and surprise filled her large honey-colored eyes. "You remember," she whispered so softly I almost didn't hear, even as close as we stood.

Okay. Not the reaction I'd expected.

"When your brother saved my life in Unseelie? I remember you there as well, though of course I didn't know it was the two of you at the time. But I put it together when I learned Eli shifted into a fox form. Thank you, by the way. After they stabbed me, I was sure I was going to die," I said, suddenly feeling my eyes get hot and prickly.

They had risked their lives to save mine.

Tarani looked absolutely horrified. "Believe me, it was Eli's choice to save you, not mine. Had it been up to me, your kind would have all died," she snarled.

"What is your problem with me?" I asked, taking a confrontational step forward.

"You think you are really special, don't you? Aurelius and Mother only spent time with you in the human realm because they thought you were a freak. Why do you think they chose you to go whore yourself out to the Unseelie prince? They knew he couldn't resist an easy target or an evil freak like you," she spit out, taking a step closer to me.

Fuck. Freak or not, I could've already had her large intestine tied around her throat if I'd wanted to. She needed to watch her tone or I would snap before it was time.

"Listen, you're a lot gutsier than they led me to believe, and I respect that, but you don't even know me," I said, tightening my jaw. "If you've got some sort of jealousy issue, take it up with your mommy."

The princess's sunset eyes locked on mine. Her autonomic nervous system's sympathetic branch was stimulated, causing her pupils to dilate—I had triggered her fight-or-flight response.

I took a step toward the door. I didn't know what her full magical abilities were, and besides that, I definitely didn't think it would help my standing here if I knocked out the princess on my second day.

"Don't you *dare* bring up my mother," she spat out, clenching her hand into a fist so tight, her knuckles were white.

"Tarani, leave her alone," a strong voice sounded from the door.

Tarani and I snapped our heads in unison to see Eli

filling the doorway, an uncomfortable look straining his face.

"She remembers everything you did!" Tarani shouted at Eli, raising her arms in frustration before they dropped back to her sides.

"Tarani, this shouldn't be done this way," Eli said warily, glancing at me uneasily. "She doesn't know, and I don't want her to."

I should have known it wouldn't have been as easy as I had hoped.

"She needs to know, at least for your own safety, Eli. She is unpredictable and weak," Tarani said, looking me up and down.

Unpredictable and weak?

While they continued arguing, I grabbed my duffel bag from under the large bed, pulling out an oversized sweat-shirt and moving closer to Tarani. As I pulled it over my head, I gripped the karambit I'd also collected from my bag and secured the circle of the curved blade's handle over my thumb, pushing it out of the sweatshirt sleeve and locking the princess's elbows behind her back. The double-edged blade pressed into her neck just below her jaw. She moved into place without resistance, realizing too late what had happened. Both Eli and Tarani gasped in unison.

"Unpredictable maybe, but this blade at your throat negates your claim of weak," I whispered. Adrenaline had sparked to life under my skin, sending tingles across my skin, and smoke flowed over my arms and into her face, dissipating as her slightly opened mouth pushed it away.

"They'll kill you for this." She smiled. "Mother will send you back to the humans as soon as she hears of this!" she barked triumphantly, sounding surprisingly unafraid when I pressed the blade harder against her throat.

I wasn't stupid. I held it flat against her skin, so I wasn't actually about to hurt her, but she couldn't feel the difference with her adrenaline spiking.

If the need arose though, it would take me half a second to do it. Some part of my instincts begged me to swipe the blade across her throat and make my life a lot easier here.

"Knock it off, both of you!" Eli shouted, stepping in close to tower above us.

"This is exactly what I mean, Aurelius! Do you see what you've done? You will both be killed before the week is through!" Tarani shouted, starting to fight back against my hold.

What was she talking about?

I didn't want to hurt her yet, and I wasn't stupid. Whatever a SunTamer could do would be far worse than anything I could. The energy in the room was explosive, each of us waiting to see what the other would do.

"Remove the knife from my sister's throat. Suns, Calypso! Sometimes I wonder if Unseelie wouldn't suit you better with the way you turn so dark," Eli grumbled.

His words shouldn't have hurt, but they did. I'd even wondered the same thing myself several times. I had foolishly thought Mendax was the only one to see my darkness, but apparently that wasn't so.

"Before you accuse me of being full of Unseelie-like darkness, remember who trained my hands." I shoved Tarani to her knees, maintaining my grip on her.

"You're nothing but a fool," Tarani said quietly from below me. "You act like you have a craving for death, and now, because of my idiot brother thinking with his dick and saving you, your lives are tied together. Forever. Now fuck off and get out of my way." Tarani burst into a glowing orb of yellow light that sent such intense heat to my fingers, I was forced to drop my hold on her.

I needed to find out more about her powers.

She stood up as the bright light faded and moved to stand next to Eli with her arms crossed.

"What do you mean our lives are tied together? I don't understand anything you just said."

My friend began to pace, running his hands through his thick, blond hair. "I couldn't help it! The pull—we were in our fox forms when I found you. I-I couldn't let you die. I was the reason you were there in the first place!"

"I don't understand. Isn't that something all fae can do? Why is that so dangerous?" I asked, gripping the warm metal of my karambit for comfort.

"No one can know what I did, Caly. Mother doesn't know. *No one* can know. It's incredibly dangerous for anyone to know what I did for you," Eli said seriously.

"And what exactly did you do?" I asked, feeling suddenly unsteady.

"Just before your heart stopped beating, Eli infused you with his power. His *Seelie royal* powers. It is forbidden in all realms of faerie to disrupt what the Fates have decided, and what's worse"—Tarani struggled to get the words out—"is now Eli's life is tied to yours and vice versa. Should one of you be killed, the other will also die." Her voice cracked on the last words.

Me? I was going to pass out. "That...can't be. Fae are immortal. I'm basically human! I'll be lucky to live another fifty years. Then will Eli die as well?" I asked, beginning to panic.

No wonder Tarani had been so upset with me.

"Fae are immortal, but that just means we aren't affected by illness and death in the same way that humans are. We can still be killed," Tarani said as she sat on the edge of my bed, her demeanor now thoughtful.

"I know, a wound through the head or decapitation. Sometimes between their wings or their belly button, depending on their kind," I responded.

"Uh...gross," replied the princess.

"I can only tie to Artemi powers, Caly." Eli stepped in front of me and gently squeezed my shoulders. His normally lively face had fallen, the smile lines by his eyes pulling down.

I stared at the small points of his ears.

"That's how I really knew you weren't human."

I took in a breath and prepared for everything to slip through my fingers before my eyes.

"I knew you weren't human as soon as Mother started telling people she blessed you with animal powers, and I hadn't even met you. She couldn't bless you with anything—she doesn't have powers beyond that of the lowliest Seelie," Tarani bit out.

I could tell her patience was waning. "Eli, I'm not—" I started.

"We think your father might have been an Ancient, Calypso," Eli said, moving closer to put this arm around me and guide me to the edge of the bed. "It's the only thing that makes any sense."

I shoved his arm off and stepped away from the bed. The rage that bubbled up when I thought about the man who left my family poked me like a red-hot iron. "What do you know about my father?" I shouted, feeling that rage start to surface.

"We don't know for sure, but from what you've told me, the timeline would make sense, and you share an uncanny resemblance to one of the newer Ancients in particular. He used to come around before he ascended. He was good friends with our dad. It's the only explanation we have been able to come up with," he said as his jaw clenched. "If it's who we are thinking, he is an Ancient, a child or grandchild of the old gods."

I couldn't be doing this. The last thing I had been prepared for today was to talk about my father with Eli and Tarani.

Trying to remain calm, I moved to the cool wall and pushed my back against it, needing something, anything, to support and hold my frame upright. "So how can I get to my father?"

"Well…Artemi are rare, and they have several powers that make them unbelievably dangerous, one of them is their connection with nature and animals. Most of them were peaceful and noncombative, which is probably one of the only reasons they were able to be destroyed as easily as they were. The ones still hidden ascend at a certain time and go to Moirai with the other Ancients."

"Just tell me how I can see him."

"I have no idea." Eli shrugged. "Ancients are only ever seen when there is a huge metamorphic event that could change the course of fate or if the Fates demand an inquisition. Even then, you must receive an invitation in order to even pass through the gates of Moirai."

I stared wide-eyed, choosing what to ask next. "Eli, I'm not what you think." I shook my head. "My sister..." I trailed off.

"As far as we know, your mother and sister were human. None of it makes any sense, and it's just a theory. I don't know much, but it seems like your father might have tried to hide you in the human realm. But either way, you most certainly are not human."

"But do Artem..."

"Art-em-ee," Eli offered.

"Thank you," I grumbled, absently touching the tips of my ears and feeling the uneven scars I'd had since I was a child.

Eli looked at his sister.

"We think someone modified your ears, cutting the tips off," Tarani said. "Artemi have slightly pointed tips. Eli told me there are scars on yours, that you thought might have been from an accident when you were little, but most likely it was your father who did it so you would blend in more with the humans. It really was smart. As for your lack of power—" She trailed off.

I felt numb. And what was worse, I had no more answers than before. No matter where I went, desolation followed.

My veins began to burn like fire. I needed to get out of here before I hurt something or someone.

"Are Artemi allowed in Seelie?" I asked. *Just hold on a little longer, just a little longer.*

"Yes, they are allowed anywhere they want to go once they have been registered. Until then, they can't use the portals. But, unfortunately, they are not safe until they ascend. There is no better place for you than here at the castle. We will keep you safe," he rasped softly, his own eyes moistening.

"Why are they not safe until Ascension?" I questioned.

"Because nearly every creature with the tiniest amount of power fears the Artemi will take their powers and leave them for dead. The more powerful they are, the more they have to lose with an Artemi alive. Every kingdom on this side of the veil fears the takeover and destruction of their courts and realms. It makes for some pretty dangerous and affluent enemies."

Great.

Something inside me snapped. "How does the tie work?" I asked Tarani, unable to look at Eli for fear I'd punch him.

"Artemi are the chain that ties all of nature together. They have the ability to manipulate nature to their will and are generally incredibly peaceful and loving." Tarani rubbed her neck with a scowl. "The blood that created shifters came from the oldest of the Artemi. Because our royal blood is so pure—"

Eli cut her off. "Pure-blooded Seelie royals who have the ability to shift are capable of tying themselves to an Artemi. It's not a known thing anymore because the only Artemi anyone knows of are gods or Ancients," he said, moving to my line of vision.

"So, what? Any shifter can save my life and tie themselves to me?" I asked as I watched him closely.

"Artemi send their powers to the child of their choosing. Every generation gets stronger, so they have to choose carefully. They could have seven children, but the most powerful parent chooses which child they send it to before they are even born. Just as only one child can get all of the powers, only one shifter can be tied to that one Artemi," Eli said. "All it takes is the tiniest amount of Artemi powers to tie with ours."

"Eli, I can't be responsible for your life. This will ruin everything!" I shouted. How could he have done this?

"It can't be undone," Tarani bit out. "The only way it breaks is if one of you dies, killing you both."

"I… This is too much. I'd like some time to think. Please leave," I begged, trying my hardest to keep it together until they left. I wanted to strangle someone.

"Calypso, please. I'm certain you have a thousand questions. Please let me stay with you," Eli said, grabbing hold of my arms.

"I have all the answers I need," I bit out.

"Remember, no one but Eli, myself, and our mother knows you are Artemi. Do not tell a soul, or you put your life at risk, which means you put my brother's life at risk. The three of us in this room right now are the *only* ones who know about the tie. Keep your mouth shut," Tarani snarled as she turned and walked out of the door.

"When you are ready to talk, I will be here for you with answers and a trip to town for lots of books," Eli said. "If you are open to a longer trip, we could also go to the town of books in Parable? That might be safest once your heart is whole though."

The town of books?

"You are undetectable as Artemi to other fae without your whole heart. Mother must have taken the part with most of your powers. It keeps you safe, Caly. And you were the one who freely gave it to her. How long has Mother known you are Artemi?" he asked gently.

"Queen Saracen has known I was Artemi since the first day she saw me," I stated.

"I wish you would have been able to tell me who you really are. It could have made this so much easier for you," Eli replied softly.

"I know," I said, nodding slowly before closing the door and sliding to the ground.

CHAPTER 13

CALYPSO

T HE STARS SPARKLED OVER OUR HEADS LIKE MAGIC DUST sprinkled through the black sky. It was a warm summer night, but the heat had receded, leaving the perfect temperature. I loved nights like these.

"I need to go. I was supposed to be back in Seelie this morning. Mom's going to be mad at me again," Eli said from his side of the blanket.

Frustration tensed my body, and it took everything not to grab our blanket and pillow pile and throw them off the roof, where we stargazed. I realized then just how much I liked him. My jaw tightened and my fists balled as I laid there.

When Saracen started bringing Eli around, everything had changed. I wanted to hate him so bad. I hated all of them.

I wanted Mom and Adrianna back.

My nails dug into the skin of my palms, taking away some of the anger. I was trying so hard to hold my anger in, but most days it felt impossible.

"Things worth having are things worth waiting for," I whispered.

"What?" Eli asked, leaning up on his elbow.

"Nothing. It's this thing my mom used to say to Adrianna and me all the time. Why can't you just stay a bit longer? My science teacher told me there is supposed to be a meteor shower tonight."

"I'll be back the day after tomorrow so we can try out the new crawfish traps in the stream. Don't put them in without me, okay?" the boy said as he folded up his share of the blankets. He stacked them neatly by the attic window we crawled in and out of.

"Okay, tell Saracen I said hi," I grumbled in response.

He didn't bother going back inside my house, instead climbing down the trellis against the back of the house before jumping to the ground with a grace I wished I possessed.

He turned back around at the edge of the forest and waved goodbye.

I could never do anything to hurt him.

Which was really saying something, because I wanted to hurt everything else right then.

Ever since Mom and Adrianna died, it had been like something inside of me had snapped into a million pieces. I wanted everyone else to hurt as much as I did—and they would.

I decided right then and there that Eli couldn't be part of the plan. He just couldn't. Maybe that made me weak, but he was the only person I'd wanted to be around since Mom and Adrianna had left me. Not only did I want to be around him, but I couldn't stop thinking about him. He was so cute. I knew he only thought about me like a friend—and that was okay.

I laid back down on the blanket with my hands behind my head.

Maybe when we got older, he'd marry me. I could be a real Seelie that way too, I guessed, instead of Saracen keeping me as her weapon.

I shook the thought away immediately. Eli didn't like me

like that, and no matter what, he'd hate me after I became an official Seelie.

He'd hate me for what was going to happen to his mom—to his whole family.

CHAPTER 14

CALY

THE NEXT DAY, I REFUSED TO LEAVE MY ROOM. I DISMISSED the food they sent. I managed to dodge the maids when they tried to come dress me. I refused to see anyone, even at the request of the queen.

Instead, I stood at one of the windows with my face pressed to the glass, fogging it up with my breath while I stared out into the land of Seelie and tried to figure out what to do. I watched the sun fade slightly as it settled for night. I watched with what felt like the same breath as it lightened once again to start a new day.

There were moments I cried so hard, I worried that alone might kill Eli and me. I could feel my heart giving out. Other times I plotted how I would burn the castle to the ground.

Eli and Tarani had said the Artemi were peaceful and noncombative.

The deepest, darkest parts of me, the parts *they* created, ached for retribution. I wanted to hurt someone. I wanted them to feel the way they had made me feel. I wanted them to cry the way I had.

But that part of me stayed locked away, only allowed to roam when it was time.

I watched the apricot-colored sea flow peacefully at the edges of town and the bustle of people hurrying along to bring fantastical-looking ships into the harbor.

Artemi—the moment the name touched my ears, it sang through me like a laugh. I hated that I didn't know more about the history of the rare species that apparently were *so* frightening to the other fae, they had been brought to near extinction.

My father.

The words felt sour. How could such a wonderful, magnificent person like my mother fall in love with such a monster?

I trailed the ridges of my ear up along the helix, feeling the tiniest line along the ridge. A line I had felt a hundred times.

I rubbed my tired, puffy eyes and returned to the messy bed, crawling under the covers and wishing sleep would finally take mercy on me and claim me.

Had Mendax sensed my powers? What tiny bit I had?

Mendax had seen me. He had seen through me from the beginning, and I couldn't help but wonder if he had known. That was silly of course.

A small smile pulled at my lips, and I let out an exhausted laugh. I couldn't help but think, for as in love with me as Mendax said he was and as unhinged as he was, what would he have done to Saracen, Eli, and Tarani if he were still alive?

He would have decimated them for hurting me. What an irony that the only person to ever truly be on my side, I had killed.

In truth, Eli had been on my side as well. If it weren't for him, I would be dead. Still, being tied to him forever was too intense. It felt like when Mendax had been bonded to me all over again. The last thing I wanted was to be chained to someone for the rest of my life, and it had happened twice. At least for my sake, only one lived.

Memories swirled in my head.

"The only fae who shift into fox are the royal children of the Seelie court, and by Seelie law, you are now tied to one of them with your life. Those bastards will never let you free. It doesn't matter what realm you go to now; the Seelie owns you. The only solace you have is that they did it on Unseelie soil, which violates a lot of rules."

Walter, Mendax's cousin, had told me that when I had first arrived in Unseelie. Of course, that was before he was dropped from the ledge of the castle to his death for trying to help me escape. Walter had been one of the very few people I'd ever considered a true friend.

My brows cinched together as I painfully recalled the kind wolf and rat shifter. Had he known? Since it was done on Unseelie soil, as he said, did that mean there was a chance we could sever the tie?

I needed to face Queen Saracen and find out everything she knew. Days of pondering, and it didn't make sense why they couldn't tell her I was tied to Eli. I felt a smile pull at my lips.

It was his mother—she would do anything to protect him. She was already trying desperately to link us together as it was. Or did she know about the tie and was attempting to be kind by letting me think it was my decision?

I laughed, knowing better.

A loud knock rattled my bedroom door.

"Calypso, let me in," spoke a voice that sounded so stern and forceful, it took me a moment to realize it was Eli.

I didn't answer but instead leaned forward to make certain the dresser I had shoved in front of the door still held. Eli was too nice and respectful to do anything more than knock.

An irritated grumble came from the other side of the door as I settled back into my fluffy pit of misery on the bed. I needed more time to plan and think about what my best course of action was.

Suddenly the room filled with a light so painfully bright, I had to shield my eyes—which was good because I did so just as a small but powerful explosion filled the room.

Eli stepped over the broken door, avoiding the wooden shards of what used to be a dresser, and walked into the room with a slight flush on his tan face.

"This shit ends now, Calypso," he spat out, crossing his arms across his toned chest.

I sat with my mouth open, dumbfounded. Sweet, gentle, golden-retriever Eli had violently blasted my door open.

"What are you doing?" I asked, still slack-jawed.

"I know you, Caly. I know that your lip curls down at a weird angle when you're focusing on doing something with your hands. I know there are exactly twenty-three freckles on your nose and cheeks." He breathed heavily in his tailored, crisp-looking white shirt. "I also know that you tie your hair up on top of your head when you're about to eat something you've been craving. I know that you had a crush on Luke Thompson in the fifth grade and that he hurt your feelings when he broke your calculator and called you a nerd." Eli's voice softened as he sat on the edge of the bed.

"What does—"

"I know that you think you can handle everything on your own and don't need anyone," he whispered, angling his body to face me better. "I also know that Luke Thompson, of the fifth grade, missed a week of school because a fox bit him and he had to get a rabies shot."

My mouth fell open again as the pieces slid into place and I remembered the uproar the class had been in. Luke had come back to school saying that a fox ran up his driveway and bit his ankle while he was playing in his garage. We all just thought he was a liar.

My eyes were opened so wide that the warm air tingled the bits it wasn't even supposed to be touching.

"I know that since I've come in this room, you've already mapped out three different ways to escape or incapacitate me, and I know that you were in love with Mendax by the way your eyes fall to the ground whenever he is mentioned."

"Now wait, just a sec—" I protested.

"I also know that you've been sitting up here spinning your mind in circles, believing that Mother doesn't really want you here and wondering what else we could be up to." Eli reached his long arm down under the bed and pulled out my leather duffel bag.

"I know that you're my best friend, no matter what ever happens, and if you want to be mad at me for tying my life to yours, then you have every right to be angry, but you're going to have to do it with me here, Cal, because I'm not going anywhere. I've waited to see you for years, and I'm tired of missing you. Get dressed. I know you keep spare clothes in this bag in case you need to leave in a hurry," he said, pushing the dark-brown bag into my lap. "And…umm…I'm really, really sorry about all of your clothes…" He trailed off, staring at the destroyed dresser and the few singed scraps of fabric peeking through the rubble. "You know what? No, I'm not! This was fate. You needed a new Seelie wardrobe with our royal colors anyway, since you are now officially a part of the family."

I couldn't help but smile even though I tried to fight it. Eli really was an amazing friend, and even though time and a few other things had put a wedge between us, I still loved him with everything I had.

"Get dressed. You can be mad at me while we go to town. I want to pick you up some books about your kind. I know how much you enjoy research, my beautiful nerd," he laughed.

"I'm not going anywhere with you," I grumbled as I tightened my arms across my chest.

"Fine. Then we will stay here, but I'm not leaving, so you might as well think of all the questions and worries you have and talk to me. The sooner you stop being mad at me, the sooner I can help, and we can go enjoy our time together."

"You can't talk about missing me, Eli. I could have been here the whole time. Your mother used me as her throwaway killer instead." My voice crackled with emotion.

"Everything I ever did was to keep you safe. I don't know half of the reasons Mother does anything she does, but from the moment I met you, I have done everything in my power to keep you safe, Calypso. That has not and will never change. That's why I happily tied my life to yours in Unseelie, and I would do it again in a minute if it meant keeping you safe," Eli said.

"I don't want to be tied to you! You don't even know what I have had to do for your mother. Why do you think I refuse to talk about it with you?" I had to look at the ground. His concern for me, when his own life was basically guaranteed to be ended now, shook me. "You and I both know it will not stop simply because I am in Seelic. How stupid do you have to be to tie yourself to the queen's fucking assassin?" I shouted, all of my worries and rage soaring out with my words.

"Pretty stupid." Eli grinned his charming, boyish grin. "But they aren't giving me the throne because I'm smart. I protect the people, and I'm powerful enough to keep an entire realm safe. You are with me now...in whatever context you want, Caly. I swear, I will never let anyone hurt you ever again."

"I need to speak with the queen. What has she said about me not showing up for three days?" I asked.

"She knows that you are having a hard time. Tarani couldn't keep quiet and told her that you were having a meltdown." Eli shrugged.

"She was the one who told me to keep quiet!" I said with a scowl.

"I know. Tarani can't keep anything from Mother. I'm shocked she hasn't told her about the tie," Eli replied. "I swear, sometimes it's like they are plotting full realm domination together."

"How lovely," I grumbled and rolled my eyes. The two of them together seemed frightening.

"Come on, get dressed. I want to take you to town. Please, please, please, Calypso," he begged, the most compelling puppy-dog eyes I could imagine accompanying it. "I made a deal with a unicorn keeper to see his mob. You'll love it."

"Sorry, did you just tell me you're taking me to see a unicorn?" It made me realize I hadn't seen an animal since I'd been in the Seelie castle. "You know, for a family that has these wild animal blessings, I see no pets in this whole castle," I bemoaned, resting my hands on my hips.

"We have the blessing to be able to shift; we don't need animals," Eli said, looking a little sheepish. "Artemi are the only ones who animals are drawn to. It's a part of you that stayed with the part of your heart you still have. Now let's go to town and get you some books and new clothes. Sometimes the merchants have pets for sale."

CHAPTER 15

CALY

Wide-open fields speckled with trees and flowers stretched along both sides of us. The frequent orange-and-black movement of the monarch butterflies that trailed along Eli only added to the unbelievable view. It looked like something from a hyperrealism oil painting. A breeze took the hair off of my sun-warmed shoulders while we continued down the dirt pathway. The small crunch under my feet and the pleasant scent of warm, fresh grass was hypnotic.

Eli really did know how to make me feel better. He always had.

"If we can't touch them, then why are we going?" I asked for the second time.

"I told you. There are several different kinds of unicorns. Some are battlecorns for the chariots of the Fates, some are for admiring their beauty, some for their magic, and many others. The unicorns we are about to see are the floricorns. They magically pollinate the stonopolis—the flowers used in our mead—and they can be quite mean."

"Wait. We can't pet the floricorns because they are mean?" I laughed so hard, I had to stop in the middle of the path.

"They are much more daunting than they sound, I assure you. They are respectable creatures though. Generally calm and mellow when left to their flowers or their mob, but they are the most ill-tempered, curmudgeonly, crabby, fierce lot when disturbed from their flowers. Not even the unikeeper likes them, but they get the job done."

"A group of floricorns is called a mob?" I was struggling to keep a straight face, but Eli's sharp, gold-speckled eyes told me it wasn't a laughing matter.

"I'm serious, Calypso. Do not try to pet one, or I promise, you will regret it. I just thought you might like to look at them," Eli said.

So onward we went to look at the scary, angry, flower-loving unicorns.

Small stone houses began to pop into view more and more until we came to an old stone fence. Bits of moss had started to climb around the edges of the sharp-looking gray stones. The fence was short, only coming up to about my thighs. The rocks had been formed into the shape of a large vertical circle in front of us. An old but clean-looking wood door stood inside the tall circle. I could easily see over the short fence, so it seemed silly to have a door in place; all that would be needed to get over the fence was to lift a leg. It was so odd and nonsensical, as so many things in Seelie were proving to be. Then it occurred to me.

"Is it a ward of some kind? Spelled?" I asked Eli.

A wide smile broke over his face. "I was just thinking of what silly things I could tell you it was." He let out a laugh, tipping his head back until he was facing the sun entirely. "But yes, the land and cottages on this side of the fence are protected by the Seelie court and its powers. Most of the houses are those of court members or employees of ours anyway. This is warded to keep everyone safe and protected. Fae villages can be dangerous and unpredictable. Suns knows the elven villages are overflowing with mischief, as are the Unseelie, and don't even get me started on Itäre. I'm sure the human villages have their own dangers." He watched as a monarch butterfly landed on his hand and crawled around with a slow fold of its wings.

"Will it hurt me to go through it? How does it know I'm allowed to pass?" I asked, looking at the round door with curiosity. I didn't fully understand the concept of magic. Unlike science, it didn't make sense, it was unpredictable, and there was no real explanation for it.

"Of course not. Your tie—" Eli flinched a little before continuing. "You're tied to me. We can go anywhere the other can safely as far as magical guards are concerned." He walked toward the door like a puppy about to be scolded. "Let's go. We don't have a ton of time."

"You want me to go through the magical door? Make me, SunTamer," I stated stubbornly. The fresh air had invigorated me, maybe a little too much, and I couldn't help but want to play around a little. I crossed my arms and planted my feet with a grin. Truthfully, I was still a little angry and had stored up too much restlessness in the room the past few days. I wanted to get a rise out of Eli.

He sighed, dropping his arms at his sides to let his head fall back dramatically. "How old are you, Calypso?" He moved in front of me and put his hands on his hips, then looked down at me with a small smile.

"For someone so smart, you're severely miscalculating the situation," he laughed, and I swear I could see it brighten the gold flecks in his eyes. "I thought you tired of me beating you years ago. You don't want this heat." He chuckled, but then his face fell. "It's been a long time since we played together, Cal. We've grown up a lot since then," he whispered. The energy between us had somehow shifted.

His frame was so large this close, he completely shadowed me from the sun. He was right—things had changed since we had last seen each other. He was strikingly different from how I remembered him. I couldn't help but admire how handsome he was standing there.

The thought felt weird, so I moved my hands up to push him back, ready to catch him off guard and show him he wasn't really as grown up or as tough as he thought. In a blur, his hands shot out to hold my own in place against his chest, and he took a final step into me.

I inhaled sharply but couldn't seem to look away as he pulled his lower lip into his mouth. I could feel his heart beating faster and faster under my fingers. My eyes took him in, from his bronze cheekbones down to the slight opening of his shirt.

A soft *thrap* sounded, startling me. The cool silhouette blocking the sun grew as Eli's feathered wings spread wide, broadening the shadow.

"You better stop looking at my mouth that way, or I'll never be able to walk through town, Cal," he whispered with a grin.

My face flushed with his words. The dancing flutter of my stomach with his closeness was undeniable. I unfroze myself and tried to move to the door, but Eli gently kept my hands in place.

"Are we going in or not?" I demanded, attempting to look anywhere but at him.

Nervous excitement flooded me.

I had always had a stupid crush on Aurelius. He was charismatic and kind. Full of self-esteem but somehow entirely selfless at the same time. No one could be near Eli and not like him.

"Haven't you ever wondered what it would be like if we kissed?" he asked, something new radiating through his eyes.

My eyes shot from his to a butterfly on his shoe.

Younger me had thought about it a lot—far more than I should have—but as an adult… He was my only real, fully trusted friend left, and I wouldn't let my brain go there. I couldn't risk losing him as my friend. There was no way I could take losing him too.

"No," I bit back a little too defensively to be believed.

"I have. I don't know that I've ever stopped."

He lifted a hand off of mine to run his fingers lightly over my forehead, pushing back my windblown hair and tucking it behind my ear. I fought against the urge to lay my head on his chest. His large hand slid into mine, and he stepped away to open the planked door and guide me through.

I followed, eyes the size of saucers and mouth hanging open like a fish.

Three hours ago, I was thinking of ways to hurt him. An hour ago, I was thinking how lucky I was to have a friend like him. Now...I was disappointed he hadn't actually kissed me.

What would it actually feel like to kiss him? What if only one of us felt something? We could be ruined forever and still tied together.

Eli tugged me along behind him by the hand, and I don't know what I was expecting—an electric shock or something, perhaps—but I came out the other side unscathed and without even an indication I'd walked through a magical ward.

I released his hand, using the excuse of taming my hair, which was being blown about even more now. I had chosen a white lace sundress that stopped just above my knees today, but I was not a white-dress kind of lady. I wasn't sure if I'd ever actually enjoyed a meal and not spilled some of it on me. I had somehow already stained it with dirt and grass just from the short walk. How could Seelie royalty wear white so often? One more reason I didn't fit in here...or anywhere.

We stopped on the top of a tall hill. Soft, salty notes in the slightly sticky sea air filled my senses as we stood, looking out onto a large shimmering ocean. The sea itself was a deep, warm orange color that glittered like Christmas lights when the sun beat down on it.

The sea from my window.

"Wow," I sighed.

It was stunning. The sky somehow matched the magical-looking sea that blended into pinks and light blues around the sun. Large white-and-orange birds flew in the horizon under the sun, dipping in every once in a while, reminding me of seagulls. A section of the water looked choppy and blurry off in the distance.

"What's that?" I asked as Eli stepped behind me. He wasn't even touching me, but I could feel the heat from his body.

"It's the Golden Sea, and those are fire birds. They are hunting for fish," he replied softly.

"Not the birds. What's that blur out there? It looks like it might be moving toward us slowly?" I asked.

My heart began to race when his hands found my waist. What was happening? This shouldn't happen.

But I also didn't want to move.

"That is just rain from the golden seas. It's not uncommon for it to rain here. It usually doesn't last for too long, and it's actually quite refreshing since the sun is a bit stronger here from the sea's reflections."

I pulled away to turn and look at him.

One brow rose as he cocked his head to the right quizzically.

"So it's a golden shower?" I said, nodding and barely stifling a giggle as I pulled my lips into my mouth. "And you say...you say you enjoy a nice golden shower, huh? That the golden shower is refreshing? Good to know." I cackled, taking off running down the dirt path.

Hearing Eli's laughter and thumping feet following closely, I slowed my pace.

The large green meadow was fenced off with thick, bolted iron panels all the way around, as far as I could see. Large pink-and-cream flowers littered the pasture, taking up more space than the grass. A small shelter covered in flowers backed up to the iron panels nearest to us. It was the oddest juxtaposition, to see the fierce black-iron panels surrounding the beautiful field and the completely flowered cottage.

"What do you think?" Eli asked.

"Why is the fence so short? It doesn't even come to my hips."

"Oh shit, here they come. Remember what I told you. Do not touch them," Eli said. I noticed he had taken on a fight stance as he looked over the hill.

No fierce, monstrous unicorns came; instead, I saw only the gray plaid of a flat cap, soon to be accompanied by the body of a weathered, old, angry farmer.

"Step away from the fence! The tyrants are coming this way! I can't stop them!" the man yelled, worry pinching his brows together.

"Are you sure this is safe?" I asked, taking another step backward.

"No," Eli said, and smiled.

He angled his body protectively in front of mine. I could still see around him, but he was clearly ready to take the first hit if something should happen.

I hated it and loved it all at once.

His body tensed as the sound of hooves grew louder, and instinctually, I moved from behind him and stepped in front of him protectively.

The thundering grew louder as the ground trembled beneath our feet. My mouth began to make the sound before I could stop it.

"Awwwwww!"

"Caly, no!" Eli shouted.

As the stampede pulled up before us, I could barely contain myself, unable to stop myself from stepping over the sturdy iron barrier.

"They are so cute! What are these guys?" I squealed.

At least seventy stocky, shaggy mini-unicorns lumbered toward me. They were adorable, none taller than three feet, and each with a fluffy coat and a mother-of-pearl-colored spiral horn parting their forelocks.

"Those are the floricorns, Caly!" Eli cried, leaping over the fence to jump in front of my crouched body again.

The floricorns surrounded us, several snorts and stomps filling the air us as Eli drew his dagger.

"Leave the prince alone, you floral bastards!" shouted the old man as he tried to move them away. "Petals has gotten me other finger!" the man yelled. "Run, Prince Aurelius!"

"Caly! Are you all right? On the count of three, shield your eyes. I'm going to—"

"I don't think I'll be able to shield my eyes," I said, wheezing a laugh at the look on Eli's face when he turned around.

Several of the mini-unicorns had made their way to me and were shoving each other out of the way to get under my hand and receive their share of scratches and pets.

"I think they like me." I smiled ear to ear. "Just be nice and pet them. That's all they want."

"Pet them? Calypso—" But before he could continue, a fluffy chestnut mare with a flaxen-blond mane charged, knocking him over. The stout equine barely missed his head with a swift kick.

"Don't hurt her, Eli!" I shouted, watching him leap to his feet, his wings spread wide and a bright light pouring through the gaps in his fingers.

He snapped his head to me with a shocked expression. "Hurt her? For sun's sake! What about m—"

The sassy floricorn took advantage of his distraction and slammed into him with the force of a battering ram again, pinning him tightly against an iron panel of fencing this time.

My hand slapped over my mouth as I tried to get up, but the lounging minis wouldn't budge when I tried to push their heads from my lap. I watched as Eli sideswiped the front legs of the mare, freeing himself and pushing her against the wall. At least his powers were not involved in their brawl.

"Yeah! You don't like that very much, do you?" he said, goading the floricorn. He put his full weight against her... and she bit into his ass with a crunch.

"Aagh!" Eli yelped.

"Okay, do you all see what's happening? You gotta let me up," I said to the ponies on my lap to no avail.

I looked up to see the crown prince of Seelie attempting to put the tiny unicorn in a headlock.

I couldn't help but laugh and realized someone was joining me with thick, crackly laughter.

"Oh, she likes you very much, sir!" shouted the old unikeeper as he held a bloodied rag over his hand.

"Likes me?" But Eli's words were muffled by the mare's armpit, where he was now pinned.

"That's the meanest girl in the bunch! She's just playin' with you though," the keeper said. "I'll move them to another field. You can watch them pollinate the stonopolis."

The man walked over to a gate and, with a great squeak of the hinges, opened it. Immediately the floricorns leaped up from my lap and trotted through the gate and into another field, this one more forest than meadow. All of the fluffy creatures left but one.

The chestnut mare remained next to Eli, watching the rest of her mob graze. When she noticed I was standing alone, she stalked over to me—and began rubbing her muzzle against me.

I made a ridiculous face at Eli, unable to contain my adoration.

He rolled his eyes dramatically. "Come on, you can see how they pollinate the flowers."

The soft unicorn walked between us, pausing at the gate, making certain we followed her in. Large pink flowers spread out in hundreds and hundreds of small patches throughout the grass and around the trees. Butterflies fluttered about, collecting in a mass on a large pine tree, giving the impression of a Christmas tree.

"There is a Seelie portal in the tree," Eli said. "See the ring of mushrooms around it?"

Clumps of large, white, toothy mushrooms were attached to the surrounding maple and birch trees. Each clump in the perfect circle dangled down, long white spines almost giving the appearance of a beard. "Lion's mane," I murmured in awe.

143

After Eli denied my pleas for a closer inspection due to limited time, he hastily moved me along to watch the floricorns do their work.

"Name's Patty," the weathered unikeeper said with a slight bow of his head.

"It's great to meet you, Patty. If you ever need a hand around here, I'd love to help with them," I replied.

"That's kind of you, miss. They sure do seem to enjoy your company. Never seen anything quite like it, as a matter a fact," Patty replied. He pointed out some of the animals closest to us, telling me their names: Nettle, Rose, Greenbriar, Honey Locust.

"All thorns, huh?" I said as I raked my fingers through the coat of the sassy mare still between us. "Let me guess: Cactus?"

Patty snorted. "It'd be fitting, but she goes by Thistle."

We watched as she walked a few paces to the nearest clump of flowers and dipped her wide head and, ever so gently, set the tip of her iridescent horn in the center of each flower. Thistle closed her eyes, a blissful expression on her fuzzy face. She looked sweet and friendly like this.

"Their horns and magic are the only things capable of pollinating the stonopolis flowers. The flowers couldn't exist without them," Patty said with a soft nod.

Eventually, we said our goodbyes, promising to return soon. I'm not certain the mini-unicorns even realized we left, they were so busy with the flowers. That was probably for the best. I think Thistle might have maimed Eli or I had she seen us leaving.

CHAPTER 16

CALY

Y OU NEED TO BE MORE DISCREET WITH YOUR ANIMAL GIFT, Cal. Someone's going to figure out what you are if things like that keep happening," Eli said softly.

"They liked you, and you aren't Artemi," I replied.

But he was right, and I knew it. I needed to think ahead. Now wasn't the time for me to slip. In fact, I shouldn't relax again until I found a way to break the tie to Eli.

"They didn't like me. Thistle did, if you could even call it that. She may be worse at handling affection than you are," he laughed. "Come to think of it, maybe that's why I started to like her—she's the unicorn version of you!"

The path ahead began to widen into a cobbled street. Each side of the road was filled with sparse, Tudor-style shops. People and creatures of all shapes and sizes bustled about from shop to shop. Merchants sang and called to people passing by, several making their skin glitter and flash in the hopes of gaining others' attention. Steam billowed from various storefronts, clearly food vendors of some sort. The air was thick with savory, appetizing scents, though none I quite recognized.

Eli's voice was stern as he spoke now. "Stay with me in town. I don't want us to get separated in the crowd. Here," he said and pulled something from his pants pocket, then placed it in the palm of my hand.

It tickled and crawled against my skin. Alarmed, I opened my hand to reveal ten jewel-toned beetles crawling timidly around my hand, each no larger than a dime. I pursed my lips in annoyance and moved to set them free in the grass with a scowl when he grabbed my palm and held it firmly.

"They are tolkiens," he explained. "Each color is a different value. I will help you learn what they are when you find something you'd like to buy."

"Your currency is beetles?" I asked, still reluctant to believe he wasn't trying to pull something.

"Gold is everywhere. It holds no value here beyond aesthetics and the family color. These are Gondor beetles. They are rare and cannot be duplicated from magic or forgery. Now, put them in your pocket before they crawl off," he said, smiling. "You can get anything you like here with that handful."

"I don't have pockets in this dress. I usually just stuff a wad of cash and my phone down between my..." I trailed off, holding the low neckline of my white dress out. There was no way in hell I was putting beetles between my boobs. I couldn't even wear a bra with how wide the cap sleeves were cut on this dress.

"Then I think your first purchase ought to be a pouch," he replied. Eli placed his hand on the small of my back and guided me toward the rows of vendors.

Turning into the stall of the third merchant, the scent of leather and tannin knocked me in the face. It wasn't entirely unpleasant, just strong. Handmade leather items filled every inch of the canvas structure, and what wasn't filled with goods was filled with shoppers.

I squeezed past several people in the tight space, hoping to get a better look.

Eli had barely reached the front of the shop when a horde of people collected around him. He smiled at me across the shop with a discreet eye roll while he talked happily with the people, patting someone's back and causing the entire group to burst out into laughter.

I smiled to myself. It was a wonder he shifted into a fox and not a golden retriever.

After thoroughly admiring the talented craftsmanship, I settled on a rich brown pouch that I could wear cross-body. Not too big, not too small—perfect for when I needed to carry some books or weapons as well.

After working my way back to the front and showing Eli my find, he introduced me to the owner of the shop—a huge, burly man with flaming red hair and the kindest smile. Eli had to step on my foot to stop me from gawking. The man's red beard was actually on fire, with smoldering flames that crackled when he laughed. He refused to accept any of my tolkiens though, and securing the beetles safely in my new pouch, Eli and I gave our thanks and said our goodbyes.

Every shop or booth we came to was a similar experience. Eli would get caught with a group of townsfolk thrilled to see him, and I would fight off the rest of the crowd to peruse the goods. I didn't mind though; it was fun to see him in his element, and the items in these shops were nothing like anything I'd ever seen in the human realm, both in quality and peculiarity.

On the outskirts of one particularly crowded area in front of several deep stalls, I spotted a tattered wooden sign labeled *apothecary* in dingy black letters with an arrow pointing left. I peered in that direction.

The street in front of it was still somewhat crowded, but it was clear that we had reached a darker, seedier side of the village, both the shops and the crowd. The people were still happy and excited to talk to the prince, but they appeared a bit more soiled and unruly. The shops on this end were situated with the sun to their backs, making this section of the market darker under the heavy canopy of shadows.

"Stay with me here, Cal. It's crowded today, and this side of the market is filled with vendors from the other realms. It's good for our trade but bad for thievery."

We stepped into the cool shadows of the next vendor's stall. The temperature immediately dropped several degrees, sending a light chill across the top of my arms, but inside, it was also packed. Shoulders knocked into mine as I felt the hum and buzz of too many people around me. Eli squeezed my arm, keeping me at his side.

"I'm fine," I said with a laugh when a large group stepped between Eli and I again. This time a small old woman and three men practically dragged him to a canvas tent across the road. Two of the men hoisted up some weird, scaled, squid-looking creature and before I knew it, they were all cheering and jumping up and down.

Suddenly the breath stilled in my throat and the hairs at the back of my neck rose. I swallowed. The thick sound of it was loud in my head. Tingles tiptoed up my spine.

I whipped my head around, knowing something would be there. I could feel it watching me.

It felt like my chest had shattered, forcing its jagged pieces into my scrap of a heart. I fell backward into several people and onto the grimy cobblestone. The crowd carried on, swarming around me like a current as I scrambled to get back on my feet.

When I did, the first thing I saw was the massive figure in the street, still and motionless, people parting around him like he was an unmovable stone in the moving stream of people. His black cloak billowed angrily as he towered above the crowd. The hood of his cloak hid his face, but it didn't matter. I could feel who it was.

Malum Mendax, the Unseelie prince, tilted his head in a chilling movement.

I fell back into the current of people, barely catching

myself from falling again. I think I tried to scream, but I was too horrified, and I don't think I made any sound. My heart slammed in my chest painfully as I scrambled to move, to get away. I couldn't think—all I could do was panic. Pure terror gripped me.

It wasn't possible.

It couldn't be possible!

This was not a horny, confused dream. He stood in front of me this very moment. Alive.

I had stood over him and watched the life drain from his eyes. I had forced my blade *exactly* between his wings, where I was supposed to. Just where he had confessed that a wound would kill him. He was dead!

He. Was. Dead.

Emotions punched me in the gut. My footing faltered, and I lost sight of him briefly, the pounding in my chest forcing my entire body to pulsate.

He was closer now, yet somehow his figure seemed unmoved in his black armor. Somehow I could tell that the shadow stared at *only* me.

You're making this too easy, pet. Run.

His words rang deep and clear in my mind, and I knew then and there that all the times I had thought I was hearing things, it had been his fucking voice in my head.

I shoved through the crowd like a madwoman, taking a hard left and ending up in a tight alley between shops, an awning covering the darkened lane. I let out a string of curses. The dark wasn't where you hid from a shadow.

How could he still be alive? And in Seelie?

Terror unlike anything I could have ever imagined put its claws into a tender place inside me.

The tie.

I had to keep him away from Eli.

I knew Mendax was going to kill me eventually, but I might be able to drag it out a little longer—he would toy with me. But he would kill Eli the moment he saw him.

My quivering hands pawed along the grimy brick wall until I felt the cold iron hinges of a door. I looked over my shoulder, only catching a glimpse of cobbled street at the other end. Tears prickled the corners of my eyes as I sent a silent prayer that the door would open, then nearly knocking a short old woman down on the other side when it did. Definitely not who I expected to be on the other end of this door, with how rough this part of the market had been.

"How the—?" the old woman shouted gruffly, surprising me even further.

Her appearance was *exactly* what I would have imagined a perfect grandma would look like, though really, what did I know? I had never had one.

The woman's puffy, gray curls were cut short, framing her creased face. Her purple sweatshirt had a brown cat with glowing hazel eyes on it that perfectly matched her own.

"Please help me" was all I managed to get free of the panic in my throat.

Wise eyes inspected me for a beat before she grabbed my arm and roughly pulled me deeper into the dimly lit room. Dark wooden racks filled the space, with ornate, antique-looking suitcases and crates overflowing from them throughout, leaving only narrow and crooked aisles to walk through.

"Move, idiot!" her warbling voice reprimanded me. She was unusually nimble for an older woman. Lithesome even. I couldn't see her ears under her poof of hair, but it didn't matter—I knew she wasn't human.

A thousand different smells overpowered me the farther we went. First I recognized pine, then damp, dirty fur—then cinnamon, lavender, something musky, and on and on it continued. Everything was too strong for me. I could taste the fragrances in the air.

The woman paused to look over her shoulder at me, a curious expression on her face. She looked at me so long, I feared she was having second thoughts about helping me.

I took a step toward the door closest to her, ready and

willing to hide myself *and her* if necessary. For a moment, I thought about going back out the way I had come, but there was something intriguing about this place that made me feel a little safer.

At my advance, she smiled, almost as if she had been waiting to see if I would step toward the door, then she leaned ahead of me and opened it herself. The shadows poured over me as her strong hand pushed me inside.

"If this isn't some shit," she said, shaking her head with a small grin. The old woman slammed the door at my back, snuffing out the last streak of light as it closed with a bang.

Moving forward, I shuffled my feet loosely, taking something with them underfoot as I slid farther in. I inhaled deeply, poring over the loose files in my brain until I could pinpoint what the smell was.

Fresh straw.

The sound of movement echoed in the dark chamber, and I froze.

Something else was in here.

Every drop of blood in my body felt as if it had plummeted to the soles of my feet. Again, the thing rustled in the darkness before I was met with a forbidding silence.

Had the old woman sabotaged me?

A few deep snorts, then what I could only guess was the sound of claws scraping lightly against the concrete. My shoulders settled a little. It was an animal in here with me. I had to be in some kind of a makeshift stall or cage. I don't know how I knew, but whatever was in here was large and friendly. Maybe it was the panic and fear that heightened my senses, but I swear I could even feel its surprise as it sensed me.

I took a step toward the animal, and the scent of straw faded into a woody, spiced fragrance.

The same scent from my room this morning and last night. Come to think of it, it was what I had been smelling since before we even left the human realm...

Realization slammed into me.

The spice and smoke fragrance of Malum Mendax.

I grabbed ahold of the wall to keep myself up. How could I have been so stupid? He'd been inside my room, watching me. My fragmented heart throbbed violently in my chest.

The dream...

I knew he was in the dark room with me now, the heady smell of him coiling around me. I could feel the fingers of his smoke trailing lightly up my leg. I could feel scentless smoke bleeding out of my arms uncontrollably, searching for him like a magnet, recognizing his smoke.

A low, lupine snarl echoed from the back.

I pressed my back against the wall and slid toward the door. I knew I could never outrun him, but I would make it as difficult as possible for him to catch me.

My knuckle finally hit the round knob, and I forced myself to stay calm and quiet my breathing. I needed to hear everything in the room, know exactly where it was.

I screamed as a gloved hand bracketed my throat to the back wall, holding me up by the neck as my legs buckled. His horrifying presence dominated the space in front of me, his smoke rolling in thick plumes over my body like it was trying to consume me. His warm breath ghosted across my face. I stabbed my fingernail into the V-shaped scar on my thumb to stop myself from fainting.

Feeling him in front of me now, I knew it had *all* been real.

Malum Mendax had been in my room, touching me.

My body couldn't decide what to feel at the realization that he wasn't actually dead. Ignoring the sense of relief that washed over me, knowing I hadn't killed him, I struggled to focus on the bigger problem—he knew everything now.

And he was going to kill me for attempting to assassinate him.

My stomach tightened to the point of pain. I was going to be sick.

I felt his stubbled cheek brush against my face before his deep voice softly rumbled into my ear.

"Do you know what happens to pets that run away from home, *Calypso*?" His hand around my neck pressed me harder against the wall. "They get punished."

Hearing him use my real name and not the nickname I had given him summoned goose bumps across the back of my neck.

He knew my real name. How did he know my name?

If he knew my full name, he could crawl inside of my mind and impel me. He could make me do *anything* he wanted.

I had watched him take down a monster as big as a house simply by impelling it and forcing it to take its own life. I couldn't even imagine what he would do to me—the obsession that betrayed and tried to kill him.

His hand released my neck to skate down my clavicle.

"You're—you're dead," I forced out breathily, trying to jump-start my brain into action. Something was happening in my chest with his closeness and the realization that he wasn't gone forever.

"Only on the inside," he whispered across my skin, hovering his lips just above where my neck and shoulder met.

He was touching me, but the room was so dark, I couldn't see him right in front of me. All of my senses amplified, taking in his heavy breathing and the hushed sounds of his clothes moving. I couldn't stop my fingertips from stretching out to graze the heavy fabric of his cloak.

I heard the slip of leather against skin. A glove being removed. I flinched but couldn't escape with his hand still pressed to my breastbone, keeping me in place. His bare fingers skimmed along the side of my neck so slowly, he may as well have been counting every pore.

Mendax let out a deep sigh. "Make me alive again, Caly."

The sound of cracking and shattering echoed through the darkness. The creature from the back let out an angry snarl.

Mendax's hand fell away from my chest, and my instincts

finally emerged—I didn't waste a second before I reacted. I no longer needed to hide who I was from him. He would learn quickly that the real Calypso was a far cry from the helpless Callie Peterson he was obsessed with.

I moved quickly, ready to slam my hand into his face after precisely angling my movement for enough momentum from the rotation to break his nose. As soon as I swung though, my hand only touched empty air.

He was gone. Whether from the room entirely or just no longer in front of me, I had no idea.

I grabbed for the doorknob as I heard the large animal rush closer. I got the sense that he wasn't going to hurt me. It felt like he was coming to help me. Still, I couldn't be one hundred percent certain, and I wasn't ready to risk mine and Eli's lives on a feeling.

The knob jangled, but I finally managed to turn it and fall out into the dimly lit space from before. And then I ran, following the light until I almost tripped over the gray-haired woman sitting on an old wooden chair at a small table.

"You look like you've seen a ghost," said the woman with an unvexed expression. Her wise eyes held mine, giving the impression she knew a lot more than she was letting on.

Still panting, I took in her and the store with fresh eyes. We were closer to a door at the back, but I could see the front of her shop. It was filled with women. Glass jars of every shape and size with worn paper labels lined the walls. The strong smell of florals and spice returned to me as my breathing slowed.

"This is the apothecary. You run the apothecary," I said, putting the pieces all together.

"What gave it away? The large sign or the herbs?" she asked sarcastically. She nodded at the plethora of amber-glass jars on the table next to where she stood and lazily scratched her arm.

I moved toward the exit, still panicked. "I need to find Prince Aurelius," I mumbled, touching the side of my face.

I could still feel Mendax's mouth on my skin.

"I fucking knew it!" she shouted at me. All of the women in the store snapped their heads to us briefly.

"What?" I asked in alarm.

"How have you stayed hidden? I can barely pick it up from you. If I didn't know better, which I damn well do, I'd believe you to be a human," she laughed, a deep rasp that sent her into a coughing fit. She wheezed before taking a drink from the teacup in her hand and scowling.

The tea smelled familiar. I winced from the pungent floral aroma before my eyes widened in shock.

"*Ricinus communis,*" I stated. "Castor bean."

Her gray eyes stilled before she canted her head, giving me her full attention. "How—"

"It's in your tea. I can smell it," I said, watching her movements.

"Does it taste familiar, Artemi?" She was taunting me.

Every muscle in my body stilled.

What was I supposed to do now? My gut told me to kill her, but I needed to know how she knew first. I needed Eli.

"You drink a lot of poison?" I asked, moving to sit in the wooden chair next to her. I needed to know what all she knew.

The woman raised her teacup as she eyed me. "Business is bad, and unwanted fae keep breaking into my wolf's bedroom. Can't take it anymore," she said sarcastically.

Wolf's room? That hadn't sounded like any wolf I'd ever heard. I looked around the shop at the faces of the shoppers as they read labels and darted sideways glances at the front door.

"Business doesn't look bad. I wonder, do fae have morgues? If so, you should warn them that a large number of husbands and lovers are about to be dead." I turned back to her. "How did you know what I am?"

She wrinkled her brow at me before the lines softened and her eyes grew sad. "I've been around," she answered.

I watched the crowd filter through the shop, noticing a younger woman with the same complexion and dorsal hump

155

in the structure of her nose as the old woman. She wore an apron and walked around, talking to the women, measuring out their purchases, and taking their money.

"You're over-steeping your castor beans. I guess probably the aconite as well," I said as I leaned back, getting a little more comfortable. I needed to gauge her reaction.

"You don't know shit about sh—"

"I'm guessing that you're practicing mithridatism: self-administering small amounts of the poisons you're selling in an effort to develop immunity in case one of the many enemies you or your clients have tries to poison you," I stated. My terrified and chaotic nerves were settling with the calm distraction of something I knew and knew well.

The woman's face creased with a small smile.

"You've been over-steeping your herbs while doing so, though, and giving yourself liver damage." I paused to look at her arms. "From my guess, it's probably pretty severe. Your body is unable to develop a metabolic tolerance, so it's causing cirrhosis of the liver."

Her smile fell as she stared at me with glittering eyes, absently scratching her arm.

"I'm also guessing you have a bile salt buildup, and that is what's causing your skin to itch so badly." I stood up from the chair as I realized something was happening on the street in front of the shop. Had Mendax returned? Had he even left?

I couldn't leave though—I was still anxious to get answers. "I also know the woman over there in the tan apron is your daughter. It would be awful if something happened to her. Now why did you try to kill me by throwing me in with your wolf, and *how* can you tell I'm Artemi?" I glared at her.

My pulse quickened as all the women in the store fled out onto the street, hearing the commotion themselves. Shouts and screams rang out like a chorus as the pounding of running feet echoed in from the street.

"There isn't time, girl," she replied, unfazed by my threats and whatever chaos was about to happen. "I do a lot of business in *all* the realms, and I've been around for far too long. I know exactly what you are, and that is why I put you in my wolf's room." Her eyes turned cold suddenly. "Have you ever wondered why the only two kingdoms at war in all the realms have two queens and no kings?" she asked, standing now as well.

The street outside was getting louder and more panicked. "How do you—"

"You really should know more about someone before you threaten them. You see, I know things too, child. I know that the queen isn't the family member who is going to destroy your heart. There's a lot more to know than they allow these Seelie sheep to believe. Nearly everyone outside of Seelie knows the truth. You've never wondered why the Seelie and Unseelie queens hate each other so much? Or why it is that they *both* happen to have dead husbands?" She lowered her voice, coming closer. "He's nearly here."

The energy in the room pulsed as screams rang out in the street, louder now. I didn't care—a bomb could have gone off and I wouldn't have moved. I needed to know how this stranger knew so much about me.

"You seem like a smart girl. What's the main reason women want to poison their husbands? Or the reason two seemingly intelligent women fight? Wake up, child, and use that brain of yours. Get out of Seelie before it's too late for all of you." Her voice shook as she finished her sentence.

Heavy footsteps slammed down at the front of the shop, and both of us snapped our heads around to see a group of armored Seelie guards enter. Eli pushed through the middle, panicked.

"There you are! Thank suns you are all right! We have to go. There has been an attack on the royal grounds. It's not safe for you—for us—to be out of the protection of the castle now. We have to hurry," he commanded, breathing heavily. His handsome face was flushed as he glanced around, realizing where we were. He narrowed his eyes

157

on me. "Why are you here?" There was the barest hint of accusation in his tone.

His sharp citrine eyes fell on the old woman. My best friend clenched his jaw before looking back at me with an expression I'd never seen.

"Versipellis." Eli gave an unfriendly nod to the old woman.

"Does she have need to poison you, Prince? She was buying a pet, dummy," she said as she squeezed my hand. "Jag, go to the back and box up that good-lookin' critter we got in a few weeks ago. The little one from the wolf room. It must be the little one," she called to her daughter in the corner.

The brown-haired girl paused a second to stare at her mother before hurrying to the back and returning with a small cardboard box.

"Caly, we have to go now," Eli said impatiently.

"Thank you, uh, Versipellis?"

"Ver-sip-ellis, that's right, and my daughter is Jag." She winked at me kindly.

I took the box from Jag and tried to read the old woman's eyes.

Eli stepped forward and grabbed my arm, impatiently pulling me toward the door. "Now!" he shouted.

Outside, I put the small box gently in my new pouch, thankfully I had gotten the larger one. I felt something weighty shift and heard the scratch of claws on cardboard. Had she actually given me a pet?

"Thank you. I'll take good care of him!" I shouted back through the open door.

"Lovely! Our dear friend Alistair will be *so* pleased to hear his friend is going to such a prestigious home. His last owner tried to drown him! Poor thing looked like a drowned rat when he came to me," the woman said with a sly smile. The brown, embroidered cat on her sweatshirt winked at me.

Wait, what? Alistair?

She couldn't mean the nine-tailed panther from the

Unseelie castle, Mendax's personal assassin—well, at least until they made him leave for refusing to kill me. How many Alistairs were there?

Eli continued to pull me down the street like I was a misbehaving toddler, several guards on either side of us. People ran past in both directions, shops shuttered and doors bolted. Canvas tents were quickly torn down. Some of the people looked terrified, while others looked furious.

I realized I hadn't even told Eli about Mendax yet. I had been so terrified and panicked, but as I sat and talked with the old woman, I had become distracted.

What was I more scared of: the Unseelie prince, who had become obsessed and convinced himself he was in love with me, or what would happen to me once the queen and Eli found out Mendax was alive?

Eli had warned me that if Mendax wasn't dead once I crossed over to Seelie, then I would be killed for betraying the queen.

I thought about keeping it to myself that Mendax had been here, but it was obvious, with the chaos, everyone already knew. I needed to tell Eli.

"I saw him," I whispered.

He continued to move me along, still keeping ahold of my upper arm as we ran up the cobblestone path. We were taking a different way than we had come. "Saw who?" he asked. His tan face was flushed, but he didn't look as alarmed at my words as I had expected.

"*Him*. Mendax. I saw him in the crowd at the market when you were across the street. He came for me, and I ran—"

Eli stopped abruptly, his amber eyes hard as they darted over my face.

"Calypso, you *couldn't* have seen Mendax. You killed him. You *swore* you killed him," he said frantically. He was holding both my arms now, his grip tightening enough that it was starting to hurt, even over the adrenaline. Years of training triggered my reflexes to break his hold, but I pushed them aside. I wouldn't hurt Eli even if I could, which I honestly wasn't sure about anymore.

"I know, and I *did*…or at least I was sure I did, but I'm telling you, I saw him. He shadowed into the back room after I—"

"Did he hurt you?" Eli cut me off, immediately softening his grip on me. He looked at each of the guards who had circled us with a hard glare, and they took a step away and turned their backs to us.

"No, he didn't hurt me, but—"

Eli cut me off again. "Then it wasn't Mendax, Caly. It doesn't matter how fond of you he was before. Mendax is an impulsive psycho with a ferocious temper and a need to dominate. Even if you hadn't actually killed him like you thought, he would never have let you walk away alive. Never." His toned chest rose and fell heavily as his breathing evened back out. "Besides, we have moles in Unseelie, and they all say he has been gone. It wasn't him," he finished quietly.

"He wasn't in Unseelie because he's been hunting me, Eli! He is following me. What about all of the chaos? You said there has been an attack?" I asked.

"We don't know what is responsible for the attack, but it was near the royal portal just outside of the castle. Which means the attackers are here, and from the way they…did what they did, they wanted to make a point." Eli dropped his hold on my arms and placed one hand gently on the small of my back as we began our speed walk again.

"A point, huh? Something like *I'm not actually dead and I'm back to kill you all?*" I asked angrily.

Why was he not believing me? I felt like a child telling their parents a ghost lived in their closet—only my ghost was very alive and dangerous.

"This isn't a joke, Calypso. You should have seen what they did. On my land!"

"What did they do?" I asked. "Do the Seelie royals have any other enemies?"

I scanned the sunny expanse of field to my left, paranoid and unable to shake the feeling of eyes pressing into the back of my skull.

"Yes, of course, but both our biggest adversaries use butterflies and moths as their symbols, so that doesn't help decipher who it was."

"What do you mean? I know Unseelie claim the luna moth but what does that—" I started.

"The Fallen fae," he said, interrupting *again*. If he did that one more time... "They are the expelled Seelie. Besides the Unseelie, the Fallen fae are our largest enemies. I'll explain what they are another time, but they claim the deadhead moth as their symbol," he stated.

"What do the moths have to do with the portal attack?" I asked. There was a scuttle in my purse from my new pet.

Eli stopped to look at me, his eyes full of both anger and sadness. "The Seelie guard at the portal was skinned alive, hung from a tree, and wrapped in a cocoon of his own flesh." Disgust was clear in his voice.

"Oh..."

Eli quickly grabbed my arm again and hurriedly moved us, but I was tired of being treated like a child.

"I know what I saw, Eli!" I shouted, ripping my arm out of his grip.

"No, you don't, Calypso!" he snapped as he moved in front of me and pushed his face closer to mine. God, he was fast. "NO, YOU DON'T!" He took a deep breath, but I could see the panic was still coursing through him, even as he lowered his voice. "Because if Mendax is still alive, then that means that you didn't kill him. And if you didn't kill him, then that means you will be killed. Not only are you on Seelie soil without paying your allegiance to the court, but that would mean you betrayed and lied to the royal house."

I flinched at his words.

161

"How does that even matter anymore? I'm not human. I'm allowed to be here anyway. And as for paying my allegiance, I've paid with my own fucking life already!" I shouted back.

"As far as everyone in Seelie knows, you are human, and believe it or not, as dangerous as that is, it is far more dangerous for anyone to know you are Artemi without enough power to do more than call off a few creatures' attacks."

Neither of us spoke for a moment as we stood in panicked silence.

Eli's face and voice softened. "Sierra," he called to the captain of his guard, keeping his eyes locked on mine. "Alert the castle that Queen Tenebris, the *only* remaining Smoke Slayer, has broken through the wards and is inside of Seelie as we speak. Lock down the grounds to level three, and sound the alarm. Everyone must go to their concealment stations." He paused a moment. "Let the people of Seelie know they are no longer safe. There is a monster in our realm."

By now, the mystery creature inside my purse was clawing frantically at the box, trying to get out.

"What the fuck kind of pet did you get?" he asked as we both stared at my noisy pouch.

I widened the opening of my purse to grab the top of the stiff box. "I got a…" I braced myself and opened the tabs to peer inside. "Oh my god," I said, my vision blurring as I locked my knees in place before I could fall.

"What is it? Must be something cute," Eli said, moving to look at the creature.

"It's—it's a brown rat. A brown rat with sweet eyes." I swallowed the hard, thorny lump of emotions in my throat that I couldn't show and scooped up the very familiar brown rat.

"Ew, he's big." Eli cringed at the rat crawling up to tuck into my neck. "You know, if you just want to cuddle something furry, I'd have been more than happy to shift into my fox to snuggle you," he said with a smirk. "What are you going to call that thing?"

Brown Rat grumbled at him and burrowed farther into the back of my neck, under the curtain of my long hair.

"His name is Walter," I said, unable to stop my shaking voice as a tear dripped down to my chin.

Mistaking my emotions for fear, Eli straightened to his full height and gave me a wink. "Don't worry, Caly, nothing can get inside the castle. It is warded far beyond any other power. As soon as we are inside the walls, we are safe. I promise," he stated.

I supposed now wasn't the time to tell him about those nighttime visits from Mendax.

CHAPTER 17

MENDAX

Inside the Seelie castle, I paused to kick the marble pedestal below the statue, knocking over the bust of some ancient, dead Seelie. My wings quivered as I walked down the hall to Caly's room. Neon sun bounced off my black cloak. The statue behind me toppled onto the marble floor with a crash as I continued my stroll toward my pet's chamber.

No glamour concealed me now. I was bored of hiding, and I was sick of this place.

I stopped abruptly outside of Prince Fuckhead's to take a hard look at the white-wood door of his room. He would be in there. Everyone in the castle was asleep. I knew because I had watched them all.

Ever since following Caly to this reprehensible place, I had watched everyone in the castle. How else was I to learn what their level of pain would be when they died?

Everyone would die. The more they were involved in hurting my Caly, the more they would suffer. The ones who made her leave me would hurt so fiercely, so relentlessly, their ghosts would weep for an eternity.

I heard nothing from inside the fae's room.

Aurelias confused me. Caly seemed to actually like him, even be close with him.

For that alone, he would suffer severely.

I'd never had feelings like this before. I didn't know what to do with them, but I did know even the most minuscule thought of her finding joy in the company of another male made me yearn to pull the veins from someone.

I was also struggling to figure out exactly how involved with this he was. He was spineless and weak, always had been, mostly doing what his mother told him to like a good little marionette as she pulled the strings. Oddly enough though, I'd seen him lie several times to his mother in defense of Caly.

The Seelie prince had a bigger target on his head than the others. Sometimes, he made her smile—the only reason I hadn't killed him already was because he made her smile and laugh like no one else...including myself.

In my wildest dreams, I couldn't have imagined the beauty that emanated from her face when she smiled. It started deep in her devious blue eyes as an innocent sparkle, but before I could even prepare for it, the laughter emerged, happy and rapturous. Three lines formed at the edges of her eyes. Four would collect on her left side if she was exceedingly happy. If she didn't try to stop the smile and pulled her lower lip into her mouth, then her nose would wrinkle just above the cluster of freckles shaped like the Tardeki stars.

I wanted to make her smile like that.

My queen smiled a lot around Aurelius. Therefore, I found myself divided between watching him bleed out or watching him make her smile more. I would ascertain what it was that made Caly smile, and then I could kill him.

I let out an impatient breath and continued walking to her room.

As it stood, I doubted I would be able to end the night without killing him. Unlike him, I was *not* soft and gentle, and it was probably best if my pet learned that now. She would most assuredly be easier to make smile after she cried anyway.

I stilled outside of her door, hearing a quiet shuffle on the other side—there were two heartbeats.

I ground my teeth together, and my jaw popped.

One heartbeat was quiet, but the other pounded fast—someone angry and full of adrenaline.

He is fucking dead.

If Aurelius touched her with his breath, I would sever his wings and cave in his skull.

Hurrying, I closed my eyes and shadowed inside of her bedroom.

It was quiet. Still.

The room was dark now that the blinds she had made covered the windows. I smiled at how much she liked the darkness. I was about to give her every morsel of darkness she needed.

Caly was lying on the bed with her hair in a messy knot on top of her head. Her eyes were closed, and the blankets pulled up under her chin. She was asleep.

On the bed to her left, the covers were pushed back and showed a large, man-sized imprint.

My back strained and jerked with force as my wings shot out. The tips of my fingers tingled. I twisted around, knowing he was in here.

Already the smoke and flesh of my body fought. The smoke was the victor, as always. I let the darkness take me and familiar inky-black smoke rose, the hood of my cloak shadowing me even further.

I hoped he pissed himself when he saw me.

I released a displeased growl when I didn't see him in the room. I knew he was there—I could feel his angry heart pounding.

I snapped my head in the other direction as something slammed into the center of my back, knocking me down. Tangled in my cloak, it took me a second too long to rise. Aurelius, apparently having shifted into his fox form, took the opportunity to sink his teeth into my side.

From under the cloak, I shadowed, leaving both it and

my shirt behind, and rematerialized a few feet away. He and I had fought one another many times, but not once had he fought me shifted.

I cracked my neck and urged my smoke out, ready to suffocate the bastard, when I saw the massive gray wolf snarling at me from atop my abandoned cloak.

It was Walter, my cousin and friend from Unseelie.

"What in—" I began.

Walter sprang at me as a snarl ripped from his chest. I fell back into the wall, feeling his teeth around my throat. I grinned. "Go on then, get it free from your system, shifter. I deserve worse for leaving you in this Seelie rat nest so long. No pun intended, of course."

I shoved the wolf from my chest, noting the way he purposefully drug his nails across my bare chest as he went.

He shifted in a blur, transforming himself into the large fae I had grown up with.

"You dropped me off the roof of our fucking castle! You piece of shit," he ground out with nearly the same growl as his wolf's.

His furious brown eyes ripped into me. At well over six feet tall, Walter wasn't a small fae. We had trained together since we were kids, and I knew that he could still get a blow in if he wanted to. He was one of the few that could.

"Get over it. I knew there was a portal there," I said, stepping into him. "Why are you in Caly's room?" I asked, feeling my anger flare again.

"Leave. Now," he bit out, stepping into me.

What the fuck?

"Listen, I'm certain you've been the scary bad boy to all the Seelie ladies, must've been nice to be feared for a change." I pressed my chest into his. I was still a few inches taller. "But if you try and get in between me and my pet, you may as well have died because I'm going to kill you," I said, giving a small shove to his chest.

My neck cracked, my head whipping back when Walter

landed his punch square on my jaw. I could feel the dimples in my cheeks popping with my smile. "Do that again, Walter. I dare you," I whispered, tilting my head at him.

"I know you could and obviously would kill me, Mendax. But you are going to have to if you want to get to Caly. I'm sorry, but I won't let you hurt her anymore. I don't know what happened after I left, and I can't fathom how she managed to get away from you. I imagine it must've been bad, considering you entered Seelie to kill her—"

"I need her, Walter. I'm inescapably in love with her."

His mouth fell open as he stepped back.

"She isn't who you think she is. She killed me. She's magnificent," I said, feeling the creases tug at my eyes as they always did whenever I thought about her darkness.

"She what?"

"Well, she thought she killed me until earlier today," I said as Walter nodded, his mouth hanging open again.

"You mean you know what she is? How?" he asked, the shock clear on his face.

"Of course I know she's an assassin. I knew it the whole time. If you recall, I'm the one she tried to assassinate," I grumbled.

"No, that's not what I—" He shook his head.

"We bonded, Walter. She will be my queen as soon as we go home to Unseelie. First, she wants to get the other half of her heart."

"That's not what I me—"

But my thin patience was nearly gone. "She is mine, Walter. That is the only thing you need to understand. Take her with you to Unseelie tonight. She may fight it, but I will take out the Lumin guard stationed at the portal and get you two out. I need you back at the castle as soon as possible. I dislike leaving Mother alone with all of the Fallen's recent activity—"

"Mendax, no," Walter interrupted, surprising me. "Caly, she's...she's Artemi." His eyes were as big as plates.

My entire body went cold. "No, she—"

"She is not human, Mendax. She is a fucking Artemi."

"It's impossible," I answered immediately. "We would have known. Alistair would have…" But I trailed off, recalling my panther friend's declaration that he couldn't understand it, but he wouldn't harm her.

"They are holding half her heart hostage—the half with her powers. That's why my shifted form is so drawn to her," he added.

She couldn't be Artemi. That meant—

"I found Versipellis at the docks. Remember, the old Seer who runs the apothecary in town? The cat shifter who was close with Alistair? Well, that smart old lady sold me as a pet—"

Something sharp whipped across my cheek at the same time something cracked into my stomach with such force it sent me to the floor. I felt the cold, black blood drip from my cheek as I shadowed a few feet away from the attack.

Caly stood next to a stunned Walter in her plaid sleep shorts and white T-shirt, braced and ready for a fight. She instantly refocused on me when I reappeared, adjusting her stance and raising her tiny weapon as she prepared to charge at me.

Holy Tartarus below. I had never been so fucking excited in all my life.

"Weird. In all our catching up tonight, Caly, you somehow forgot to mention that you two are in love." Walter smiled, shifting glances between the two of us. "I wouldn't have snuggled you so much had I known."

A deep rumble ripped from my chest. He had snuggled her?

"*He* is in love," she snapped at Walter. "I hate him! He's been following me, scaring the wits out of me!"

She charged at me, moving my arm and stabbing her curved karambit deep into my side.

"Fuck, that hurt!" I bellowed. I kicked her legs out from under her, and she fell to the ground with a growl.

Walter sighed and rolled his eyes. "I'm going to leave you

two to work this out while I search the castle for her heart. I'm drawn to her powers as a pure shifter, so I will have a better chance of finding it than you two anyway," he said as he shifted into his rat form and scurried over to the door with a squeak.

I walked over to the door to open it, but Caly had somehow gotten there first and wrenched it open, smashing it into my head and splintering the wood.

Fucking Kaohs, I wanted her.

"You are detestable!" she exclaimed.

Walter scurried down the hall, while Caly took off in the opposite direction.

"Running to your golden boyfriend, huh? He won't be able to keep you from me," I goaded, stalking after her with thundering steps. "Go on then, love, make it easy for me to slaughter him. Shall we do it together? Our first couples activity?"

She stopped dead in her tracks.

It gave me enough time to grab her around the waist and throw her over my shoulder. My hand squeezed her round ass cheek before slapping it as hard as I could.

She yelled, then blasted the back of my knees with her fists, forcing me to fall to the floor.

"I thought you were dead. I thought I killed you," she said shakily before she punched me in the face.

I scowled at her. I was trying to be gentle with her, but I could only restrain my temper for so long. She was mine, whether she liked it or not. Whether she liked me or not. "And I thought you were human. Still, I will not be without you," I said, prodding my jaw with one hand while the other held her ankle tight as she tried to squirm away.

I released her ankle for a fraction of a second as I stood.

Before I could grab her again, she rolled out of my reach and leaped to her feet with the grace of a fucking cat. "I'm not going anywhere with you, you psycho," she said, taking a step toward me.

Never had I witnessed her in such a striking, undisguised manner as she was now.

I needed to touch her.

I shadowed in front of her and pushed her back against the wall. My bare chest rubbed against her thin T-shirt, and I shuddered, nearly crying out with joy at the feeling of touching her again.

"You will come with me, pet. It isn't an option, and we both know you don't really want it to be." I leaned down until my face was barely half an inch from hers and closed my eyes. I needed the feel of her in front of me. I *needed* her lips.

Caly bashed her head into my face. She grabbed ahold of my arm and twisted it so hard, it would have snapped like a twig had they been weaker human bones.

My love was out for blood, and I would give it to her.

My smoke shot out to grab her, but she had already started to run down the hallway.

"I don't belong in Unseelie with you. I need to be here," she cried, running down the stairs two at a time.

I was so close to her, I could smell her lavender shampoo as I stalked behind her.

"You belong with me. In the Elysian Fields with Aether or the depths of Tartarus with Kaohs—you will always be mine. Always."

CHAPTER 18

CALY

M ENDAX WAS INSIDE THE CASTLE.
Alive.

And he loved me. Still.

My heart knocked against my chest in tandem with the pounding of my bare feet down the stairs. I needed to put as much distance between Mendax and Eli as possible. For all our safety.

What was I supposed to do now?

I should find Queen Saracen. Certainly she was powerful enough to get rid of Mendax without getting Eli involved and killed.

Fuck! What if she hurt Mendax? Did I want to get rid of him?

The sound of unhurried footsteps stalked me—I needed to decide what to do, and fast.

The castle was eerily quiet. The sun that cast from the ceiling was now as dim as a reading light. There were no signs of life in any of the rooms I ran past.

Even the staff were asleep.

I stole a glance over my shoulder to see Mendax

confidently striding after me. His mouth was set in a hard, determined line, his ice-blue eyes stabbing into mine.

Anger surged through me as my stomach fluttered. I *hated* how much it got to me when I heard him tell Walter he loved me and that he'd come to take me back. No one had ever wanted to take me with them.

Why could nothing ever work out right for me?

I shouldn't have even been the one to have to kill Mendax. I shouldn't have ever even been trained as Saracen's assassin. I should have never let them trick me into giving up my heart.

I was tired of being controlled with lies and manipulation. Maybe all of *them* should learn what it felt like to die inside.

I stopped running.

Maybe they should all just die.

My smoke flared to life, pouring off my arms the instant I glanced back to lock eyes with Mendax again. A cruel smile pulled at the dimple on his handsome face.

I continued to walk, taking a right down the hallway and barreling through the large doors of the throne room. I looked around at all of the barbaric art surrounding me. The people of the wall murals began to mumble quietly.

My hand went to pull the door shut just as I felt him shadow behind me. My eyes shut at the feel of his body so close. I pretended to be preoccupied with closing the door, as if it was possible for me not to feel how close he was.

My grip tightened around the karambit. Slowly, I moved the sharp point of the blade in the direction of his stomach. A small, controlled breath silently left my mouth. Widening my stance slightly, I leaned my body closer to the door and acted as if I were listening for him on the other side.

As the queen's assassin, it had been my job to end him, and I had failed. He couldn't be here. If she found out he wasn't dead, it meant I would die. And if I died, Eli died—the only person I cared about saving.

"You will leave tonight and return to Unseelie with Walter," he stated. "I will retrieve your heart and bring it with me after I finish killing each of them for what they've done to you."

Icy breath caught in my lungs, chilling my heated body with a new fear. "You will not hurt them. I still need them. You hurt them, and I will spend every second of the rest of my life trying to kill you," I promised through clenched teeth.

Mendax stepped toward me with a grin. "What part of that threat was supposed to dissuade me?"

In theory, the Unseelie prince was more powerful than me in every respect, but so was everybody else. I wouldn't let that stop me. It was kill or be killed, and I would use everything I had.

Knowing the rotation of my torso would have an effective mass far greater than my arms would, I turned quickly. With the proper rotation, I was capable of imparting up to four hundred percent more force into my strike.

Letting out a loud grunt, I slammed the double-edged karambit deep into his shoulder.

The prince fell back as I pulled my weapon free from his body, his blood speckling the floor with black dots and lines.

"I can't leave with you. I-I won't. I don't want you. It's my heart, and I will get it on my own, and then—"

The dark silhouette of his body stepped toward me, unfazed by the fresh wound on his shoulder. "And then what, pet? You will be the smoking puppet of the Seelie court? Don't be so gullible," he growled.

"Gullible! I am their family. They—"

He stepped nearly flush against me, but I refused to move back. Focusing on his cold eyes was significantly harder when his midsternal line was staring me in the face. Tiny grooves of striations in between his pectoral muscles tormented me. The devil—Kaohs, whatever they called him here—knew exactly what he was doing when he made Mendax so alluring.

"They are using you," he said with a twitch to his brow. He reached for my shoulder, but I shoved his hand away with my forearm.

Our tussle continued further into the throne room.

"Using me for what?" I asked. "I can't do anything. I have been nothing but a burden to them. Queen Saracen looked out for me when my mother and sister died. What have you done for me? Manipulate me," I said. "Try to kill me. Forced a bond that was unwanted. If it hadn't been for Aurelius—"

He fisted my hair, yanking my head back to press his face over mine. "Aurelius will be a pile of debris within the hour, you have my assurance of that."

I struck Mendax in the face so hard, two of my knuckles split. The shot felt good—at least until I saw something wild crackle to life in his icy eyes.

His wings widened and grew with the same wavelike motion a snake would make if it coiled around your neck. With a violent yet graceful sweep of his leg, mine were knocked out from under me. The throne's armrest was the only thing that stopped my fall. The dark prince shoved his fingers against my chest, and I fell back to sit on the queen's extravagant throne.

Placing one hand on each armrest, he trapped me.

"Go on then, take your place on the Seelie throne. Is that what you want? In this realm, you are only wanted as a weapon, my love." He blocked my knees in, stopping my move to knee him in the dick.

"I've been her weapon in the human world nearly all of my life. At least this way I get a crown, and my family along with it. What's the difference?" My voice trembled with emotion.

For a moment, neither of us spoke. His eyes darted around my face. "The difference is, with your heart and powers restored, you will be a *full-blooded* Artemi at her disposal—tied to the Seelie realm, knocked up by her tree stump of a son, and therefore unable to ascend with the Ancients. Combine all that with the powers you've gained from me, and you will be the most powerful weapon the realms have ever seen, surpassing even me. Convenient how all that worked out for her, don't you think?"

He stepped back, giving me a bit of space to breathe.

I opened my mouth to retort, but nothing came. The truth was, I didn't know anything about Artemi, or really much of anything. It was impossible to think of myself as anything but human. I felt human.

"And what is it you want with me then? You want me to be your weapon too?" I snarled.

Since arriving in Seelie, I hadn't understood much of anything that was happening. I didn't know who I could trust. I had no understanding of their magic, customs, or what was actually expected of me.

One thing I did know was that Mendax saw things in me I thought were invisible to everyone else. Just being near him sparked something inside I'd tried so hard to fight.

Every cell in my body had exploded with relief—and fear—when I had found out he was alive. I was helplessly drawn to him. Telling myself not to be didn't change a thing.

"I don't need a weapon. The Seelie do. I want you as my lover and queen."

I stood, my bare legs brushing against his. Both of us were breathing heavily as we waited to block or strike whatever the other's next move might be.

Fuck! He was loathsome and horrible, and I wouldn't be foolish enough to let him ruin everything I'd worked so hard for.

I would not have a weakness. Not now, with everything at stake. I took a step back before I struck out to kick him in the liver. Before I could register that my kick didn't land, my back slammed against the painted wall behind the thrones.

Mendax pinned both of my wrists above my head and pressed his body against mine.

The painted figures of the wall mumbled in shock.

At least seven of the white-robed figures started running from across the room, turning the corner and racing up the wall to where I was pinned. Black movement caught my attention in time to see several of the huge, shadowy figures of the

176

painting glide toward us from another section. Several of the others, including most of the more plain-looking ones, began to climb the walls in a grotesque rhythm I'd never seen before.

Sweat beaded across my skin as I watched all of the creatures climb to the top of the domed ceiling, where they each gave me one final, hollow look before jumping out the sun-filled window in the most morosely terrifying way.

I gasped, looking around at the white walls with unease. Mendax and I were all alone now.

"I was going to be gentle with you, pet, but I'm starting to think that's not what you really like. Do you want me to be rough, Caly?" His deep whisper felt like a threat.

We were breathing heavily, blood smeared all over the both of us. I would have been scared witless from the mural had a bigger, more dangerous monster not been pressed so close against my body.

Danger and power rolled off him while he held me in place. The adrenaline and fear in my system mingled with his closeness, creating dangerous arousal. The prince of night's wings were spread wide in a commanding span of black smoke.

My body pushed into him. His words might as well have been an incantation that turned my insides to jelly.

I swore under my breath, realizing I was staring at the shape of his lips. "I-I have to kill you," I stuttered, bursting forward to fight against my feelings as much as to fight him.

He pushed me back, slamming my wrists back against the wall so hard, my blade clanged onto the marble floor at my feet. My mind marked where it had landed as Mendax pressed against me, sending all of the air out of my lungs.

"I knew what you were the moment I saw that fire ignite in your eyes in the Unseelie forest. I knew when I showed you where to stab me. You're the only one who doesn't understand what you are," he said, kicking my legs farther apart.

It felt like he was looking straight into me. I had no fucking clue what I was anymore. How could he?

177

"And what exactly am I?" I bit out.

His hands dropped from my wrists to cup my face, the tip of his nose brushing mine. "You are an alluring rose with secret thorns. A droplet of rain fighting to quench and to drown," he said, looking deranged and enthralled all at the same time. "You are my only care in life."

I was so tempted to give in and taste him *one* last time. The adrenaline and temptations were so intertwined. Instead, the need to protect Eli flared, and my fight-or-flight instincts overtook my lust. Fight won.

I wrapped my arm around his waist, two fingers digging into the open wound on his shoulder and rotating him so his back hit the wall, freeing myself.

He groaned, pushing forward to grab me, but I anticipated his move and ducked out of his reach. I grabbed my karambit off the floor.

Smoke shot from him and wrapped around my arm to pull me back. His smoke seemed to awaken my own, and it began to pour from my sides and mingle with his. But the tendrils attached to me slithered and widened the smoke from Mendax that gripped my arm, allowing me to slip free and back away.

"You made it. You're alive. Go home then! Why are you here?" I shouted at the top of my lungs.

He watched our smoke spiral and mingle together. "You know why I'm here," he stated.

"You don't love me! What don't you understand? You are the monster of death that lurks in their nightmares, and I was the fool tasked with destroying you."

"If I'm the monster and you the knight, then Aurelius must be the damsel in distress. Tell me, do you ever grow tired of letting him think you are the princess in the tower and not the dragon that guards it?"

I charged at him as anger flooded my system, overriding any rational thoughts or training I had. Once again, Mendax had seen through parts of me no one else did, and it infuriated me. How could he possibly understand me so well? He didn't even know me.

This was nothing more than feelings fighting now.

He launched toward me at the same time, easily blocking every disorganized blow I threw.

Onyx blood smeared across his sweaty torso, and bags were under his eyes. I had never seen him look so worn down. I knew now it was from spending every moment stalking me. The familiar burn of anger pushed me, and my hits grew more strategic, smoother. I wrapped my arms around his waist, shoved my chin into his chest, and upset his center of gravity, knocking him to the ground.

I went to kick him in the ribs, but he grabbed my ankle and pulled me down. I grunted in pain as the hard marble floor cracked against my knees.

Rolling backward, I looped my thumb into the hole at the handle of my blade. Mendax was already on his feet with a lustful look dancing across his stupidly handsome face.

I was about to make that face a lot less handsome.

"You continue to call me the villain, but what of the golden prince? You want him to be your hero, Caly?" He grinned and wiped the blood from his lip with the back of his hand.

"Hero, maybe not, but he will be my king," I bit out. "And I am to be *his* queen."

Seemingly unbothered by my taunts, he shadowed in front of Saracen's ornate throne and causally leaned against the side of it. "You are the keeper of my soul, no matter what castle you choose to reign over," he said calmly.

I stormed toward him with my blade raised high. "It is *not* reciprocated. I hate you!" I screamed as I felt all of my buried emotions slither to the surface.

A war thundered inside of me with the constant push and pull of what was good and what was bad—it cut into my soul. Every inkling of doubt and deceit I had ignored were brushed from the corners of my anguished mind to lay as a pile of kindling. Rage and heartache lit the tinder.

I lunged.

Mendax grabbed my wrists and stepped into my body before I could slice into his neck. Our bodies pressed together, smoke and heat coiling around us. Even his fastest movements were executed with a calm confidence.

Frustrated, I panted, aiming daggers at his eyes with my glower. The three shades of his blue irises watched as I grappled with all the feelings I didn't want to bear.

Malum Mendax dropped his hold on my wrists—including the one that still held the karambit.

"I am nothing more than a soul without residence since you left me, and I refuse to bear a life without you. Should I die, let it be by your hand, so that your touch is what I remember when I haunt every single dwelling you inhabit. Soon enough, you will meet with me again in Tartarus." His voice softened while his eyes steeled. "Go on, Calypso, make your life better and finish me off. For good this time." His right dimple popped. "It makes no difference to me if I'm dead or alive when I chase you."

I moved the curve of my blade to the side of his neck defiantly. He didn't think I could do it.

I pushed it into his flesh, feeling the blade break through.

Unrelenting calm came from his eyes. He was serious.

Mendax loved me.

I could have cut his throat right then. It would have taken two and a half seconds of pressure to have him dead and out of my life for good—to sever his carotid artery and saw his head off. All of my problems would be fixed. Well, at least the ones that involved him.

My blade was sharp enough. I knew that for a fact.

Both our chests heaved to opposite beats as the blood and sweat from his chest painted my front. A clang echoed through the empty throne room as I dropped my weapon and pressed my mouth hard against his.

I had tried so hard to fight it, but I could try no longer. The last drop of self-preserving willpower left through my mouth as I opened it to allow Mendax's tongue in.

My moan was muffled as Mendax consumed me. Electricity sparkled through me while my hands fumbled, pulling him closer.

His hands matched mine in our frenzied battle for control, hungrily wrapping his fingers around my neck and pulling me tighter against him. Nothing could have separated us as we kissed each other in a way only our souls could understand. Flesh and bones tangled as we each fought to touch more.

A new battle had begun.

His tongue teased mine, forcing entry while he grabbed a fistful of hair at the base of my neck. The sting only added gasoline to my fire, and I bit his lower lip savagely.

Never had I been so turned on. I couldn't think—only feel.

Roughly, I shoved him against the hard back of the throne, tugging his neck down, closer to me. Even the warm, muscled softness of his neck was sexy. My other hand plundered the hard ridges of his chest, devouring the way his warm, dirty skin felt against my fingers.

Spinning us and taking back control, he slammed my back against the cold gold throne with a force that should have frightened me.

I moaned, and I swear I felt it come out of my pores. I was anything but frightened.

Mendax let out a snakelike hiss when I raked my fingernails down his chest, leaving marks beaded with blood. He pressed his body harder against mine, trapping me between him and the large throne. I could feel how hard he was. The tip of his substantial length threatened to peek out of his waistband. My own sex clenched in response to seeing the teasing outline.

Strong hands found my waist and hoisted me up, wrapping my legs around him and as he bent down. The domineering fae set my head on the back of the throne, while my butt rested on the front edge, never once removing his lips from mine until my back was fully on the seat.

Only then did he pull back slightly, still holding each of my thighs around him.

"I will not be gentle, so do not expect it," he stated, hovering just above my mouth.

Then he kissed me so deeply, my lower stomach clenched and quivered while my hands tangled in his black hair.

His grip on my thighs dropped, but I stayed in place, hooking my legs around him. He stood to his full height and traced over me with wild eyes.

Every part of my body wanted to sprout more limbs to pull him closer to me.

His large, rough hands moved to grip each side of my night shorts. Instead of trying to pull them down, a sharp tear cut into the silence as he trailed his palms down my legs, the remaining fabric falling off me and leaving me completely vulnerable and at his mercy on the throne.

He leaned over once more to push the pad of his thumb into my mouth. His pupils were almost completely blown. I locked hungry eyes with him and swirled my tongue around his thumb, tasting the smoky saltiness of his skin as I bit down eagerly.

The intense look that had been plastered on his face cracked, and a small grin pulled one side of his mouth up, causing that dangerous dimple to show when his eyes ravaged my exposed body. My hands tightened on his forearms as I took in his muscled chest and stomach, still filthy with his Unseelie blood and sweat.

The hand not in my mouth moved to press between my legs. A low, gravelly moan rumbled as he pushed his body against mine. More of his fingers found my wetness, and I thrust forward impatiently.

Watching him as he towered over me was too much to take.

"This cunt is dripping wet, Caly. Am I supposed to believe you don't need me after feeling this? You're a liar." He said it with cocky grin as he pressed two fingers inside of me and dragged the other hand down my outer thigh, leaving scratches in his wake. "My *filthy*, fucking liar."

I could see in his wild eyes that he was struggling to control himself.

A shiver wracked my body as the hand not inside me reached up and pinched one of my hardened nipples. I gasped, but it somehow turned into a moan. I needed to touch him so badly, but it was impossible. At this angle, he stood with full access to me, but I was only able to reach him when he bent down to me.

Long fingers slowed their thrusts to an agonizingly slow tempo. He continued to circle and massage my clit with his thumb, applying just enough pressure that I thought I might combust if he didn't move faster.

I strained to pull myself up with quivering stomach muscles but was quickly stopped with a large hand on my throat.

"Fuck! Then do it already," I growled at him.

Darkness flared in his eyes, and his hands dropped away from me completely. He took a few steps back and dropped my legs with a broody expression.

Furious, I stood up from the throne. What the fuck had happened? And what was I even doing? Frustrated and slightly embarrassed, I shoved his unmoving chest and got in his face.

"What's the matter?" I bit out. My eyes watered from anger. "I'm not an innocent, pushover human anymore, so you don't want it? Is that it? Or do you only want it when they're scared of you? Afraid of someone dishing it back?"

He let out a slow, ragged breath. Before my eyes caught his movement, I had already been thrown back down on the seat of the throne. The towering shadow tightened my thighs around his waist, leaving my ass raised above the seat.

"I was trying not to break you. Remember that. Now, be a good pet and sit."

The smoke of his wings shadowed me almost completely, giving his figure a spine-chilling look.

Mendax undid his pants, letting them hit to the floor with a rustle as his large cock sprung free. For a moment, I began to rethink things. He was huge. The pink tip of his cock strained in his grip as he fisted himself. He was malevolent and intimidating as he stared down at me—a predator who's just overpowered his prey.

"Grip the throne, and don't let go," he rumbled.

I reached behind my head and clutched on to each side of the queen's throne as commanded. He could have asked me to juggle, and I would have found a way.

The smooth tip of his warm cock glided over the seam of my entrance. Slowly, he rubbed his tip along the lips of my pussy, swiping the beaded drops of pre-cum against my tingling center.

I was panting now, trying to push myself onto him.

He froze and moved his length away from where it touched me. "What if I hurt you, Caly?" his deep voice whispered. "What if I lose control? I don't want to hurt you."

His words startled me. Malum Mendax did not worry about hurting anyone. Ever. In fact, he enjoyed hurting others. Craved it.

The feelings threatened to cut me in two. So I responded like I always did when I felt things I didn't want to feel. I got pissed off.

"Have you turned soft, Mendax? Afraid to *fuck* me?" I grumbled, a new level of frustration possessing me.

His eyes smoldered. "Inside and out, there isn't a single part of me that's soft. Especially when you are involved. You really should remember that."

He slammed into me.

A pleasure-filled gasp tore from my throat as I clenched myself around him.

"So fucking wet, Caly," he mumbled. He slowly pulled out of me before he pressed himself inside again. Deeper and deeper with every heavy thrust.

Every single millimeter of my body lit up with sensations

as waves of pleasure rippled through me. I could feel how it felt for him. The explosion of carnality when inch by inch he slid into me.

The bond—it was ecstasy.

His thrusts were pounding into me so hard, I would be bruised, and still I wanted more. Rougher.

"Get up," he growled, pulling out of me and taking a step back.

I stood up, confused, and stared hungrily at his glistening cock as it throbbed under the sunlight.

He flipped me over, and a strong hand pressed the back of my neck down so my face smashed against the velvet cushion of the throne.

The Unseelie prince pushed into me from behind, letting my neck go to grip my hips savagely. Our skin clapped loudly as he slid himself out of me to drive into me harder and harder with every thrust that followed.

Oh my suns. I could feel all of his feelings as well as my own.

It was too much. My skin was going to implode and come on its own if I took one more thrust.

A wild scream tore out of me as I arched my back and ground against him like an animal.

"I'm going to come! Oh, Mendax!"

Mendax swore in response, slamming into me slower as trembles prickled over my skin with the building of both our orgasms.

The dark prince collected my hair in a bunch at the base of my neck and pulled, lifting my head up off the seat as he slammed into me. Delicious pain tore into the flesh of my shoulder and neck as he peppered my body with feral bites and licks, thrusting so deep that his black wings pulsed against the air, stabilizing his body and helping to fill me completely.

Still pressed against my back, he yanked on my thighs in search of a way to get deeper inside of me. I bit the cushion, feeling the overwhelming climax rise as his thrusts slowed.

"Fuck!" I shouted as he spanked my ass cheek, the sting and tingle the exact amount of pain and pleasure to push me over the edge.

I exploded with an orgasm, shouting out incoherent words into the velvet cushion I bit down on.

"That's it, my love, squeeze this cock. I can feel every part of you," his deep voice rasped against the shell of my ear.

"Oh my suns" was all I could mumble as he slowly moved in and out the smallest bit.

As soon as my orgasm ended, he pulled out of me and bundled me up into his arms, turning me around and pulling my dirty shirt off. The fire relit inside of my hungry body when he pulled my nipple into his hot mouth. The sensation of our bare chests touching felt like it expanded my cracked heart somehow.

Still holding me in his arms, he sat on the throne, leaving only enough room on either side of his legs for my feet.

"Sit on my cock, hellhound. I want to watch you take me," he commanded with a whisper.

I needed no encouragement—I grabbed ahold of his huge cock and angled it at my entrance, slowly lowering myself all the way down until he was fully inside of me again. It stung slightly, but quickly tipped into euphoria while I watched his face contort with pleasure. Pleasure that I was giving him.

I planted my hands on his muscular shoulders and used my legs to bounce, setting my own pace and rhythm.

"That's it. You're in control," he whispered, biting his lower lip as his hands roamed across my breasts and stomach.

"Malum!" I cried out, feeling the surging tension in my belly tighten again.

At the sound of his first name, his hands flew to my hips, slamming me down deeper. My head rolled backward, and I let the pleasure consume me as he continued his deep thrusts.

"Keep taking me, Caly. I want to watch your face when you feel me inside of you, filling up every part of this lying cunt with cum. Then I want to watch it drip from this decadent pussy. Come for me, my goddess. Come on my cock," his gravelly voice pleaded.

I continued rolling my hips, our eyes locked on to one another's.

Trembling took hold of my body, and I fell forward, onto his chest, muffling my scream into his shoulder with a bite. He held me firmly against his chest, letting out low groans into my messy hair as his nails dug into my back and hip while he continued to buck into me. I felt his thick cock pulse as he spilled, filling me so full, hot liquid had already drizzled down to my inner thigh.

I gave a silent shout-out to Fate that I had been taking my contraceptive teas the last few nights.

Then something akin to shame and embarrassment flooded me. I had been taking it because I thought something might happen with Eli. I had wanted it to.

The doors of the throne room slammed open. We both jumped up, ready to fight.

"Stars above, where the fuck are your clothes? Blood and iron, *not* on the throne? You didn't. Oh, come on." Walter shook his head, taking a second to turn around when Mendax growled at him.

"It's in here. The other half of your heart is in here. I can feel it," Walter said, ignoring us standing naked to walk to an empty corner and pace back and forth.

Mendax and I looked at each other.

"I'm taking Caly to her room. Shift into your rat form so no one sees you. I'll return in a moment," Mendax said. "We will find the heart."

He scooped me into his arms, ignoring my protests about leaving and shadowing me back to my room.

I opened my eyes in my dim bathroom, ready to yell at him.

"It's my heart. You can't just ignore me and do whatever you want," I barked at him. "You will ruin all of this for me. You're a prick, you know that?"

187

He set me on the vanity and proceeded to wet a washcloth, ignoring me completely.

"You can't just show up, alive suddenly, and think you can change everything. You can't. I'm not leaving to go with you. I-I have to stay here."

He pushed my legs apart, stepping between them and pressing his lips softly against mine, tender and gentle, unlike the bruising kisses in the throne room.

I felt the warm washcloth run over my scratches and wounds while he cleaned the blood off of my skin.

"Fine. You don't want to go with me?" he whispered against my lips but not moving away. "Then I'll stay here and unleash death and destruction on this castle and realm until you are ready to leave with me."

Then he vanished in a puff of black smoke.

Oh no. What had I just done?

CHAPTER 19

CALY

S EVERAL DAYS HAD PASSED SINCE MENDAX HAD REAPPEARED.
And I had been jumping out of my skin at everything
since. Every time I smelled a fire or a candle being extin-
guished, I became a lunatic, trying to protect whoever was
around me at the time. Chef Samuel, unfortunately, thought
I was unbalanced, but I certainly didn't blame him. Twice
during breakfast in the kitchen, I tried to coerce him and Eli
to break through the window and climb down the exterior
of the castle to get to safety—induced by the smell of mulled
cider burning in a cauldron on the fire.

Walter, though, had apparently been given strict instructions to stick by me. Luckily everyone believed him to be my
new rat companion.

It was one of the best feelings I could think of, to have
Walter around. Besides just being an unbelievable friend, he
also knew Mendax better than anyone, and there was a chance
he could be the only thing capable of helping me keep Eli
alive. On more than one occasion, he had helped calm my
mind about what was happening between Mendax and me.

Even with basically being a brother to Mendax and hating

the Seelie fae, Walter was there for me. From the moment I had met him as Brown Rat in the Unseelie dungeons, I had felt a deep friendship with him. I'd never had someone I could lean on so fully and openly and know they were going to still be there. Even Eli now felt like a stranger to me sometimes. He'd changed so much since I'd last seen him, and though once an innocent crush, it now felt like we were opposing poles of neodymium magnets, being attracted to each other. It just felt so...permanent now. Of all the things I thought I would do once I became a part of Seelie, marrying and ruling wasn't one of them.

My worries only continued to grow. In a house full of fox shifters, I still couldn't understand how they didn't pick up on another shifter right under their noses. Walter reassured me several times that he was such a pure-blooded shifter, it would be impossible for anyone to tell, shifter or not. He also guessed that that could be another reason he and I were so close. Walter said that even though the broken heart inside of my chest had only a crumb of powers, it was still there and drawn to his pure blood.

I still hadn't spoken to Queen Saracen yet. I was planning what to say. I needed to tell her that the game was over—a part of me was avoiding her for fear she would somehow find out about Mendax being alive, and the other part of me was avoiding her because I needed to figure out my next move before I went to her. Another part of me was avoiding her because I knew she would want to discuss the ceremony in which I'd get my heart put back together again, and then she was going to test me to see if I still possessed some of Mendax's power. Well, with him still alive, I knew how that was going to go. She'd make me marry Eli in front of every-one, and together, we would leave the ceremony as king and queen of Seelie—if that was even possible when you were bonded to an Unseelie.

I wasn't ready for any part of it.

What would happen if they restored my heart and nothing

happened? What if it killed me? I heaved out a breath at the thought. At least I would be with my sister.

I would talk to Saracen only once I had figured out what to do.

I swallowed, and it felt like cut glass sliding down my throat. I knew she would kill me, which would kill Eli, and then she'd probably figure out a way to actually kill Mendax. I needed a plan that would keep Mendax, Eli, and myself all alive. I also had to get my heart back before she found out about everything and it was too late to get it back.

This would all be over soon—it had to be. I was so, so tired of this.

"You better snap out of it before we get to the hills," Princess Tarani barked as we continued walking up the path and through the forest.

I glanced to my right, shaking my head free of all the thoughts running through it that I couldn't seem to sort out.

When I had tried to tell Eli that Mendax was back again, he had refused to listen, claiming it was Queen Tenebris who had attacked the guard at the portal. I knew he wanted to protect me, but it wouldn't do us any good if Mendax was traipsing around the castle, just waiting to be found out—or worse, waiting to kill them all. I hadn't seen him, but that didn't mean anything. One rarely sees the ghost in their attic, but they know he's there. Mendax still didn't know about my tie to Eli.

I had told Walter everything last night but swore him to secrecy. It felt like I'd been wearing a thousand pounds of armor and finally got to remove it for a few minutes.

Something pressed against my arm, and I jumped nearly a foot in the air.

"Wow, you've really been on edge the last few days, Cal. I promise the threat is taken care of. I wouldn't be taking my two favorite girls riding if I thought it was dangerous," Eli said as he let go of my arm.

"I'm still certain the threat is closer than ever," I said, glaring at him.

Tarani looked between the two of us, doing her best to figure out what was going on.

The sun beating down on my bare arms burned my skin as the three of us continued along the path. Eli had been determined to get me out of the castle, claiming that my anxiety was from being cooped up too long. He knew I was an outdoorsy type and found something in nature I couldn't find anywhere else.

"How much farther are we going?" I wished I had brought a light jacket to protect my arms from the sun. When Eli had told me we were going to the pits to collect horses, I had no idea we would have to walk so far.

"What's the matter? Tired already? Boy, if the Ancestors could see their prized secret Artemi now," Tarani said with a smirk.

"Knock it off, Tarani. I brought you along so the two of you could get to know each other, become friends," Eli said, wisely moving between us.

"Thanks, but I don't need friends like her."

"What's that supposed to mean?" I asked, moving to get behind Tarani. Ever since arriving in Seelie, Tarani had done nothing but push my buttons, and I had had enough.

"It means no one wants you here. You're just her puppet anyway," Tarani bit out, stepping into me to put her nose into mine.

Had she not been jeopardizing my stay here, I would have really liked her bite.

"Enough!" shouted Eli as a blaze of gold emanated from his skin. His golden wings flared out from his back. "*I* want her here, and we all know Mother wants her in the family— probably more than she wants you, Tarani." Eli winked at his sister to soften his words, pushing back in between us.

"Trust me, I know. It's only because she will be the only Artemi not to ascend in history, and the Seelie will dominate the other realms," Tarani snapped.

"Look, Tarani, it's no secret that I wish for Caly to be

my wife and a part of this family one day, and if Mother has her way, it will be soon, whether you want it or not. Either way, you will *not* speak of her like that in front of me, unless you want to be expelled from the castle with the Fallen," Eli boomed at his sister.

My belly flip-flopped hearing him say he wanted me as his wife. It sounded just like I had once imagined it would.

Tarani glared through narrowed eyes, looking like she was ready to shout back, but instead of responding, she closed her mouth and stormed off into the forest.

"I'll go back to the castle. You go get her," I said. "She's just being protective of you."

"It's fine. She just needs to cool off a little. She knows how to get to the hills on her own. We'll meet her there once she's calmed down," Eli said, taking my hand in his.

Oh god.

What if Mendax was watching? If he saw Eli touching me, he would kill us both.

I pulled my hand free and gave a tight smile when Eli looked at me, puzzled.

"Eli, you know we can't really get married," I said with an airy laugh.

"Why not?" He guided us under a large oak, into the shade, giving my skin a much-needed break from the sun.

"I'm not going to accept that deal with your mother. At the ceremony to get my heart back, the smoke will still come. Mendax is still alive. He and I are bonded, and that's why I still have the smoke. That isn't going to change once my heart is repaired. I'll form a new plan to get my heart back from her, but I can't marry you. I need to find another way. I can't hurt you," I said as I traced my fingers over the deep grooves of the oak's bark.

"You hate the idea of marrying me that much?" he asked, looking surprisingly wounded. "Cal, I love you. I always have, and I always will. Having our lives tied together doesn't matter to me when I was never going to leave your side anyway. I would do anything for you. Let me take care of you," he whispered.

My eyes could have bugged out of my head. It was as if my teenage fantasy was coming to life—except...

"It's not that—"

"He really is here, alive, isn't he?" he asked as he grabbed my arm and turned me around to face him.

"Yes. I told you he was."

"And that is why then?" He began pacing in front of me. "You cannot love him. He is evil! How could someone as good and sweet as you love a monster like that?" he shouted.

"That!" I shoved my finger at him. "That is why I could never marry you. You stopped being my best friend over ten years ago! A letter here and there doesn't keep things the same. You don't even know me, not really." I switched places with Eli and began pacing while he stilled. "How could you? Because I don't tell you anything about who I really am."

"That's not fair, and you know it! I was barred entry after what happened with Commander Von—after I found out what he was doing," Eli said.

"Don't put this on me. I never told you to fight him and get yourself banished! I was handling him just fine on my own," I spat out.

"From where I stood, he was the one doing all the handling," he snapped back. "I'd have killed him if mother hadn't sent him to Malvar."

My chest tightened remembering the day Eli had shown up to surprise me, and instead found my trainer taking certain liberties with me. I barely remembered, I had become so good at flipping a switch and going numb. Sometimes I think it might have been the best training I received from him; other times, I wondered if I had ever turned the switch back on.

"You have no idea what I've had to become." I stopped pacing, having lost all the steam from my rant. The Seelie prince walked a few steps from the shade to stand in the sun, turning to face me with a hard look in his eyes as he

194

reached between his shoulder blades and grabbed ahold of the neckline of his shirt.

"I'm sorry I didn't know you were Artemi sooner, Caly, but even if I'd have known, I wouldn't have told you. You're not from this world. You don't understand how dangerous it is for an unascended Artemi to be found. There is no way you can understand my reasoning. You have no idea how much I fought my mother on taking your heart when I thought you were a human. Now, I think it was probably the best move, for your safety. I'd never even known you could take half of an Artemi's heart. Before he passed away, my father was best friends with your father. I believe that's how mother knew to save you before Queen Tenebris could get to you."

He finished pulling off his shirt, and for the first time since we were kids, I saw his bare chest.

"But the truth is, you don't really know what I've become either." Eli's large, golden wings stretched wide behind his firm body. Streaks of deep, brassy gold covered him. There were barely more than a few inches between each of the lightning-like marks. Texture in the gold shone through, brightening under the sun's rays. Seelie bled gold. These were scars.

Eli's chest and back were covered.

I struggled to contain the violent ocean of pure rage that coursed through me. My teeth creaked against the force of my jaw. I would slaughter whoever had done this to him. Add them to the fucking list.

I moved behind him to see that his broad back and shoulders bore even more marks than the front. My finger-tips carefully skimmed over the scars on his pectoral muscle, then followed the vein of gold to another branch of scars that stopped just below his neck. My eyes blurred with hot tears. Eli had gone through all of this without me here to help. Whoever hurt him would experience a pain so severe it would need a new name. "Tell me who fucking did this to you, Eli. They are dead," I thundered.

"Mendax, the crown prince of Unseelie did this to me."

Eli's honey-colored eyes held mine. "The man you choose over me. He is responsible for these marks."

"What?" The air was punched from my lungs.

What had I done?

"The Smoke Slayer and I have had more than our share of battles. Many of them at the commands of our mothers… many of them not."

He stepped into me, and my palm heated against his tan abdomen.

"Neither you nor I know what the other is actually capable of, do we? We've both kept things from the other. It doesn't mean anything now. I have been in love with you since the day I met you, when you told me you hated me," he chuckled softly. "I will be anything for you. I love you, Calypso, and if I need to fight the Unseelie prince for you, then he should be warned. Every battle we've endured prior will be *nothing* compared to the lengths I am willing to go through to ensure you are happy and safe—with me." He bent down to press his warm, sun-kissed lips against mine.

It felt like summer. Like rolling down a grassy hill and laughing until your belly hurt. Like the feeling you got when the first rays of spring sunshine danced across your melancholy winter mind. The kiss was so light and gentle, filled with feelings and tenderness I'd never felt from anybody before.

Nothing about it felt wrong or shameful. For the first time since my mom and sister died, a bit of warmth spread through my cold insides, blanketing the dark, angry parts of me with the feeling of home.

Eli moved his head back to end the sweet kiss but stopped with his lips separated only a breath from mine, his eyes still closed. As if he couldn't physically move away from me.

"Feuhn—Kai—Greeyth," he whispered.

Eternal love and friendship.

My mouth would have lifted in a genuine smile, but for

a moment, I forgot how to move, so instead I looked at him for a few seconds without my walls or masks.

"Your lips feel like happiness and sunshine," I muttered. I didn't want to move for fear I would lose the feeling.

"You taste like sadness. Or a rainy day that doesn't know light should be in the sky," he whispered against my lips. "Allow me to be your umbrella, Cal. Let me keep the rain from touching you ever again."

We stood still for a few beats before he stepped back, folding his wings and replacing his shirt. My very confused, ashamed eyes trailed over my best friend's lean, flexing muscles.

Suns. What was I doing? I had fucked the Seelies' greatest enemy not long ago. The very same man who had scarred my best friend's body like an old cutting board—and I had wanted it. Shame drowned any good feelings. I had thought about leaving with Mendax after I got my heart and telling him everything, stupidly thinking he would be perfect to help me with what I still needed to do. What the fuck was I doing? Mendax was evil, Eli was good. I needed to be good.

Mendax was lust, danger, and passion, but with Eli, I could be different. Everything could work out so perfectly—even better than I had hoped. I could finally get my heart back and be happy.

"Come on, we should meet up with Tarani. I want to make sure she got there okay. I'll explain how you trick your horse on the way. Tarani's probably already gotten hers."

"Sorry, what?" I said, certain I'd misheard him through the myriad thoughts that pounded away in my skull. I stepped away from the shade and back into the blazing sun and winced as soon as the light hit my eyes.

"There will be shade once we are at the hills," Eli said sympathetically.

As we walked, my mind flickered back to Walter, at the castle where I had left him. I knew that his goal while we were gone was to try to figure out why he kept sensing

Artemi powers in the back corner of the throne room when there was nothing in there but creepy murals of an eerie, empty battle and thrones.

"How much longer until we arrive?" I asked, breaking the silence.

"The forest of the hills will begin shortly," Eli replied.

I got the distinct impression that he was avoiding telling me any more about the hills than he had to. "I still don't understand why we have to go into the forest to capture a horse. I happen to know the castle has a paddock full of horses. The Unseelie had skeletal unicorns in theirs. They were incredibly cool."

At the mention of Unseelie, Eli shot me a look. "That is exactly what I'm talking about. In Seelie, we respect our horses. We prove to them that we are worthy of their strength and loyalty. The Unseelie simply capture and cage anything they decide they want."

He had no idea how true his statement was.

We pressed on as the forest grew denser and more beautiful, with bright, flowering trees and pines.

Looking ahead on the path, I understood exactly why it was referred to as the pits.

"Let me guess, we're here," I said as I stared down into the wide-open pit that seemed to have appeared from nowhere. The spongy, green moss around the edge of the hole camouflaged it, making it virtually impossible to see. Glancing around the shaded forest, I saw no other holes in the ground.

"Yes we are here, and watch out—the pits move. They usually don't show this far out, but it looks like they are being temperamental today," he said. His jaw tightened. "We need to find Tarani. Stay by me. You won't see them if they appear in front of you, and if they even cause you to lose your balance, they will be relentless," he said before he moved in front of me.

As we continued through the forest, I moved to the side, feeling stupid for letting him shove me behind him. I had eyes. I was able to see a hole the size of a house just as well as he could.

"You hear that? What is that?" I asked Eli.

He turned around, his eyes as wide as saucers. "Shit! That's Tarani!"

We took off into the forest, my short legs struggling to keep up with Eli. Tall trees with bushy tops appeared to move as we ran. Were we running that fast? Or were the trees really moving?

A deep rumble started, vibrations buzzing up my ankles, making my whole body quake.

"Come! You have to move quicker, Caly!" Eli shouted just as a pit the size of a minivan opened right in front of me, nearly taking me down with the rubble and dirt that it swallowed.

I leaped to the side just as there was another shout off in the distance, this one more panicked.

Tarani was in trouble.

"Go without me!" I screamed at Eli, praying he would leave me behind and go to his sister.

"I've done that before. I'll never you behind again," he stated as he ran back several feet, trying to get to me.

"Fucking go, Eli! Stop trying to rescue me every five seconds and go get your sister. I can make it out of here on my own," I hollered. "Stop treating me like I can't do anything."

"Fine, stubborn ass. Keep running and don't stand still, or they will sense it and open under you. Go back out the way we came!" he shouted.

Eli was panicking as he spun back and forth between me and his sister's screams before letting out his own gruff shout. His golden wings spread with a sharp *thrap* before he took off running in the direction of her voice. Mystified, I watched as my best friend rose gradually into the sky. Eli could fly.

I had had no idea he could actually fly.

Of course I knew he had wings. Beautiful, sparkling

wings that I could picture a god or archangel having, but I had never thought they could actually carry his weight. Still a science nerd at my core, it felt terribly wrong. The weight should have been too uneven, and how did they just seem to disappear into their skin when they were not in use? Mendax's wings of smoke did the same thing. Magic made no sense.

I realized I had stopped running and was standing in the still forest—precisely what I had been instructed not to do.

I made a mental note to ask him more about his wings. Maybe Eli would humor me and let me run a few tests on them, for the sake of placating my curious mind. I knew he would. He would do anything for me. Sadness gripped my chest, thinking about how much he would hate me soon.

Another shrill scream sounded, shaking me out of my thoughts.

Was that a growl that came after?

This time the shriek came from my left—not the way Eli had flown.

Logically, I knew that I shouldn't wander off into a forest I was unfamiliar with, especially one with creatures I knew nothing about. I glanced around. The humid air was heavy with the aroma of woody earth. Everything was peaceful— bright-green moss and grass, pink and yellow flowers I didn't recognize. It was beautiful in a way that you couldn't imagine being real.

I stiffened immediately, hearing the high whine again.

I knew better than anyone that if something dangerous appeared beautiful and calm on the outside, it was far more twisted and devious than anything that looked spooky and ominous. Those who hide their darkness under a mask of beauty and good are filled with the worst kind of evil—the kind that will betray and trick you once you trust it.

Feeling the ground beneath my feet tremble, I bolted to my left.

I felt a pull in that direction. It wasn't in the hopes of saving Tarani—honestly, it'd be easier for me if she died now.

I would be fine. I'd continue running while I paid close attention to the ground.

When the pits opened, it was silent aside from the crumble of the dirt and roots caving in on themselves. Even the birds of the forest were annoyingly quiet when it happened. No squawking and flying off—they just watched from the trees.

I nearly plummeted into a small pit before I fell backward, throwing my weight behind me as hard as possible. I rolled away from it, panting as I pressed against the nearest tree.

Fuck, that was close. Maybe Eli was right, and I shouldn't be out here.

The pit closed slowly. The ground sealed over with fresh, spongy moss as if it had never happened at all.

Holy hell, they closed. Did that mean if you fell, you were eaten up by the forest dirt?

A tree nearby creaked loud and long. Several in the distance groaned and creaked almost as if in answer.

I peered around the other side of the tree that I leaned against. My fingers touched the dark, textured bark. It was beautiful, but not a tree I recognized. I would ask Eli if I could go through the castle library. I desperately wanted to learn more about nature in these realms. For all I knew, I was about to climb up a creature right now.

I pulled myself up the lowest branch, feeling the stretch and pull of my unused muscles. I continued to climb until I was able to look out and see a good distance.

Pits of all different sizes pocked the moss-carpeted floor, exactly where I had been about to run. I never would have seen them.

A low growl and a yip echoed through the trees again. My eyes finally found a large hole at the edge of my vision. Dirt and rocks crumbled along the inside edge. Something was unsuccessfully attempting to climb out.

Tarani.

I cracked off a small stick from the branch I was crouched under and held my hand out, my pointer finger following

201

the direction of the pit with Tarani. I firmly pressed the small stick's round end onto the top of my hand until indents were left in the same pattern of the pits I could see along the forest floor. It would serve as a pit map, but it would only remain accurate if I was fast and made it before any closed or more opened.

Shimmying down the rough bark, I was incredibly thankful I had worn leggings under my sundress as I dropped to the ground and pointed my finger in the direction of the pit. My confidence increased as I dodged several pits and successfully made it to the large hole at the end of my hand map. Sweat dripped down my back as I skidded to a stop just at the edge of the hole and dropped to my knees.

The pit was shaped like a cone, the top wide and spacious, but as the pit deepened, it grew narrower, until the pointed base of the steep hole came into view, nearly a quarter the size of the opening.

"Tarani!" I called as I peered over the edge of the pit.

Deep, deep down, in the very small base of the pit was the most beautiful red fox desperately trying to climb up the dirt wall of the pit and falling back with a yelp.

"Oh my god." My eyes caught movement at the opposite side of the base.

A humungous grizzly bear was crouched, watching Tarani climb and fall.

"Tarani!" I shouted again, causing both the bear and Tarani to look up. "What are you doing? Shift into your fae form and use your wings to fly out!" I yelled, wondering why she hadn't done it already.

I glanced around the sky. Surely Eli could hear us? He could fly down and get her out easily.

Snarls and growls rose from the pit, drawing my attention back down. Tarani had fallen too close to the bear's area and it had gone for her.

"He looks like he might be an adolescent. Just give him space!" I shouted. This was not going to end well for her. Black bears were excellent climbers, shy, and generally quick to retreat when threatened. But this wasn't a black bear.

Tarani was in the pit with what looked like a massive grizzly. They were not good climbers and were incredibly aggressive when threatened. Unless she pulled out some serious powers soon, she wasn't going to make it out alive.

"Shift, damn it!" I screamed at her. I don't even know why I cared. I didn't want to like her. One more fucked part of the plan.

She looked up, and I saw the fear and pleading in her eyes. Was she unable to shift for some reason?

She hit the opposite wall with a soft thud as the bear slashed at her with his long claws. Her fox form slid down the dirt wall to lay in a lifeless heap on the ground.

"Tarani!" I bellowed. "Get away from her now!" I snarled at the bear.

To my surprise, it looked up at me. Its brown eyes were filled with sorrow as he hunkered down once again, on the opposite side of Tarani.

"Eli! We're over here!" I screamed into the forest, cupping my hands around my mouth like a megaphone.

Just leave. Go back to the castle, I thought. *This is retribution being served up on a silver fucking platter.*

I grumbled as I punched the dirt next to me. None of this was working out like it should. I was too weak with Tarani and Eli. I flipped over on my belly and let out a shaky breath, letting my feet dangle over the edge a second before pushing myself into the pit. I clumsily slid and rolled to the bottom, nearly crushing Tarani's lifeless fox form as I fell next to her.

"Wow," I mumbled under my breath.

The bear was huge from up there, but huddled on the other end of the small space, he seemed absolutely giant. I had assumed he was a grizzly, but seeing his larger-than-normal body reminded me that I didn't know a thing about the fae's creatures beyond bits and pieces that I'd heard; it meant nothing that they looked like things I was familiar with. For all I knew, it could shoot fire out of its eyes.

"What the fuck are you doing?" Eli's voice thundered down into the hole.

I looked up to see his handsome face leaning over the bright opening. "Tarani! What hap—" His eyes landed on the bear next to us.

"Of course you'd show up right after I drop myself down here!" I yelled at him. I ran my hands over Tarani's fluffy body, checking for any damage that I might recognize.

"Is she—"

"She's okay, strong pulse. I think she just got knocked unconscious," I replied, unable to stop myself from petting her soft, orange fur. She *hated* me and would probably try to murder me after she knew I had pet her like a dog.

So I rubbed her belly for good measure.

"What were you thinking? The pit could close any second! This isn't the human realm anymore. It doesn't matter if you killed a few incompetent fae for my mother. You *don't* have any powers and are going to get us both killed being so reckless! Or did you already forget we are tied together? Probably forgot all about me again. As soon as you saw Mendax—who might I remind you, you couldn't kill because you are as powerless as a human!" he screamed.

Deep down, I knew he was panicking at seeing both Tarani and me at the bottom of a pit that could close at any second, killing all three of us in a second, but his words sparked like a firecracker inside me. He had no idea what I'd managed without power.

"What are you doing?" he asked, his voice softening as he watched me take a step back to look around the pit.

"Getting out of here," I replied flatly.

"I'm coming down. Move to the side by Tarani. I don't want to anger the eval. It must be hurt, because there is no way it wouldn't have killed you two already otherwise, especially you. I don't know how you and I are both going to get out of this alive." Eli glared at me. "Which means we both won't."

I had already lifted Tarani's lean body and was in the process of draping her limp form around my neck, so I could grip her legs on either side of my chest.

Eval...what was difference between evals and grizzlies? I wondered.

"Stop. What are you doing?" Eli shouted. I could hear the frustration in his voice. He sounded like he was talking to a toddler who wouldn't do what he asked.

Irritation created soft whorls of smoke that flowed off my arms.

The eval lifted its head and wiggled its large black nose to sniff at my smoke before it let out a growl so rumbly that it caused bits of loose dirt to drop from the sides.

Interesting. It didn't seem to like the Smoke Slayer smoke.

"Caly!" Eli yelled.

I adjusted Tarani on my shoulders, stood to my full height, and locked eyes with the eval. His brown irises roamed over me, still inhaling the smoke that trickled off my arms and hands and tilting its head as if it was confused. The eval turned around and pushed its head against the dirt wall, leaving its large brown butt to face me.

Umm...okay.

Tarani was light enough. I could do this. Just like at the mall, where they had those yellow spiral wishing wells that I would drop my penny into and watch as it continued to circle around and around the bright plastic side, until it dropped down the bottom of the funnel. Well that's what I was going to attempt. Only the opposite.

When an object moves in a circle, it must have an acceleration component perpendicular to its velocity. The magnitude of the acceleration increases, causing the speed to increase and decrease as you increase the span of the circle. Basically, I should be able to use centripetal force and run around the interior walls, eventually getting to the top. But this would only work if I could go fast enough and gradually rise at a steady pace.

I heaved in a breath and ran diagonally, stepping hard against the wall just above the dirt floor and taking wide steps as I increased my speed. As I neared the eval, my steps faltered, and I began to fall, catching my balance just in time and landing in a crouch back on the floor where I had started. Was it too wide?

"I have to run right above you. *Please* don't hurt us," I begged the eval.

This had to work. I said a small prayer that I wouldn't mess up, which would not only startle the giant animal, probably causing it to lash out, but the fall alone could kill the both of us...the trio of us.

"Caly, stop!" Eli shouted.

I needed to be faster and not let running above the eval make me nervous. If I could create enough speed, the total magnitude of the normal force would increase. With a larger frictional force, I could get us out, running around the edges of the cone as it widened.

I took off, letting Eli's earlier words fuel me. I didn't need him or Mendax. I didn't need anybody, and I needed to remember that.

My ankle cracked at an odd angle while I struggled to get started around the circle. I changed my grip on Tarani, moving all four of her thin legs into one hand so I could balance better as we accelerated around the wall. If I couldn't keep this speed, we would drop.

"What the—" Eli said as I got closer to the lip where he was crouched.

Finally near the top, my ankles throbbed and my arms quivered, but I flung us onto the edge, slamming against the earth as large hands gripped my wrists, helping to pull me up. The mossy edge of the pit slid against my tired body until only the tips of my tennis shoes dangled over. Hurrying for fear the pit would close at any second, I pulled my knees up, away from the edge, shoved Tarani's body from my shoulders, and rolled over, panting.

"How did you—" Eli began.

I moved my eyes from the blue sky above to see Eli holding Tarani's limp body, staring at me with an open mouth.

"Physics," I grumbled, dropping my head back down for one more second before standing up. "Why couldn't she shift? Couldn't she have flown out?" I asked.

"Sometimes fate toys with us, and our animal form won't allow us to shift. She must have been terrified. Evals are no joke," Eli whispered.

He had lifted Tarani to hold her in a bright ray of sun that peeked through the trees. As soon as the sun touched her fur, it glimmered like each hair was full of magic. She moved her head to the side to soak in more of the strong sun.

My shoes compressed the deep moss as I stepped back to the edge of the pit.

"Okay, be ready for me. If this closes, I'm sorry for every-thing. Know that I loved you, even when you're being an ass," I said, sitting on the edge of the pit, dangling my legs back down.

Hands clapped over my shoulders and pulled me back. "What the fuck are you doing?" Eli barked.

"The grizzly or eval—whatever it is, I'm going to help get him out," I said, shoving him off of me. It was stupid, but so was saving Tarani.

"What? You can't do that. You can't carry him out. He's six hundred pounds at least! You will kill us both! And for what? An eval?" Eli gawked at me like I had grown a second head.

"I don't think he'll hurt me. I can sort of feel it. I think," I said softly.

"You can't feel anything, Caly! You don't have any of your Artemi powers yet. They are tucked away safely in the castle," he said while he rubbed his forehead. "Just because a lot of animals like you, doesn't mean they all will."

My jaw dropped. "You know where my heart is. You've known this whole time?" My throat tightened until I was barely able to finish the words.

"Yes, I know where it is, but that doesn't mean I can get to it. You're the only one who can get to it."

"Why wouldn't you help me get it then?" I asked. This is what happens when you love someone and trust they will keep you safe.

"I didn't know that you were planning on stealing it back before our ceremony. You are though." His eyes flashed. "You were planning to steal your heart and leave with Mendax, weren't you?" He was shouting now, hurt and anger carving lines between his eyes.

"I wasn't planning to do anything with Mendax, but why should I have to marry you in order to get my own heart?" I shouted back at him. "It's *my* heart! I was told I would be considered a Seelie royal upon my arrival. No marriage required." I watched the muscle feather as his jaw clenched and he took a step back as though I had wounded him.

"Forgive me. I was unaware you held such objections to marrying me," he stated. "Perhaps then, once I put Mendax to death once and for all, it will lessen your struggle. After all, he's in my realm, stalking my family," he said with chilling calm.

I stared at him for a minute. I had been so worried about Mendax killing Eli, I had never once thought about the possibility of Eli killing Mendax.

How had this gotten so complicated?

I turned my eyes back to the pit. Now more than ever, I needed to be around an animal. It sounded stupid, but it reminded me of my sister, and it was the only time I felt any peace. Right then, I would risk a mauling for that kind of calm.

Sliding my legs over the edge of the pit, I tried to flatten my back against the wall, in the hopes of using a playground-slide position as I slid down. Unfortunately, a large rock grated against my spine, forcing me to coil and tumble until I fell to the bottom.

"Calypso! No!"

Before I could stop him, Eli dove into the pit, spreading his gilded wings to hover above me. The eval rose, filling the crowded space with its large frame and letting out a growl so forceful, spit flew from his open jaw.

"Eli, go back with Tarani. If she doesn't wake up soon, another pit could open under her. I can handle this," I said, standing up to brush the dirt off my leggings and ripped sundress.

"You think I'm going to leave you here?" Eli said, swooping over to grab my waist. "You have no defense. It *will* kill you! It's not a puppy!"

"You are going to leave me here because I chose to do this on my own. I have already proven time and time again that I am not even a little helpless, so stop thinking that I am, and trust me. As my best friend, would you ever want me to marry someone who doesn't believe in me?" I said, angling myself between him and the eval.

Eli closed his mouth, pressing his lips together tightly, obviously attempting to filter out the millions of things he wanted to say. "Fine," he bit out as his eyes darted over my face. "But only because I know that if I simply grab you and fly from here, I would be no better than Mendax, and *when* I do kill him for everything he has done to you—and believe me, I will—I want you to understand that he and I love you in much different ways."

He removed his hand from my waist after a light squeeze and flapped his wings. "The instant you ask for my help, I will be waiting," he whispered before he kissed my cheek.

The eval snarled and charged at him just as his wings flapped gracefully and he rose to the top.

Nervously, I moved back as the animal's brown eyes focused on me. *Don't fail me now, Adrianna, for the love of Aether in the Elysian Fields, do not fail me now.*

"I won't hurt you, I promise," I said softly as I took a step toward the bear. "You have to trust me though. You are much too big and heavy to carry, so you are going to need to run like I did around the sides in a circle until we reach the top," I whispered, taking another step. "I will go behind you and push if you can't move fast enough. Can you even understand me?" I questioned, feeling a little stupid for trying to have a conversation with a scared otherworldly creature.

I couldn't explain it, but I knew that it was the eval that had led me to the pit, not Tarani.

The walls started to vibrate slightly, knocking small pebbles and dirt off the sides. The pit was going to close.

"Caly! It's too late! Leave it behind!" Eli shouted, standing at the top with his wings spread. He couldn't help it—he was going to try and get me before it closed.

"Follow me now! We don't have time. Whatever happens, do not slow down!" I shouted at the bear.

Retracing my previous steps, I ran up the wall a few feet and began to pick up speed. I glanced back to find he was already following behind me, right on my heels. "That's it! Follow my speed!"

I couldn't believe it. He was bounding after me on all fours. Somehow, I knew he understood me. I could feel the dust of his thoughts—not very strong but enough.

The walls of the pit shook as they began to close in. The vibration was making it hard to keep my footing, but the circle tightening made it easier. At last, I made it to the edge where Eli stood.

I leaped onto the bank just as before, but before Eli could grab my hands I turned back to the pit. The monster of a bear clawed at the edges of the pit, but it was closing in around him too tightly. He couldn't pull his weight up.

"Help me!" I pleaded.

Grabbing ahold of the thick folds of skin and fur at the eval's neck, I pulled with everything I had.

Eli was at my side in an instant, pulling up at the bear's back.

With a final heave, the eval managed to get its footing against the back wall and pushed itself up, as all three of us rolled farther from the closing edge.

"What the—" Tarani said, standing in her human form to stare at us all panting.

I had somehow rolled on top of the large bear. He—I could feel it was a he now—gently pushed his huge paws against me, pulling me into an embrace and licking my cheek, nuzzling into me happily.

"Oh, now stop that. No need to get all gushy. You're welcome," I giggled, lightly swatting his nose away.

I relaxed against his fur to pet his giant head, feeling closer to my sister than I had in a long time. I missed her so much.

He wiggled his large head into the crook of my neck happily. Had he been a dog, his tail would have been wagging.

My gaze rose to see Eli and Tarani gaping at me.

"Apparently she has more Artemi powers in this part of her heart than we had thought," Tarani mumbled.

CHAPTER 20

QUEEN SARACEN

THE PAST

I'M SORRY, HOW DO YOU KNOW CALYPSO AGAIN?" THE WOMAN
asked.

"Oh, forgive me," I said, shaking her hand. "I'm a neighbor from the other side of the meadow."

The loud, mechanical cars drove past the sidewalk we were stopped at as the nervous-looking woman angled her head at me. "I thought Darcy owned the farm? Is he okay?" she asked as she moved the little one in front of her closer.

"Oh, yes, I'm his mother's sister's daughter-in-law." I waved my hand and gave a wide smile. "Sometimes even I can't keep it straight. Anyhoo, I heard Caly has a birthday coming up, and I wanted to do something special. Eight really is such a fun age."

"You're the lady who Cal saved in the field last month!" the little girl exclaimed.

"Adrianna, don't point please."

"Oh, she's perfectly fine! Listen, I'm glad I ran into the both of you. I have a gift for Caly at the farm. I'm sort of crafty, I suppose you could say, so I made it. The last thing it needs is just a little splatter or two from the both of you to make it really special. Would you mind?" I smiled sweetly.

The mother was immediately put at ease. "Wow, that's really sweet of you. Adrianna and I would love to be a part of that. Caly's been getting into some trouble lately. I'm sure she's told you," she said.

"Cal's just mad at our father. She really isn't bad like they say," the child added.

"Adrianna," the mother scolded, obviously embarrassed. "Umm...anyway, yes, we will drop these flowers off at home and run over to the farm."

"Actually, the art is at a studio up the road. It's very secluded. They haven't even paved the road yet. Let me drive us so your car doesn't get stuck."

They nodded and smiled as we crossed the street to the nearest SUV, happy to be doing something nice for Calypso.

I used the dismal amount of magic I possessed to start the car's engine as they buckled their seat belts—safety first.

Calypso's mother caught sight of the empty ignition and froze, giving me an anxious look.

"Keyless start. It's amazing what they come up with these days," I chuckled as I pressed harder on the pedal. It was too late for them to change their minds now.

"You know, I just remembered, we have something we need to do," the woman said, finally listening to her gut.

By now I was driving down a back road out of the small town, gaining a speed the street had probably never seen.

"I'm sorry, but I really can't let you get in the way any longer," I singsonged. "She doesn't belong with two humans anyway. She will be the hero of the Seelie realm. The Elysian Fields won't be able to keep her out," I said proudly. "Not that she'd be refused anyway, being Artemi. Becoming Seelie royalty alone would have secured that. The Elysian Fields are like your heaven," I said to the child, my voice filled with saccharine. "Unfortunately, the two of you will not be meeting her there anytime soon. Humans don't belong," I snarled.

The now-terrified mother looked back at her young daughter, bracing herself against the dashboard. Turning to me, she said. "You know." She turned her flushed face to her daughter again. "Adrianna, I'm so sorry. I'm so sorry, honey. I'm so sorry," she sobbed.

The car bounced and swayed. The view blurred like watercolors as it flew by us in shades of green and yellow.

I veered off the road, aiming us toward the old bridge and gunning it once I had lined the car up with the brick wall at its base. I pressed the cruise-control button.

My wings began to spread. I was ready to take off just before the car would crash.

Unable to hide my smile, I glanced behind the seat to watch the little girl as I shrunk myself, letting my wings fully unfold. I couldn't fly with them, but they would grant me a soft landing.

The girl sat calmly, a marked contrast to her mother's hysteria. Her sad eyes stared at the incoming wall with a look of defeat. Her little blue eyes filled with tears.

"What did you do?" Adrianna whimpered just before the car smashed into the wall.

CHAPTER 21

MENDAX

N O. I'M NOT LEAVING THIS REALM UNTIL THERE IS A LEASH attached to her throat and she is latched to my side."

My fist slammed into the doughy gut of the dead Seelie hanging from the tree in front of me with an echoless thud. His headless body swayed back and forth in the cheery sunlight. It must've been the tenth Lumins guard I'd killed in half as many days. After killing the first one, chaos and panic rippled over the realm, but then nothing. They were either trying to keep it quiet and hide my arrival, or they were planning something knowing I was very much alive.

"Leave her, Mendax. Now. Are you really about to throw everything away in Unseelie for an Artemi? After what they did to our kind?" Queen Tenebris scolded. My mother shifted the black-feathered skirt of her ball gown, lifting it from the mossy forest floor with a look of pure disgust.

"I will never leave her. Human, Artemi, it makes no difference now; her only classification of concern is that she is mine," I snarled as I clenched my fists, attempting to keep my rage in check.

"Fine. Grab the bitch and bring her back with you to

fight the Fallen fae. She'll die before you cross the front forest." The dark queen opened her palm to let one of the many luna moths that had followed her through the portal land on her hand.

"She is a powerful enemy with deceit in her blood. Don't you see? Either way, now Saracen has the advantage. Somehow the sneaky whore did it. Let's say you do manage to find and restore her heart and powers. Who do you think she is going to use them against?" She stepped close to me, dropping the hand with the moth. "The man who is trying to tear down and murder the people she calls family? Or perhaps she will use her powers against one of the Smoke Slayers who is credited with forcing her entire race to die or go into hiding? Yes, that seems promising," she said with a glare.

"I would harness that tongue of yours," I stated as black-blue smoke clouded my feet. "Her reciprocation of my love is unneeded. I would never require her to hold the same attachments as myself because it is an impossible feat. I am possessed with a cruel and bloody love that collapses and suffocates, squeezes and rips until scars and bruises are the only traces left. She is the noose that hangs me, the rope that strangles and chokes at my soul, and no one—not her or anyone— could ever be left as breathless as I am."

Queen Tenebris's sharp blue eyes held pain before she closed them. Her raven-black hair was wrapped elaborately around the black crown on her head.

"That is the greatest downfall of a Smoke Slayer—once we feel our soul has chosen, we cannot exist without them in our grasp, no matter how undeserving they are. Believe me, I understand, but our souls are infantile and demonic. Have you learned nothing from what we went through with your father? How could I have not recognized her?" She was shouting now, her own ashy smoke pouring from her in a silent plea. "The Artemi are too powerful to be allowed to return. Unseelie will be the first thing she destroys."

"You are the one who has left the castle while it's under attack," I growled back, frustration bleeding into my words.

"I left to retrieve you! This is *exactly* what Saracen wanted—to distract you while the Fallen take our castle. You're an idiot, and not the son I raised, if you think for one moment she doesn't know you are within her walls. With an empty throne and a tired queen, the Unseelie court has never seen a more vulnerable time, and here you are trying to bed the enemy!"

"Return to Unseelie. Tell Dirac to get his father's army. They have the Ladon. We won't require such measures against the Fallen, but it will send the desired message. At any rate, his father's dragon will be heartily fed when he returns," I said with a grin. That would terrify the Fallen.

My mother looked up, sadness in her eyes. "Mendax, the Fallen have gained control of the Lindwrym."

"The Lindwrym? How?" I asked.

My skin itched with frustration. I cast a stream of smoke over my mother's head sharply, breathing only when it cracked into a squirrel eating on a log behind us. With a small clap, it was consumed entirely by the black cloud.

I needed to kill something. Now.

"They have grown more powerful since you have been gone," she whispered. "We think they are under new leadership." She didn't need to say who she thought could be behind it.

"Return to Unseelie. Do exactly as Dirac tells you, and for star's sake, listen to his instructions if your powers are needed." I turned to face the unsightly gold castle, only a speck in the distance. "I will return to Unseelie tonight. Caly will be safer in the Seelie realm, at least until I can find her heart." Even as the words poured from my mouth, fury and pain rippled through me at the thought of leaving her here.

"Listen to me, you must find her heart and destroy it before she gets ahold of it and receives her powers, or I promise you, my son, she will ruin every piece of you there is left," Queen Tenebris bit out with a stiff jaw.

"She already has."

We nodded goodbye. Mother stepped into the ring of mushrooms and disappeared with a puff of smoke, and I started the walk back to the Seelie's castle, killing every living thing that presented itself to me.

The thought of adding any amount of distance to what I already felt from my bonded made the splintery crumb of a soul I had ache. I couldn't risk her death in Unseelie. If it was as bad as Mother made it out to be, Caly couldn't be there without her powers. Still, I couldn't bear to leave her here... unprotected. The goose bumps on my skin prickled with the need to violently slaughter something and release a fragment of the rage that burdened me.

Aurelius.

My pace quickened. I didn't bother to shadow back, hoping the walk would make some of my impulsiveness ebb a bit. I didn't care who saw me. It was vital that I feel his life slipping away under the force of my calloused hands. I needed him to be gone and away from her once and for all.

Fuck her for making me her fucking keeper.

I hoped that she had left the castle, because right now, I wanted to kill her too. She could wait for me just as easily in the netherworld of Tartarus. I wondered if they had officially marked her a Seelie royal or if she had enough Artemi in her that it would count; humans couldn't go to Tartarus or the Elysian Fields, and I wasn't going to run around trying to pull her out of human heaven or hell.

Was that a fucking eval?

The barbarous creature snarled at me. It was lucky I thought it was some new gargoyle when I passed it, or it'd be dead too. What the fuck was an eval doing at the front door of the Seelie castle?

I turned back around to look at the large animal for a minute, contemplating if I wanted the fight or not. It snarled at me, flashing its long teeth. It had an odd stare, one I'd swear I'd seen before. The creature stilled, growing as stiff as a statue.

I didn't have enough time. I had people who needed to be killed.

Servants screamed as I charged into the entrance, the giant double doors slamming loudly when I pushed past them and continued down the hall. It didn't matter who saw me. What could they do? She was the only one who could ever hurt me.

Platters and trays clanged to the floor, the cymbals in a terror-stricken orchestra. There would be no more lurking in the Seelie castle now, but I didn't care. It was beyond my abilities to care about anything but her.

Screams pierced the still air of the castle from every direction. The harsh light pelting my face only fed my irritation. Apparently the walk to the castle hadn't helped calm my rage. I couldn't recall a time I had ever needed to make something hurt and bleed as much as I did right now.

A door shut with a crash at the end of the hallway near Caly's room, and the man himself stepped out, looking around for the cause of the excitement. He didn't look surprised to see me, which meant that my Caly had already told him. I hoped she'd told him how hard I'd fucked her on his throne too.

Not a word was said before we each took off, running head-on toward the other. This—the fighting of our worlds and the weight that rested on us as the sons of enemy families—had long ago reared its ugly head, but this—this was different. Both of us would destroy the realms for her if she let us, but it would be impossible until the other man was gone. Forever.

Aurelius was too strong a fae to impel, or I could have made easy work of him. As it was, I was filled with so much hostility, all I wanted in this life was to destroy him with my own hands.

We slammed into one other, each throwing a punch. Both of us had been highly trained, but none of it showed through as we hurled ourselves at one another. Dents and cracks sequined the walls and doors as the brawl moved into the smoking room.

"Let Calypso be. You are no good for her," the golden prince shouted. He moved around me too quickly, tackling me around the waist and slamming me into the wall. Gypsum and wood sprinkled and fell around us. I landed a punch to his side, feeling the bones of my knuckles connect with his ribs.

"And you are what she needs, huh? That goddess is a serrated wraith of darkness just waiting to be fed. She's not some dumb embellishment, made to pump out heirs and go dancing with. You don't even see the darkness inside her. She was made for me and me alone." I grunted, taking a rather strong hit to my stomach.

"I will not let you near her, Mendax. She doesn't know this world. She doesn't understand what a cretin you are. But I do. You are just like your father, and I will take a sword to my neck before I let you hurt and manipulate Calypso like Thanes did to my mother!" he snarled before he elbowed me in the face.

I didn't know or care what it was his mother told him about how the Fallen were created. He would never understand what his mother had done like I did. He was a pampered, spoiled child. He had no involvement with any of it.

I, on the other hand, had been forced to take the life of a man I loved and looked up to more than anyone. I had been a part of it.

I would never say that I was nothing like my father because that was a lie. I was very much like him. I just wasn't as obvious.

In the many, many times the Seelie prince and I had fought, not one of those times had he fought me as hard as he was now.

I laughed softly, feeling the blood trickle from my split lip. "How is daddy Felix? Still rotting in the grave where your mother put him?" I ducked, barely missing the ball of sunfire that ignited the wall a few feet behind us. "Perhaps you should be more concerned with how close she is to your mother. Calypso probably holds more poison and hate in her veins than I do," I bit out through clenched teeth. I punched him in the eye so hard, he fell back into the wall, knocking a tall shelf of books to the ground.

He rose with a scowl. "I don't know what rumors muck around in Unseelie, but my father was poisoned by the maid, you dense, gullible candle," he said, panting.

Aurelius's warm-shit-colored eyes told me he was telling the truth. He had no idea what had really happened. I knew Saracen had lied to her realm, telling them my mother and father had forced her, which had started the big rift between Seelie and Unseelie, but I figured her own kids would know the truth. I almost felt bad for how witless Aurelius and his sister were.

Almost.

My wings made a soft creak at my back as they extended as wide as they were able.

Aurelius's own wings widened in return. His hand glowed orange with light as he pushed it to block my smoke.

I shadowed to his side, catching him off guard. He burned my chest with a quick blast of light as my smoke wrapped around him like a snake, binding his arms and legs in a suffocating cocoon. He burst with light as he fought and struggled against the smoke, falling to the floor behind the leather sofa.

"Leave her alone, Mendax! You touch a freckle on her, and I swear to suns I'll—"

"You'll what?" I taunted as I gripped his throat. His pulse quickened under my hand. Once he was gone, Calypso would learn who she belonged to. "You'll do nothing because you'll be dead, annoying someone else in the Elysian Fields."

Aurelius's eyes widened as if he just remembered something of importance.

My knuckles bent and my fingers folded, excited to feel his heroic gleam finally extinguishing under my grip. She was *mine*.

221

"Stop! Wait, you can't kill me! Wait! Please—"

I pursed my lips and blew out a puff of black smoke that trailed across his mouth, cutting off his petulant whines. Of course he would be a whiney, weak fae at the end. That shouldn't surprise me.

"Tell me," I croaked, "how do you make her laugh? I don't want her to lose that." The smoke dissipated from his mouth at my command.

He gasped, "You can't do it! I'm tied to her, Mendax. I'm tied to Caly. I did it to heal her in Unseelie. If you kill me now, you will kill my girl!"

I recoiled, glaring at him in disbelief. I could feel myself going off the edge of sanity.

"No!" I roared, smashing his face into my knee. "You can't—"

"I can and I did. Caly is Artemi, but she has no powers… well, only a tiny amount. I tied my life to hers in Unseelie," he spat, getting the words out as fast as he could. "After you fucking tried to kill her, you piece of shit. You nearly killed my wife!" he shouted with renewed anger as he continued to fight the constraints of smoke around him.

My knuckles cracked across his cheekbone, leaving a smear of golden blood to trail over his tan face. "She is not your wife!" I shouted as the blood pounded through me.

I had to step away from him. I was going to do something I couldn't undo, and I *could not* lose her.

"Aaarrrrggghhh!" I thundered. A shock wave of my power shook the room.

The door banged open, and icy relief doused my hot skin. Whoever was at the door would be taking every drop of rage I had hoped to relieve with Aurelius. They were about to be in a lot of pain.

Walter's shaggy, brown hair popped into the doorframe.

"Mendax! They have alerted the Lumins Army. They are coming for you!" he shouted.

"Good, let them come. My need for relief will likely not be satisfied until I drain the blood of an entire army."

"You ogre! It's not you I worry about. Caly loves Prince Aurelius, Mendax. She has been through more than the both of you will ever understand, and she doesn't deserve this. She has her own reasons for being in Seelie, and if you get in her way, she will retaliate. She already hates you," Walter stated, glancing to Aurelius, tied up with ropes of smoke on the marble floor.

"So you think you understand her better than we do, better than me? Huh, shifter?" I said through clenched teeth.

How much more could a person take? Was this what love was? I wanted to rip my own heart out and put a blade through it.

"I think that I'm the only one here thinking about her and not myself." Walter narrowed his eyes at me. "You have alerted the entire castle that you are alive and that she was unsuccessful in killing you. As far as Seelie is concerned, Caly never completed her task of allegiance and has betrayed the entire realm, and the ones she calls family here. You just doomed the woman you claim to love."

"It seems you have an awful lot of adoration for someone who is not yours, brother." I'm not even certain I said the words out loud before I had him tied in twin ropes of smoke, lying on the floor next to Aurelius.

They both wriggled and strained against their cocoons as I stood over them.

I commanded the smoke to adjust them until they were leaned against the edge of the love seat. My glare attempted to burn a hole through their heads as I tied the ropes tightly behind their backs, restrained legs in front of them.

I needed out of here before I murdered them all. Too much rage still boiled under my skin. I was going to combust if I didn't get it out. Now.

"Apparently, there is still a question of who Calypso belongs to," my rough voice grated out.

Racing heartbeats roiled like a symphony in my head as I walked out the door, leaving Prince Puppet and Walter bound and gagged in the smoking room.

The thud of my boots reverberated across the hallway.

A collection of poorly armored Lumin guards at the far end froze upon seeing me.

I grinned at them and opened my hands, sending a barrage of smoke into the air that twisted and morphed until it formed three antlered wendigos of smog. The demon creatures overtook the guards, easily ripping and tearing into the weak-armored fae.

Screams and grunts rang out around me as I walked, a tendril of rage trailing after me.

I shouldn't be near her yet, but I needed to see her before I left.

My mind strained under the pulsing rage. I whispered out a shield barring anyone from entering the hallway. It wouldn't hold for long, but I didn't need much time.

I shadowed into Calypso's room.

CHAPTER 22

CALY

I PULLED THE THIN TANK TOP OVER MY HEAD, LETTING THE soft, gray fabric of my nightshirt drag against my damp skin.

After our return from the pits, I couldn't help but be angry with myself. Saving Tarani was not my responsibility. I wasn't even supposed to like Eli, but I'd failed there too. Marrying him would make things move so much quicker, but I couldn't. I just couldn't do that to him.

The shower had helped my sore muscles but not my mind.

It wasn't until I burst into my empty room and was hit with the familiar jolt of disappointment that I figured out why.

Walter was waiting in the room for me, alone.

Every time I walked in since Mendax had left, I'd expected to see him talking with Walter on my bed. Had wanted to be with me one final time. I could never bite or scratch Eli in bed. He would know in two seconds what a twisted monster I was, and then he'd leave me too.

I didn't get the feeling Eli was vanilla, but I would bet an entire ocean of tolkiens that he would worry if I told him how dirty I *really* liked it. Still, I couldn't help but wonder what being with Eli would be like. Would it be weird?

A shadow flickered in the bathroom corner, and for a second, I almost looked to see if it was Mendax.

But it wasn't, and it was for the better. He wasn't mine. He wasn't even a friend. He was a problem that needed to be solved. He couldn't be here. Not now. He would ruin everything I had waited my whole life for.

A thought I'd played with reared up: What if I did go to Unseelie? A part of me missed the dark castle, even after all of the horrors that happened while I was there. What if I went there? With Mendax? If anyone could help me, it would be him.

My neck cracked as I bent my head to my shoulder. *No.* This wasn't the time to be sloppy. I would never trust anyone ever again, not fully.

I squeezed my sister's ashes and tucked the pendant back under my shirt, then shook out my folded cotton pants from their heap on the counter.

Sudden warmth ran over my back and down my thighs as someone pressed against me from behind.

I dropped the pants to the floor with a gasp, immediately filling with excitement as Mendax pressed his chest against me and linked his hands over mine on the counter.

"I am leaving you here and returning to Unseelie," Mendax said haughtily into the shell of my ear.

"What? You're leaving?" I mumbled in shock as I turned to face him.

The sharp edge of the counter bit into my ass as he stepped into me, caging me between his hands still resting on the sink. His icy-blue eyes were angry as they trailed up my exposed legs, pausing on the black thong I wore.

"You're disappointed?" He smiled slightly, causing his scarred dimple to crease.

God, he was gorgeous.

"I'm just..." I didn't know what to say. I was very disappointed he was leaving me. Shocker—even he didn't choose me.

"The castle is under attack. The Fallen are too strong now. I need to return," he murmured breathily. "They have gained control of the Ladon dragon and—"

"They have a dragon? But...the castle? Will you—will it be all right?" I asked.

I couldn't hide the feelings that tore through me at everything he just said. What if something happened to him or Walter?

He looked furious, even though I could tell he was fighting to control it. The pulse in his neck tapped wildly. Even his eyes looked like weapons as they glared at me.

I realized his wings were spread.

Uh-oh. That meant one of two things. Danger and power rolled off him like I'd never seen.

My stomach tightened with lust.

"I'll come with you and Walter. Maybe I can help?" I said so softly I wasn't sure I had even made a sound as I stared at the small lines on his lips. *What the fuck am I saying?*

He let out a breath as though it had been trapped inside his chest. "I-I can't take you with me. Not until we get your heart. It's not safe for you to be there. I can't risk something happening to you. You'd be the only one without any powers," he stated.

There it was.

Once again, I was only a weak, powerless fool.

"I can't lose you. You're the only reason I fight. Those thrones belong to us. I will return for you in a week's time."

"No. I'm going with you," I said defiantly. I was so sick of everyone underestimating me.

"You will stay."

"Fuck you. I—" I shouted as the wind was taken from my lungs. He slammed me against the wall and pressed his face down against mine.

"Be *very* careful, little hellhound. I haven't a thread of control left, and I'm contemplating killing you as we speak. If I am unable to have you all to myself, then maybe no one should have you," he rasped.

"You know I'm tied to Eli?" I breathed.

He smiled a cruel smile before he roughly lifted me up and over his shoulder, carrying me out of the bathroom. The door slammed against the bedroom wall, knocking the painting down as he carried me through the room and into the hallway.

"Where are you taking me?" I snapped.

I was a little frightened of him like this. He was coming undone, and he wasn't just anyone. He was a Smoke Slayer with the ability to slither inside of your mind. At his core, he was a predator, and he always would be. When you are at the top of the food chain, everyone else is prey. The question was simply when he would get tired of playing with you, not if—never if.

I didn't know if he was about to fuck me or kill me, and at this point, one might cause the other. Regardless, I wasn't going to go down easily—for either of them. What fun was that?

I reeled back and punched him in the back as hard as I could.

"If you're thinking about fighting me, don't. I am not Aurelius. I *will* hurt you, and I *will* like it. Be a good girl, and later I'll give you a knife to stab me with. You know how much that turns me on, hellhound," his husky voice rumbled.

That was where I had stabbed him before. The thought sent a shiver coursing down my spine. I knew Mendax felt it too by the way his hand tightened over the back of my thigh.

Not once had I ever truly wanted him dead, but that didn't mean I wouldn't kill him. There were a lot of people dead who I wished were still alive and with me. What I really wanted was to tell him all my dirty little secrets and light the heavens on fire after he handed me the lighter—but I couldn't. I wouldn't.

I just couldn't trust him. That was the problem with villains: you could *never* trust them.

Muffled groans and cries caught my attention.

What the hell?

A hazy wall at both ends of the hallway blocked a small army of Seelie guards from stepping any closer, but they were trying. Shouts and bangs echoed back and forth as each end fought to break down the barricade.

My stomach dropped. "They know you're here? What— what happened? Where is Eli?" I asked, gripping his wings in a panic.

He stilled immediately.

Smoke, barely visible, rose from my palms and melted into the smoke of his wings, which had begun to whorl and coil over my hands and arms like a sensual caress.

Somehow time stopped.

The next moment I blinked, and my thighs were wrapped around Mendax's waist, my back pressed against the hall wall. The Unseelie prince shackled just below my jaw with his large hand.

He was fast.

"What happened is you infected my soul and placed yourself in an exceedingly dangerous position. The sole person I would ignite the entire world for is tied to the one person I would give an entire world to burn."

He pressed his body into me so hard, it was difficult to think. Icy-blue eyes glowered down at me, causing the small scar above his brow to crease slightly.

Like always with Mendax, tension pulsed low in my stomach as I homed in on the feel of him pressed against me. It was impossible to think about anything but how deep he could fuck me at this angle.

I was broken and dark, and that just proved it.

Horror washed over me when I saw the Seelie guards again. Every one of them paused to watch the dark prince pin me against the wall. They would think we were working together to betray Seelie.

"Get off of me. Is this all payback for what happened in Unseelie? Well, congratulations, you have just ruined everything. All that I've worked for is ruined because of you. They'll kill me before I can get even get to him. You have no idea what you've just cost me!" I screamed, pushing my throat against this hand as hard as I could.

His face showed no hint of remorse as the creases of his eyes wrinkled slightly. "Pet, if you think I've ruined your life, you don't give me enough credit. Things are just getting started." Mendax tightened his grip around my throat, squeezing out air as he leaned down to brush my ear with his mouth. "And I promise you, there is no other threat to your life. I will be the only one that kills you."

My eyes ping-ponged between his face and the guards to my left.

"What's the matter? Afraid they'll see me do this? You belong to me now. You are my possession." He moved the tips of his fingers over my mandible and angled it toward him. The hand not on my jaw squeezed my ass.

My eyes darted to the guards. There was no getting out of this alive.

Mendax squeezed my face as his mouth hovered barely an inch from mine. His hand trembled slightly, and I got the feeling it was because he was trying not to snap my neck.

He pressed his mouth to mine in a devouring kiss, still holding my face.

There was probably a puddle beneath me, I was so wet.

He pulled back and turned my face to the side, toward the guards, as he pressed his mouth to my ear. "*No one* touches my possessions without consequence."

He licked the side of my face with one long swipe before he turned my face back to him. Unbridled rage twinkled and danced in his pale eyes, causing me to question just how far he had been pushed this time. I'd never seen him as ready to strike out as he was now. He looked absolutely feral.

Malum Mendax had snapped.

"Where is Eli?" I asked again, suddenly a lot more worried.

I was alive, so I guessed he was too, but that didn't bring

me any comfort considering the look on Mendax's face right now.

He grabbed me around the waist, tucking me under his arm, into his side, as if I were a sack of potatoes, and carried me down the hallway until we entered the smoking room. He kicked the door with his large black boots, sending it ricocheting off the wall before loudly slamming it closed once he had stepped through.

The angry fae carried me past a large set of mahogany shelves lining the back wall before he dumped me on the ground.

I didn't trust him at my back right now, not like this. Refusing to take my eyes off him, I watched nervously as he picked up a decanter from the dark wood bar and poured a glass to the brim with deep-purple liquid.

"You couldn't have at least let me grab pants?" I grumbled as I clamored back onto my feet.

"You won't need those," he stated, casually moving to hand me the purple drink and return to pour himself another. "You will, however, need this," he said with a sinister smile.

"You should find a new drinking buddy. I'm not interested. All hell is breaking loose out there," I bit out, angrily pointing to the hallway.

"You've got it all wrong, pet. Hell is in here, where the devil is." He winked. "Last chance to drink your mead," his gravelly voice purred as he walked past me.

In my brief encounter with the libation, faerie mead had made me do some wild things—including dry humping my best friend.

Pounding and mumbles caught my ears.

The Seelie guards must have been getting closer to breaking through the barrier. It would only be minutes before they entered and I was killed, taking Eli with me. It had all been for nothing.

My nails clicked against the glass before I tipped back the pretty liquid, draining the glass.

I would need it.

I turned to Mendax.

He had positioned himself on a small leather love seat with legs spread wide and an arm draped casually over the back like he owned the castle and everything in it.

And then I saw them.

Eli and Walter sat on the ground, bound and gagged with familiar black smoke. Their backs leaned up against the small sofa positioned at a ninety-degree angle from its twin. The one in which Mendax leisurely sat in.

Eli struggled and fought to undo his bindings; his wide eyes stared at me in pure horror. Walter looked more relaxed, not moving except to lock eyes on Mendax with irritation. Whatever was happening didn't seem like it was a surprise to Walter, who knew his cousin far better than any of us. I noticed that both he and Eli didn't shift into their animal forms to get away. Whether they were unable to or they simply knew better than to try was beyond my knowledge.

I clamped my mouth shut, turned around, and walked back to the counter to pick the glass decanter up. Popping the top out, I lifted it to my lips and proceeded to gulp down several huge swigs of the liquid.

"Kiss me," Mendax ordered, his low, rumbly command rippling across the stale room.

"Get fucked," I fired back, setting the decanter back down. Already, I could feel the faerie mead's effects lighting every nerve in my body. What did it matter now?

"You first," Mendax purred while taking a drink.

I moved past the umbra of darkness to kneel beside Eli, giving Walter's thigh a gentle squeeze. The shifter had become something different to me over the past few weeks. It felt like he was the only one who heard me sometimes. Foolishly and for reasons I couldn't explain, I had let Walter inside my solitary box of demons. I had shared everything with him. He was the only person I'd ever told my plan. I cried on his chest the whole night. Snuggling with him in his wolf form

232

had been one of the most enjoyable and comforting things I'd ever done.

Eli grunted in pain, folding forward. My gasp cut like a knife through the room. Ribbons of charcoal cut into the skin of his neck, tightening as his face paled.

"Stop it! You're killing him!" I shrieked, holding on to Eli's broad shoulders.

My skin heated and prickled all over. Whether it was the effects of the faerie mead or the fact that Mendax was killing me right alongside Eli, I couldn't say.

"You're going to kill us both! Is that what you want?" I screamed. Frantically, I struggled to pull the smoke away from Eli's throat, but my attempts only appeared to be make it tighter.

"Kiss me," Mendax commanded.

His voice was calm, but that was the only thing about him that appeared relaxed. Blue eyes watched me like a hawk while his body pulsed with thinly veiled rage. The tension and power surrounded him like a heavy cloud. His eyes were locked on where my hand touched Eli's chest.

This was nothing but a dick-measuring competition. Was this because he had to leave me, or had something else happened?

A *thud* filled the room as Eli's body fell to the carpet.

"Enough. Stop this," I screamed, trying to hold Eli's limp body up. "You sick fucking psycho, stop. Please!"

Walter closed his eyes, and a strained snarl escaped his lips; he was obviously in pain as well.

"You are, aren't you? You're killing all three of us," I said, a heaviness in my own chest.

He couldn't. I wouldn't let him hurt them like this.

Hysterical, I ran to where Mendax reclined and hurled my fists repeatedly into his hard chest until I fell to the ground between his knees, now fighting for breath as I continued to try to whale on him.

Eli and I were barely clinging to life.

"*Kiss me*," his deep voice rumbled as he leaned forward, his face now only a breath away from mine.

If my eyes alone could have killed him, they would have in that moment. But I was in no position to be stubborn right now, and unfortunately, I always wanted to kiss him.

My hand struggled to grasp the black tunic stretched across his chest, but I pressed my mouth to his. I couldn't believe I was kissing him while Eli lay crumpled and dying.

Immediately, my senses filled with the woody taste of spiced smoke sweetened with mead. As soon as our skin touched, a storm erupted inside of me. I felt invincible.

Loud gasps filled the air to our right, and I pulled away, seeing Eli had regained consciousness and Walter's warm eyes were open, giving Mendax an angry glare.

"This is a game to you," I whispered, still holding on to his shirt. "Our lives mean absolutely nothing to you."

Wood splintered and cracked as Mendax moved his hand from the now-crushed armrest of the seat.

"Your life," he said, leaning back once more, "and death mean more to me than *anything*. Because of that, I must leave you here." In his other hand, the drinking glass shattered with a high-pitched crunch. Obsidian blood dripped between his fingers as he dropped the bloody shards to the floor.

The broken pieces of my heart clenched.

He didn't want me to get hurt in Unseelie, but leaving me behind with Eli and being unable to kill him was making him crack.

All the more reason why I couldn't be with him. Ever.

"Mendax, you and I, we couldn't… We would never work," I said, still kneeling in a tank top and thong between his strong legs.

It didn't matter what I really wanted—it had to be this way. He had to leave me alone; he'd already messed everything up.

Eli had chosen to tie himself to me. He even knew where my heart was located. I hated to do this to him, but he would have to help me finish things. God, would he hate me once this was all over with. This was what I deserved for falling for him when we were kids. I never should have let anyone get that close.

"Mendax, in some other lifetime—"

"Stop talking and use that sinful mouth for wiser things," Mendax ordered.

"What don't you get?" I asked, shocked by both his words and the way my body ignited lasciviously at his order. The mead was definitely doing something. "Leave me here, and don't come back. Move on, Mendax. I have nothing for you. *I* am nothing. You have been bonded; you can become king now! Why do you waste your time with me? I am a weak, powerless monster," I screamed, wiping tears away with the back of my hand.

Mendax slid himself down from the couch until he was eye level with me, cupping my face in his palms.

"What do you not understand, Calypso? I will lie, cheat, steal, and kill just to be close enough so I can taste the spent breath from your lungs. You are my only soul. Without you, I am merely a hollow cavity of flesh, a ghoul that will haunt and track your every step and gambit. Whether you accept it or not, you and I belong together. No two creatures were ever made more perfectly for one another," he whispered against my lips while his hands held my face tightly.

"I can't be with you. I have to be a good person—a true Seelie. I have to be able to enter the Elysian Fields! Unseelie go to Tartarus when they die—I can't go to Tartarus. I love Eli, but I think I'm somehow in love with you," I blubbered as hot tears poured down my cheeks and over his hands. "I can be a good person, you can't. You are the Unseelie prince, for sun's sake! I need to end up with someone like Eli."

Standing up, he brushed the shattered bits of glass from his black pants. Both of his irises were blown now; muscles pulsed and flared in his jaw, causing him to appear more tense than he was before.

Pushing onto my feet, I snagged Walter's eyes. He gave a small nod of reassurance. I stepped closer, afraid to look at Eli. We could carry an entire conversation without words, and I was scared to death to see what his eyes were saying now.

I froze when the husky voice rolled over me.

"So you're a good person and you end up with someone like Eli? Is that right? The hero?" he questioned. Reclining on the sofa again, his muscular legs parted, his arm stretched along the back.

"I—"

"Well, *good girl*, come get on your knees. Your good guy is about to watch the bad guy slide his cock down your throat." He swiped his thumb across his full lower lip with a devilish smirk. Blood from his lip smeared across his shadowed face. "Every man in this room knows you want it. Don't waste time pretending otherwise."

My eyes rounded in shock. "Fuck—"

"Do it now, or I'll kill Aurelius," he cut me off.

Everything in the room stilled until my thundering heart was the only thing I could hear. Mendax meant every word, and all of us could feel it.

Eli shifted slightly in the corner of my eye when I slowly stepped between Mendax's legs. A quick glance at Walter and Eli caused my cheeks to redden when my knees landed on the cold marble. Heat washed over me as I touched the warm closure of Mendax's belt.

Walter turned his head away. My eyes snapped to Eli's. His handsome face was full of intensity and frustration. The chivalrous gaze almost concealed the lust in his eyes when they took in my nearly naked body kneeling before Mendax.

Walter looked back when I fumbled with the leather belt before pulling it all the way off. Folding it, I moved to tuck it under the sofa. Later, I would use it to choke Mendax for what he was—

"Give me the belt." Mendax grinned, removing it from my hands.

I wasn't sure if the faerie mead was to blame for my reaction when I saw Walter's and Eli's eyes hungrily looking at me, but I had to clench my thighs together for fear they could see the effect it had on me.

The guards down the hall continued to yell and fight against the shield; they could barge in at any second. It made me feel...dangerous.

Wanted.

Free.

I tied my hair up in a knot on top of my head and nervously lifted my eyes up to Mendax's while I timidly ran my palm over his crotch. Feeling the hard outline of his cock under my hand caused me to squeeze my thighs together again and hope no one noticed.

But every eye in the room watched me.

It was perfect.

Feeling more confident now, I pulled down his pants until his thick cock sprung free.

My hand wrapped around his shaft, feeling the warm veins and soft, velvety skin rub against my palm. The tip was rosier. A droplet of pre-cum glistened under the dim lamps of the smoke-filled room.

Greedily, my palm moved up and down the length of him.

"I said your throat."

My eyes darted to the left to see he had removed the smoke from Walter's and Eli's mouths. It looked like they hadn't noticed that their mouths were unrestrained, as they were simply hanging open. Their hungry eyes were busy watching me.

My eyes flicked back to Mendax, and I wondered if he realized the smoke was off their mouths, but his amused eyes answered me.

Watch how they hunger for you. We are infatuated with you.

A sharp breath cut through my lungs at Mendax speaking through the bond.

Powered by curiosity and horniness, I licked my lips and moved them over Mendax, covering his shaft with my mouth until I gagged. I hadn't taken all of him, and I doubted I could. But suns, did I want to unravel him.

A hand brushed the base of my neck, sending chills across my skin. He gathered the few locks in his hand with the rest of my hair. The action sent a million tiny tingles all over my scalp and body as I slid my mouth back down his length.

I grew more and more eager, nearly forgetting anyone else was in the room. Mendax's small, almost inaudible moans made me suck and hum deeper, with the hopes of causing another one.

"You are everything to me, Caly," Mendax said through a shortened breath, his hand pulling at my hair. "I'm going to be rougher with you, pet. Will you be a good girl and take it?"

I pulled my mouth free from his cock to shoot him a challenging glare. I nodded, maintaining eye contact with him while I spit on the head of his cock and slurped my mouth around him, watching him hiss and curse when I lightly dragged my teeth along his sensitive skin.

His hand tightened painfully around my hair, holding my head in place as he fucked my throat. I struggled to breathe, gagging as my eyes watered and tears ran down my face.

"She is not yours, Aurelius. She will never be yours. For eternity, she is only mine." He let out a breathy heave of air while he continued thrusting into my throat. "Do you see how divinely she takes me, Walter?" he growled breathily. "It's because she is fit perfectly for me every way. Can you see how flawless she is? Her throat was made to fit my cock. If you ever so much as think about doing something to ruin that, I will rip out your throat, brother or not."

Mendax tugged my head back, away from him, and his cock pulled out of my mouth with a wet pop.

"Lay back," he rasped. "Remove the rest of your clothes and lean against that chair." He nodded slowly to a wing-backed chair, diagonal to the sofa the men leaned against.

"I—"

"Now, pet. I can't hold the guards forever, and I still need to make certain a few things are understood before I leave you." He peeled his gaze from me to focus on Eli while he tucked himself back into his pants, leaving them undone, so his still-hard cock was barely concealed.

Eli glared back at him in a silent challenge. The corner of Mendax's mouth quirked up into a self-assured grin.

"You will never be able to deter me from loving her. Without killing the both of us, you will never *ever* be able to tear us apart from one another. Our tie is as unbreakable as my love for her." Eli clenched his jaw as he looked to me. "And I don't need to make an embarrassment of her to prove that."

I flinched. My nails dug into my palms until they bent, shame tingling my cheeks for having experienced any pleasure at what was happening, embarrassed that I had somehow let my untamed bits and pieces peek out in front of him. I didn't want Eli or Walter to think of me that way. I wanted to be good and wholesome in their eyes—not the broken, empty murderer I really was.

I needed to officially be deemed Seelie.

Embarrassment and shame tried to take me, but the faerie mead drowned it in a pool of need, leaving me only with a throbbing ache between my thighs.

Power.

An embarrassment. Eli's words echoed in my head.

My eyes snapped to Mendax, who was watching me with a tight smile.

You need to learn as much as they do the power you hold over them...over me. I will not leave you here without me until they understand—you are the one in control while I am gone.

They are both fighters. They will respect and bow to your every whim and command if you dominate them.

They have no control over you or anything that you do.

Butterflies tickled my insides.

The beat of the guards pounding down the walls of the hallway felt like the heavy beat of drums.

To Walter and Eli, it appeared that he was claiming and dominating me, but he wasn't—at least not entirely. He was showing me how much power I held without actually possessing any powers.

Mendax let out an arrogant chuckle. "For being her best friend, you really don't know her at all."

My neck cracked, it had snapped back to look at Mendax so quickly. He calmed my hazy worry with a knowing wink.

"Yes, she's always laughing and smiling with you, isn't she? Oh no, wait. That's me," Eli bit out. "You bring her only anger and pain. She'll get tired of that real quick."

Mendax's wings flared, sending a haze of smoke tumbling through the room. Eli's bindings cinched, causing him to let out a groan.

"We get the point, brother," Walter grumbled, sounding bored. "We will not touch her. Now recall your smoke, and we will return to Unseelie. They are in need of us."

"Calypso, I advise you to take your clothes off before I tear them off," Mendax snarled, keeping his eyes on Walter.

I peeled off my shirt; my sister's pendant swayed across my chest. My nipples pulled tight at the cold air and hungry eyes.

"Walter, you will stay and protect her. I'm unsure how Queen Saracen will retaliate knowing that Caly didn't kill me. I need you to keep her safe. You're the only one I *almost* trust." Mendax's voice softened while he slowly looked my body over.

"What do you expect me to do, Mendax? Be her cellmate again? She is as good as dead here now that they think she betrayed them, and you know it," Walter spat.

"Do anything necessary. A dungeon cell might keep her safe and alive. I will handle everything else when I return. Make *certain* she is not hurt."

Mendax turned to me. "My queen, touch yourself while we watch. Our attention is fully yours."

Completely naked, save for the ashes of Adrianna that hung from my neck, I stood fully on display in front of the three handsome fae.

With confidence, I sat down in front of the large wing-backed chair, feeling the soft fabric brush my back. The pounding rhythm of the guards' efforts and the heavy breathing of the men poured into my ears in a sensual song. Even the small *tink* of my necklace shifting around on its chain lent its own erotic harmony. It felt so good to sway my hips to the song, slowly rolling my body like one long wave while my fingertips inched down the front and sides of my breast and stomach. I watched all of their darkening eyes while my hands caressed over my stomach once more, this time dipping down between my legs.

Every place their eyes touched, my body felt it like a pair of hands gliding over my skin.

Mendax leaned back farther onto the couch, letting out a low hum of approval while he freed himself from his undone pants, grabbing his cock roughly, his eyes boring into my skin.

"Isn't my queen fucking beautiful, Aurelius? Walter?" said the Unseelie prince hoarsely. "She is the *only* thing of value for any of us now, do you understand? To you, she is *everything*, and you will stop at nothing to keep her out of harm's way."

"Of course, but—" Eli spat.

"Come on, pet, don't be shy now. Spread your legs and let us look at the sacred cunt we all worship," Mendax cut in.

I pointed my toes on the floor and spread my knees wide, eager to see Eli's shocked reaction. He had only ever thought of me as a gentle, delicate girl and was always trying to shelter and protect me. I wondered if his thoughts had changed now.

My eyes trailed up the well-built body of my best friend and met Eli's heavy stare. I had expected to see him shocked and embarrassed as he watched me touch myself, but instead, his face looked rigid, angry, and *full* of lust—like he was having a difficult time not touching me.

Holy, fiery suns.

I didn't think I could get more turned on than I was that second.

"She's worth everything. Isn't she, Aurelius?" Mendax's gravelly voice ripped into the tense room, the words spoken with a sharp and dangerous edge.

Aurelius nodded, moving his eyes from me to shoot a deadly look at Mendax.

"Let her actions feed your lustful eyes and my warning fill your thick skulls: Should either one of you touch what is mine while I am gone, it will be the most regrettable decision of your short life. That I promise you. As for you, Aurelius." He paused for a moment, struggling to speak through a snarl. "I swear to the stars, even if I can't kill you, you will wish I had," Mendax growled.

A low moan slipped out of me as my fingers continued their task. Mendax was evil; there was no doubting that, but having my hero, my villain, and my most trusted companion watch hungrily as I touched myself was making me melt in a puddle of arousal.

All I had ever wanted was for someone to love me and never leave, someone to protect and care for me without overlooking what I was capable of on my own.

Right now, I had three someones. Through the cloud of lust, I realized how incredible that was.

"Tell her how beautiful she looks, Walter," Mendax whispered, though there was no mistaking this as a command.

"She—ugh—you're beautiful, Caly. I think we should leave, Mendax?" Walter said with a polite nod.

"Look at how he watches with hungry eyes, pet. I want you to crawl over there and give Aurelius a taste of what's mine," he said with a demented smirk.

The dimples popped on both of his cheeks.

A shiver crept up the back of my neck, and my mouth fell open. Was this a trap? Mendax was far too possessive to allow another man, especially his enemy, to touch what he thought was his.

242

My insides swayed with a foreign, euphoric feeling while my curiosity grew. Was he testing us for some reason? Was this really just to see how I reacted with them? I didn't know, but I wanted to see both of their reactions when I did it.

The polished floor squeaked, tugging against the skin of my leg as I slowly crawled to where Eli was bound.

"Seriously? You are so fucked up." Walter shook his head at Mendax with a scowl.

Mendax canted his head to the side and gave a wolfish smile.

What was he going to do if I touched Eli right now? I didn't want Mendax to hurt him…or me.

"Go on, straddle him, love. He's all tied up. He can't hurt you," Mendax chuckled, knowing that wasn't a deterrent for me.

Euphoria clouded my reasoning. In the back of my mind somewhere, I *knew* I shouldn't be doing this, especially not with Eli and most certainly not right in front of a tense, raging Unseelie on a hair-trigger, ready to kill every one of us.

My eyes caught Eli's, and I hoped to gauge what was going on in his mind, but his eyes had locked on the ceiling. I bit my lip hard, the painful pinch causing me to let out a sigh as pleasure tingled over my mouth. The tang of blood should have grounded me a little, but unfortunately it only made me more aroused.

Hearing a rumble of appreciation, I snapped my gaze to Mendax.

"I knew you were made for me," he said joyously. He stood up, fastening his pants as he walked over to the bar and poured another glass of mead, then took a long drink.

"On fae, mead makes them calmer, removes some of their stress or anxieties. But non-fae, especially humans or those without powers to absorb the magic, they get encouragement for the things they stifle. Many of them die because they can't stop dancing, and it kills them." He held up the glass with a wink. "It brings out their natural…more primal desires, if they have any. You may have the half of your heart with no powers, but it is still an exceptionally fiery half, it seems."

I turned back to Eli, who was still staring at the ceiling. Suddenly I hated that he wouldn't look at me—even though I was touching his thigh, and it was probably a trap. I also hated how much Mendax thought he knew me.

Determined to spite them both, I threw my leg over Eli and seated myself on his lap, tightening my knees against his hips. My fingers felt the warmth of his skin through his thin white shirt. He tightened his jaw, still refusing to look at me. I wanted him to look at me. I wanted to feel his eyes on mine.

I knew it wasn't because he didn't want me. I could feel his hard length pressing through his pants against me.

"This is your chance, Aurelius. She's all yours," Mendax said as the binds of smoke evaporated from around Eli's body, freeing him completely.

"Do. Not. Touch. Her." Walter bit out the quiet warning to Eli as he continued to glower at Mendax.

Suddenly filled with nerves, I pulled my hands back from Eli's solid chest and turned my head to look at Mendax.

"I don't—"

Mendax's body turned to black smoke, disappearing from where he sat, before reappearing so close, my bare back pressed against his legs. I gasped as he fisted the back of my hair, wrenching my neck so that I was looking straight up at him.

"So you are aware as well, this will also be the *only* time you are ever allowed to touch him again, so you might as well get it out of your system now, pet," he purred before lifting his glass to his lips. "Perhaps you need another drink."

My neck wrenched farther back. I could feel the tingle and pulse of every hair on my head as he bent to tower over me, where I kneeled on Eli. Mendax's sky-blue eyes and evil mouth were only a few inches above mine. He lowered his bottom lip, and cold mead poured from his mouth into mine. I fought to swallow with my neck at this angle and began to choke and gasp for air before he finally let go of my hair. I straightened, swallowing the remnants while sending streams of purple liquid down the front of my bare chest and splashing on Eli.

"Let him have a taste," Mendax laughed as he returned to the couch, looking maniacal and devious.

I ran my fingers over the dribbles of mead on my chest, then down over top of my sensitive clit, rolling my hips when my fingers made contact. Eli's length pulsed underneath me, causing me to groan.

"Eli," I whispered.

Softly, I grabbed his face with my left hand in the hopes he would look at me. Movement caught my eye when his hands flexed at his side, still looking at the ceiling.

"*Trust me, friend.* Don't do it, no matter how badly you want to," Walter warned again sternly.

I pulled my two fingers from inside myself and lifted them to Eli's handsome mouth, pressing them inside.

His eyes flickered closed and his hips bucked ever so slightly. He grabbed my wrist, keeping it in place while the other went around the small of my back and pulled me against him. He swirled his hot tongue around my fingers with a soft groan. Eli's face was now only a breath away from my own.

"You don't have to do a *thing* he says, Calypso, and you also have no worry from tempting me. Not a sundown has come in this castle that I haven't been tempted by you and not acted upon it. I swear to the Ancients, I will do nothing that will put you in danger, and I will get us both out of here," he whispered, finally looking into my eyes while holding his hands up in surrender.

The energy in the room tensed as Mendax and Eli locked eyes.

"You may experience the fire of Caly's love now, but you've only just fallen." Eli's gaze turned to mine. "I've been burning for years. I can take the heat."

Straddling him in all my nakedness, my jaw dropped.

Eli was my hero; he always had been.

Mendax was my villain, and he always would be.

Deep down, I knew I loved them both. But the problem was, who was I? Did I belong to the night or the sun? Was I a hero or a villain?

Stunned, I glanced to Walter, still tied next to Eli.

"Don't look at me," Walter responded with a sparkle in his eyes. "The Artemi ancestors created my entire lineage. You are almost a goddess to me, and I love you in a powerful way. I respect you far more than these two *ever* could—but if you willingly sit naked on my lap right now, Mendax will have to kill me for what I'd do to you." He grinned.

My panicked eyes shot to Mendax while my horny brain tried and failed to form a plan that could keep Walter and Eli safe.

"Don't worry," Walter replied softly. "Mendax already knows this. He also knows I'm as loyal as a—well, wolf—and I'm not the one you really want. My desire is to be a source of friendship and to bring you a sense of comfort and—I don't know—home when you need it. You never have to *be* anyone around me, and I will always be here for you. Even when it's the angry you or the imperfect you. I will always be here for *you*."

Even with faerie mead pulsing through my veins, my cheeks heated at both of their admissions. I shifted myself off of Eli's lap.

Still untied, Eli reached out in a flash and grabbed a large shard off the floor where Mendax had shattered his glass.

Worry shot into me watching Mendax's wings widen from their slacked position.

I moved between the two of them, even though that was arguably more dangerous. Eli tossed the jagged glass to me just as the smoke returned to overlap and tighten around his body, leaving only his head free from the full cocoon of smoke.

My training was so ingrained that I immediately snagged the glass and was about to whip around and face the dominating man behind me, but before I could turn, he was on me, pressing firmly against my bare back.

Through the delirium of lust and mead, my years of brutal training lay in wait and the hand not holding the glass came up to block my throat as something moved over my head.

Mendax's belt.

I tried to shove my forearm out to loosen the restraint, but he was too strong. He pulled the belt tighter so that my left wrist was now pulled against my neck painfully, yanking me back against him. Delicious tingles prickled around my neck and coursed down my body, brimming with such potent ecstasy, my teeth chattered.

Fighting against the intense pulsing between my thighs, I remembered the glass in my free hand and moved it down to stab his side. Mendax grabbed my wrist with the hand not holding the belt.

"So their words affected you?" he murmured into the crook of my neck.

A sharp pull of the belt forced me to gurgle and gasp. He pulled my earlobe into his mouth, dragging me backward until we were at the edge of the love seat.

I pushed my wrist away from my neck, and I felt the belt slacken slightly.

"Enough. This has gone too far. You have toyed with me enough, Mendax. Release us *now*, or I will carve your flesh into a chessboard and challenge Eli to a match," I snarled.

I was fighting it but was more turned on now than before, and I had a suspicion it had nothing to do with the mead.

"Do you know the primary difference between a hero and a villain?" His warm breath brushed my ear. "The hero refuses to cause pain when given the choice, but the villain," he rasped as he dropped hold of the belt and spun me around to face him, still holding my wrist. "The villain knows pain only allows for more pleasure."

He held my wrist tightly, no doubt leaving a mark on my skin, pulling me down to him while he returned to his

247

favored seat. Gracelessly, I fell onto him chest first, tossing my thigh over his lap and straddling him to gain any footing and recover my upper half. My intent was strong; I was filled with determination—but as soon as my bare, throbbing skin brushed against his barely clothed length, I stopped thinking completely.

This close, his whole visage was hostile and blanketed with grim captivation.

I could feel the firmness of his desire nearly parting me. At this angle, there was no possibility of hiding how turned on I was. I'd likely already left a wet spot on his pants.

Mendax moved my wrist until it was at his throat and pressed it firmly against the top of his black tunic. The glass I had previously refused and now couldn't drop was forced against his skin, pressing out a few small beads of black blood. My mind swirled like a hurricane, while my tongue felt dry from panting. He shifted slightly, his hardness brushed against my bare center again, and it took every grain of fight in me not to roll against it.

"Do it. Carve the flesh that makes you feel everything you wish it didn't," he whispered.

"I've stabbed you twice already. Do you really want to play a game of chicken with me, Prince?" I said huskily, wishing it was from the belt still hanging from my neck and not arousal.

His eyes darkened, glistening with so much danger, I could hardly find the blue. Pushing my wrist down, he slowly dragged the glass down the front of his chest, slicing open his shirt and a shallow layer of his skin.

I grimaced and tried to pull my hand away, but he continued his ministrations until his muscular chest was under my palm instead of the shirt.

"I'll eagerly die loving you, Calypso," he said, grasping my hip and pulling me forward so the base of his cock pressed against me.

My eyes rolled to the back of my head, as it felt like a thousand sparklers had ignited inside me. A moan escaped

248

my throat and I rocked forward, the tip of his velvety skin cresting his pants to tease my wetness.

"I—gods, I am in love with you, Mendax," I panted, completely lost to the ecstasy.

He swore while grasping both my hips, lifting me just enough to free his hard cock.

"Yes!"

I cried out in pain and pleasure, feeling a thousand tingles enrapture my body when he pushed inside of me. Lost in the feeling of him sliding deeper into me, I hadn't realized I was still squeezing the glass until red blood dripped down my wrist and Mendax's chest, where the sharp edge had sliced into my hand.

"I will return for you," he whispered. "From the deepest corner of Tartarus, I would return for you."

I continued to ride him, experiencing the euphoria of fully letting myself go. "I won't be able to go with you then either," I muttered with a smile.

"You will," he grunted, closing his eyes as his head fell back against the sofa.

"Oh god, Mendax."

A symphony erupted in the room. Everything twinkled and faded around me as the strongest orgasm of my life rippled over me like an atomic bomb.

"That's it, beautiful." He quickened his pace. "Remind them who you belong to."

His hands tightened on my hips, holding them against him, moaning as he came inside me. I felt his cock pulse as hot cum filled me.

The dark prince groaned when he pulled out of me. His cum dripped out and down the inside of my leg, and he moved his hand to catch it, wiping it up with his fingers and rubbing it all over my pussy. His palm massaged the spent cum all over me until I was gripping his shoulders and moaning.

"Come all over my hand like a good girl—that's it."

Another orgasm slammed through me while he continued to rub his cum back into my sex.

With his other arm, he gently moved me from his lap onto the couch, kissing my forehead as he stood.

Mendax walked over to where Eli sat bound and gagged.

Embarrassment reddened my cheeks when I realized he had been so close and angled against the chair so he couldn't look away as Mendax and I fucked.

The ribbon of smoke was removed from his mouth as Mendax stood over him with a smile.

"I'll ki—" But it was all Aurelius got out the second his mouth was free before Mendax cut him off by roughly grasping Eli's jaw, wrenching it open, and smearing his cum-soaked hand aggressively onto Eli's face, shoving him backward with the force.

"Have a taste of that too, sunshine. Taste me all over her now? That's the only way it'll ever be from now on, so fuck off."

He turned to Walter and released his smoke from the shifter. "Walter, find her heart. I will return once Unseelie is safe. As of now, we will work together to keep her safe." He scowled at Eli. "Hear my words, Seelie, because it will be the only warning I give you: Calypso is mine and mine alone. Whatever demon, god, or witch I need to find to sever your tie to Caly, I will. Know that the *instant* I can kill you without it affecting her, you are dead."

Mendax shadowed in front of me, lifting me into a tight embrace and kissing me tenderly on the mouth. "Until I see you again."

He tightened his squeeze on me for a moment before giving Eli and Walter a hard look and fading into a cloud of black smoke, taking with it Eli's bindings.

The halls thundered with movement, and the door was blasted open with a ball of orange light.

The guards had come to kill me.

CHAPTER 23

CALY

PRESENT DAY

W E NEED TO SPEAK WITH MY MOTHER BEFORE THIS GETS out of hand."

Eli had been pacing continuously ever since we had arrived in the queen's chambers. Walter, ever the shifter, had returned to his rat form and escaped the guards, continuing his quest for my heart.

"I would definitely say this is already pretty out of hand," I mumbled, still feeling the aftereffects of embarrassment at what had happened in the smoke room.

The Seelie guards at the back of the brightly lit room stood as still as statues. Every time I took a step near Eli, they swayed, ready to pounce.

When the guards had swarmed into the smoking room, I had been prepared to be killed on sight. I had been too afraid to look at Eli after what had just happened, assuming he would probably welcome my death by then. In his eyes, it would likely be preferable to being tied to me.

Instead, Eli had run in front of me protectively and, to my amazement, spread his wings to hide my naked body from the guards, allowing me to keep my dignity somewhat while he unbuttoned his mead-splattered shirt and tossed it over his shoulder to me.

Even when the guards had demanded they take me, Eli had taken my hand and walked with me to the queen's chambers.

I couldn't help but think everything could have been so much easier had I not made out with the enemy in front of the guards. Though it wouldn't have changed the fact that they knew I'd not killed Mendax.

"You should leave. If you stay, your mother will think you are a part of this," I whispered.

"There is nothing to be a part of. You tried to kill the Unseelie prince as ordered and failed. We have been trying to kill him for ages and have all failed. It was foolish of her to think you could kill him without powers anyway. If anyone is to blame, it is her for giving you such an outlandish test of loyalty," Eli grumbled as he paced in front of a large mahogany desk.

"I don't think that's what's going to be the problem," I mumbled.

Eli plopped down to his knees in front of my chair, grabbing the armrests and making me jump.

"I'll kill them—the guards who saw you with him. No one will ever know."

I rolled my eyes at him. "You and I both know you aren't going to murder an entire army of innocent Seelie," I said.

He deflated slightly. "You know, I'm not as heroic as you apparently think. Which is really a shame, 'cause I quite like the thought of being the one who gets to save you," he said with a small grin.

"I-I'm sorry about what Mendax did to you in there, and I'm sorry you had to see some of that...but I'm not sorry it happened. I know that's probably not what you want to hear. Do you promise you're not hurt?" I questioned.

Eli paused a moment before standing. "Not where you can see it."

With a bang, the double doors slammed open, causing everyone in the room, including the guards, to jump and straighten.

The blond queen strode in with her large monarch wings billowing behind her, more beautiful than any faerie-tale painting I had ever seen.

My heart rate began to rise as it always did when I saw her, while I struggled to swallow the new lump in my throat. I'd only ever seen her wings spread a few times, and none of them were pleasant.

No matter what, I needed to convince her to let me stay until I was a Seelie royal. I had to.

"Your Majesty, I—" I began.

"Is it true?" Queen Saracen slammed her fist into the front of a glass display cabinet behind her desk, shattering the center shelves. The pieces fell to the white marble floor like crushed ice. "Is Tenebris's son, *the Unseelie prince*, still alive? And on my side of the veil?" she shouted.

"She didn't know he was alive. He followed her here—she told me, but I didn't believe her. It's my fault—" Eli took a step toward his mother.

"Leave," Saracen bit out while she stared him down.

"I'd like to stay with Calypso. He tricked and manipulated her. It wasn't her fault!" Eli tried again.

"Guards," she called, keeping her scowl on Eli. "Take my son away from the *traitor* before she poisons his mind more than she already has."

Eli turned toward the guards as they timidly approached him. His wings snapped out as he took a challenging step toward them. The way he towered over them in height and muscle was almost laughable, especially with the power he exuded with his beautiful wings spread.

How did I always manage to get myself into more and more trouble?

"It's fine. You should go. Make sure Tarani is okay," I said softly, still unable to find my voice.

"I suggest you listen, or your fate will be the same as hers," Saracen said from behind the large desk.

Eli's gaze volleyed between the two of us before he gave a small nod and walked toward the door. He stopped at its threshold. "Do not hurt her, or you will regret it, Mother," he stated, not unkindly.

Her white gown rustled as she stood. Her beautiful orange-and-black wings fluttered dangerously.

"Do you think it wise to threaten me, Son?" she challenged.

It felt like even the air in the room stilled.

Eli's gaze hardened. "I'm not threatening you, Mother. I have tied myself to Calypso. Unless you wish to kill me as well, you will not harm her," he said matter-of-factly.

"I don't believe you. You would never be so reckless. Look what she's done!" Saracen's voice began to grow.

Eli nodded respectfully to his mother and me before stepping out of the room, apparently at ease that he had secured our safety.

The queen gave a nod behind Eli, and the guards filed out behind him.

A prickle of unease tickled my neck—I didn't like that they had followed him. Something about it was wrong.

The last sentry left, and the doors closed, locking the silence back in place.

"Clever," Saracen crooned.

"I thought I killed him," I said flatly. "I stabbed him between the wings. He was in a lifeless ball on the dirt when I left."

"Clever of you to bond yourself to the dark prince and tie yourself to the prince of light... Who could hurt you now?" she singsonged, ignoring my previous statement.

"Neither one of those were my choice!" I shouted, feeling the anger rise up.

The queen's eyes dropped to the tips of my fingers, where they had started turning black as lines of smoke caressed my knuckles.

254

She fluttered her wings in an annoyed fashion, pushing the smoke away from her.

"You have two choices now," she stated, still focusing on my hands. "You will either reattempt your task of loyalty and finish the job, or you will be sent to Malvar with the other traitors, where you will pay with eternal suffering for your lies and betrayal. Commander Von is in charge over there. You remember him of course."

Shudders wracked my body hearing his name again. "No," I replied softly.

"No?" She squinted until her pretty face looked like a raisin.

"That's right—no. Had you actually wanted me to succeed and complete my hit on Mendax, you would have told me what I was stepping into. Empower me as an official Seelie right now, and I will do *anything* you ask of me, Saracen."

She stared at me a moment before sitting back down at her desk. Her crinkled-up expression softened slightly under the glow of the ceiling.

"*No one* understands the ease with which one can fall in love with the Unseelie royals like I do," she said. Widening her arms in a stretch, she let a bit of tension roll off her shoulders, tucking her wings away as she looked around the room, as if checking for someone. "You, my dear, will never have the title of a Seelie royal now. Even as a child, you were too devious for your own good. I think it's time you learned some things about our relationship, for after today, I will never see you again."

No.

No. Don't panic and do something stupid. Things could still change. Whatever it is can always change. I can still become a Seelie royal. I can marry Eli.

I was filtering my thoughts and actions so microscopically, it was like time stood still for a moment, like some other version of me was watching.

Fiercely needing comfort, my fingers trembled around my sister's ashes.

"I was madly in love with Mendax's father," the queen continued.

"King Thanes," I whispered, feeling foolish. The multitude of puzzle pieces began to fall into place, answering decades-long questions.

"Never in your life, Calypso, have you seen a pair more in love." She smiled softly as she spoke.

Something in her eyes turned my stomach. "What about your husband? Eli's father?" I asked wearily. The strange glassiness in her eyes warned me to tread carefully.

Her smile faltered, and she stared off into the empty corner. "She killed him," she whispered. "Because of Mendax's mother, I lost everything."

"You forget who you converse with, my queen. You've already told me it was your hand that ended King Felix's life," I reminded her.

"You will kill Queen Tenebris, the Unseelie queen, or you will be killed," she stated sharply.

"I—you can't kill me; I'm tied to Eli. And I can't kill Tenebris." I gripped the chair.

"What is a loyalty task if it doesn't prove one's loyalty?" she bit out. "You want to be a Seelie royal, then kill Tenebris."

"You know I can't kill a Smoke Slayer. I've already proven that. But I know you well enough to believe that even you wouldn't hurt your son," I said.

She smiled so wide, I saw every one of her beautiful, white teeth. "You think you *know* me?" she laughed. "Not even my kingdom knows me. You will wish for your death, child. How long have you and the dark prince been working together?"

"We haven't been working together, Saracen! I thought he was dead! We were bonded—"

"That explains why you still hold his powers," she said, nibbling on her lower lip. "It's a shame they got to you, Calypso, though I can't say I'm surprised. You were always a monstrous little thing. I loved you like my own child—perhaps more than my own children. An unascended Artemi with no one but me and my son?" A frown pulled at the corners of her mouth. "I had imagined you would be powerful, but I was naive to think that your evil could never be turned on me. I had such hopes for us. Too bad you'll be of no use to anyone now."

"You—what?" I thought the faerie mead was mostly out of my system, but I was struggling to make sense of what she was saying. "You don't mean that. You're upset with me, and I'm sorry," I stated firmly. "I messed up, but you can't just kill me because I couldn't complete an impossible task! I have done everything you have ever asked of me just so I could be here with you and Eli and become a Seelie royal. You can't take that away because you sent me to kill a fucking Smoke Slayer and I failed!" I shouted. "Family doesn't do things like that."

"I am not your family, Calypso," Saracen said. "Your family is dead. Their remains disintegrated into the soil after the crash. You have nothing and no one, and do you know why? Because fate gifted me an opportunity, and I took it. I killed your little human family," she said.

I was trembling. Hearing her words made my insides fill with explosive, hair-trigger anger. "Why did you have to kill them? Why not just steal me away?"

Flashes of Saracen telling me about the accident played like a movie in my mind. The way her vibrant wings fluttered slowly behind her. How much it hurt my ears and heart when I hugged her. The knit purple hat with the cartoon ninjas I wore.

I remembered everything.

"How else was I going to get you pliable and willing? I'm no imbecile; take a powerful creature and use them against their will, and they will hate you, turning on you the moment their leash slips." Saracen straightened proudly. "Take that same powerful creature and become the only one they rely on for everything, craft and knead their little clay mind

257

until they love and cherish you, and they will do anything for you—including dominating all the realms."

Her words struck a thousand nerves as they poured into my head. I was going to be sick. I couldn't let everything fall apart like this. Not when I was so close!

"Send me to Moirai with the Ascendants. Let them deal with me!" I tried.

"You would have made Thanes's and my dreams a reality. You could have salvaged what was lost to the Fallen." She turned and ran her finger over the books on the shelves to the right of her desk. "You could have been everything."

"You're upset with me, and I understand, but the plan isn't over. I'm not working with the Unseelie. I-I can still take them out!" I cried, scrambling to fix things. In the end, I would destroy anything and anyone if I had to.

"The plan is over." She nodded. "It has been for a while. I was just too set in my ways to realize that. I am old and tired. The time for a new generation is upon Seelie. Tarani will take the throne as queen. She has the guile needed. We will exist within our own realm. I've decided after all these years, I am without the need of an Artemi weapon."

Tears blurred my eyes as angry panic surged through me, threatening to still the mangled heart in my chest. I threw myself to the ground at Saracen's feet with a frustrated scream while salty tears ran down my cheeks..

"She screamed, you know....your mother. She sounded a lot like you," she whispered.

I couldn't take any more of this.

"I remember bracing myself to see what horrifying wrath your father would send down upon me for killing his lover and child." Her smile widened as her head canted to the side. "I suppose that's foolish though. Why would he care? His Artemi blood only went to you, and he obviously didn't want you either. Though I suppose without your full heart, there's nothing he can do anyway."

She patted my head like a dog before walking to a shelf and running her fingers over the old leather tomes there.

My hand instinctively skated over my hip for my karambit, only to graze bare skin—I was still wearing only a tank top and underwear. How could I kill her?

I knew she was stronger than she looked. All fae were.

If my training had taught me anything, it was that you never struck out of impulse or outrage.

"Your head should be so full of planning and calculating, you don't have space in there for emotions." Commander Von's shrill voice crawled through my head.

I would do anything to never see that fae ever again. I had been ten when he arrived in the human realm to begin my training. I was also ten the first time he broke my nose and fed me the fae we had killed for dinner.

"Don't look at me like that. You would have done the same to get back at your enemy. I guarantee you would have. How else was I to get my revenge on Tenebris?" She clucked at me.

Sounds muffled. Colors blurred. I backed farther away from the woman.

What could I do now? Even if I abandoned everything, I would be wanted and recognized all across Seelie. The tie to Eli wouldn't matter now; he had doomed himself from the start.

"You're worse than I even thought!" I shouted, barely recognizing my voice as everything I'd planned unraveled before my very eyes.

"Says you," she laughed. "How many kills did you make without a purpose or for training, and guess what?" she whispered with a smile. "You loved doing every one. Your darkness exceeded my every expectation. Except when it came to Mendax, of course. I should have known. You were the perfect little me in every possible way. It's only fitting that you want Thanes's son," she laughed. "Truly, this is my fault for training you so well. You now think you can betray me and join the Unseelie?"

"That's not what happened!" I screamed.

"You are lucky that you are tied to my son and he may be needed, or you would be dead right now, Artemi or not."

I looked around for anything I could use for a weapon, but all logic vibrated out of my head with rage.

"You will never get the other half of your heart. It will be destroyed the moment you step foot in Malvar," she said. "Or maybe I'll keep it as a reminder on my bookshelves—a conversation piece, if you will. You foolish child, had you not betrayed me, everything in this land could have been yours. You never should have crossed me."

Standing up, I caught the glint of a letter opener in a cup sitting on her desk.

Her dress swished against itself as she walked over to the corner of her mahogany desk, where a beautiful clear- and frosted-glass chess board sat.

"Let me see Eli," I said. I needed to tell him everything. He needed to know.

Suddenly the door burst open and the guards poured back in, all circling me this time.

"Goodbye, Calypso. Too bad you didn't get to tell every-one goodbye." She tsked, moving her frosted queen on the chessboard. "I've taken matters into my own hands. The Unseelie castle is crumbling to dust as we speak. You see, while the future Unseelie king was gallivanting around my castle trying to breed with you, I was placing my pawns." She nodded to the open doors. "Do you know what happens when the opponent leaves their queen unprotected?"

One of the guards stalked toward her carrying a burlap sack, stopping just in front of her. Another small nod from the queen and the armored guard opened the bag, pulling out a large, hairy stump. Pale-green moths scattered, escaping from the burlap.

"They get overtaken, leaving their would-be king an easy target."

The guard readjusted his grip on the thing, collecting

more of the black hair to reveal a beautiful, pale face with icy-blue eyes and red lips.

Queen Tenebris.

The guard held Queen Tenebris's severed head out at me.

My stomach cramped, and its contents spilled out of my mouth, dribbling down my chin as the taste of acid coated my tongue.

"It wasn't the Fallen fae who attacked the Unseelie castle, it was you," I whispered, gripping the wall behind me to steady myself.

"Do you know the best part of being queen?" she asked. "My people believe anything I tell them. The Fallen have long been trying to gain a hold on either of our castles. It was hardly a stretch for everyone to believe it was them. When they find us at Unseelie, we will yet again be saving the day and claiming it as Seelie to keep the evil Fallen fae from gaining control."

Queen Saracen smiled wide as she grabbed ahold of Tenebris's bloody head.

I brushed off a tickle on my face and realized the luna moths had flocked to me, all landing on my body as if I were their owner.

"We intercepted the dark prince just prior to departure. There wasn't much left of his head, but we grabbed this." The guard shuffled to dig through the burlap sack.

His meaty hands landed on their prize and he lifted out a chain.

A chain with my tooth attached to it.

"Noooo!" I screamed.

I landed on the floor, but it felt like my heart had dropped further. Agonizing sorrow took hold of me while I struggled to breathe. My mind eventually defaulted to an all-too-familiar numbness as I stared at the dangling tooth—*my* dangling tooth.

"Fantastic. I want whatever is left of his head. Tell Victor to make a display by the throne so everyone can see the

Smoke Slayers are all gone for good—well almost," she said, looking at me with a smile. "Take her to Malvar."

The guards stalked to where I had backed myself into a corner. I let them take me without a struggle, scenes from my childhood and my time in Unseelie playing over and over again as I stared at the woman I had fought so hard to please all these years for nothing. *Nothing.*

One of the guards roughly gripped my bare ass as they shoved me out the door. I didn't care.

Tenebris was dead. Mendax was dead. My mother was dead, Adrianna was dead, soon I would be dead.

Eli would be dead too.

I wasn't an official Seelie, and my time was running out. I wouldn't get my heart back in time.

I had nothing.

I was nothing.

CHAPTER 24

CALY

M EET ME BACK HERE AT THREE OR YOU'LL SLEEP IN THE alleyway again," Commander Von barked out the window of the rusty Buick LeSabre.

The lights from the yellow and purple neon signs glinted off his shaved head, my own mousy reflection staring back from his aviator sunglasses. Responding only with a solemn nod, I stepped back, into a puddle where the glistening black asphalt had crumbled away.

The large fae removed his hands from the steering wheel with an emphatic drop to his lap.

It had only been a few months since Commander had taken Cecelia's place in the home, but I had already learned not to give him access to my back.

He looked out over the top of his aviators in a silent dare as I glared at him.

"What did they do?" I asked hesitantly.

This had been the first hit I had struggled with. It was a double tonight: two elves who had done something to cross the queen, what I didn't know. That wasn't the part I was struggling with though. It was an elderly couple that ran a bar in a less-than-ideal part of the city.

Pain radiated across my face, and I fell back onto the gritty pavement with an animallike cry.

"It's not your job to know why; it's your job to know their weakness and how to kill them. Do not question the queen's reasoning again." Commander pulled back the hand that had just punched me in the face and wiped it across the front of his shirt before driving away, leaving me curled up in a fetal position on the ground. The late-night drizzle had picked up once again, slowly covering my black dress in a heavy dampness.

"Hey!" the scary fae shouted only a few feet from where he'd taken off. "Bring me back her tongue, or I'll use yours again!" His deep, throaty laugh traveled on the wind as he drove away.

I lay in the puddle and cried. For how long, I had no idea. Time had been different ever since Mom and Adrianna left me. Everything felt endless and long. It was getting harder and harder to stick with the plan, but every time I felt like crying and breaking, I knew I couldn't.

I would never get back up, and then I'd die a dopey human.

I thought Saracen had started to have doubts about me going to Seelie. Last week she had shown up right when I was dragging that Peter kid's body into the woods.

"I didn't order this hit," she said, crossing her arms and tapping her foot.

"I know—he said I didn't have any parents because I was so ugly," I responded flatly.

"We agreed that you would stop killing everything that looks at you sideways once training began. That was the deal if you wanted to be my assassin here. I had no idea what a vicious, little thing you were," Saracen scolded. "I'm starting to wonder if you are a demon of Tartarus, instead of a peaceful Artemi! I thought you were just angry about your mother's and sister's deaths. It was a great idea for me to have an assassin here, and I thought it would help you let out a little anger, but I'm starting to worry you're too dark, child. When your powers come, you will be an absolute weapon of destruction if you continue like this. You're ten and already have the countenance of some of the most horrendous fae I know. I could never trust that you wouldn't turn your powers and hate against me."

I froze. I had thought this would work.

"I'm only practicing. I just want to get better so I can go to Seelie with you and Eli," I said flatly. Too flatly—I needed to make sure to put more emotion in the next words. "I would *never* hurt you. I love you."

"I don't know, Calypso. They aren't just going to let a bloodthirsty Artemi wander around Seelie. They would send me to the Elysian Fields before I could even empower you to be an official Seelie royal," she said, sitting down on a tree stump.

"Elysian Fields? You seem sure you won't be going to Tartarus," I grumbled under my breath as I kicked leaves over Peter's arm.

Saracen let out a snort of laughter. "I agree. I'm likely better suited to go to the fiery pits of Tartarus." Her head shook slowly. "Thank the Fates, all Seelie royals automatically go to the Elysian Fields, regardless."

I dropped the rope I held. "I'll complete a huge test. Something that all of the people will be affected by, so they know I fight for Seelie only," I said frantically. "I'll do anything you ask! Whatever it is, I'll do it, and then you can empower me as an official Seelie royal. I couldn't turn on Seelie then."

"That still doesn't mean you won't turn your powers on me once you get them," she said as her body shifted away from me.

"I'll—I'll give you my heart!" I cried out.

"You've been near Commander Von too much. I have no cannibalistic tendencies, my dear," she replied with a grimace.

"No—no! It's an Artemi thing. I've heard about a witch who can split your heart in half. It's an option when the

265

power bestowed on the Artemi is too great and they can't bear it any longer. Usually if there is a lot of power, they get it before they're eighteen and able to use it. I'll find a witch and she'll take the half with the dormant powers and give it to you! You'll have full control of me until I've proven to be a part of your family and court." My chest rose and fell with excitement.

She wrinkled her brow at me. "Why have I never heard of that before?"

"Because it's a transfer of powers, and they don't want anyone to know that they can do that. Artemi can even give weak elders small bits of their power if they get sick or need it. There are lots of things no one knows," I stated.

Now, in the dirty street, blood had poured from my face down to my dress. My nose was broken and throbbing, pain radiating from my eyes and head. I just wanted to lie down in the puddle a little longer and pretend I wasn't here. What was I doing? I was only ten. I'd nearly flunked science last year and gotten Ds in everything else. Why on earth had I thought I would be able to pull off this plan? I wasn't smart, I wasn't strong. I was nothing.

I looked over at the alleyway, where a small black cat was sitting and watching me.

Adrianna had loved cats. Every shirt she owned had kittens on it. She had even managed to get Mom to iron on little cat patches all over her book bag.

The place where I guessed my heart might be already felt hollow. No matter how much I lashed out, it never filled.

No, I wouldn't let them down. I wouldn't let myself stop until the person who killed them died.

The black cat coiled around my legs, shoving its soft, little head at me until I was forced to sit up in the parking lot so the cat would stop pushing against my swollen face.

A car slammed on its brakes, honking and veering right before hitting me. Had I been lying down, they would have never seen me.

"Agh! It's a ghost, man," the driver shrieked to his passenger as they screeched away.

"Thanks," I said to the cat, patting its raised rear end.

I knew why the cat was drawn to me, but it was still weird. I didn't think I'd ever get used to it. I didn't want to.

The dainty feline started to walk down the alley, but then stopped and came back in a huff to shove my legs.

I needed to get to this bar and kill my marks or a broken nose wouldn't be the half of it. Commander dressed me in the usual, a cutesy dress and a pair of tights. If I showed up like this, they would probably run from me like that car had, and I needed them to let down their guard.

I stood up and grabbed my pounding head as the rush from standing caused more blood to gush from my nose. I had to get cleaned up a little.

"All right, I hope you're taking me somewhere with a sink," I muttered, following the pleased cat down the alleyway.

We continued down several long side streets and corners, scaring every person in the alley who was attempting some sort of nefarious activity and sending them screaming and running the other direction, until we eventually came to a small hole-in-the-wall shop with a flashing neon sign that said "Psychic Readings."

The cat pushed open the cracked door and snaked in as a bell jingled loudly. It was as good of a place as any to get cleaned up, so I opened the door and walked inside to find the cat coiled up on a purple-haired woman with at least four facial piercings.

"Well, well, well. Look what my cat dragged in," she said with a stern look. "Tell me who to put a hex on while I clean you up, little girl."

"You're a—a witch?" I asked, glancing at the cat and hardly believing my luck.

"Yeah, honey, but don't worry. I'm not the scary kind like in the movies."

The cat leaped down from her lap as she stood and moved behind the beaten-up glass counter of the register.

"Seelie."

Startled at my words, the witch whipped back around to me, recognition filling her brown eyes.

"I knew you were a real witch," I muttered triumphantly as I hugged the little black cat.

"Well, this makes more sense," she said, tossing me a cloth with strong-smelling oils all over it.

"Can you split my heart? I need to give it to someone, and it's important that I can physically hand it to them," I pleaded, deciding on taking the blunt approach.

"Split your heart? Body modifications like that are incredibly unreliable and difficult. There's a reason why you never hear about it being done, kid, especially when it comes to vital organs. That's why those witches in Hanabi got burned for splitting those Marongs' hearts once their powers started killing them. Besides, it only lasted a short amount of time." She grimaced at my blood-smeared face. "Here, let me help." The witch slowly moved toward me, as though she was afraid of scaring me, and grabbed the cloth.

If she only knew.

"How long does it last?"

She stared at me for a second. "Depends on what you are, but usually only until the red circle passes the moon."

"What does that mean?" I asked.

She laughed. "No one knows what it means unless you're a witch. It's about twenty years."

"Please, I need you to try on me. I have to hand her my heart," I pleaded. "Please."

"I'll have to call my grandma. She's better at—"

"No. No one else can know I was here," I said, cutting her off. I needed to make sure this didn't get back to Saracen.

"Okay. Then it's going to cost you," she said with a smile.

I giggled appropriately and palmed the karambit in the pocket of my cardigan.

Unfortunately, it was going to cost her a good bit more.

"What are you? I can't see your ears under that hat. Elven? You know, over two streets, there are the sweetest husband and wife who are elven. They own the Hobbit Hole Bar on second street," she said warmly.

Moving aside a deep red curtain that acted as a door behind her counter, she paused and waited for my answer.

"Okay," I said with false intimacy, "but you can't tell anybody."

CHAPTER 25

CALY

I WATCHED THE HEAVY RAYS OF SUN MOVE THROUGH MY CELL and be replaced with the orange-red of Seelie dusk.

They would be coming soon, just like they had every night for the last several weeks. Goose bumps pricked up my arms at the thought. My dry, bloodshot eyes stared out into the sky, unable to blink. It felt like it had been forever since I'd started hearing the distant cries of the others day in and day out. Maybe today would be the day they actually came for me.

Sitting at the very peak of a beautiful mountain, high above the tallest tower, and nearly in line with the clouds, stood Malvar. The place I would breathe my last breath.

The opulence here was used to break your mind, to make you feel safe when you weren't. My mind had broken a long time ago, accompanied by several other body parts.

The sun shifted again, and I knew it would only be a few more hours.

Malvar was not what you expected to find when you heard it was a prison for some of the most dangerous fae out there.

Gorgeous crystal chandeliers swayed slightly with the

breeze that swept in from the open room. The cells were three sided. As soon as you entered a cell through the barred door of the hallway, you faced open sky. There was about twenty feet of polished marble flooring between the back wall and the edge of the room. It was completely open to the elements, and at various times of the day the sun beat down and cooked the room. At night the sun shifted to the other side of the mountain, leaving it bright but cold, but that wasn't the worst thing that happened here.

I heard the tapping of boots on marble and tried to listen harder. It was the slower guards.

A beautiful feast of meats than I'd ever seen before, and refused to touch, would be brought in and set on the table next to a spread of fruits and cheeses. They did this every evening and left it until you couldn't eat anymore.

When I had first arrived at Malvar, I thought there had been a mistake. How could this place be terrifying and bad? It was beautiful and almost cozy looking—if you didn't look at the three walls of iron bars.

But like everything else in life, sometimes the most beautiful things are the most hideous.

The Seelie prison was set up in levels along the mountain. The worst and most dangerous of the inmates were placed in three-sided cells atop the mountain, where I was, while the rest were held in cells inside the bottom half of the mountain.

I didn't understand why they put me up here. I didn't feel dangerous anymore. I felt weak and stupid. How could I have let everything slip through my fingers when I was so close?

A breeze flowed through the open chamber, bringing with it the scent of rotting corpses.

"Hey, puddle," whispered the familiar voice of my neighbor.

Just as every other time, I ignored him.

Since being here, the occupants of the neighboring cells had changed several times. With no real privacy, you could sit and watch the other person through the bars all day if you wanted to.

It irritated me when they tried to speak to me. It was a waste of breath to talk to anyone ever again.

I should have stayed in Unseelie. If I was going to Tartarus anyway, I would have preferred it to be at the hands of Mendax. I wished I'd stopped pretending and let the darkness consume me with him by my side. I should have trusted my gut and told him everything. He would have helped me—I knew he would have. I wished I could have told Eli the truth about everything also, let him know how much I loved him. I hoped Mendax had died knowing how much I truly did love him.

"Puddle, I have an idea."

I had an idea too.

I rose from the floor where I sat, steadying myself against the bars at my back. The wind tickled hair across my face as I took a step toward the open edge of my cell. Another step and I could see what looked like a whole world below me. We were so high up.

"She moves!" came the high-pitched voice of my other neighbor.

Everything I had ever loved had hurt me in some way. Every time I was strong when I wanted to crumble, every time I fought when I wanted to cower… It was for nothing. I had been put here.

I had missed so many perfect opportunities to kill Saracen. I should have just taken one of them. I had planned on killing her at the ceremony, after she empowered me as an official Seelie and restored my heart. I was going to kill them all. I could have a million times over. Everyone but Eli. When I was thirteen, I swore I'd never hurt him. I loved him so much back then, it hurt. He was the only one who wouldn't die. I should have done it without my heart—it's not like I planned to be alive for long.

My tired eyes stared at the red-and-gold sky. Tears wouldn't come anymore.

I missed Walter so much. Had he managed to escape the castle? He never even got to say goodbye to Mendax.

I took another step. Soft fur grazed against the sole of my foot; I numbly stepped over the large heap.

I was nothing.

Even science, the only thing that had kept me sane for years, now felt wrong. In fae realms, nothing acted with any predictability. Much like its inhabitants.

I had been holding on to the thought that Mendax was somehow still alive. I could only imagine how broken he must've been for them to have been capable of taking him down. He must have lost it seeing his mother's dead body and knowing he hadn't been there in time to stop it.

He'd been with me.

My throat tightened at the emptiness I felt from our bond.

I never should have fought myself about him—he was never my villain.

"Edin, I don't like the way Puddle looks," the male voice called to my other neighbor.

"Okay, ass," the girl grumbled back.

I took another step, hearing the bones and tendons crunch and snap under my feet. Only another six inches or so left before the edge. The tangerine sun heated my skin as it moved, now nearly behind the mountain. Puffy white clouds passed just below the ledge, steadily moving as the gusts of wind propelled them. "Edin..."

"Even the animal power is too much for me. I will never make it to him, and I will never make it to her," I whispered to myself. One more step and I would be done with all of this.

"Puddle, I have an idea for when they come tonight. Get away from the ledge—this will work. I saved broth from dinner. We will rub it on you. It will work—Edin!"

"You really that stupid?" the girl named Edin demanded. "You think you'll die and plummet to your death if you step off that ledge? I don't know what the hell you are, but you must not either. If they put you this high up on the mountain, you won't die from the fall anyway and you'll be back staring at the sky in a few hours."

"I'm nothing," I breathed.

"You know what's so great about being nothing?" asked the man. "You can become whatever you want."

I lifted my foot, fighting the suddenly strong wind.

Heavy footfalls rang through the hallway. They were here. I was too late.

"Edin!"

"It doesn't matter anyway; they're here," she said with a shaky voice.

Giant white objects pelted into each of the cells. Blood-curdling screams ricocheted through the space.

My foot instinctively hit the ground as my head snapped to my right. The curvy, black-haired girl had been pinned to the ground by the creature.

Cries of pain made my head snap in the other direction, where a similar scene was unfolding. The brown-haired man who called me Puddle had been pinned by another of the giant birdlike creatures. Soul-tearing screams sounded from the rest of the cells around and below us.

My eyes flashed back to the sky, where the feathered monster flew straight at me.

I turned around and walked to the middle of my cell. The sound of screams and tearing flesh pressed into me from all directions. One thing I could never numb out was the unforgettable sound of flesh being ripped.

The monstrous birds mauled the people, each viciously fighting to rip out all of the prisoners' internal organs, leaving pools of blood and bones in their wake. Soon, after having eaten their fill, the birds would fly off into the orange evening sky, their white feathers painted various shades from the blood of their victims.

The first hour of morning, the prisoners' bodies would be fully restored, completely intact, left with nothing but the fresh memory of the carnage from the previous day. Then they would spend the rest of the day counting down the hours until another painful massacre that evening.

Angrily, I watched one of the large creatures land in my cell. They were mythical looking, like eagles with feathers as white as fresh snow and bodies the size of a train car.

The creature flared its taloned feet and skidded to a stop right in front of me.

I couldn't take another one. Why hadn't I just jumped? Even an hour away from this hell would have been worth it. Besides, it was possible that I didn't have enough power to live through it. I still didn't understand why the queen hadn't destroyed the other half of my heart yet, and she most certainly hadn't, or I would be dead.

Hot tears fell like rain down my face as I looked at the monster.

"Do it!" I shouted, feeling the spittle fly from my mouth.

Its sharp, yellow-and-black eyes softened as it looked me over. No longer raging and ready to shred me.

I lifted my tank top and uncovered my stomach. "Please!" I bellowed hoarsely.

The bird of prey lay down in front of me, bending its head and nudging my legs as I furiously shoved it, hoping to anger the feathered beast into attacking me.

My knees cracked as they hit the floor, and I tried with every fiber of my being to shove the animal away from me. The bird's eyes flicked over me; the feathers of its head softened as it laid its body down, continuing to calmly nuzzle me.

Sadness poured from its concerned eyes as it turned their efforts toward tucking me under one of their expansive wings.

"Go, please! Please!" I howled.

Unable to see more than a white blob through my tears, my hands gripped its silky feathers.

The door of my cell opened. Breathless sobs shook my body. I reached as deep as I could and collected every bit of strength I had left to make the calm bird leave the cell.

Hollow bootsteps permeated my cell.

Commander Von.

My mind tried to black out, blurring and darkening at the edges, attempting anything to protect me from what it was about to see.

Orbs of light shot out from behind me with a whirring sound, hitting the creature just before it went limp in my arms.

The commander chuckled from inside the cell door.

"I suppose one way or another you suffer, traitorous bitch," he chuckled as he closed the barred door with a loud clang. "You must've missed me a lot to have come all the way here to see me. Guess you didn't mind my cock as much as you thought."

I cried until morning, buried in the feathers of the slain animal, cursing everyone I could think of.

Every night, the creatures appeared from the sky, and then left after destroying their chosen inmates.

All but mine.

The beautiful creatures came every night, and every time, each and every one of them refused to hurt me. Eventually the commander or guards would enter, killing the animal and leaving its body in my cell. I would then spend the rest of the night and the following day using all of my strength to push its lifeless body over the ledge, only to repeat it all in a few hours.

Once they had discovered the giant, white birds wouldn't touch me, they began sending in various other animals, and to my horror, not one would touch me.

So many animals had died for refusing to hurt me. The irony was, as it turned out, that was the worst punishment they could have crafted for me. Every part of me that could have possibly been broken had been.

It made no sense.

The creatures in Unseelie had had no problems hurting me. Why, now that I was locked in Malvar, had there been a change? Was it just the Seelie creatures?

I only had four months left to retrieve the other half of my heart before I would die anyway. Even if the queen didn't destroy it, I was basically dead already.

"Puddle, are you doing okay over there? I thought of another idea…but I'm not sure if you'll like this one," my neighbor said in a low voice.

I didn't bother to look at him; he had lasted longer than most of the prisoners in that cell, but it wouldn't matter. Eventually, Malvar would weaken their magic, and their wounds would kill them—if they didn't injure their head first. I learned that most of the more powerful fae, shifters, elves, and several others had to have a really severe head wound to die: something they couldn't recover from, like a caved-in skull.

Most of the prisoners of Malvar would ram their heads into the ground or put a chair leg through their eye sockets.

I looked at several lionlike creatures lying dead and rotting a few feet from the corner I now sat in. They had been the hardest to stomach yet. Commander had allowed me hours with them. Buried in their soft fur, I had almost felt whole again, like I could actually do something and get out of here. Like there had to be a way to get to my father.

"Puddle?"

I moved a few feet, barely registering my surroundings. I was no longer alive even if I wasn't dead.

I curled myself into the fur of the bloodied creatures, ignoring the stench of decomposition, and closed my eyes. I would lay here in the bodies of those who had died for me and silently try to coax Aether, the god of the Elysian Fields, to take me, even though I wasn't Seelie.

Hot, almost scorching hands pulled at my forearm as another slid under my legs, lifting me up.

"Come on, Puddle. I'll help you move them," whispered the stranger.

I didn't fight. I didn't do anything. I just lay there.

"Edin—"

"I'm already here," snapped the familiar female voice.

"Oh, shit," replied the man, setting me back down on the floor in my corner.

"Why are we doing this?" asked the woman.

"Because I think she's the one they are talking about. Look at her, she doesn't even know what she is capable of. Come on, we were just like her once," he said.

"Fuck. Fine, but only because I'm tired of smelling rotting animals."

The bronze-skinned man bent slowly and put his oddly warm hand on my forearm again.

"Anything you want to do or say to them before they are gone? I don't know what your kind does for burials," he said softly.

For the first time ever, I really looked at the two strangers.

The woman stood impatiently with hands on her hips while she looked down at the animals. Her short, white hair—a striking contrast to her dark skin—was buzzed on the bottom, while the rest coiled in tight curls that stopped at her chin on one side. My curious eyes took in her curvy body before landing on her rounded ears.

"You're human," I whispered.

She snorted, revealing one of the brightest, most charismatic smiles I had ever seen.

"Once," the man laughed. Standing back up to his full height and brushing his long, pin-straight, black hair over his shoulder.

"You're human too," I murmured, seeing his ears.

"About as human as a blowtorch," said Edin with a laugh.

The man nodded at the woman, and they began to push the dead animals to the open edge.

"They didn't deserve this," I sobbed.

"Here's a pro tip: the ones who deserve this are the ones who run this shit," Edin grumbled, struggling to push the giant lion.

"The animals deserve more than just being dumped

off the mountain," I cried, imagining the sounds of their bodies hitting the rocks. "I don't know what else I can do. It's not like I can build a pyre in here," I said with strangled sobs.

The two strangers abruptly stood to look at one another.

"Absolutely not," Edin stated.

"It will take four minutes, and no one will know," said the man gently.

"Sid, no. Ugh, can't you follow orders for once? I knew I should have picked Roach for this," she growled.

"Come on," he pleaded.

After reluctantly agreeing to whatever the man was asking for, Edin walked over to the corner beside me.

"Okay, Puddle, why don't you say a few words for the animals?" he instructed with a nod. The man stood over the largest animal, wearing only his torn and bloodied trousers.

Wait.

"How did you guys get in here?" I asked, suddenly feeling more alert.

"It wasn't rocket science. We climbed around the bars," Edin said as she played with one of the many earrings that coiled up her ears.

"Why would you risk—" I began.

"Okay, Puddle, words now, if you have any," he commanded gently.

Not knowing what I planned to do but too tired to fight my own mind, I walked over to the lion and closed its beautiful eyes, planting a kiss on their head. I said the only prayer I knew. Something my mother had sang whenever one of our pets died or we crossed paths with a dead animal in the road.

As I sang the weird words under my breath for the first time in twenty years, I realized they made no sense, and I didn't even know what they meant. Something about the words that flowed from my mouth felt right though, so I continued to say it to each slain animal. "Okay." I nodded, beginning to push the large animal.

"Step back," Edin said gently as she guided me to the back of the cell.

"I'm Sid by the way." The stranger smiled kindly as sympathy poured out of his narrow-set brown eyes. He held out his palm and a bright, round flame rolled across it.

My mouth opened as I watched the athletic-looking man from my neighboring cell conjure flames. He kneeled before the animals and bowed his head, holding his arms out wide. Blue-tinged fire shot out from his body, covering every part of the ground in front of him.

Sweat beaded and rolled from my temple as the intense heat blew against my face and arms.

Edin put her arm out, pushing me as far back against the cell bars as the two of us could go.

The flames continued to grow, the blue tips licking the ceiling above.

"Sid, that's enough," Edin said cautiously.

The figure covered in flames didn't move as the riot of fire began to spread closer and closer to us.

"Sidney!" Edin shouted, stepping in front of me.

The fire continued to rage, the tall flames pushing through the cell's bars and crawling into the cavernous hallway, leaving only a small circle around us free from the blaze.

My old way of thinking tried to enter my mind, telling me I could close off the air supply to the flames or lessen the conflagration, but I pushed it out and away.

That me was dead in every way, and hopefully I would be too by the end of this.

"You motherfucker." Edin grit her teeth as she moved toward the fire and Sid.

I didn't care enough about either of them to do anything.

Edin wiped the back of her hands on the sides of her dirty beige shirt and stretched out her arms, opening her palms one in front of the other next to her mouth as if she were about to blow a kiss to Sid.

White speckles flew from her palms and over the flames in icy gusts.

My skin chilled instantly, sending a shiver through my body from my sweat that froze.

She moved, now directing the swirling snow not onto the fire that crept around us but instead at Sid.

Feeling the blast, Sid whipped around with wide eyes. The flames halted immediately, leaving only a few to dance across his hands and arms. He brushed the last few from his shoulders, shooting a sheepish look in Edin's direction.

Only a handful of small flames remained on the floor, flickering across the piles of ash where the large creatures had lain only moments before.

Stepping aside with an exaggerated bow, Sid cleared the way. Edin's chest rose before sending out a huge icy breath of wind and sleet across the cell, causing all of our hair to whip back while it took the piles of ash and flames off the ledge, into the crisp mountain air.

The pair smiled at one another, then they both turned to look at me. Their faces seemed full of life with a glow that wasn't there before. Sid had a hint of pink deepening his warm skin, while Edin's dark cheeks were now dusted with a frosty blush.

"So you're definitely not human," I said in awe. "What are you?"

Sid looked at Edin with a boyish smirk, turning his large brown eyes to me. "Lightmires," he said just before he dropped his smile completely.

Lightmires… Why was that word so familiar? I couldn't seem to place it.

"You've probably heard us referred to as the Fallen fae."

CHAPTER 26

CALY

Y ou're Fallen fae? Why are you helping me?" I asked
wearily. "How can you use your powers inside the prison?
I thought they were neutralized by the mountain?"

My legs pressed against the bars that separated my cell
from Sid's.

After the fire, the pair had returned to their cells, easily
stepping around the last bar at the ledge like they weren't
dangling over the tallest mountain in Seelie.

"Our powers don't adhere to any of the realms' rules.
It's what makes us so scary," he said with a wink. "I'm not
supposed to use them here though. Probably why I got a little
carried away, ya know? Just felt so good to use them again.
And as for why I'm helping you, I have a feeling we can help
each other." He stretched his arms, resting his hands behind
his head as he looked out into the orange sky.

"I can't help you," I mumbled.

"Aren't you the one they thought killed Prince Mendax?
Didn't you build a bomb in his bathroom or something?" he
chuckled, leaning up to look at me.

"It doesn't matter. He's dead," I said, my jaw tightening.
My stomach clenched painfully at the thought.

"You love him? Is that why you worked with him?" he questioned.

"I didn't work with him," I grumbled. "But I did love him. I was stupid and foolish and didn't listen to my gut when I should have." I turned away from Sid, pressing my back against the bars. Edin was asleep in the corner of her cell.

"So which side are you on? Guess I should have found that out first, huh?" I could hear the smile in his voice.

I let my heavy head drop down. "Neither," I whispered, wiping a stray tear from the corner of my eye.

"Weren't you supposed to marry the Seelie prince?"

"Yeah" was all the response I could form.

We continued talking as the sky turned deeper shades of orange and red, signifying that it would be time for the bird to arrive again soon.

"What if you rip out your own insides? Ya know, make the guards think the roc did its duty," Sid said nonchalantly.

"I already tried. The roc, as you called it, stopped me. They won't allow me to hurt myself. Besides, it's likely that I'd pass out from blood loss before I was finished," I replied.

"You two are fucked up," Edin called from her cell.

Footsteps echoed behind us, getting louder the closer they came.

"Fuck." The skin around Sid's eyes tightened. "I hear claws on the ground, Puddle. I think they're bringing you another creature again."

Air filled my lungs and pushed out my ribs painfully. I tried to brace myself to watch another sweet animal die at my feet.

The cell door slammed open, hitting the bars behind it with a clang.

"You better fucking destroy her, or it's a sun pellet between the eyes for you, dog," the commander goaded.

A yelp and snarl sounded as he kicked whatever creature had just stepped into my cell.

Every part of me sank lower than I thought it could go. I couldn't handle any more animals being hurt. My eyes blurred as I continued to stare at my hands between my knees.

The footsteps echoed back down the hallway.

I couldn't take it anymore.

"The fuck?" said Sid next to me.

As I cried, the creature seemed to grow taller in my blurry peripheral.

"We really need to stop meeting like this." A warm and soothing voice blanketed my skin.

My head snapped up as hope rippled through me like it was going to light my insides on fire. "Walter!" I gasped.

My gaze found the kindest chestnut-colored eyes. I tripped to my feet, unable to believe what I was seeing.

"You know, I do enjoy other activities, ones that aren't always helping you escape from a dungeon," he said with a broad smile.

I ran to where he stood and hurled my arms around him.

"Caly, outside—"

"Mendax," I breathed, pulling back to look into his eyes. "It's not true? He's not dead?"

Walter's throat bobbed with a rough swallow as his forehead creased.

"I'm afraid it's true." He lifted my tooth necklace from where it now hung around his neck. "I was able to get his necklace from the queen's quarters. Unseelie are still fighting, but the castle has been destroyed. Mendax was gone before it came down," he said softly.

"That can't be, Walter. He's just hiding!" I bit out, looking at my tooth. It looked wrong hanging from Walter's neck. It belonged on Mendax.

Walter pulled me into his chest.

"We both know he wouldn't hide while his home was being destroyed. He's gone, Caly." Walter's voice cracked with emotion.

"You need to leave Seelie." I squeezed Walter tightly and

inhaled the clean smell of his shirt. "Saracen is going to make Tarani queen. She's been grooming her. No wonder Tarani is so awful. It's a wonder Eli turned out as sweet as he is. I have to find a way to get to Moirai before my time runs out with my heart," I said, feeling tears run down my face.

"If by sweet, you mean extremely tough and manly in a roguish sort of warrior way, then I agree."

I froze.

The Seelie prince stood outside of my cell door. Blazing yellow light swirled from his fingertips and into the door's keyhole. He pushed open the cell door and stepped in, pausing to look at me with sad eyes.

I ran to Eli and threw my arms around his neck. It felt so good to see familiar faces.

"Puddle? You still okay over there?" Sid called with a hint of concern in his tone.

"Yeah, Sid," I replied.

Eli stirred. "*Puddle?* Is he insulting you? Why is he calling you a puddle?" he asked, tensing under my arms.

"I don't know," I replied honestly.

"Caly, you need to see what's outside." Eli's voice cracked as his eyes filled with emotion.

"We need to leave now. I need to find a way to Morai," I responded flatly.

Eli laughed for a second before stopping when he realized I was serious. "Moirai? The land of the Ascended and the Fates? Why? You can't get in without an invitation, Cal. There's never been a way to get there unless they send for you," he said gently.

My shoulders fell. "Then how do I get them to send for me?"

"What are you talking about?" The golden prince brushed my hair away from my face tenderly.

"I'm going to die, Eli, and you're going to die too now because of the tie. I'm so sorry." I bit the inside of my lip to stop from crying more. "You should have tied yourself to someone worth dying over. You—"

285

My argument was cut short when Eli's lips crashed down on mine.

Ripples of emotion surged through my body as I felt everything possible. Anger, happiness, sadness, love, hate—everything.

It was like a blanket cocooning me, every possible feeling contradicting one another as I kissed him back, until true realization slammed into my head.

I pulled away abruptly. "Mendax is gone."

Eli held me tighter. "Yes, and I'm only sorry about it because it hurts you. It was for the best. You cannot be tied to me and bonded to him. One of us had to die. It went against the Fates for you to be connected to us both. I'm so sorry for what my mother has done, but we found it." Eli smiled, glancing at Walter. "We finally found your heart. Turns out it wasn't at all where I had been told it was. I was going to steal it for you before Mendax stormed the castle."

He slowly leaned back down and kissed me with so much feeling and tenderness that my eyes began to water.

"You move quick. I guess with one dead, why not, right? Has she seen all her fans?" came a familiar voice from the open cell doorway. Tarani stepped into the crowded cell.

"No," I whispered as I looked at the small princess.

I probably could have passed her in the street and not recognized her without her fancy dress on. Instead, she wore dark training breeches and a dark, long-sleeved top.

"Tarani's going to help us," Walter said with a nod toward the Seelie princess.

"Tarani, what are you…" Edin's harsh voice sounded from the next cell.

"Edin," Tarani stated with a nod.

"No, Tarani is being trained by your mother to take over as queen. She's in on all of it!" I said as I pulled out of Eli's embrace. "She's bad, Eli. Saracen is already pulling her strings."

I glared at the princess, refusing to take my eyes off her.

"It's not what you think——" Eli started.

"She's been working with Saracen! She's not who you think. She's been hiding everything from us," I bit out.

"Well, she's not wrong." Tarani laughed. "Edin, team C is still at Unseelie. Be ready to make a move tomorrow night. Listen for the signal," the small princess barked.

"Tomorrow?" grumbled Sid from his cell.

What the fuck?

"What is going on?" I felt as though my knees would give out at any second. I was attempting to put the pieces together, but none of it made any sense.

"It seems Tarani is a bit more of a leader than any of us knew," Eli said with a tinge of resentment.

"What's going on is not *every* child was fooled by Mother's lies," Tarani stated as she lifted her shirt to show a small black tattoo of a deadhead moth between her ribs.

"Honestly, we don't need to see that," said Eli, scrunching his face.

"What is that?" I asked.

"It's the mark of the Fallen," said Sid from behind us. He stood by the bars of his cell with his right arm raised high, gripping the iron bars. The same tattoo was visible on his underarm, just before his armpit.

"Tarani, you're..."

"I am. I may not have been created the same way, but one of the two monsters still made me and tried to use me. It's not right what is happening to the kingdoms. Seelie is supposed to be happy and full of sunshine and goodness, not trickery and lies. Unseelie is where the dark souls find peace. They are different, but there is no reason why we cannot live in peace as we once did." She clenched her fists tightly. "They deserve to pay for what they did to the Fallen. Both sides deserve to pay, and what better way than having the Seelie king's sister on your side?" She smiled at Eli.

"The Fallen were not who attacked the Unseelie castle, like Mother is saying," Eli offered.

"I know." My jaw popped in an effort to stop the tears that threatened as I looked to Walter. "She told me all about what her army did when she played show-and-tell with Queen Tenebris's head...along with Mendax's necklace."

Walter's round eyes looked so sad, I couldn't help but go to him and wrap my arms around his waist.

"I'm so sorry, Walter," I whispered.

He squeezed me back. "Was it only Mendax's necklace? No body parts?" he asked. A hint of something in his voice.

"Yes, only the necklace," I said, feeling hope warm through my system. "The one with my molar on it." I pulled back abruptly to look into his eyes. "You think he could be alive, then?" I asked.

"No. Quite the opposite," Walter said somberly. "He could have faked a wing or a body part, but he would never have let someone take the only piece of you he had left. I know him too well. I'm afraid he is gone, Caly." He quickly brushed away a tear from his red-rimmed eyes as I nodded, chastising myself for having hope and finally accepting what I didn't want to.

Mendax was truly gone now, and I had been so busy trying to please Saracen and the Seelie court that I had let the man who could have been my soul mate die.

The smallest flicker of anger came to life inside me.

"We don't have time for this," said Sid gruffly. "They will be coming soon."

"He's right. What's the plan?" asked Edin.

"Take out the guards and get Sidney and Edin out of here. Get them to safety," I said softly, feeling the flame inside me die before anything productive could come from it.

Tarani chuckled. "They don't need help getting out. They were stationed here with the intent of being close to the castle when the time came to overtake it." She gave a nod to Eli. "Which happens to be right now."

"Walter and I found your heart, Caly, but it's spelled. It will only be unbound by your own flesh and bones. Even with our tie, I could not pull it from the magic that guards it." Eli smiled at the shifter. "It let Walter get way farther than me. I guess the tie can only do so much."

"The Fallen will help capture Mother, and because I am her daughter, they have reluctantly agreed that she will be moved to a prison where I can hold her, instead of killing her, but we need your help and your word that once your heart is restored, you won't use your powers against the Fallen," Tarani said, chiming in.

"Fine. You have my word," I said, turning to face the red sky.

"Caly, once we get your heart, you'll...you'll be able to do a lot more than you think. You could really change things here for the better," Eli said softly.

My plan can still work... The thought niggled at me like a worm. It was something I had sworn I would never do, and it meant hurting Eli. I knew poor Eli would marry me and make me a true Seelie royal...

"Caly...once my mother is gone from the castle, Tarani will be announced as the new Unseelie queen by the Fallen. They have chosen her to rule those who are choosing to stay in Unseelie," Eli said sadly. "Until we can establish that we are a peaceful realm once again, I will likely be under a lot of...challenges...and..." he rambled on, running his hands through his golden hair.

"He wants you to be his queen," Walter said with a smirk.

I inhaled sharply as my mouth fell open. No! He couldn't do this to me. I couldn't do this to him. Butterflies danced in my belly. Maybe I could change the plan somehow. Maybe there was some way we could be married and he would not get hurt.

"It's just that we are forever tied, Caly. It is unbreakable, whether we like it or not, and well, I will be nowhere near as strong as you, but you cannot ascend because you are tied to me anyway, and I know you chose Mendax, but..." Eli stepped close to me, the vision of Prince Charming.

"It would say a lot that you stood with the Fallen," Tarani began.

"I'm not a mascot. Have none of you considered that I might not be very powerful once my heart is restored?" I asked as I wrinkled my brow in frustration.

"Artemi are unmatched in power, Caly. That's why the Smoke Slayers killed most of them and went extinct, except for those who ascended to the Ancients. At least as far as we know," Eli said.

My heart skipped a beat as it plummeted to my stomach. "The Smoke Slayers are the reason the Artemi went extinct? *They* are the reason the Artemi had to be hidden?" I whispered.

"To be fair, Artemi are the reason the Smoke Slayers also went extinct...well, *now* they're extinct as far as we know." Walter bit his trembling lower lip.

"Don't be anybody else's gun, Puddle, trust me. Be your own," Sid muttered.

"Why do you call me Puddle?" I asked.

Sid's tan throat bobbed as he swallowed roughly. "Because when you first arrived, you reminded me of a puddle: still and gloomy. You can never tell how deep or shallow a puddle is just by looking at it. All it takes is a bit more rain and the puddle becomes a pond, then a lake. It grows when everything else drowns."

"That's quite the glorification of a—" I started.

"I saw it in your eyes—the same fight I went through when Thanes turned me into a monster. You just have to decide what kind of monster you're going be—the kind that makes puddles with their tears, or the kind that drowns the ones who caused them. You're a weapon no matter what, just like us. You just have to decide who the wielder is," Sid said.

"What happens to Unseelie now?" I asked as I looked back at Walter, wondering how he felt about the Fallen taking over.

"I will return to help Tarani in Unseelie as soon as this is sorted out. With both Mendax and Tenebris gone, there is no one else to claim the throne. I believe the Fallen's intentions are good and that it's time they finally had a realm or two to call home," he said with a nod to Sid.

"Stay with me in Seelie, Caly," Eli pleaded as he gripped me by the shoulders.

"No, I can't. I have to go to—"

"Marry me. Not because my mother ordered it and not because I'm begging or because it will make you a queen. Marry me because you love me as much as I love you." He lowered himself to the floor and planted one knee as his warm eyes filled with emotion.

"I'm sorry.... Is he doing what I think he's doing? In a prison?" Edin chimed in, sounding disgusted.

With horror, I looked to Walter, who only shrugged in answer. This would be the most monstrous and horrid thing I had done yet. I would deserve to rot in Tartarus...but the next part of my plan would happen.

"Yes," I whispered. "But let it be known to all that I loved Mendax with every beat of my mangled heart. He may have been the villain to most of you in this room, but he loved me in ways I couldn't comprehend—in ways I didn't know a person was capable of loving—even if it was shown in a way most wouldn't recognize. No doubt should *ever* enter the mind of anyone here how much I reciprocated that love. Even if I was unable to show it."

Everyone gave a short nod.

The cool breeze off the mountain had picked up, whipping all of our hair violently. I looked to my hands and silently begged them to produce his smoke one last time. The smoke that would let me know he was still alive.

Just as every other time I sought out the obsidian wisps, it pulled at my heavy heart to see absolutely nothing across my skin but freckles.

"We need to go before it's too late. Tarani and Walter have everything we need to perform the wedding ceremony. We need to be married so we can take the crown tonight," said Eli with a soft expression. "I will never be sorry I'm the man who gets to treasure you. You were always going to be the last battle between Mendax and I, and I would have done everything in my power to kill him. I suppose at least this way, you will not hate me for being the one who took him from you. I will spend every day with you, my best friend as well as my soul mate." His eyes were soft and full of understanding. He knew I loved both of them, and he was doing his best to be a respectful victor.

"Caly," Walter said as he put his large arm around me and steered me out of earshot of the others. "I still consider you the sister-in-law I never got to have, and I will dedicate my life to making sure Mendax's soul knows that I have kept you happy and safe. I know this is a lot and that you are not yourself right now, but I am still Unseelie. Say one word and I will pull a Mendax and kill every single one of them and get you out of here," he whispered with a dangerous look to his dark eyes. "I have kept close tabs on all of them, and though Mendax would kill me for saying this, Eli truly is a good, wholesome man who loves you deeply. I have spent many a night wandering the Seelie castle, and I can attest that Saracen kept him completely in the dark—just as the rest of Seelie doesn't know even half of what she did." His knuckles went white as he clenched his fists at his side.

"It's fine, Walter. I've known Eli since I was a child. I know that he's a good person. I have always loved him—not in the way I loved Mendax, but I don't really think that type of love can exist in the world without causing it to end."

"One of them was always going to die over you," he said solemnly.

"That's not necess—"

"It is, Caly. Your father has more pull than you can imagine."

"What does he have to do with anything?" I barked at him, angry to hear my friend soil his kind mouth with talk of my father.

He looked at me in surprise. "You cannot be tied as you are to Aurelius *and* bonded as you were to Mendax. The tethering of souls can't work that way, Caly. It would pull until there was nothing left of you. One of the three of you was always going to die. Only an Ancient could have made it last as long as it did."

My eyes welled, burning my nose.

"We are out of time," Tarani whispered breathlessly. She stared into the sky.

Curses echoed off the gold bars between our cells.

"Go. Take Eden and Sid," I said hurriedly.

"Caly's right, we need to get into the castle tonight, and I can't have you and Sid mangled, with no strength before we need to make a move. It's time. Grab the others. We take the crown tonight, and she will not be an easy victory." Tarani's back straightened and her chin lifted. "We are not strong enough to take Malvar *and* the castle on the same night, so do *not* get caught."

How had I only thought of her as a delicate princess? I had done to her exactly what so many had done to me: judged her solely on her appearance, blinded by her fine dresses. She radiated a sense of command that seemed so natural, I couldn't imagine her being anything other than a queen.

One by one, we fled the breezy cell and ran into the dark hallway. Where were all of the guards?

I swayed weakly, catching my balance against the rough rock wall of the hall. Another time, in another world, I would have been embarrassed being so sapped of strength. I hadn't cared about anything enough to eat, and now I was paying the price.

My dirty hands trembled. I stared through the bars at the bloodstained floor I had just walked out of. Tucking a strand of hair behind my ear, my fingers trailed across the scarred, rounded tip.

The problem with using broken weapons is that they backfired. After Eli and I were married, as soon as I got to the castle, I would break the spell, pull my heart from the flames…and leave.

Little did the Seelie know that, by the end of tonight, their new king and queen would be dead.

A thousand times, I had prayed for death in the cell I was leaving. Every time the creatures were killed because of me, I begged and pleaded that I be taken instead, that I would just be allowed to die.

And soon I would be.

Heat bloomed inside of me, likely from the simple exertion after having been sedentary for so long in my cell. Regardless, my eyes snapped to my wrist, my chest filling with hope as I searched for Mendax's smoke.

But again, there was nothing.

God, did I need to feel his smoke on my skin. Just *one* last time. It wasn't in my mind tight enough. I hadn't savored it the last time like I should have. What if I forgot how it felt?

I fought tears and looked up at the ceiling. A few strays dripped down into my ear. I was so tired of crying.

Warmth slid against my palm as lightly calloused fingers linked between mine.

Walter squeezed my hand. His brown eyes looked as sad as mine felt. He already knew everything about my plan, so I had no doubt he had figured out what I had to do now. I braced myself to give him some bullshit explanation or tell him something that would ease his worried expression, but none came.

Instead, he just held my hand tightly, letting me know he was there and understood.

Being a shifter of such pure blood, Walter had a connection with me that was different than anything I could have with the others. Even if my animal powers were minuscule, it was like he could peer inside of me and feel what I felt, understand it. The connection I had to animals, the way I felt whole in their presence, like we were a part of each other— that's how I always felt with Walter.

He cleared his throat. "Caly shouldn't be at the castle now. I'm going to take her to the human realm to hide."

"What? *No*," I said with an angry look at Walter's puppy-dog brown eyes.

I tried to pull my hand away, but he held it firm, giving me a stern look.

"You're right," said Eli. "It's too dangerous for Caly to retrieve her heart with the queen still there. She'll be out for blood and will try and destroy it before it falls into anyone else's hands, including Caly's." The soon-to-be king turned around to face us, glancing at our clasped hands. "But she's not leaving this realm. We will get my mother out of the castle while Caly waits in a safe location, and then she can come inside and get her heart."

"Yeah, I don't know how to tell you guys this," I said as I tapped my pointer finger to my lips. "But I don't take orders from either one of you."

Eli scowled. "I will make certain your heart remains protected during the battle inside. I won't let anything happen to it. I still believe I can release it from the flames somehow, and you are going to need it now more than ever with what is about to happen in Seelie. Being that we are tied, my soul flows through yours. If your heart is spelled only to release to you, it doesn't make sense why I shouldn't be able to collect it," Eli said, a defeated look on his face, as if he had let me down. "If I cannot retrieve it for you, then I will at least protect it until you can get inside to it."

The six of us continued down the hallway at a steady pace until Eli led us through a deep alcove and down a set of comically steep and windy stairs, the steps so small, only the very back of my heel could fit on each iron plank. This continued, all of us hustling down more stairs and more hallways, until it dawned on us.

"Where are the guards?" Edin asked, halting the group.

"I just assumed you guys took them out when you arrived?" I replied, looking between everyone's frozen features.

"No, we assumed we got lucky and that they were all on another floor or something," Walter corrected.

"They know we're here," Tarani hissed. "We have been—"

"Listen," Eli barked, tilting his head to the side, looking extra foxlike.

Distant rumbles and thuds were muffled down the hall, by the front doors of Malvar. Tarani gave a nod before Eden, Sid, and she left for another hallway.

Walter's grip tightened painfully on my hand. "Go, now!" he shouted to Eli.

Eli's eyes shot to Walter's for a tense moment. "Please keep her safe. Do not leave Malvar until the guards reenter, and for sun's sake, do not let her near the Seelie castle until it is cleared and I am king."

"What is happening? Wait... I thought you needed me to be your queen? You can't just leave me!" I shouted at Eli's back as he ran down the hallway.

He stopped, whipping around to shout back, "Unlike Mendax, I do not *need* you to take the throne in order for me to become king. I *need* you as my wife...it just so happens that makes you a queen."

His words knocked the air from my lungs. When I reopened my eyes, Eli was at my face with golden wings spread wide.

"If I fail, and this is the last moment I get with you..." His eyes looked glassy. "I'm sorry for everything I did wrong, Calypso." Tears streaked his lightly stubbled jaw. "I'm sorry I wasn't there for you more in the human realm. I'll never forgive myself for it. In every part of my soul, I am filled with remorse that I played a part in your sadness. I despise myself for being so selfish in wanting you with me, that I allowed her to send you to Unseelie in the first place."

"Aurelius—"

"Please, Cal," he muttered as his head dropped. "Do not leave me with that name."

"Eli," I whispered, finally understanding everything he

was saying. "You are a fool to think you could have stopped me from going. I'm not sorry about any of it."

I stepped into his hard chest and slid my hands up his tan neck until the tips of my fingers touched his pale hair. "In every way, you have proven yourself to be my hero and friend," I said, looking between Eli and Walter. "I have already lost someone and their love by not embracing my own feelings. I may never get over the love I had for Mendax, but I will never make the mistake of not allowing myself to feel again. I love you, Eli."

"As much as I hate to interrupt....whatever it is that's going on, we need to get out of here now," Walter remarked.

"You aren't leaving me in another realm while you fight. We will *all* go to the castle together," I argued.

"No," both men replied at once.

Everyone gasped in surprise as the entire prison shook. The floor beneath us trembled like an earthquake, nearly knocking us all to the floor.

"Go!" Walter shouted at Eli with a stern look. "Help them!"

"Help who?" I yelled.

Loud, high-pitched noises rent the air. You could feel the desperate energy from inside the quiet prison. It sounded like a war had broken out.

"Take her to the crypt," Eli said with a sad look at Walter before he sped off down the hallway once again.

"Geez, harsh way to tell your fiancée goodbye," I grumbled.

"It's where your heart is being kept. It's in the crypt under the castle, guarded and spelled with blue flames and about every form of fire and magic block imaginable," Walter explained as he grabbed ahold of my hand again. I couldn't tell if he did it to comfort me, himself, or simply to keep ahold of me so I couldn't run off. I suspected it was all three.

"That's why you could feel it in the throne room..." I trailed off.

Walter looked at me appreciatively for a long moment. "Yes, your heart is directly under the throne room. There is a hidden door to the crypt behind one of the paintings."

I pulled Walter's hand in the opposite direction, to follow Eli.

"No, you cannot go out there yet, Caly," he said, pulling me away from the battle sounds.

Only they suddenly didn't sound like just weapons and fighting alone.

I heard snarls.

Heat singed inside my chest, and I snapped a look to my left, through the open prison cell next to us. The woman stood, staring out at the eerily empty sky.

The roc hadn't come to feast on the prisoners. Where were they?

I inhaled sharply as my eyes snapped to Walter.

"Caly, no!" Walter shouted after me as I slipped my hand free and took off toward the doors.

He caught up to me in half a second, but he only tried to stop me with the look in his eyes—and something hidden within them told me he secretly wanted me to see whatever it was I was about to.

"I'm sorry" was all he said.

CHAPTER 27

CALY

THE PAST

I STUFFED THE LAST CORNER OF THE TOASTER WAFFLE IN MY mouth as the screen door slammed behind me with a creak and a bang. Adrianna and Mom had gone into town, and I didn't want to waste a minute of this time.

The dew-covered grass dampened the bottoms of my feet as I ran out back. I passed the place where those fairy things had been. That had been so cool.

The pretty gold fairy told me I'd be seeing a lot of her, and I couldn't wait. She was so neat. Adrianna had been getting so annoyed with me because I couldn't stop talking about how I had saved a real-life fairy.

I wondered if she would come to school with me for show-and-tell. *That* would definitely get me more friends. I didn't know why everyone always seemed uncomfortable around me.

My legs picked up speed over the flowers and tall grass.

"Hello!" I sang out to a nearby squirrel.

He would come to my lap and snuggle—I knew he would right now.

This was my favorite. It was the only time I felt like

anything liked me, well, besides for Mom and Adrianna—they had to like me though.

My own father didn't even like me enough to stay. I was glad I didn't remember anything about him. I didn't need him or anyone else. Mom was enough for me. Mom was everything to me.

I sat down excitedly, moving my legs to standard crisscross-applesauce position, when all of a sudden, my skin started to tingle. The power in my veins felt like it was being pulled out, but somehow it also felt like it was being pushed back in. My stomach hurt like I had swallowed an anvil. What was going on?

My powers pulsed, and then all of these bright, flashing lights came into my vision. Voices stuttered in and out of my head.

Was I inside a car? I listened harder to the voices, gripping the tall grass to balance myself.

"I'm sorry, but I really can't let you get in the way any longer."

Who was that? I knew that voice.

"Hello?" I shouted.

"She doesn't belong with two humans anyway. She will be the hero of the Seelie realm. The Elysian Fields won't be able to keep her out."

Wait, that was the pretty fairy! Why were they in the car? How come they'd left me behind?

My vision continued to pulse, hurting my head. What was happening?

"Not that she'd be refused anyway, being Artemi. The Elysian Fields are like your heaven. Unfortunately, the two of you will not be meeting her there anytime soon. Humans don't belong."

What? Why was the fairy talking about the Elysian Fields?

The anvil in my stomach flipped.

No. She was too beautiful and kind to be bad.

But Mom's face was terrified.

Tears prickled my eyes, soon falling from around closed lids.

Why was Mom so scared? Why couldn't she stop the car? It was going too fast! No!

I stood up and ran toward the house. I had to do something! I had to help them. The fairy was bad. How could she be the bad one when she was so pretty and nice?

The door slammed behind me as I grabbed the house phone. Who should I call? Mom was the only one I knew to call for help. But I had to do something. The car was going faster.

I frantically ran around the house, trying to figure out what to do. I couldn't call the police. I didn't know what I was seeing, and I didn't have anybody else. The only people I had were in that car.

"What did you do?" Adrianna cried.

"Noooooooo!" I bellowed.

My body dropped to the ground in a pile of Mom's gardening supplies next to the back door.

No. No. No. No. No.

It couldn't. They couldn't.

No!

She had hurt them.

The fairy had hurt them, and it was all because of me.

I stared at the ground next to where I had fallen.

I didn't blink. I didn't cry. I just stared, thinking about what she had said to them.

Hours passed. I shifted my legs. They had gone completely numb. I couldn't even use them. I palmed the garden shears as I moved to my hands and knees and crawled out the back door.

My legs prickled and stung as I stood, my walk turning into a run.

The neighbor's house was pretty far away, but I could make it. I needed to get help.

She had hurt them.

Someone was coming on a bike. They could help me.

"Please help me! My mom and sister are hurt! I-I think they are dead!" I cried before realizing the bike rider coming closer was Kyle Pierce. The mean kid from down the street.

"What? They didn't want to be around you either? Left just like Daddy?" The boy snickered. He pulled his bike in front of me to block my path.

"Please! This is serious. Go get your mom. I'm running to the Wetzels. Please help me!" I cried.

"Please help me, please help me," he mimicked.

"Stop it!" I screamed as I tried to walk around him.

Kyle was a year older than me and was always picking on me. Mom even drove me to school so I didn't have to ride the bus with him.

"You're such a nerd, you know that? That's why no one hangs out with you. Because you're an ugly nerd!" he shouted at me.

Who would drive me to school now?

Mom was gone. Forever. Who would stop Kyle from bullying me?

No one. Because I had no one.

I was all alone. Everything was up to me now...

The gardening shears slammed into Kyle's stomach, making him fold over.

She had hurt them.

My father was to blame for this. *He* did this. They *both* did this to them!

I hit him again with the shears, this time in the back. He yelled, but I couldn't hear anything. It felt like I was underwater; everything was muffled and dull sounding.

A little bit of hope swelled inside of me as I continued to stab and stab.

I could make it alone. I didn't need anybody.

I turned around and walked back the way I had come. Still holding the bloody garden shears, for the first time in hours, I felt like I might be okay.

302

My mind turned over and over and over until a plan hatched.

"If it's worth having, it's worth waiting for" came Mom's voice from my inside my head.

She was right.

Creak, bang! The screen door slammed behind me as I walked into the house. The quiet air of no one home dug into my chest.

Turning into the bathroom, I stared at my blood-splattered face and dress.

It was like I was looking at someone I didn't recognize—someone new. She looked similar to me, but she had a different light in her eyes. She had the look of someone who was capable and smart. She could handle things alone.

I stared blankly at my new hollow eyes and raised the kitchen shears to my ears. It shocked me when I felt nothing as I worked. I cut the next side. Blood ran down the sides of my face, and I had to sit against the wall for a few minutes because my vision blackened.

When I woke up on the bathroom floor, I knew it wasn't a dream and I was still all alone.

Mom and Adrianna never would have left me to lay on the floor like this.

There was so much blood everywhere, so I showered, making sure I used the rubber mat inside like Mom wanted.

My ears were still bleeding when I got out, so I grabbed a tube of superglue and glued the big cuts shut. I'd seen Mom do this on cuts from the garden sometimes. I hoped it'd work.

I taped them up with some Band-Aids just in case and then grabbed my purple beanie off the counter to hide them.

A knock came at the back door, and I froze.

"Knock, knock! Calypso, honey, I have some terrible news. But don't worry, everything's going to be fine."

It was the fairy, but I was ready.

CHAPTER 28

CALY

T HE DOORS TO THE OUTSIDE OF MALVAR MADE A LOW, METAL-
lic creak as they opened. I pushed with all of my strength
as it crawled open. Walter grabbed the thick iron.

I could hear Eli's voice as the space between the doors
widened.

The sound of steel against steel sliced through the air as a
whir of shadows and movement broke across my vision.

A silent cry filled my lungs so sharply and painfully, it felt
as if my chest would be concave from here on out.

Eli's strong back and wings glinted and sparkled under
the red sun while he fought to kick and slice at the Seelie
guards—his own guards. The scene registered slowly. He was
fighting, but it wasn't to free Tarani or the rest of the Fallen,
like I had suspected.

Thousands of creatures had surrounded the entrance
to Malvar. The steep stone steps were the only space free
of the battle that waged on the sloped earth below—the
battle spanning the field between Malvar and the small town
adjacent to the Seelie castle. Everywhere my eyes touched,
they saw a new animal, creatures I could never in my wildest

thoughts have imagined. Some looked almost demonic, with black, curved horns, others gentle and fluffy. Silver unicorns with black, daggerlike horns and serpents with large textured wings.

Blood and tufts of fur rained down on the battlefield, as the animals fought against what, by the sheer volume, could only be assumed to be *every* Seelie guard within the royal forces.

"What is happening?" I cried, turning to Walter in horror.

A loud, gritty sound like a jet engine blared from above us. The entire mountain seemed to erupt in rage.

Walter jumped into the battle, knocking over a row of guards as they fired long gold cannons from the platform at the tall steps of the prison, where we had come out. Glowing balls of red and orange seared into the crowd of animals, combusting into wounding light. Shrieks and cries poured from the wounded animals and guards on the ground as the fight raged.

The mountain shook, sending bits of sediment from the sturdy prison tumbling down onto the platform outside the doors.

What the fuck was that?

Dusty air filled my open mouth as my stunned eyes focused on the sloping sides of the mountain behind me. Four black dragons with sharp-looking wings crouched against the dark mountain terrain. I whipped back around in time to see Eli hurling long sticks of light at the guards who had surrounded the animals in the distance.

He was helping the animals, not the royal guard. The guards weren't listening to their own prince.

Eli looked like a god doused in gold as the wind thrashed at his hair. His powerful wings shimmered against the sun as they flapped, taking the soon-to-be king a few feet over to snap the neck of a guard as soon as he landed. The guard's glowing, orange sword dropped in front of the animal they had been about to stab at the front of the crowd. The animal's eyes lifted to mine.

The eval I had saved from the pit—I recognized him immediately.

"They fight for you because they sense that you cannot," Walter said, ripping out the throat of a guard who tried to grab me. "But they still sense the Artemi in your heart."

"But—"

"They were here when we arrived, though fewer in number."

Dozens of flying, white roc hovered in the air, like car-sized seagulls. Instead of swooping into the sea for a fish, the roc dipped into the ocean of bodies, pulling free armored guards to tear apart.

Streams of gold and crimson swirled on the ground, leaking out of the many, many dead bodies lying there.

What were the Seelie doing? It wasn't enough that so many animals had died in my cell?

"Noooo!" I bellowed into the wind, falling to my knees. I couldn't watch any more animals die for me.

"Grab the Artemi bitch! Kill her while you still can!" someone yelled from behind me.

A forearm as solid as a metal pipe wrapped around my throat, lifting me from the ground.

My nails tried to dig into their flesh, but it was protected by armor.

A growl I'd come to love rang out from behind me. Walter had shifted to his wolf form but, from the sound of it, was also being restrained.

"Don't fight me, or I'll cut a smile into that Artemi face that you can wear in Tartarus," the guard warned as he scraped a severed dragon claw down my cheek. I winced in pain as the sharp, hooked claw snagged on my skin.

The realization hit that this might be my last fight.

Light shifted in the sky as Eli dove for me, but the guards had been one step ahead in expecting the prince to do just as he had. At least fifteen men restrained him, but not before our eyes latched together like magnets.

This would be it—the end of both of us.

The large man who gripped me stumbled back, tightening his forearm across my throat as he gripped my hair tightly and pulled me against him.

I closed my eyes and prayed Eli and Walter could escape.

Anger began to pulse softly in my system. I refused to see one more animal slain at my expense.

A thundering roar sent a shiver up my spine as a large dragon crawled down the rocky ledge in our direction. I could only hope he fought with us and not the Seelie guards, but he looked so terrifying, a part of me doubted the dragon was even from Seelie.

Emerald-green slits watched us as the guard turned our bodies to face the serpentlike creature.

"Move another claw and her blood spills!" the grating voice shouted.

It was too late.

Shrill laughter skittered up my spine like roaches as my old trainer came into view on the platform. Commander aimed an odd-looking gun at the dragon and fired, sending a golden ball of light the size of a basketball hurtling at the creature.

MOVE! I silently urged him.

The orb exploded into his shoulder, destroying half of his body as the rest of him tumbled down, crushing at least fifty more creatures beneath it.

Including the eval.

His sad, round eyes held mine as he dropped beneath the dead dragon.

"NO!" I cried out in despair over the commander's laughter.

The commander's stride ate up the space between us. I had sworn if I ever saw him again, I would kill him.

Anger pushed through my veins as I looked into his familiar face. The same face that taught me never to give anything away with my expression. He kicked away one of the dead animals with his black boot. The same kind of boots that taught me never to leave my ribs or my face open. The commander laughed his arrogant laugh. The same laugh that taught me to never let on how good I was because I might have to use it against them.

My eyes remained on the commander as he took the last steps forward, placing the cold barrel of a gun against my forehead.

"She should have killed you the minute she found you," Commander Von growled as he moved his finger over the trigger and pulled.

Nothing happened.

My breath stalled as I waited for Mendax to leap from the shadows and save us all.

Nothing.

The longer I watched the commander, the more my darkness leached to the surface. What did it matter if I let it take me over now? There was no way Eli and I could get married in time anyway. Especially if we both died right now. For the first time in twenty-one years, I let the darkness out to play.

My eyes held tight to Commander Von's as I struggled against the guard who held me before stopping to smile at my old trainer. He scowled uncomfortably at my expression and pulled the trigger again, letting out a string of curses when nothing happened. Frustrated, the guard removed his hands from me to grab his gun.

"No, do—" the commander tried as I watched and savored as the most delicious, deep fear suddenly crawled onto his face.

I couldn't help but smile as I reached behind my back and palmed the severed dragon's claw, bumping the gun from the guard's bumbling hands as I did. In the blink of an eye, I had the claw in my mouth and the gun tucked in my armpit as I grabbed the dagger from its sheath at his belt. I moved fast, slamming the blade under his chin and into his head before I stabbed three vital organs left exposed by their shitty armor. Before the guard even had a chance to drop to the ground, I threw the blade into the neck of the guard holding Walter, who quickly finished freeing himself. I shot the gun, hitting the guard on Eli's right arm with a large orb before chucking the gun to Eli and turning back to the commander.

"You fuckin—" Commander Von began.

I slammed my fist into his nose before he could finish, shimmering gold blood pouring out. There were better ways to break his nose, but I didn't think any of them would have been as satisfying.

He was much faster than me, landing two hard kicks to my side.

"Caly!" Eli shouted.

Using the dragon's claw as a karambit, I sliced open his neck, then lifted his arm to stab as deep into his armpit as the claw would go.

The large fae growled angrily. "So I see you picked up a few things."

He made a move to kick me again, but this time I swept his leg, causing him to fall. I was on him in a second, pressing the tip of the claw into the front of his brain, just enough so the point nudged into his anterior cingulate cortex.

Completely immobile now, he let out a cry of pain that made my skin shiver in excitement.

I got comfortable, sitting on his chest, my legs stretched out and relaxed.

"I did pick up a few things since our training," I said with a grin.

I checked his pockets, moving aside his limp arms to dig around until I located a short Swiss Army knife–type gadget from his utility pouch. "This will do," I said softly.

He didn't care what I said though because he was too busy screaming in pain.

"This right here?" I muttered as I pressed the thin pocket-knife blade into a different part of his brain—not enough to kill him, but enough to do a different kind of damage. "Well, you see, this is the primary somatosensory cortex." The commander made a strangled sound as his body went completely still aside from his eyes rolling back in his head periodically. "I know, it's a mouthful, isn't it? They are the pain centers of your brain. Fascinating, right? Now hush, or you're going to miss this next part, Commander." I bit my lower lip, pretending to think. "Now, what was it you always used to tell me? Oh yes: one man's pain is another man's pleasure. Boy, are you gonna like this," I said sarcastically as I twisted both blades into his skull.

His body jerked before it went flat, literally dying from an abundance of pain his brain couldn't override.

I pulled the dragon's claw free before I drove it back down into the top of his skull. Over and over again, I did this until a hand pressed lightly to my back and I turned, claw at the ready.

Eli and Walter leaped back, eyes wide.

"You—you good?" Eli asked nervously.

"Mendax is rolling over in his grave with a stiff dick somewhere right now," Walter said, looking much more relaxed with the scene before him than Eli. "You good?" he asked, mimicking Eli.

I licked the dragon's claw in one slow swipe as I stared at the mangled commander on the ground. Even his blood tasted bitter.

"So good," I replied with a wink.

I took a deep inhale, smelling a hint of smoke. I whipped around, the corners of my mouth already quirked, expecting to see Mendax standing behind me.

The dark-gray wall of rock was the only thing that caught my smile. But I could have sworn I smelled him just then.

My eyes dropped to the ground behind me to see a charred tree limb had fallen on the platform.

Agh.

Eli and Walter had managed to take most of the guards on the platform, but below, the fight waged on.

Something cracked inside my chest suddenly, and I felt the blood run from me as the deep sound of a muffled thud filled my hazy head.

No!

"No!"

One of the last guards below had shot me in the stomach when we weren't paying attention.

Urgent hands lifted me.

"No! Cal!" Eli's panic skittered through his tight grip.

I had fallen from the edge of the platform and onto the ledge below. Eli pulled me against his chest. His heart was thrumming...too fast.

"Calypso Petranova, please, please don't leave me."

Eli's heavy breathing feathered across my forehead.

"Walter!"

My head fell to the side, and I fought to open my eyes.

Growls and snarls filled the silence as I took in the crowd. The animals were overpowering the guards easily now. But the clink of cannons made my body tense.

The guards struggled and panicked for a few more seconds before taking off into the crowd. The cannons wouldn't fire, and they were significantly outnumbered.

I choked suddenly.

Large hands grabbed my shoulders, trying to stop the sharp, jerking movements as I struggled to get down and walk on my own.

"It's okay... It's okay." Walter's comforting face moved in front of mine.

"She's been hit pretty good." Eli trembled.

"Do you have your powers?" Walter asked.

"No, and she—*we* will be dead in a few hours if we cannot get her heart now. It's too much for her little bit of heart. We have to get it now." Eli's voice cracked.

"What happened to your powers?" I rasped, fighting to hold my head up. I just needed to get my breath and I would be fine. Men were always babies about getting hurt.

I felt the cold air push back the hair from my forehead. The smell of clean, fresh soap and sunshine hovered in my nose. Eli readjusted my weight, pulling me tighter against his chest.

"We need a new plan. We have tried a *thousand* times to free her heart. The castle is under siege right now. You have no powers and are dying right alongside her." Walter's angry voice seemed like it rattled against the mountains.

"But she needs it! She needs me." Eli's voice quivered. "She needs me, and I will never ever let her down again."

My chest seized painfully, but I think it might have even had my heart been whole.

Warm drops fell on the clammy skin of my face, and for a moment, they felt like sunshine peeking through gray clouds, but they weren't rain; Eli was crying.

"You have become an unlikely friend, Aurelius—Eli. I cannot let you, Seelie or not, get caught in the battle between the Seelie crown and the Fallen. Tarani is forgiven because she works with them. If you enter that castle, you will not make it out." Walter's voice softened.

"I am the crown. There is no amount of friendship that could erase the dangers placed on my head now, but the castle is my home, and the real war is between my mother and sister. My mother will be placed in the castle's oubliette, and Tarani will take the Unseelie throne." Eli let out a shaky breath. "In truth, even with my sudden lack of powers, it's still safer for me to go than anybody else."

"Take this, then," Walter said with a grunt, ripping Mendax's tooth necklace from his neck with a smile and handing it to Eli. "Mendax would want to have been a part of your death."

"Ha-ha," Eli said, palming my tooth.

"Put me down. What happened to your powers, Eli?" I murmured as I tried to find my voice.

"No. I like carrying you, and you'd never let me if you weren't too weak to fight me," Eli said as the three of us continued down the mountainside. "Just don't get all wild looking like you did back there with the commander, and as for my powers, with the wound to your stomach and only half a heart, you are dying, which means that we are dying, and what little power I have left is keeping us alive with our tie."

Walter's warm brown eyes snagged mine, and for the first time, I realized how much I had come to love and trust him since meeting him as Brown Rat in the Unseelie dungeon. His proud, dancing eyes felt like balm to my soul right now. In some weird, unconventional way, Mendax, Eli, and Walter had all become family—a home to me that wasn't bricks and beams.

I grabbed ahold of Eli's tunic, trying to wiggle my legs down to the ground.

He held me firmly, staring out into the distance as we all continued walking farther away from the creatures and closer to the castle.

"Put me down. I'm better now," I lied.

In truth, I was terrified. Not of dying, but of running out of time.

There was something unwavering that burned inside me now, unleashed and stronger.

Hate.

I had just had a taste of what it felt like to let the monster out of its cage, give it a lick from the spoon, and I knew that if I could only get the rest of my heart, then I could have the whole fucking bowl to myself.

It was time to make the ones who had wronged me pay.

My heartbeat pounded in my ears as fast as a rabbit's while heat blazed through me with such force, my toes curled to stop from screaming in Eli's arms.

Eli's steps faltered on the dirt slope, startling me out of my vengeful thoughts.

"For star's sake," Walter said, grabbing me from Eli before he could drop me. "Is it from Calypso?"

"Is what from me?" I rolled my eyes. I could have walked now had they let me.

"The Artemi have been feared and hunted into extinction not by simply being capable of controlling and bending nature, but because of what their powers can do to others," Walter said, nodding to where Eli had stumbled to the ground.

"Make a handsome fae flop on the dirt?" I said with a grimace.

"You hear that?" Eli groaned and swore. "Handsome."

"An almost *mortal*, handsome fae flop on the dirt," Walter replied. "Artemi's most terrifying ability is to take another immortal's powers, rendering them as useless as a human... No offense. I know your mum and sister were both human." He tightened his mouth into a line with a flinch as he looked into the sky as if he were solving a math equation.

"It's more likely from our tie than your powers," Eli said, returning to where we stood. "Though I'm scared to even see what kind of powers you get once your heart is repaired. You're not just a hidden Artemi that never ascended; you're *Zef's* fucking daughter."

Zef.

My father.

I shoved out of Walter's grip to slowly walk. It really wasn't that bad.

Both men protested, but when they tried to grab me, I pulled the dragon's claw out, and they backed off quickly.

"Zef was the King of Artemi when it was still a realm of its own. He is the Titan of the Ascended," Walter answered. "He's easily the most powerful Artemi to exist, which means his daughter is going to have a fuck-ton of powers."

He was also the one who chose which child got the Artemi powers and the one who was going to have to pay for that decision.

"The Ascended are the grandchildren of the old gods— the closest thing we have to gods and goddesses now, next to the Fates—and your father happens to be the Titan of the

Ascended, the King of Gods," Eli bit out angrily. "And you, not having the other half of your heart and powers, were never able to ascend."

Silence filled the air as we continued to walk, no one knowing quite what to say as we prepared for what was to come when we arrived at the castle.

Eli cleared his throat. "If it's all right with you, we will perform the wedding inside the castle as soon as my mother is removed."

"You can't really think she will remain locked up?" I started. "I know she doesn't really have any wild powers, but look at her. She hasn't let that stop her yet. Maybe the Fallen should—"

"She will be locked away with the utmost precautions. She has done horrible, horrible things, but I will not allow anyone to hurt my family, and that includes my mother," Eli thundered.

Acid rage poured through me. "She deserves to pay for what she has done," I ground out through clenched teeth. Heat flared in every pore of my body as low thuds pounded through my ears. Hot, enraged tears filled my eyes.

Walter tried to squeeze my hand, but I shook him off. I couldn't help it—she had raised me to be cold-blooded.

The evening sky was as dark as it got in Seelie, with deep reds and oranges sulking above the treetops.

"She will pay, I promise you that. But not with her life. Not everything needs to end in death." Eli's tall frame stepped toward me. The charming fae put his hands on the sides of my face as his emotion-filled eyes poured into mine. "You don't have to hold on to the evil side of you any longer," he whispered. He leaned down to lightly brush his lips across mine.

My own lips pushed into his, tasting his sunshine before I pulled away, caught off guard by the tenderness I felt in the kiss. I pushed back into him before he could move. It felt like the whole world—and all of my pain—blurred into the background.

"I want to marry you, Eli," I whispered. "As soon as we get into the castle, I want to make it official."

I loved him, and our lives were literally tied together already, but mostly I wanted to do this because it was the only way I could ever see my sister again.

He smiled so hard, even the creases of his eyes made new smiles when he leaned in closer. "You have a heart of gold, Wife." He pressed a kiss to my lips, then my forehead. "Once we are married, all of this darkness will be gone from inside of you. I will do *anything* to make you happy," he said as he pressed his mouth to mine in a sweet kiss.

"Married or not, my darkness and I will still come inside her," added a deep, gravelly voice I would recognize anywhere.

Malum Mendax.

CHAPTER 29

CALY

L IKE AN APPARITION, HE LIMPED UP FROM THE CASTLE'S PATH. His black armor barely held on to his body in most places. Bloody scratches and bruises covered his dirty face and body. His broad, muscled chest rose and fell with labored breaths, and his defined jaw clenched with effort as he stopped next to Walter.

"Mendax!" Walter rasped, throwing his arms around the giant fae.

Malum fought a smile and lost, patting his brother on the back with a wince before pushing him away.

"You're alive! Where have you been? But...Aunt Tenebris? Is she...?" Walter asked, his face hopeful.

"No," Mendax said as he turned his stare to mine. "Mother is dead, and I nearly was too. The Fallen vultures invaded after the Seelie army left."

I couldn't think enough to form words. There in front of me stood the man of my dreams and nightmares. How many times could one person play dead? Perhaps *he* should have been given the nickname of *pet*.

"How did you—?" Eli asked, sounding dumbfounded and irritated.

Mendax moved his eyes to where Eli's hand gripped my waist.

"I have quite the number of deceitful, non-law-abiding friends in dark places." He tipped his face to Walter. "I was in Eromreven before I went to Itäre. Eletha guided me."

Eli seemed taken aback. "Oh, sure, you were in Eromreven. Just relaxing in Eromreven?"

"You saw Eletha?" Walter said with obvious interest.

Mendax smiled and cocked his head, ignoring Eli to stare at me. "She owed me."

"How was she? How did she look? Did she speak of anyone?" Walter asked, suddenly more flustered than I'd ever seen him.

Eli's gaze went to Walter, shocked.

"You just went and hid in the underworld's playground? You made friends in Eromreven and just left, did you?" Eli said in disbelief. "Sounds horrifying."

I tried to remove my hand from Eli's chest, but he clapped his hand over it and locked eyes with Mendax.

"Unless you're of the dark, then it's not so bad," Walter countered with a smile. "It's the other realms' version of heaven and hell. The dark finds peace in Tartarus, while the Seelie who stayed on the path of good rest in the paradise of the Elysian Fields."

"Unless you are a Seelie royal, in which case you are guaranteed admission into the Elysian Fields no matter how bad or evil you are," I chimed in unexpectedly.

Mendax watched me with interest. "Yes, and it is the same for the Unseelie royals," he replied. "They are automatically granted admission to Tartarus, no matter how good they have been." He stared straight through me while everyone else just watched.

"Adversely, they work as the other realm's punishment or peace, depending on what would be most torturous or joyful to that particular fae," said Eli.

"So, you went to hell and came back," I mumbled, unable to peel my eyes from him.

"I've told you from the beginning, there was nothing that would stop me from returning to you," Mendax answered.

Tension crackled like lightning between Eli and Mendax.

"We've located her heart. It's in the crypt below the castle. It's spelled to only open for her, and she needs it now. She was held at Malvar, and then the animals came to help her." Walter paused. "You should have seen her, Mendax. She eviscerated a man with a claw from a fucking Ladon dragon," Walter said proudly.

"I will get her heart. The castle is halfway in ruins already," Mendax said sternly.

"I'm already getting it," Eli bit out. He released his hold on me to move toward Mendax. "Seeing as our souls are tied and it's *my* castle." Eli's boots hit the toes of Mendax. "I'll be getting my *wife's* heart."

"Is this true, my love? Did you promise to marry another while I was gone?" Mendax asked with a hint of amusement in his voice.

"I…I… You're alive" was all I could say.

"She has," Eli growled, "and I will not allow you to hurt or confuse her. She has been through enough, Mendax. *Leave.* Let her be happy. You and I both know that you only want her because of our rivalry. You want me, as a Seelie, to pay, so you take away the only thing that makes me happy." Eli tightened his fists. "Right now, you stand before the new king and queen of Seelie. We will be married as soon as we get inside the castle."

Mendax calmly placed his hands in his pockets and turned his amused expression to me. "If you think a wedding will deter me, then you don't give my feelings for her *or* my lack of morals enough credit, Aurelius," he said with a handsome grin.

"Well, while you two pissheads have a cock fight, I am going to the crypt, and I'm not leaving until I get her heart, because if none of you have fucking noticed, she's still dying," Walter grumbled angrily as he looped his arm in mine and urged us down the path toward the castle.

"He's alive," I whispered to Walter, still in shock.

"Barely," he replied. "Look at him. He's in worse shape than you."

Mendax was at my side in a second, lifting me up and cradling me against his hard body. "Are you all right?" His warm chest rumbled under my cheek.

A sigh slid from the back of my throat at the feel of his heart beating against me. "Are you all right?" I asked, feeling the staggered pace of his limp as he carried me.

His smoky gaze trailed over my face. "Almost."

"Cal, when you want down from this ogre's grip, say the word," Eli grumbled, walking beside us.

"Thank you," I said, reaching out to squeeze his shoulder. "But then who would carry him once he plummets down the hill on his shattered leg?"

All four of us smiled, pushing the tension away for the moment. We had things to decide, but for the moment, we all knew we were stronger together.

"Give her to me, you stubborn ass," Walter growled after watching Mendax limp along.

"Mine," Mendax said with a scowl and small smile as he moved a few paces ahead of the others and palmed my ass.

"Stop that right now," Eli growled, moving next to us.

I couldn't help but smile at Eli.

"He is going be my husband," I said in a light, conspiratorial tone to Mendax.

"Not if I have anything to say about it," he whispered loud enough for all to hear.

As the journey to the castle progressed, my body weakened.

Several of the animals that had fought at Malvar passed us as they returned to wherever they had come from. Several times, they tried to join us, but eventually they wandered off, likely annoyed with our slow pace. Dragons flew over the treetops, sending a welcome breeze down upon us as we neared the Seelie castle.

The entire castle was surrounded by people of all different shapes and sizes only seeming to have two things in common: a very human look to them, and deadhead moth marks decorating their skin, or scales, somewhere.

Several of them coiled fire or sparks in their hands. Some appeared nearly see-through, while others, instead of skin, looked covered in a haze of static-like air. Not one of them that I saw carried a weapon, and I got the very distinct feeling they *were* the weapon.

"I'm going in to get the heart and make sure they don't hurt Mother," Eli said with a somber look at the castle.

"I will come," I said as I slipped from Mendax's arms, only swaying a small amount.

"No," the three men said in unison.

"You stay here, where it's safer." Eli struggled to swallow. "Walter will join me in case...in case something happens to me and you need your heart faster."

"What about the marriage?" I blurted. "We should do it now."

Eli smiled at me before straightening to his full height and looking at Mendax. "As soon as we get everything settled, you will be my wife."

"Oh, okay, of course." I nodded. "Come get me when you're ready to let me attempt to get my heart. Please don't die."

Eli glanced between Mendax and I.

"One of us must die anyway...for the other two to live. My death would only make things easier for you," he choked out.

I squeezed him so tightly I thought I might pass out. My face and fingers tingled with exertion, but I couldn't pull away. "You will not die. Either one of you," I said, pulling Walter into the hug. "Leave the heart if it is a question. It doesn't matter anymore."

"She's right. Who will I fight if the two of you don't return?" Mendax said before slapping Walter on the back

321

and slapping Eli's cheek lightly. Eli straightened and moved toward Mendax until Walter stepped in the middle.

"I will return when I have your heart and the queen has been detained," Eli said, taking my hand.

Wait for me, his eyes begged.

My hands looped around his tan neck. I pulled him down to me to press a kiss full of thank-yous and sorrys onto his lips. I tensed slightly when I felt Mendax's eyes on me, but he didn't stop me.

With a solemn nod, Walter and Eli left us at the edge of the forest, where we watched their forms grow smaller until they disappeared behind the crowd of Fallen.

"All right, let's go," Mendax said, pulling me into the cover of the surrounding woods. "There's a portal in the forest just down the path if we cut through that field."

I knew about the portal. It was the same one Eli had shown me by the floricorns' pasture.

"What?" I pulled back slightly, still trying to keep my eyes on the castle's entrance.

"It's very likely that they have one off of their rooftop, same as ours, if you'd rather climb. I'm fairly certain that's how Saracen and my father kept their affair so secret," he said nonchalantly as he pulled my body against his.

I hissed in pain as he touched the wound on my stomach. In return, he rolled his eyes like I was being dramatic.

"We can't leave them. What if they need help? You don't just leave people behind you care about," I snapped.

"Walter will bring your heart to Unseelie, and I will have you to myself. They won't need us here…most likely," he whispered against my ear.

"I'm not leaving…yet. There's a chance I'll need to get my heart…and I'm not leaving until I know Eli and Walter are all right." I stepped away from him and the camouflage of the deep forest to move back into the castle's yard.

I wasn't going anywhere until Saracen was taken care of. Protectiveness flared inside of me for Walter. Standing a few feet in front of Mendax as we both faced the castle, I kept my head still but looked to my right as far as I could, to see him in my periphery.

His dark stare remained on me in an obsessive trance— not the castle where Walter was.

How could he just leave his friend like that?

"I have been through worse endeavors with both men. Walter's Unseelie blood is nothing but piss and vinegar. It would take far more than this task to send him to Tartarus. I've come to respect and on the rarest of occasion find camaraderie with Aurelius. I do worry that he holds the key to your life, but Walter will be there." He gripped my wrist tightly. "As you so frequently remind me, pet, I am and will *always* be the villain. My desires are purely selfish. Now let's go cause some trouble and reclaim my throne before that little princess has the chance," he purred with a smile.

I turned around, pulling my wrist free, and took another step toward the castle while I stared at the man in front of me.

"Do you only want me because of Eli's interest in me? Is it because I'm Artemi?" I took another step toward the castle and away from him.

"Don't be an *idiot*, Calypso," Mendax snarled. "I had an interest in you well before I knew *either* of those things. Stop walking toward the castle."

"Did you know of my powers when you bonded to me? Your mother had seen me as a child. I doubt she recognized me nineteen years later, but there's still a chance," I croaked. Every syllable I uttered made me sick. "You seem quite adamant about making me queen." Another step back. "That's why I held some of your powers all this time, isn't it? It wasn't the bond. It was because Artemi can absorb other fae's powers when they want to, isn't it? Because I had taken some of yours without even knowing. You had to have known then."

Mendax's frustrated eyes narrowed like a predator's.

"I won't leave with you. I told you that I couldn't," I said. "I have to go to Moirai."

Both of our hands flew to our ears as a loud blast filled the air. The ground shook below our feet like it was about to split in two.

An explosion of orange light burst out from the castle, shattering hundreds of windows as glass spewed out. The pointed turret near the far end swayed slowly before crashing down onto the main structure of the castle. Sulfuric smoke and bricks of gold tumbled from the edges.

The surrounding crowd of Fallen fae stirred. With the calculated movement of an army, they flowed into the castle's opening, showing off the many different powers they possessed as they filled the opening and disappeared inside.

"Mendax, we need to get Walter and Eli out of there!" I shouted. "Walter is in there!"

"Come with me, Caly. They are fine!" Mendax shouted angrily. "I am not heartless when I leave him. Walter is the most intelligent and skilled strategist I know. His instinct is impeccable. If he cannot get to your heart, I doubt you yourself could."

"What about Eli?" I asked.

"What about him? I hope he dies. If he doesn't, I'll be forced to kill him. Why do you think I allowed him to rub his sweaty face all over yours?" Mendax smirked. "He is a man on borrowed time, Caly. Either the bond or the tie must be broken, and guess what, pet? It won't be the bond that gets severed." Mendax's deep voice grated over my frayed nerves.

Thinking he was gone forever had allowed me to see how strongly I felt for him. How much I wanted him. I had shown him glimpses of my darkest parts, and he had begged for more. I knew he could handle me. Passion and danger filled every moment we were together, and I loved it. I craved the chaos.

But there was another side of me too, and that side needed the tenderness that I found in Eli. The parts of me that wanted Eli weren't just crazed with lust or anger-fueled hate. Those parts still laughed and smiled. They felt cared for and loved. They felt good.

My untrusting mind began to spin. It didn't really matter,

I reminded myself. What I wanted didn't matter. I needed to get my heart and continue on.

I was tired of waiting.

Refusing to give my back to Mendax for fear he would grab me, I continued my backward pace to the burning castle's entrance.

"Stop fucking walking away. Do not step one foot inside of that castle, Calypso."

My chest pounded as he moved until he was only a few feet in front of me. Still, my feet continued to slowly step backward. As soon as I made it to the stairs, I would bolt.

"I need to help them...and I need my heart, Mendax. I don't even remember what it's like to feel whole," I whispered in a soft plea.

"You will have your heart," Mendax growled. "But not if you enter that..." His voice trailed off.

The energy around me shifted, and Mendax stilled completely, his eyes locked on something behind me.

"Calypso." He tried to keep his voice even and calm. "Come to me. Now," he called as if coaxing a pet off the road. The only part of him that moved were his eyes as they continued to widen.

I froze. My skin prickled with the knowledge that something terrifying was behind me.

My eyes clenched shut as I said a silent prayer to....well, to whatever god would listen. Blood pounded inside of my ears, reminding me how weak I still was.

Mendax twitched his finger, sending a small wisp of black smoke out.

"I wouldn't do that."

I whipped around to find the image of my saddest nightmares. Something cracked inside of my chest, nearly causing my knees to buckle.

"Another wisp of smoke, and you'll pick Caly's head off the ground just like your mother's." Saracen's voice coiled around me like poison.

She stepped down the two steps that separated us, hair frizzed around her stern-looking face. Her cream-colored dress was covered in soot and dirt as if she had been dragged through a battlefield in her evening gown.

A hand with perfectly manicured nails held an insanely large, glowing dagger. One of her broken and shredded monarch wings hung limply below the other.

"This is all your fault." Her voice trembled. Her hands shook the illuminated blade slightly, causing the amber glow to dance like fire in her eyes. "You ruined everything," she whispered. "I set your life up to be the best it could have ever been."

A loud bang sounded as the doors opened and Eli pushed out.

With a beating red heart in his hands.

He had it.

"Eli!" I cried out, unable to believe what was happening.

"You will not touch a hair on her head, Mother!" he shouted, placing his body between us.

"How did you do it? How did you break the spell?" the queen demanded.

Walter slipped through the door, moving to stand a few feet from Eli and Saracen.

I could have fainted from relief at the sight of both men unharmed.

Eli grabbed something around his neck and held it up—Mendax's necklace. My tooth. "Apparently all I needed was a little desperation and bone," he said, turning to cast a slight nod at Mendax. "Here, take this to its rightful owner. It's been too long apart," he said, moving to pass the crimson heart to Walter.

"No! Don't be a lovestruck idiot! She will destroy every-thing in her path, Aurelius. You don't know what Artemi can do like I do. You must destroy her and the heart," Saracen cried out as she grabbed at her son.

Eli passed my glistening heart to Walter and removed the blade from Saracen's hand, tightening his hold on her.

326

Taking two steps, Walter held it out for me.

There it was.

After nineteen years, I was about to have a whole heart again.

"Give her some space! Who knows what's going to shoot out of her once her powers are restored," Mendax said, sounding excited.

Walter gave me a solemn nod of encouragement. He was the only one who knew the truth.

I looked into Eli's kind eyes. It would probably be the last time they ever looked at me like that.

"I'm so sorry," I whispered to him.

His brows wrinkled. "Don't be sorry. You've got this," he encouraged.

I hovered the beating heart over my chest and looked at Saracen.

Taking a large gulp of air, I pressed the organ to my skin, just above where the other half lay.

The air around us stilled as everyone watched with bated breath to see what would happen.

At first, the heart did nothing. It pushed against my skin, making horrible squelching sounds, and I began to worry I had miscalculated, that possibly it had been twenty years and not nineteen and eight months...but then it all happened.

My chest burned like a fire was erupting when the smallest crack appeared in my skin, no bigger than a quarter. The heart in my hands moved to the opening and slid in, looking like a deflated balloon, until it was completely inside my chest.

The fissure sealed up with a pop, and I felt my chest fill as I gulped for breath.

It was finished.

I had done it.

"How do you feel? Are you okay?" questioned Eli as both he and Saracen gawked.

"Do you need anything?" Walter asked.

"Show us a trick, pet," Mendax said from behind.

I held my hands out to the side widely as I faced Saracen with palms spread. Slowly, and a bit dramatically, I raised them up. A smile curled the edges of my lips. Then I dropped my hands to my sides.

Each of them looked at one another in confusion.

"Nothing's going to happen." I smiled wider. "I'm human."

Everyone gasped.

I stepped in closer to a confused Saracen, my face in front of hers, making sure I could see every inch of her expression. I wanted to remember this moment forever.

"You killed the wrong daughter," I whispered, savoring her expression. "Adrianna was the Artemi."

"That's impossible," she protested.

"Artemi choose which child will receive their powers, and my father chose Adrianna."

I dug my nail into the scar on my thumb painfully.

"Because of his status, Adrianna got her powers earlier than normal. She was two, and she couldn't handle them. You can't imagine how much pain it caused her little body and mind. The pain *he* caused her, leaving my mother and I to watch her suffer. When my sister was five, we learned that she could siphon off the tiniest amount of powers to one of us, only for a few hours ever, but it was enough to give her some relief. When she would pull her powers back, everything would blur for a second, and then we could see what Adrianna saw for a minute. We used to play hide-and-seek with it."

My teeth ground together. "Adrianna had pushed some of her animal abilities into me before she went to town with Mom." I bit the inside of my cheek to stop the tears. "I saw everything, Saracen—everything. The last words I heard from my sister's mouth were her asking me what I'd done by saving you that day."

"Oh my suns, Caly," Eli murmured.

"If you saw it all, then why didn't you do something? Why wait so long?" Saracen asked.

328

I watched the small lines of her mouth twitch. "Because I wanted to hurt you from the inside out. I wanted to destroy every *single* thing you have ever loved. It was easy to wait, knowing that one day I would hurt you. The hard part was learning there was nothing you loved." My eyes caught Eli's.

"What—what about me?" he questioned.

My gaze fell to the ground—I was too scared to watch his face during what I was about to tell him. "My plan was to arrive and kill all of you the instant I was empowered as a Seelie royal. Then, I'd go to Moirai and kill my father for what he did to Adrianna."

I looked up and saw Eli's mouth drop open, hurt in his eyes.

"You were my first mistake," I said with a small tremble in my voice. "She never loved you, but I did. I made a promise that no matter how much I had to lie or kill to get revenge for my sister, I'd never hurt you more than I had to.

"The only way I can ever see my sister again is if I get into the Elysian Fields," I said, wiping at my stinging eyes. "Humans go to heaven or hell, and I-I need to tell her... tell her I'm sorry. Sorry for ever saving you in that field and bringing you into our lives!" I screamed as the rage came. "You already thought I was Artemi; this way I would get to be with Adrianna again and see my father."

Saracen looked stunned. "But the heart—"

"That was tricky. The act would have been up pretty fast when you realized I had no powers. You had just started to worry about taking me through the veil. I knew I needed something to convince you of my loyalty so I could get to Seelie—it was perfect."

Saracen smiled as she tried to move from Eli's grip, but he held her firm. "You shouldn't have told me you're a human." An eerie laugh crawled from the queen's throat. "You've made this far too easy."

The Seelie queen grabbed the glowing blade from Eli's belt and raised it high before bringing it down with force straight over my head.

From out of nowhere, Walter slammed his shoulder into mine, pushing me out of harm's way.

Before I could scream, the sickening sound of blade and bone echoed across the open land as the queen's dagger pushed deeper down on Walter's head.

The world stilled.

Shouts from behind me rang out, but it felt like everything was in slow motion.

"Walter! No!" I screamed from the ground with everything I had, as if I could move him away to safety if I felt it hard enough.

Walter faltered then, dropping to his knees while a trail of onyx blood began to swell and cascade from around the blade protruding from the top of his head. The dark stream trickled over his tousled brown hair before dripping down into his kind eyes.

Loud roars behind me seemed muffled. Somehow now only a few feet from Walter, I clutched the grass at my hands to keep the world from spinning.

He moved his eyes to mine and then to someone behind me, whom I could only assume to be Mendax by the way the shifter lifted the corner of his mouth in a pitiful, blood-covered grin. His eyes locked with mine again and he let out a soft nod, letting me know he was doing it for me, before he collapsed and his face planted against the hard platform of stone below the steps. His back rose slightly with one last breath before his body relaxed deeper onto the stone, motionless.

"Now—" The queen was cut off when I launched at her.

Eli still held his mother, obviously uncertain of what he should be doing.

"You will never take another loved one away from me! Never! I knew all along, you were really training me for this." I grabbed the sides of Saracen's face and snapped it to the right, feeling for the pop. Her C3 and C4 vertebrae cracked loudly.

"Caly! No!" Eli cried as he still restrained her.

I swung, burying the dragon's claw in the side of her head as she dropped to the ground as Walter had.

"Mother!" Eli cried out. He pulled a small blade from his belt and charged me.

I stumbled backward onto the grass as he stood above me, ready to kill me. He stilled, panting, as his eyes moved down to his mother instead.

Princess Tarani stood behind him at the top of the stairs, her beautiful face covered in tears.

Mendax scrambled forward to grab Walter and pulled his body onto his lap with rough movements. Choking sobs ripped from him as he pressed his face into Walter's chest.

The stones ripped at my knees as I crawled to them. My hands moved over the scruff of Walter's face. His brown eyes stared out, cold and unrecognizable—no longer filled with warmth and the feelings of home.

"No. God, no! Please, no," I said, running my now-bloody hands over his face and arms, certain I would find a warm space filled with life. "This is all my fault," I cried.

My eyes sought the comfort of Mendax, but there was no comfort to be found. He clenched his jaw to stop from saying something, and I knew it would have been something awful.

A few of the Fallen had found their way back outside, growing rowdy with whoops and cheers as soon as they saw the queen's limp body and the prince kneeling beside her, sobbing.

"You all should leave. They mean well, but they are still thirsty," Tarani said to Eli before turning to me. "I understand why you did what you did, and I hold no ill will, but you cannot stay in Seelie. Humans, no matter how badass they are, do not belong in Seelie," Tarani said, her citrine eyes latched on to mine.

She softened her voice as she spoke to Eli. "The castle will be yours to claim once you return. We will restore it within the month."

He continued to kneel at his mother's side, staring at the scene in front of him, frozen. He held the look of a man sleep-walking as his eyes went from the bloody blade in Walter's head to the bodies on the ground.

"Yes" was all he managed.

"The Fallen are still claiming the throne in Unseelie," Tarani stated.

Mendax didn't move.

The crowd of the Fallen's voices began to carry as they sang and danced. Several tried to pick up Saracen's dead body, starting to fight with Eli as he pushed them away from her.

"Go now. You will not want to be here for long," she urged us again.

Eli numbly walked over to us and looked at Walter. "I'm—I'm so sorry... He saved both my and Caly's life," he directed at Mendax gently. "His memory and good heart will not be forgotten in Seelie," he promised.

Hot tears poured down my face as I leaned down and kissed Walter's cheek one last time.

One last time.

Eli helped me to stand before he and I nodded a goodbye to Tarani and walked toward the forest's edge.

Mendax grunted and struggled as he lifted Walter's body, setting him as gently as possible over his shoulder.

"What are you doing?" I asked.

"You don't leave people behind you care about. Walter will receive a proper burial," he said curtly.

CHAPTER 30

MENDAX

SORROW FILLED THE AIR AS WE STEPPED INTO THE FOREST, leaving the Seelie castle in our wake. Every grasshopper and sparrow bowed their heads as we passed, and I couldn't help wondering how many of them were shifters like Walter. Did they ever get to know him like I had?

His body hung heavily over my shoulder, jostling stiffly with each pained step I took.

I had come back to find Caly as soon as I could walk. My body still hadn't had a chance to heal. I scoffed. I would never heal from *this*.

My hands shifted over the heavy, horrible, itchy fabric of his tunic. The tunic I harassed him about but he continued to wear, saying it reminded him of fur upon his skin. He felt so cold, so empty inside the shirt.

Kaohs, please let him into Tartarus and give him plenty of women and trouble, I thought with a smile.

With as much care as a man like me could manage, I set his body down next to an old ash tree, taking care to prop him up against the tree until he looked almost peaceful.

"You'll arrive in Eromreven a warrior." I brushed the

bloodied brown hair from his face. "Eletha won't know what to do with herself when she sees you."

I moved my hand over his empty eyes, feeling the tickle of his lashes against my palm when I closed them. Then, the last journey I would have with my brother commenced.

A lump as hard as a rock formed in my throat when I tried to wipe the blood off his face.

"I'll see you in Tartarus, brother," I whispered before kissing his bloodied forehead.

I firmed my expression, wiping most of the emotion away, and then walked to where Aurelius stood with Calypso.

"Light it," I ordered the Seelie.

I hated the thought of a SunTamers flames touching Walter's skin, but I had no choice. He deserved a proper resting place.

Aurelius left his post next to Caly and moved in front of the ash tree. After saying a few quiet words to Walter's body, he stepped back and held his hands up. Bright sun poured from his palms to latch on to the tree's bark. It only took a moment before Walter and the tree were nothing but bright flame.

I watched the golden boy as he returned to Caly's side, glaring at her when she wasn't looking. The fae's chin stiffened before he reached out to rub her back lightly.

The tension between all of us was explosive.

Aurelius had just watched the love of his life snap his mother's neck while he restrained her. I had just watched his mother kill Walter. It was the same as him doing it as far as I was concerned.

My patience was running thin. I didn't like the way he looked at her. But even worse, I didn't like the way *my* pet looked at him.

Especially now.

I thought the goddess was devious and enrapturing before, but now? Now I was infatuated beyond anything the realms have ever seen. How was it possible to be so completely bewitched by a human? I called her *pet*, but it was I who followed behind at her heels. I was the one with the leash tied to her short, immortal life.

I couldn't stand the thought of her dying as fast as humans did.

I would find a way to sever the tie to Aurelius before he got them both killed. I despised the idea of guarding the Seelie, but as long as he and Caly were tied, I wouldn't let harm come to either of them.

CHAPTER 31

CALY

S TOP IT. I DON'T WANT IT," I SAID, REFUSING THE ARMOR THAT
Eli tried to shove over my arms.

Both men had decided, because I was human, I should be wearing armor. Their armor. That was heavy and built for a six-foot-five fae.

"Take it. We don't even know where we're going. It's too dangerous for a mortal in the fae realms," Eli said patiently.

"I've been a human in this realm the whole time," I tried. Honestly, I was just happy he was speaking to me. I knew he was extremely upset with what I had done—all of it.

"Take mine like good girl, Cal," Mendax rasped with smoldering eyes as he tried to push his Unseelie breastplate into my arms.

The warm glow of the pyre in the distance cast a spooky vibe over the shadowed forest.

"I don't need or want your heavy armor," I said, backing away.

Mendax took up the space behind me, placing his hands on my hips just before his firm chest pressed against my back.

Eli glared at Mendax, then stepped in closer at my front,

blocking me in. "You need to take this damn armor so we can go somewhere and figure out how to break your bond."

"How to sever your tie," Mendax enunciated as he pressed more of his muscled body against my back.

"Well, then you need your armor too, since if you die, I die," I said, moving from Mendax toward Eli. "What am I supposed to do, wear them both?" I scoffed. They were being ridiculous.

"You know their armor is weak and flimsy, just like their men," Mendax purred at my ear. "Take mine. It's always hard for you."

Eli rolled his eyes but decided to use this to his advantage.

"No matter what happens, I will be here for you. Anything you need from me." Eli leaned against me, his thighs pressing against mine. "I will protect you, armored or not."

Every nerve in my body was overwhelmed with the sensation of both fae sandwiching my body between theirs. The smell of smoke and fresh citrus lingered as Eli's hand brushed over my hair. At the same moment, Mendax moved his free hand up and over the side of my neck, leaning down to whisper in my ear.

"Go on, Cal. Take it." His deep voice poured through my brain like hot soup.

"Do it for me." Eli's thumb grazed my bottom lip. "Let me know that you still love me."

My body shivered and thrummed, filled with a new energy.

A body now covered in black and gold armor.

Eli smiled down at me, beaming as he gave my arm a squeeze.

Most of my vital organs and weak points had been covered by a mix of both men's armor. "Really?" I barked as I rolled my eyes nearly into the back of my head.

Both men grinned at each other like little boys who had hidden a spider in my hair.

A thunderous crack let out above us, and the skies

darkened around the edges, revealing that the clouds above were moving closer.

One wispy-looking cloud glided down smoothly before splitting open.

We all stared in curious wonder as a black peregrine falcon flew from it, silently gliding down until it hovered just above me, opening its talons and dropping something.

My hands opened, more as a reaction than anything. I caught what I thought was a wand of glass as I watched the bird in awe.

"Should we grab it?" Mendax asked, but it was a useless question.

The falcon had already flown off, entering the crack in the cloud with a sharp cry.

I looked down at what it had given me and realized it was a rolled-up glass scroll.

Glancing wearily at Eli, I pulled at the smooth glass, not expecting it to move and being shocked when it opened into a note with black cursive scrawled over it. The letters were too hard to read against the dirt and moss of the ground, so I lifted it to the sky, where I could read it easily, and was left with no doubt that was how it was meant to be read.

Calypso Petranova,

Good day. You have been summoned before the Fates in requisition of Ties and Bonds with breach to laws 14.2 and 370.003.

Failure to appear before the Fates will result in the application of death to all parties forthwith.

Further instructions will be located in the Lake of Sheridon.

On behalf of the Fates,
Zef
a.k.a. Your Father

"Well, what does it say?" Eli asked.

"It's from my father," I said, handing him the letter, numb.

"Well, it looks like you got your invitation to Moirai after all," Mendax said as he moved to my side.

"We are going to Moirai..." I trailed off, stunned.

"No," Eli sighed. "It looks like we are going on a scavenger hunt to the Lake of Sheridon before we face the Fates... and your father," Eli stated.

"My father..."

"Has summoned us to face our judgment before the Fates," Mendax said.

"What—what will happen then?" I asked, doom souring my stomach.

"They will choose which one of us will die," Eli responded as he looked to Mendax. "And sever the bond."

"Break the tie," Mendax growled back at Eli with a look that told me we'd be lucky to even make it to the Fates without him killing Eli.

"Surely there's another way," I said with a laugh.

They both turned to me, deadly serious.

"Fae law isn't like laws of the human realm. It is written in magic. It is unbreakable and unbendable. There is no getting out of this. By the end of this, either Aurelius or I will be dead," Mendax said seriously.

Everything turned solemn and momentous all at once.

"I-I will get the opportunity to kill him," I mumbled as I stared at the glass scroll.

"Finally, right?" Mendax asked.

"Uh, what? Yeah...finally," I replied.

"Then we should go," Eli said. "Settle once and for all who gets Caly."

Our journey began as we walked away from the forest and back toward the path, our backs still warm from Walter's pyre.

"I will do anything not to lose you," said Eli, moving to my side.

"Me too," Mendax stated, glaring at Eli. "Anything."

READING GROUP GUIDE

1. Queen Saracen is not who she has made herself out to be to Caly. Why do you think Saracen is so intent on controlling Caly? What made her so evil?

2. It turns out that Prince Mendax is alive and wants Caly back. If you were Caly, how would you feel about this turn of events? What do you think Caly wants more: to be invited into the Seelie Court or to be with Prince Mendax?

3. It is noted that Calypso is Artemi at the beginning of this book. How does this affect her status in Queen Saracen's court? Could it mean something different for her relationship with Mendax?

4. Eli likes Caly far more than she suspected he did. Do you think she is torn between him and Mendax? What does she see in both of them?

5. Walter and Caly have a very close friendship. Why does Walter mean so much to Caly? Do you think his bond to her powers influences his friendship with her?

6. Saracen is the person who killed Caly's mother and sister. Why was this necessary in her mind? When it

is revealed that Caly has always known that Saracen killed her family, why do you think Caly held off from killing her for so many years?

7. Mendax is desperately in love with Caly. What do you think has made him so enamored with her? Do you think she feels the same way, even though she tries to push him away?

8. Mendax is taken for dead after Queen Tenebris is killed. How does this affect Caly? Does this show her the depth of her true feelings for him?

9. Caly is much stronger than most people believe her to be. Why do you think so many people, even her friends, repeatedly underestimate her?

10. Mendax is alive at the end of this book, and it comes out that Caly is indeed human. Why does this make him love her even more? How do you think Mendax and Eli will get along now that they are both bonded to Caly?

ABOUT THE AUTHOR

Jeneane O'Riley is a #1 bestselling author of whimsically dark and romantic fantasy books. Her love of storytelling began when she was a small child, dreaming up glorious fantasies to fall asleep to. As she grew older, her love of storytelling remained, but the tales became more dangerous and full of toe-curling tension.

She is a hobby mycologist and nature enthusiast who resides in Ohio, at least until she can locate a proper bridge to troll, or perhaps a large tree spacious enough to hold her smoke show of a husband, her Irish wolfhound, pet dove, and, of course, her three children.